A Humorous Erotica Collection

STAND UP, LIE DOWN COLLECTION

A Humorous Erotica Collection

CHASTITY VELDT

4 Horsemen
Publications, Inc.

Table of Contents

CHASTITY VELDT

Molly in Milwaukee

Stand Up, Lie Down Collection

TABLE OF CONTENTS

CHAPTER 1

Jake Nilsen parked his truck in front of Pretzel's Comedy Club on a Wednesday afternoon and slammed the door, thinking, *Shit, you're not supposed to start a story this way.* He locked the door with a key fob. *Oh well, what are you gonna do?*

Jake looked at his watch: *12:30.* He opened the door to Pretzel's and stood for a moment, letting his eyes adjust to the dim lighting.

"We're closed," came a woman's voice from behind the bar.

"Really? I thought there was a matinee," said Jake.

"No, we don't really do matinees at a comedy club," said the woman.

"I—I know," said Jake. "I was just kidding."

The woman laughed. "That's funny. You should be a comedian."

"I am, actually. My name is Jake Nilsen, and I'm the middle this weekend."

"Oh! My name is Randie," said the woman. "Randie Sanders." She reached across the bar and shook his hand.

She had long, slender fingers, and Jake was careful not to squeeze too tightly. Randie looked admiringly at his slender waist and broad shoulders, and she could just about make out that little valley between his pectorals in his form-fitting t-shirt. Jake ran his fingers through his hair with his left hand as he waited for her to let go. Randie's nostrils flared slightly as her gaze traveled up and down his 6'2" frame, lingering on his flat stomach.

Jake smiled. "Randie Sanders? I'll bet that's easy for people to remember."

"No, why?" asked Randie.

She was about 5'6" and built like a long-distance runner, slender and willowy. And, as Jake quickly realized, a bit of a ditz. Randie's shoulder-length strawberry-blonde hair was pulled back in a ponytail, and she drank him in with her big hazel eyes.

"Never mind," said Jake. "I'm looking for Sherry."

"She's in her office. I think she's eating lunch."

Jake stared at her for a moment. "I don't know where that is. Could you show me?"

"Oh, sorry." Randie stepped out from behind the bar, "Follow me." She was wearing a runner's tank top, running shorts, and running shoes.

She must be a runner, Jake thought, because he wasn't that clever either.

His eyes zeroed in on her slender hips and tight little ass. She turned around to make sure he was following, and Jake had to snap his gaze back up off her butt. Randie turned back and continued walking, smiling to herself, and put a little extra wiggle in her hips, putting each foot directly in front of her like she saw the models do on her favorite TV show. Jake readjusted his pants as his cock began to swell imagining the things he would love to do with, to, and for that ass.

She knocked on the office door. "Sherry, this is Jake Nelson—"

"Nilsen," he said.

"Nilsen. He said he's our middle."

"Yep, until Sunday," said Sherry. She looked at Jake then back at her sandwich. "Looks like you caught me in the middle of lunch. Do you want some?" proffering half a sandwich that only had a couple bites taken out of it.

"Er, no thanks. I just wanted to check in and let you know I was in town, and to pick up the key."

"Oh, sure." Sherry wiped some mayonnaise on a paper towel and fished a key out of the desk drawer. She tossed it to Jake who caught it and stuffed it in his pocket.

Randie followed his hand and stared at his crotch. *Shit, is that his dick or is he just happy to see me?* she thought.

Sherry continued, "Randie can take you to the club apartment. It's a block down the street over a taco joint. You've got the place to yourself this weekend. The opener's a local, and the headliner demanded a hotel. Fucking prima-donna-douchebag."

"I'd better take a couple of towels for him," said Randie.

She turned and squeezed past Jake, who was standing in the doorway, grinding her ass against his crotch. She grabbed some towels from a cabinet and squeezed past him again, sliding her nylon-clad ass along his crotch one more time. Jake kegeled his dick and made it jump, which made Randie gasp a little. She turned and gave him a wink.

"I'll show you the way," she said, smiling a little and looking down at his crotch.

"Jesus, get a room, you two," said Sherry, returning to her sandwich.

"...And the bathroom's over there, and you can choose whichever bedroom you like." Randie was just wrapping up the tour of the club's apartment, so Jake picked a bedroom and dropped his duffel bag onto the queen-sized bed.

Many comedy clubs provide an apartment for their out-of-town comics to stay in while they're working at the club. Some club apartments are real shit-holes, but this one was a decent looking place, and Jake said so. They were standing in the kitchen, Jake leaning against the bar that separated the kitchen from the living room.

"Thank you. This is one of my responsibilities for the club, making sure the place stays nice. And anyone who fucks that up doesn't get invited back later. So keep it clean, buster," she said, poking him in the chest with each syllable. "Wow, you really are strong," she said, and ran her hand over his chest muscles then his shoulders.

"Well, I run a lot and work out when I can. I used to be a swimmer in college and I still do that a few times a week when I can find a pool."

Randie stepped closer, still squeezing his arms, and running her hands over his chest. "I'll bet you have to be careful when you squeeze a woman, huh?"

Jake encircled her in his arms, crushing her to his chest. "I'll be careful," he said.

He leaned down and turned her face up toward him, pressing his lips lightly to hers, then a little harder as she freed her arms and wrapped them around his neck. Her tongue slipped between his lips and slid over his, exploring his mouth with the thoroughness of a blind dentist.

Jake slowly slid his hand down and cupped Randie's ass, massaging it slightly, and drew her closer. She pushed up against his swelling cock and began to breathe heavily as he kissed and licked her neck, flicking his tongue into her ear.

"Oh, God," she breathed. She rubbed his cock through his jeans, stroking up and down, trying to feel the outline of it through the denim. "Oh my God, that thing is huge."

Jake began to tug at her tank top, lifting it up. Randie raised up her arms to help him finish. She took off her sports bra as he peeled off his t-shirt. He began to massage her small-but-full tits and lightly squeezed her nipples. Randie moaned and began to kiss him again, enjoying the sensation of her naked skin on his. Jake continued to massage one of her breasts, even as he held her tightly to him.

She reached back down and began to fumble with the button and zipper on his jeans. Randie slid his pants down and his cock sprang out, all eight-and-a-half inches pointing straight at her. *(Jake measured it when he was in college. All guys measure it. Don't let them lie to you about that.*) She reached down, wrapped her long fingers around the shaft, and began stroking it. Her hands were a little cold and Jake gasped at the pleasure of cold fingers on his hot meat.

"I don't know if I can get all this in my mouth," she said, stroking it with both hands, "but I'll sure try." She spit on one of her hands to provide some lubrication.

Jake started to slide his hand down her shorts, but she grabbed his wrist. "Uh-uh. You can't fuck me; I have a boyfriend."

"Alright," he said, wondering at her logic, "but do you want me to make you come?"

"Yes, please," she groaned, releasing his wrist; he began to rub her pussy with his middle finger.

"Oh," she moaned. "Ohhhh. Oh fuck, that's so good."

Jake turned her around and together they slid off her running shorts before pulling her back against him, his cock resting in the crack of her ass, even as he massaged her tit with one hand and rubbed her pussy with the other. He slid his middle finger over her clit, gently probing the folds of her pussy, exploring the length of her slit. Randie gasped as he pulled his finger out, now wet with her pussy juice, past her clit again. He slid it back in, deeper, deeper, and slid it out again, following the same path up her lips and over her clit. With each slide, up and down, Randie moaned, "Ooohhh... fuuuck... ooohhh... fuuuck..."

She reached back and began to stroke his cock, feeling a drop of pre-cum on the tip. *Or was it pre-come?* She could never remember how it was actually spelled.

As Randie began to moan a little louder, Jake spun her around, kissed her hard on the mouth for a few seconds then lifted her onto the bar. She gasped at the cold Formica on her bare bottom. He massaged her tits while they kissed, caressing them gently, rubbing her nipples between his fingers and pulling lightly on them as they got harder. Then he gently guided her back, so she was propping herself up on her elbows.

Jake lifted her legs, rested them on his shoulders and positioned himself so his head was between her thighs. He kissed and licked the insides of her thighs, even as he slowly slid a finger in and out of her slit.

"Ooh… ooh… ooh," Randie breathed as Jake slid his finger in and out. His kisses grew closer and closer to her mound until he finally found it, withdrew his finger, and began to slide his tongue inside her.

"Ooooooooh," groaned Randie. She grabbed his hair and pushed his face harder into her wet cunt.

Jake sucked her pussy lips into his mouth and drove his tongue deeper inside her, flicking it over her clit. Randie's torso glistened with sweat as Jake slid one finger back into her pussy again and reached up with his other hand to massage her breasts, tweaking her now-hard nipples. He flicked his tongue faster, traced circles around it, and slid a second finger into her pussy.

The faster he flicked his tongue, the louder she got, until she was screaming, "Ohfuckohfuckohfuck!"

She grabbed his hair with both hands as he slid the full length of his two fingers in her cunt, in and out, in and out, licking and flicking her clit with his tongue.

"OH MY GOD! ... I'M COMING! ...*CUMMING?* ... COMING!" She mixed the two spellings in, just to be sure. "AAAAAAAAAAAAAAAHHH!" Her body jerked and spasmed as wave after wave of orgasm washed over her.

When she came, she fell back onto the bar, and she lifted Jake's head by his hair.

"Holy fuck," said Randie, "let me catch my breath because you deserve a reward for that. My boyfriend can't even make me cum that way." *Or is it 'come that way?'* she wondered. "He doesn't even go down on me.

While he waited, Jake slowly licked his finger, tasting her juices as Randie watched. He easily lifted her off the bar. They kissed for a few minutes, and she could taste herself on him. She also felt his throbbing dick pressing against her pussy, and she was so tempted to slip it inside her.

But I do have a boyfriend, she thought, *so I can't.*

Instead, she knelt in front of him, wrapping her fingers around his cock. She kissed the head a few times and gave it a few licks before slipping it into her mouth.

Jake groaned as she sucked on the head, then took it out with a light *pop*, and licked the sides of his shaft, first one side then the other. She put her mouth on his dick again, this time sliding it toward the back of her throat.

He watched as she gobbled down *four, five, six* inches before she gagged. She slid her head off his meat and then tried again more slowly—*four, five, six, nearly seven*—and held it for a few seconds before sliding it out and gasped for air as if she had been underwater. Then she wrapped both hands around his fuckstick and slid them up and down, twisting as she went. She did that for several seconds before returning her new favorite toy back into her mouth, sliding her head up and down on his dick, holding at its deepest and sliding it back out.

Then she put her hands on his hips and began pulling and pushing him, fucking her mouth on his shaft. Jake got the idea and began rocking his hips back and forth as Randie held her hands up to keep him from hitting her gag reflex. Even with all his muscles and that fat cock, Jake was very tender and careful with her.

He continued to slide in and out of Randie's mouth, his dick tapping the back of her throat. With every thrust and tap, she made a small noise: "*GULK... GULK... GULK...*"

"Oh, God," said Jake, his breathing getting ragged, "I'm coming... I'm going to come..."

Or is he saying, I'm cumming... I'm going to cum, Randie wondered, trying to shove his dick as far into her mouth as she could.

She held his balls in her hand and they tightened, letting her know he was almost ready. Randie clamped onto his hips as he began to moan, holding half his cock in her mouth and licking the underside of the head.

"UHHHHHHHHH! UHHHHHHHHH! UHHHHHHHHH!" Jake grunted and spasmed as he spurted shot after shot after shot into Randie's eager mouth.

She held him there for several more seconds, flicking her tongue over his sensitive head, causing a few more spurts, and she swallowed it all before cleaning him off.

Jake slumped back against the bar. "That was amazing," he gasped. "I don't know if I've ever come so hard."

"Me either," said Randie. "You have an amazing tongue, Jake Nelson."

"Nilsen. So now what?"

"Well, we can't have sex because I have a boyfriend. He lets me go down on guys once in a while as long as I don't fuck them."

"Ah," said Jake in understanding, although he didn't.

"Plus, I have to go back to work, so maybe we should just end this chapter here, so it won't be awkward."

"Good idea," said Jake.

CHAPTER 2

Molly Moser was bored. Dead bored. Thursdays are always boring in a bookstore, especially in the spring—especially after lunch. Everyone wants to be outside enjoying the sun. They don't want to be inside reading a book.

Hell, they don't want to be outside reading a book either, thought Molly. She wished she could take a nap in the back, or even settle in the easy chair and close her eyes for a little while. *But Aunt Judy said that we had to be ready for customers at any time.*

Not that Judy was ever ready for customers. She was usually out at Chamber meetings or luncheons for the Ladies' Auxiliary or some networking group, which is where she was *this* afternoon. In fact, Aunt Judy was never really at the store, except on weekends or when they had important authors come in for a book signing. Then Judy became the face and voice of *Lost in Pages New & Used Books*, chauffeuring the important authors around, emceeing the readings, and speaking with all the customers.

Molly just sat behind the counter and rang up everyone's purchases. She thought about moving the easy chair behind the counter so she could see the front door and hear the bell. That way, she could look like she was reading in case Judy came back sooner, but no one could see her right away. Cleaning up some piles of books and the stool behind the counter, she tried to figure out how to drag the easy chair from its current spot without scratching the floor. The door opened and the little bell tinkled.

Shit, she's not back already, is she?

Molly popped her head up from behind the counter and looked for whoever had come in, but there wasn't anyone. She pushed her long brown hair behind her ears and adjusted her glasses.

"Hello?" Molly called out.

"Hello?" came a man's voice. The owner of the voice stepped out from behind a bookshelf. "Hi, sorry. I was just over there."

She studied her customer carefully, like one of her favorite literary detectives. He was tall, muscular, and was wearing faded jeans and a tight t-shirt.

"No problem, can I help you find anything?" replied Molly.

A little too tight, she thought with a tinge of disapproval.

"Oh, no. I'm just looking. I love to get lost in old bookstores."

"Well, we're not that big, so hopefully you don't get too lost," said Molly.

The man was in his late 20s or early 30s with a thick head of whitish-blond hair, cut short, and he wore gold-rimmed glasses. He reminded her a bit of Tony, the first German terrorist that Bruce Willis killed in *Die Hard*.

"Have you ever been here before?" asked Molly.

"No, I'm from out of town. I'm here at Pretzel's Comedy Club for the week."

"Are you a comedian?"

"Yes, I'm Jake," said Jake. He stayed several feet back from the counter so she wouldn't feel nervous.

"I'm Molly," said Molly. She reached out her hand and he stepped up to shake it. "So, what do you like to read?"

"It depends," said Jake. "I like old mysteries, like my grandfather used to read—Ellery Queen, Raymond Chandler, G.K. Chesterton, that sort of thing. But I also like fantasy stuff. You know, swords and sorcery, Patricia McKillip, Katherine Kurtz, Tolkien."

Molly began to change her assessment of him as he talked. She examined him a little more closely. Jake was built like a swimmer, but leaner. He didn't seem to have any tattoos and his eyes were such an icy blue, she thought she could see her breath. She flicked her gaze down toward his crotch, but she was embarrassed that he'd notice.

Molly became aware he was waiting for her to answer. "I'm sorry, what?"

"I said, 'what do you like to read?'"

"Oh, I like mysteries too, cozy mysteries actually. And I like to read young adult on occasion, and some romances." In fact, she couldn't wait for Jake to leave, because she wanted to dig into that new Honey Cummings "steamy romance" novel on her secret Kindle app on her phone. She'd started reading it in bed last night and fingered herself until she came and fell asleep. Molly wanted to re-read that scene again, maybe after she'd had a chance to trim her nails a bit.

"Can you point me toward your mystery section?" Jake asked.

"Oh, you'll love exploring there. We just had a few big boxes of old mysteries added. There were a couple of older people who had died, and their families just dropped the books off last week. I just finished putting them on the shelves a couple days ago. I think I saw some Rex Stout paperbacks in there."

"Great! He's my next writer to dig into," said Jake.

As they walked back to the mystery section, talking about her favorite authors, Molly's arm brushed lightly against Jake's a couple times. She could feel the light tickle of his arm hair, giving her goosebumps. Jake admired Molly's figure with some side glances. She was short, about 5'3", not skinny, but not what you would describe as plump either. *Healthy,* his grandfather would have said. Her long brown hair, parted in the middle, was pulled back behind her ears, and hung down to her shoulder blades. A pair of brown tortoise-shell glasses framed her brown eyes, which were the color of the root beer barrel candies he'd loved as a kid. She wore a short-sleeve sweater which stretched across her ample breasts, and she wore a short skirt above her knees with knit stockings to keep warm against the chilly spring; spring in Milwaukee still meant 40-degree mornings. Jake couldn't quite make out the shape of her legs, but they seemed pretty toned as far as he could tell.

Molly took him to the S shelves then wandered back down the other way, stopping at the A's. As Jake perused the Stout collection, Molly came back with a book in her hand.

"Ellery Adams," she said, holding the book out to him.

"Oh, another Ellery," Jake said, studying the cover. "Thank you."

"Well, I'll leave you to it. Let me know if you have any questions."

Molly walked back to the counter to finish cleaning up the space. Jake watched her walk and appreciated what he could see. Her skirt covered up her ass, but he could make out the general shape underneath.

"MM-hmm," he grunted quietly under his breath.

Molly took a quick glance behind her and smiled at him. He smiled back and watched her walk the entire way, skirt sashaying with every step.

Several minutes later, as Molly was starting to struggle with dragging the easy chair into its new position, Jake appeared and set several books onto the counter.

"Okay, how did you do?" She sorted through the books. *Two Chandlers, three Stouts,* and she was pleased to see her Ellery Adams book was on top.

Molly rang up the total and Jake handed her his credit card.

She looked at it and asked, "What's your last name? Nilson?"

"Nilsen," Jake corrected.

"What did I say?"

"Nilson."

"I can't hear the difference."

"Basically, the Nilson's are pig rustlers and sheep fuckers. Except on weekends, when they're sheep rustlers and pig fuckers."

Molly snorted a laugh and clapped her hand over her mouth. "Oh, my God, that's so embarrassing," she said between her fingers.

Jake laughed with her. "No, no, that was cute. It means I caught you off-guard and it was really funny."

She smiled and lowered her hand.

"By the way, do you need some help with that chair? I'm sure you can manage, but I thought I would offer."

"Actually, yes, if you don't mind. I just want to put it over in this corner."

"Sure, no problem." Jake moved behind the counter and squeezed past Molly, her breasts lightly brushing against his stomach.

Molly's breath quickened and Jake's dick hardened a little. He quickly turned toward the chair and picked it up effortlessly. He stood up straight, holding the chair in front of him, and Molly felt herself getting wet, thinking about him crushing her with those beefy arms, kneading her breasts with those strong hands.

"Where do you want me?"

"Huh?" Molly was a little startled.

"Where do you want me to put it?" Molly could only point in the general area, so he turned and set it into its new position.

He turned and looked over his shoulder and thought he caught her staring at his ass. "Is this alright?" he asked.

"Back a little, so it's almost against the display case," Molly gulped, stealing another look at his ass. "Perfect."

Jake stood up and moved aside, gesturing to the chair. Molly sat down and tried not to look like she was staring at his crotch. She imagined sucking his cock and was seconds away from reaching up to stroke him. Jake could feel her gaze and his prick swelled to life.

"It's perfect," she said, just as the bell over the door tinkled. Molly sprang up out of the chair and saw that it was her Aunt Judy. *Fuck, Prudie Judy*, thought Molly.

"Hey, Aunt Judy," Molly called.

"Hello, dear." Judy removed her coat and scarf, stopping at the counter. "Who's this?"

"Oh, uh," stammered Molly.

"Hi, I'm Jake. Jake Nilsen," he stuck out his hand. "I was just helping Molly out with her chair."

"Nielsen?" asked Judy.

"Nilsen," corrected Jake.

"I see," said Judy, a little coldly. She was in her early sixties, dressed in a lavender pantsuit and wore Magnifique perfume like she'd gotten a BOGO coupon for her birthday.

Jake could sense the temperature change. "I should get back to my place," said Jake. "I have to go over tonight's material before the show and catch a nap." He picked up his books and stuck his hand out to Molly. "I enjoyed talking with you. Thank you for the books and the recommendation."

Her small hand fit inside his big, warm hand and she remembered the old saying from her college days, *'You know what they say about men with big hands?'* "I enjoyed it too. Thank you for your help. Let me know what you think about Ellery Adams."

Jake shook Judy's hand, mumbled a "Nice to meet you," and left, the bell tinkling over the door again.

"Who was that?" asked Judy.

"Jake. He's a comic performing at Pretzel's this weekend. He stopped by for some books and we got to talking."

"I don't know if you should associate with a *comedian.*" She said *"comedian"* like she meant *"leper."*

"I'm not associating with him, Aunt Judy. He bought some books and helped me move the chair."

"Why are you moving the chair anyway?"

"Because I got tired of sitting on the stool, and it hurts my back after a couple hours. This way, I can still see the front door without getting any workplace injuries."

At the phrase, *"workplace injuries,"* Judy stood a little straighter. "That reminds me, I met this very nice young attorney at my networking event today. He just became a junior partner at Gorman & Mendoza in their tax division. I think you should meet him."

"Oh God, Aunt Judy, please stop fixing me up with people you meet at your business events."

"Look, honey, when your mother died and left you her half of this bookstore, she also made me promise that I would find you a nice man to settle down with."

"Yeah, but not another attorney. The last two attorneys you hooked me up with were such boring duds. One guy didn't even smile, and he didn't read anything that wasn't a law journal. The other one was just two-steps above an ambulance chaser. I swear, he had on at least three gold chains."

"Well, being an attorney is a nice, reliable profession with plenty of job security for your future. And instead, you're interested in a standup comic?"

"I'm not interested in anyone. This was literally his first time in the store. Besides, I don't want to settle for anyone. I like my life like it is. I've got my apartment above the store, I have my books, and I have plenty of friends to hang out with. I don't need to complicate that with a relationship. In fact, the last thing I want is a relationship."

"Alright, dear, I won't push any new attorneys on you. After this one. His name is Tad Ackroyd, and he's expecting your call."

"Really? Tad Ackroyd the tax accountant?"

"Well, that's just a bad choice on his parents' part."

"Fine, leave me his number and I'll call him Monday."

"Why Monday?" Judy gathered up her coat and purse.

"Because if I call him now, he'll want to do something this weekend."

Judy sighed. "Alright, just don't go riding that comic into the sunset this weekend."

"Aunt Judy!" Molly gasped and giggled. "I was planning nothing of the sort."

"I know, I just had to say it, for your mother's sake." Judy headed toward the door again. "I'm meeting Betty Anne Schmidt for coffee, then I'm off to my executive women's dinner. I'll see you tomorrow." She kissed Molly on the cheek, and Molly resisted the urge to wipe off the lipstick that she knew was there, at least until Judy left.

Once the bell tinkled again, Molly settled down into the easy chair with her phone, found her Kindle app, and opened up her new purchase, *Beau and the Professor Bestialora*. Thumbing to the place where she'd brought herself to a satisfying orgasm last night, Molly slid her hand up her skirt and under her panties.

Pushing his hand into the front of her underwear, he found the pink valley and flooding river awaiting him. Two fingers fell into the heated depths of her folds and she collapsed into him, her nipples hard against his chest even through his shirt.

"Oh, God," Molly whimpered as her fingers found her own *heated depths of her folds.*

CHAPTER 3

Friday morning, Jack woke up early, at least what constitutes early to a standup comic, which is more like 10:00, and decided to go for a run. He thought about going for a swim, using his YMCA membership to get into the local Y, but he saw it was clear on the other side of town, and he didn't feel like driving that far.

He put on his running togs and thought about asking Randie to join him, but he had met her boyfriend, Kurt, at the bar the night before, and he seemed like a nice guy. He felt a little guilty about going down on Kurt's girlfriend the day before and shooting his cum in her mouth, so he decided he would just leave that one alone. Also, Kurt was a local MMA fighter and more than a little scary. Jake didn't want to risk pissing him off.

So instead, he decided to run on his own and see if he could work out some of his urges. Jake got dressed, putting on a pair of compression shorts under his running shorts, and added a t-shirt from a comedy club in Fargo, North Dakota called The Cellar. A quick check of his phone showed that it was 50 degrees outside, and

Jake knew he would get too sweaty if he put on a long-sleeved shirt. Besides, having grown up in Minnesota, he enjoyed working out in the cold weather, and 50 degrees was a warm spring day to him.

He stretched for a few minutes in his apartment, bending over, trying to touch his head to his knees. He wasn't as limber as some of his yoga friends, but he could nearly manage. As he bent over, he was struck by a thought: *If I were able to suck my own cock, does that mean I'm gay, or just masturbating?* Then he started riffing on a few jokes about it and wondered if he could work that into a bit for an upcoming routine.

Outside, Jake studied his map on his mobile phone. Randie had told him he might enjoy a run through Washington Park, which was three miles away, so he plotted a route on his phone, put his earbuds in his ears, and turned to start—

"Ow, shit, watch it!" shouted a shape as Jake collided with it. He nearly knocked the person over but managed to catch them in time and keep them from being slammed to the ground.

"I'm sorry! I'm so sorry!" Jake stammered, moving the person into view. "Oh, hey, it's you." It was Molly from the bookstore. "Are you okay? I'm really sorry. I didn't know you were there, and my mind was elsewhere. I'm so sorry."

"I'm fine, I'm fine," she said. "Really, I'm okay. Don't worry about it. You caught me in time."

"Are you sure? I didn't bruise you or anything?"

"No, no, maybe just squished my boobs a little bit."

"Sorry," said Jake.

"You're, um, you're still squishing them," she said, looking pointedly down at Jake's arms and her chest still mashed together. He was still holding onto her so she wouldn't fall over.

"Oh, sorry! I didn't mean—" He let go, held her by the shoulders, and stepped back, making sure she wouldn't fall before he let go.

Molly laughed. "No, it's fine, I'd be more upset if you had just let me fall."

"You're sure you're okay?"

"I promise you, I'm fine." Molly was wearing an olive-green sweater and some black jeans. "It's my day off, so I was just going shopping and to run a couple errands for Prudie, then meet a couple friends for coffee."

"Prudie? I thought her name was Judy."

"Oh, it is. I just call her Prudie Judy because she's such a stick in the mud. She's always trying to fix me up with guys she thinks are appropriate but doesn't let me go out on dates with anyone she doesn't approve of."

"Like who?"

"Oh, artists, musicians, writers. She owns a bookstore but doesn't actually approve of the kinds of people who make the stuff she sells. Unless someone important comes for a reading or something, then she fawns all over them."

"I don't think she likes me either," said Jake. "I detected a real frostiness when I met her."

"Yeah, I caught that too. I think it's because you were in the sacred space behind the counter."

"I promise I'll be careful next time I'm in your sacred space." Jake groaned inwardly, hoping that didn't sound as forward as he thought.

"Did you read any of your new books yet?" Molly asked, not wanting the conversation to end just yet. She had caught the double entendre but figured he hadn't meant it since he didn't leer at her the way most other guys would have.

"I finished one of the Rex Stouts before the show, and got about a third into the Ellery Adams before I went to sleep."

"Wow, that's a lot."

"Well, I was up until 3:30 or so. It's a good book and I couldn't stop. I finally quit when I fell asleep and dropped the book on my face."

"Three-thirty? What time do you usually go to bed?" Molly asked. She thought midnight was staying up late, and usually went to bed after the 11:00 evening news.

"Usually around 2:00 or 2:30, depending on whether I'm headlining or not. If I'm a headliner I don't get out until 12:00 or later, and sometimes I'll stay and have a couple drinks with the other comics. Last night, I was the middle, and I was done by 11:30. I've worked with the headliner before and we toured together a few months ago, so I decided to head back to the apartment early."

"What's the 'middle?'" asked Molly.

"There are typically three acts at a comedy club. The opener is the comic who opens the whole show. They're usually local or regional and they're at the start of their career. The headliner is the main attraction, generally a national act, or from a larger region. Then, we have the person in the middle, hence the name."

Molly felt herself get wet when Jake said *"hence." Dear God, I love an educated man!*

"The middle only does 30 minutes, but the headliner does an hour," he was saying. "They're better than the opener, but not as good as the headliner."

Molly started to shiver and rubbed her arms. "Aren't you cold?" she asked, staring at his biceps, which were stretching his sleeves. She wanted to feel his arms back around her again.

"Maybe a little, but I'm about to go for a run, so I'll be alright in five minutes."

"Oh, sorry! Here I am pestering you about comedy and you're probably sick of thinking about it."

"No, not at all," he reassured her. "I enjoy it. Tell you what, how about I stop by the store when you're there tomorrow, and I can tell you more about it. Maybe we could get some coffee after you close"

Molly smiled. "That would be wonderful."

"Excellent, I'll see you tomorrow." He shook Molly's hand and started to run down the street, starting the timer on his runner's watch.

This time, it was Molly's turn to watch Jake's tight ass, and to see him turn around and look back at her.

"LOOK OUT!" she hollered, and he quickly turned back to avoid running into a signpost that sprang up out of nowhere.

Chapter 4

For all his athletics and exercising, Jake couldn't resist a good hot dog. Or even a bad one. So he ate two for a late lunch at a hot dog joint he'd passed during his run the day before.

He'd had a pretty good set the night before. Friday nights were always good nights at a comedy club because people were getting off work and wanted to cut loose and have a little fun. The late crowd was usually a little better than the first show because they'd had dinner and a few drinks and were a lot looser.

Of course, that also meant a few drunk assholes who decided they wanted to be a part of the show. Last night wasn't too bad, and Jake had learned how to handle hecklers over the years. Usually it was just some response to "you suck!" or someone blowing the punchline to a joke, and Jake could handle them pretty easily with a cutting remark. Not too harsh though, or you could quickly become the bully and get the crowd to turn on you.

Last night's heckler was a little different though, because he thought he needed to offer his input about Jake's set. As Jake was talking about life on the farm, the guy started kibitzing from his seat.

Finally, Jake had had enough when the guy shouted, "I had a cow bite me once."

"Really? You usually have to pay extra for that in the city." The crowd laughed, and so did the guy. It was all the encouragement he needed to keep contributing.

"They pay me after they see what I'm packing," hollered the guy, standing up and grabbing his package. The guy's wife pulled on his arm to make him sit down.

"Are you saying the cows pay you to have sex with them?" Jake asked from the stage. "Like, are you their cow-boy-toy? You like a little beef bangin'? Does that make you horny?"

The crowd laughed as the guy's face turned red and he balled up his fists.

"So, do you work freelance, or do you work in a whorehouse? Who's your MOO-dame?" The laughs got louder, and the guy got madder.

"Man, I'll bet the Cleveland Steamers you get are HUGE! Do they pay extra for that too?"

"Goddammit!" the guy roared. He grabbed his wife by the hand, who had been laughing along with the crowd, and he stomped out of the club.

"Jeez, that guy looked pissed. I hope he can steer straight," said Jake, as the crowd broke into applause.

Jake took another bite of his hot dog and smiled. He was especially proud of that Cleveland Steamer joke. He wrote that into his notebook, along with a couple other joke ideas he'd thought of, then pulled out the book that Molly had recommended.

Molly. She was a tough one to figure out. She seemed so quiet and reserved, like the good girls he grew up with. They went to church, were heavily involved in band and youth group, and got good grades. They were the do-gooders in his hometown of Mankato, Minnesota, but you could sometimes count on them for something more. When he was a senior in high school, Jake remembered fingering Sheila Jorgensen in the woods at a bonfire in fall one Friday evening after a football game. She had gasped and clutched at his arm as she came, kissed him on the lips and ran back to her friends when she was finished. He had spent the rest of the evening trying to hide his boner from his friends, even though he was sure Sheila and her friends were whispering and giggling about it.

Molly reminded him a little of Sheila Jorgensen. He wondered if he even had a chance with her, or would she quickly pull away and slam her knees shut as soon as she had to touch his dick.

He liked Molly because she was smart and seemed to enjoy reading, but he couldn't read her much beyond that. She was shy, dressed to hide what were obviously large tits, and never seemed to know exactly what she wanted.

Oh well, he thought.

It wasn't like this hadn't been a good trip. He'd met some nice people, found a great bookstore, and even gotten a blowjob from the hottest bartender in the club. But still, the thought of Molly riding him flashed in his mind, or him laying on top of her with her legs wrapped around his waist as he drove his cock into her wet pussy crept into his mind. The images gave him another erection, and he tried to will it back down. He read his book again and waited until it was safe to stand up. He walked outside, climbed into his truck, and drove back to the club's apartment, then walked to Lost In Pages.

An hour later, Molly and Jake were sitting at a coffee shop a few blocks down from the bookstore, and he was armed with a few new pulp novels from the store. They ordered lattes—Molly had hers with a touch of lavender—and they sat at a small table. Since it was in the 60s, she was wearing a low-cut tank top under a cotton, button-down shirt, on which she had unbuttoned the top three buttons. Jake could see her deep cleavage and got a very good idea of the size of her breasts. He fantasized about holding them and feeling their weight, licking and kissing them all over. He made it a point not to stare, but he did sneak the occasional glance. Otherwise, he focused all his attention on her and watching her candy-brown eyes.

At one point, she stood up to get a couple napkins, and she leaned forward so he could see her beautiful mammaries hang down and watch the gap between them grow. He imagined them hanging and swinging as he plowed her from behind. She did the same when she sat down again, and he wondered if she was doing it intentionally.

Which she was. Molly knew he had sneaked an occasional glance, and she knew she had nice breasts that drove men wild and could imagine his hands and mouth smothering them and kneading them. The thought made her juices flow and she clamped her thighs together to resist the urge to finger herself right there. Molly had had sex before, especially in college.

She wasn't particularly sexually active, having had no more than six or seven partners since she'd first had sex at the age of 20, and none in the last two years. But she loved to masturbate and would often read erotica, or occasionally watch a porno on her phone after she'd had a few glasses of wine. Most of her real sexual partners had been a bit disappointing. She remembered sleeping with her first boyfriend on her 20th birthday, who thought he was giving her some kind of gift. She was a junior at the University of Wisconsin–Madison and he had been in her creative writing class. He wanted to be a poet and he called himself a feminist. They had gone to yoga together a few times, and she had attended a couple of his poetry readings at one of the local coffee shops. For her birthday, he took her out to a vegan dinner (he'd had a Groupon) which she'd hated (she loved a good cheeseburger!) and as the evening was coming to a close, he asked if he could "take her flower." She almost kicked him out of her dorm room, but she'd had a few shots of schnapps that they had snuck in, and she thought she liked him at least enough for that.

Still, it was a disappointment because he hadn't lasted for more than 30 seconds and he'd wept when they were finished, thanking her for "such a beautiful gift." He had even pulled out and come all over her sheets. She had to sleep on a towel that night, after telling him she had an early class the next morning and he needed to leave. She blew him off after that, and chalked her first time down to a shitty lover. She later learned he had used that "take your flower" line several times over the last three years, mostly with freshman girls who thought he was deep and sensitive. Other partners had been better, but not by much. A couple of them were just run-of-the-mill lovers who would do their pushups on her then fall asleep after filling her up with their *come*. (Molly felt the correct spelling of the word was *"come,"* for both the noun and verb, and *"cum"* was used by men who used too much body spray, and texted *u up?* messages with eggplant emojis.)

After a while, Jake had to head to the club, so he offered to drop Molly back off at her apartment. When he pulled into the parking lot behind the bookstore, they sat in Jake's truck for a few minutes. It was already turning dusk outside since it was still April in Milwaukee. They twisted to face each other, and without saying a word, Molly reached up and put her hand on Jake's face. She leaned in for a kiss, and he gently pressed his lips to hers. When he lifted his head again, she pulled his head back down and kissed him harder and more fervently, darting her tongue into his mouth. Jake hesitated for only a second before intertwining his tongue with her own then gently capturing hers between his teeth.

Molly took her hand off Jake's face and slid it up his thigh, toward his rock-hard cock. She ran her hand over it and gave a sharp little intake of breath at what she felt. Jake slid his hand up toward her breast, slowly, questioningly. When she didn't stop him, he cupped her firm mound, squeezing and caressing it. They kissed harder and deeper, and she squeezed his dick and slid her hand up and down, trying to give him a hand job through his jeans.

"What are you doing for dinner tomorrow?" she whispered.

"It's Sunday, so we only have one show tomorrow at 7:00, and I'll be done by 8:00."

"Come over for dinner," she said quickly, kissing him deeply twice more. "And bring some wine. There's a door to the stairs in the back of the building. Just ring the buzzer." She gave his cock a final squeeze. "And bring this."

She gave him one last kiss and got out of the truck before she changed her mind and mounted him right there in the parking lot. Racing upstairs, she took off her pants and fingered her soaked pussy until she came twice, moaning, "Oh, Jake, fill me up with your cock. Oooohhhh, fuck me, Jake, with that big throbbing monster."

CHAPTER 5

The buzzer in Molly's apartment sounded a few minutes after eight, and she hit the intercom button: "Yes?"

"Hey, it's Jake." Molly hit the button to release the lock and a few seconds later, there was a knock at her door.

Not sure how to greet him after last night's groping, she played it safe and kissed him on the cheek. Anticipating a fun night, she wanted to give him easy access, so she wore her favorite skirt and a spaghetti strap top that was a little low cut. She also had on her special bra that accentuated her cleavage but didn't spill her tits out.

Jake was wearing his "work clothes," which was basically just a dress shirt and sport coat with jeans and tan leather Oxfords; he removed his shoes at the door and hung his coat on a hook.

"I brought wine," said Jake, holding out a brown bag, trying not to stare at her luscious mounds.

She pulled out the bottle and examined the label; it was a nice merlot that she'd enjoyed before, but not that often, because it was a bit pricey.

She thanked him with a deeper kiss then said, "I wasn't sure what you wanted for dinner, so I thought we could just do takeout, if that's alright."

"That would be fine. Do you want to have a glass of wine before we decide?"

"Sure. I'll put on some music if you could open the wine." Molly opened her favorite music app on her phone and turned on her favorite jazz station, plugging it into a small speaker.

Meanwhile Jake located the wine opener and glasses. He poured them each a glass and joined Molly on the couch. They made a quick toast, took a drink, then set their glasses on an end table. She sat close to him, and when he put his arm on the back of the couch, slid over and cozied up to him. They chatted for a few minutes, and Molly rested her hand on Jake's thigh. She watched his erection grow and remembered how it felt under her hand last night, so she slid her hand up toward it. She even thought that she saw the front of his jeans twitch! Molly couldn't wait any longer, so she raised up and kissed Jake hard on the mouth, slipping her tongue into his mouth as it writhed and curled around his tongue.

After a few minutes, she gasped, "Oh God, I want you."

Jake groaned in response. "Not as much as I want you."

Molly swung a leg over Jake's lap and mounted him, facing him, and continued kissing. "Ooooooohhhh," she moaned as he kissed and licked her neck and bit her ear lobe.

She pulled his head harder onto her neck as his nibbling gave her goosebumps. Molly began to grind her pussy on the raging hard-on she could feel through his jeans. She was hitting the right spot on her clit, and she rocked back and forth.

Jake had moved down from Molly's neck and began licking at her cleavage, massaging her tits with his hands. He kissed the top of one breast then the other before returning to her cleavage, sliding his tongue deep inside, licking straight up to her chin and kissing her on the mouth again. He lifted her shirt up over her head and she raised her arms to help him. Reaching behind her with practiced ease, he unclasped her bra.

Molly was more than a little impressed. *Usually I have to do that for the guy.*

Her breasts separated from her lacy brassiere as she eased it off her shoulders, holding her hands in front of her breasts, slowly exposing them. Molly grinded her wet pussy on his sheathed cock, soaking both her panties and his jeans.

"Holy fuck," murmured Jake as he watched Molly unveil her perfect, heavy breasts.

He put his hands back on them, trying to hold as much in each hand as he could. Jake leaned down and took one nipple into his mouth, sucking it until it became hard like a pencil eraser. Then he focused on her other nipple, licking it, gently sucking until it was a twin to the first. He pinched and tweaked the other one, keeping them hard.

Molly's pussy and panties were soaked, and she couldn't stand it anymore. She stood up and pulled her skirt and panties off in one motion, stepping out of them. He gazed at her nearly hairless mound, bare except for a small thatch right above her pink pussy.

Jake reached out and lightly stroked her slit, just once with a long finger.

Molly lunged for Jake's zipper, and fought to free his throbbing prick. He lifted his hips and helped her take his jeans and underwear off, then he pulled off his socks, because nothing is as unerotic as a naked guy in dark socks.

"Holy fuck," echoed Molly, finally seeing Jake's full eight-and-a-half tent pole, which was cleanly shaven. "I want that inside me. Will it even fit?"

"I'll go slowly," Jake said.

Molly climbed back onto Jake's lap, facing him once again. She tucked his cock so it was pointing downward, and she could feel the length of it on her pussy. Resuming her grinding back and forth, her pussy lips glided over the top of his hard shaft. She was so wet, her juices were running down to his balls, and he got a delicious chill as they cooled. Molly moaned as her grinding brought a delicious friction to her clit, an orgasm building.

"Oooohhhh… oooohhhh… OOOOHHHHH!!!!" she shrieked as her first orgasm overtook her sliding her cunt over his cock.

She collapsed onto Jake's chest his cock still pinned beneath her pussy.

"Fuck, I haven't come like that in years," she said into the nape of his neck. "That deserves a reward." She slowly slid back off his lap, pushing his legs apart. Kneeling before him, taking his big prick in her small hand. "I can barely get my hand around it. That's going to be a tight fit, but it's going to fucking fit," she growled deep in her throat.

Molly jerked his cock a few times then licked the underneath side of his shaft, from the base of his dick all the way to the head. She kissed it lightly and traveled back down one side, up the underside, and back down the other side. Molly jammed Jake's meat into her mouth a few inches, clutching the base with her hand. Jake groaned as she sucked his cock, suctioning so hard her cheeks pulled inward. She continued the suction as she lifted her head almost completely off his dick, before sliding it back into her mouth more than halfway. Again, she slid her head back, providing suction all the way, and Jake shifted his head a bit so he could see her cheeks hollowing out.

"Oh, fuck, that looks so hot," he groaned. "That feels so wonderful."

Molly slid Jake's prick in and out of her mouth, pulling it with her vacuum-sealed lips working the lower part of his shaft with her hand. Stroking his cock as she sucked him, her mouth and hand worked in tandem. She moved faster and faster as Jake bucked his hips under her ministrations.

"Aahh! Aahh! I'm going to come, Molly" Jake warned. "Look at my eyes," he pleaded. "Look at my eyes when I come in your mouth."

Molly looked up as she continued to piston his prick into her hot mouth, and Jake locked eyes with her.

"Oh, Molly, baby, I'm gonna... CO-O-O-OME!"

As soon as the first rope of come left Jake's cock, Molly held his head in her mouth and pumped her little fist furiously on his shaft, jacking three, four, five spurts of his milky, salty gel. She continued to suck and stroke. His spasms subsided except for a few after-shocks and tiny spurts. Molly swallowed deeply and cleaned him off like an ice cream cone.

"Holy shit balls, Molly, that was amazing!" Jake said, slumping back into the couch. "Give me a second, and then I'm going to return the favor."

Molly was a little surprised, *only one other guy has ever eaten my pussy.*

Jake stood up and told her to sit on the couch. Padding over to the kitchen, he got an ice cube from the freezer and popped it into his mouth. He returned to her and pulled her ass toward the edge of the couch. Jake separated her legs and began to massage the insides of her thighs with his powerful thumbs, working his way slowly up to her pink folds until he parted her pussy lips with his fingers. He leaned in and, with his face just a couple inches from her wetness, slowly blew cold air on her hot pussy.

"Ohhhhhhhhhh," she breathed and inhaled deeply. "Ohhhhhhhhhh," she moaned again as he did it a second time.

Molly moaned even louder as he stuck his cold-but-still-hot tongue into her cunt and licked upward to her pink pearl, flicking it with his tongue a few times. He returned back to her folds and slid his tongue deep inside her wetness, tasting her juices. Jake swirled his tongue around a few times before returning his attention to her clitoris, sliding his middle finger inside her. Molly whimpered as Jake sucked her clit and fucked her with one, then two, fingers. He raised his head, lips and cheeks glistening with her juice, and looked into her eyes. Massaging her tits with his left hand, he fingered her cunt with his two fingers and his thumb rubbed her clit.

"Fuck, I'm going to come," she said. "Make me come with your mouth and look into my eyes, too."

Jake did as he was told and returned his mouth to her slit and suctioned her clit between his lips, flicking his tongue over it.

"OH, FUCK! THAT'S IT! EAT MY PUSSY, JAKE! MAKE ME COME WITH YOUR MOUTH!"

Molly could barely keep her eyes open as she was overwhelmed with an even bigger orgasm than her previous one. Her juices flooded out of her pussy and over his hand. When she stopped bucking and writhing, she looked up and saw him licking off his fingers.

"I love to taste your pussy," he said, sliding a finger into his mouth and cleaning it off.

She took his hand and sucked the other finger, tasting her own juices. She looked back down and saw that Jake was already getting hard again.

"I want you inside me," she breathed. "Put that fucking monster inside me and fuck me with it."

Jake stood up and put his cock close to her mouth. Molly slid it into her mouth and pumped up and down on it a few times as deeply as she could, coating it with her saliva.

"Now, fuck me, Jake. PLEASE!"

Jake kneeled back down, put one hand on Molly's belly, thumb on her clit, and guided his cock toward her wet pussy. He slid his head in and she gasped sharply at the sensation. He slid a couple of inches in and she keened a little.

"Gently," she murmured.

He nodded, keeping eye contact.

Jake waited several seconds so she could adjust to this thick new invader. She nodded and groaned with delight as he slid in a couple more inches. He felt a little resistance, so he slowly pulled out until just the cock head remained inside, then slid back in, inch after inch, until he was at his previous depth. Again, he slid out and back in just as slowly, out again, in again, out again, and in again a third time. He continued this several more times, getting his cock coated with her juices and getting her used to the motion. After several seconds of gentle thrusting, he pushed in a little more. Molly arched her back and opened her mouth in a silent scream as he finally buried his cock up to the hilt.

"Oh, God, it's in me. I can feel your giant prick inside me. It's so—OH!" Jake made his dick twitch inside her pussy, making her jump. "Fuck me with it," she begged. "Please fuck me with it."

Jake slowly slid his cock out as he had before, resting only the head inside her pussy lips, before sliding it slo-o-o-owly back into her love tunnel. It slid in more easily, and Jake buried himself completely once again. He began pumping her now, not as gently, but not so rough. She felt the smooth, steady glide of his big shaft splitting her up the middle and exploring her pink, wet depths. He gripped her forearms, and she did the same, pulling her to bury himself deeper.

"You're so tight," murmured Jake, between thrusts. "Your pussy feels like velvet. I love your hot pussy, Molly."

She loved hearing him use her name when he talked dirty. "I love your big cock, Jake," Molly answered. "It feels so good inside me."

Jake continued to fuck her this way for a few minutes, now placing his hands on her breasts as they shook and wobbled with every thrust. They listened to their ragged breathing and the *slap, slap, slap* of Jake's body against hers.

"Let's change," said Jake.

Molly nodded her agreement, and Jake stood, pulling out of her warmth. He turned her around and guided her onto her hands and knees onto the couch, angled so Jake could slip into her pussy from behind. He guided his cock back into her sopping cunt—"ooooOOOHHHH" she moaned when he slipped all the way inside her—then grabbed two handfuls of her ass and started fucking her from behind.

Molly's big tits hung down and began rocking and swaying with each thrust. Jake reached underneath her, kneading them with his hands. He used them to guide Molly, pushing her back into him, causing her to fuck him from the front. Their bodies slapped together several times before Jake raised up again, and grabbed Molly's hips, pulling her back even harder, thrusting forward to meet her, his front slapping into her ass.

Molly grunted with each thrust before she said, "I want to ride you. Sit on the couch and I'm going to fuck you."

Jake noticed how sweaty they were as Molly guided his throbbing dick to her sopping entrance. He rubbed her glistening tits, using her sweat as a massage lubrication. Jake kissed her hard on the mouth and she moaned into him as she slowly lowered herself onto his magnificent dick.

Molly raised and lowered her hips, slamming down onto his lap, driving his cock up into her throbbing cunt. She grunted with every thrust—"Unh! Unh! Unh! Unh!"—giving an extra grind as she came down each time, rubbing her clit against his pubic bone, until she began to moan. She gazed deeply into his eyes, fighting the urge to close hers while she came.

"Ohhhh, fuck... I'm going to come again, Jake... I'm ... going ... to ... come... OH, JAKE! ...JAKE! ...JAKE! FUCK ME WITH THAT GIANT COCK! OOOOOHHHHHHHH!"

She collapsed against his chest again like she had nearly an hour ago. Only this time, she was full of Jake's meat, riding it like she stole it. Even as she came, she couldn't stop thrusting because she knew he was getting close.

"Oh fuck, Molly, I'm gonna come. I've got another load for you. Just tell me where to come and I'll do it for you, baby."

"Oh, oh, oh, oh. Come inside me, please, Jake. I'm on the pill. Shoot your hot come inside my pussy!" Her velvet pussy clamped down on his cock, squeezing it even as he continued to thrust from below.

"Look at me," she gasped. "That's such a turn-on. Look at me again when you come inside me."

Molly and Jake were breathing like they had just run a marathon. Sweat dripped off both of them and mixed at the point of their union, lubricating Molly's pearl where she was still grinding into Jake's body, bouncing up and down on his dick.

"Ohhh, this is it," moaned Jake. "This is it. I'm going to come for you."

"That's it, baby," said Molly. "Fill me up. Fill up my pussy. Let me see your eyes when you shoot inside me."

Jake held his forehead to Molly's and gazed into her eyes, even as she grunted every time she landed on his dick. "FUCK! FUCK! AUUUGGGHHH!"

Molly screamed as Jake's hot semen filled her, each throb of his shaft released another white rope into her battered pussy. She held onto him as he shuddered with every spasm of his essence depositing deep inside her. The two stayed locked together, his cock still inside her pussy even as their juices mingled. They kissed and Molly whimpered as she rocked her hips slightly, enjoying the sensation of release as Jake's slowly deflating manhood retreated from her folds.

"Fuck, that was amazing," said Jake.

"Oh, for me too," Molly answered, kissing him deeply.

She buried her face into his neck as they panted and recovered.

After several minutes, she said, "Do you feel like dinner?"

"Definitely. What are you in the mood for?"

"We can order Chinese, and have it delivered," she said. "I know a great place near here." She stood up, and Jake gazed at her naked, glistening form, admiring the curves of her hips and her full, heavy breasts.

"I just need a shower first," Molly said. "And I want you to join me."

"I'd love nothing more," said Jake as Molly led him by his growing cock toward her bathroom.

THE END

CHASTITY VELDT

Irene
in Indianapolis

STAND UP, LIE DOWN COLLECTION

TABLE OF CONTENTS

CHAPTER 1

The smell of freshly ground coffee hit Jake's nostrils the second he opened the door to Cool Beans Coffee in Indianapolis on a late Monday afternoon in May. He imagined himself floating in on the tendrils of the heavenly smells, like they did in cartoons whenever someone cooked a steak or baked a pie. Standing in the entry for a moment, breathing deeply, he inhaled the heavenly aroma.

He was something of a coffee snob and always liked to find the local shops in any new city he visited. After driving for a couple days from his hometown, Mankato, Minnesota, for a gig in Indianapolis, he needed to get some of the road fuzz off his tongue. Showing up a day early, he had time before he needed to check in at the club and let them know he was there.

Jake Nilsen was a standup comic who toured the Midwest and Southeast performing most nights. He mostly lived out of his truck, although comedy clubs tended to have a club apartment where they would let comics stay while they were in town. He was 6'2" and exercised regularly. Jake had been a swimmer in college and still swam whenever he could but would always made sure to run for a few miles regardless of where he was. Thanks to his light blond hair and gold wire-frame glasses, people often remarked he looked like Tony, the first terrorist killed in the *Die Hard* movie. He still had his swimmer's build and wore his t-shirts a little tighter than he needed to.

Jake had been in Milwaukee a couple weeks ago,[1] spending a few nights as the middle at Pretzel's Comedy Club and having wild monkey sex with a woman named Molly. He went home to Mankato for a week before heading to Indianapolis where he was going to be the midweek headliner at Cracker's Comedy Club, as well as emceeing their Tuesday night open mic. He hated open mics and wondered how drunk he could get without being fired before his Wednesday night gig. Except they were paying him an extra $100 to be the emcee, and when you were a working road-comic, you didn't turn down any cash.

The coffee shop was mostly empty this late in the afternoon, so Jake thought he might read a little. He had some time to kill before he needed to meet with the club owner and had a couple books he had picked up in Milwaukee he wanted to finish, so he stepped up to the counter to order.

"Hi, welcome to Cool Beans," said the woman behind the counter.

"Thank you," said Jake, "it's my first time here."

"Crossing over from the charred side, are you?" asked the woman whose name tag said *Bianca*.

"Excuse me?"

---

[1] See *Stand Up, Lie Down #1: Molly in Milwaukee*

"The charred side. You know, 'the big guys.' Corporate Coffee." Bianca made air quotes when she said that; her fingers were long and elegant.

That must mean she's got a big dick, Jake thought and tried not to smile at his juvenile joke. "Oh, no, I'm not from here. So this is all new to me."

"You mean coffee? Don't they have coffee where you're from?"

"Well, of course they have coffee. I mean, I've never been here to this place. Or this city."

"No kidding? Where are you from?"

"Mankato. Uh, Minnesota. I'm just here for a show. I'm Jake, by the way. Jake Nilsen."

"Nilsson?" said Bianca.

"Nilsen," said Jake.

"I'm Bianca." She stuck her hand out and Jake shook it.

Bianca was tall, nearly six feet, tanned from plenty of outdoor activity, and looked like a former athlete who had put on a few pounds. She was curvy and fleshy, but when she squeezed Jake's hand, the muscles in her forearm flexed and he realized she may have lost her tone, but not her strength. Jake watched her forearm flex under the dragon tattoo wrapped around her arm. He slid his gaze upward, taking note of her full breasts under her t-shirt and apron, pausing briefly at her full lips, then rested on her improbably green eyes.

Contacts? he wondered, although he didn't care: *her eyes are gorgeous.*

Her black hair was tied back into a long braid that hung over her shoulder and draped over her ample bust. Faint crow's feet around her eyes that, as a comic, Jake knew meant she laughed and smiled a lot. He guessed her age at around the mid- to late-30s.

"Do you know what you want?" Bianca asked.

"Just a latte for now, please."

"Anything to eat?"

"I don't know. What do you have?"

Bianca handed him a small menu and said, "We do sandwiches, some soups, and we have pastries."

"Well, I skipped lunch, so maybe I should eat. What do you recommend?"

"We have a grilled three-cheese panini and chili on special today."

"I'll have that as well," He paid with a credit card, and Bianca talked him into joining their coffee club.

"I have a feeling we'll be seeing a lot of you this week," she said, turning to make his latte. "I'll bring everything out to you."

Jake sat down at a table, pulled a Rex Stout book out of his backpack, and began to read. He was soon immersed in the story and was a bit startled when Bianca set a plate and mug down in front of him. The sandwich was excellent, and he dipped it into the chili between bites, something he had done as a kid. He ate slowly and resumed his reading. Engrossed in the book, he didn't notice Bianca wiping down tables nearby and watching him as he ate, taking a bite, turning a page. Finally, as he finished, she came back.

"You said you were in town for a gig. What are you, a musician?" she asked.

"No, I'm a comic."

She smiled. "Really? Tell me a joke."

"When is a door not a door?"

"I don't know."

"When it's ajar."

Bianca stared blankly at him. "That's not funny."

"It's my first day," Jake said.

Bianca threw her head back and laughed from her belly, which jiggled a little and thrilled Jake. He was not fond of women who felt they had to titter quietly or be "ladylike," *whatever the hell that meant.*

"Okay, that was pretty funny."

"To tell you the truth, I'm more of a storytelling comic, rather than a one-line comic. I don't just spin off one-liners like Mitch Hedberg. I tell stories that get laughs as I tell them."

"That sounds interesting. I'd like to come see you perform one night."

"Well, my first show is on Wednesday, but I'm emceeing the open mic tomorrow night. I won't be doing too much there, so you probably want to skip that. Plus, open mics tend to be, well... not good."

"Then why do they do them?" She pointed at the other chair and raised her eyebrows questioningly.

"Please," said Jake. "Open mics are a cheap way for a comedy club to get people in the door without paying high-priced comics to show up, especially since people typically don't go out in the middle of the week. But that's where every comic gets their start too."

"Even you?"

"Even me. We all go to an open mic, suck terribly, then go back the following week. We keep going back, sucking terribly, and eventually sucking a little less. After a while, we get good enough to perform a ten-minute opening set for fifty bucks at some shitty comedy club."

Bianca leaned forward and put her chin on her hands. The move pressed her breasts together, and Jake wished she had been wearing a V-neck shirt. "So, what's the difference between a successful comic and those people at the open mic?"

"Honestly? It's that second night. Anyone can go suck at an open mic one night. But the people who go back, they're the ones with the desire. They know they won't get laughs for a while, but they'll come. So they work at the craft, they're always writing jokes, always studying other comics, and trying to get better. Eventually, they get into the game and one day, they decide to quit their job and go out on the road."

"How long have you been doing this?" asked Bianca.

"Let's see, I did my first open mic seven years ago, right after I graduated college, and I've been a full-time road comic for two years. I'm just getting to the point where I can middle in some bigger cities, or headline in some small ones."

"Middle?"

"That's the second comic in a three-act night."

"Oh, so not the guy between the top and bottom in a three way?"

Jake snorted into his latte and sprayed foam onto his upper lip; Bianca reached out and wiped it off with her thumb.

"So are you performing tonight?" she asked.

"No, I wanted to get here today. I went home to visit my family for a while and decided to leave a little early."

"Really? Why?"

"My family is still not too supportive of my career choice. They wanted me to be a lawyer or join the family business and be a farmer. But I've been able to support myself with my work, and I did enough farm work when I was younger to last two lifetimes."

"And is that how you got those great pecs?" Bianca had to resist reaching out to run her hands all over them.

"No, I was a swimmer in high school and college. I still swim. In fact, I wanted to ask you if there was a YMCA in town."

"Sure, about three miles north of here. I'll give you directions before you leave."

"That sounds good. I should probably go in a few minutes anyway. I have to check in at the club and get the key to the club apartment."

"Oh, that's too bad. I was enjoying talking with you," said Bianca. "Any chance you'd want to continue the conversation over dinner?"

"That would be great. I don't have any plans for the evening, so whatever you wanted to do would be fine with me."

"Well, we close up here at 7:00, so if you meet me here at 8:00, that will give me time to go home and change, and I can take you to one of my favorite sushi places. It's just a few blocks away."

"Great. I'll see you then."

Jake walked a block over and found Crackers. He went inside and introduced himself to the bartender.

"Oh, you want Sherri," said the bartender, Gavin. "I'll take you to her." Gavin guided Jake to the back room where Sherri was sitting, looking at something on her laptop. Gavin knocked on the door and said, "Sherri, this is Jake Nilsen, our emcee and headliner for the week."

"Nilsson?" asked Sherri.

"Nilsen," said Jake.

Sherri ate a cookie from a tin of Danish butter cookies. "You want a cookie?" she said, offering up the tin and blowing a few crumbs out of her mouth.

"No, thank you," said Jake. "I just ate."

"Suit yourself. So you want to get into the club apartment, I suppose. Well, here's your key; there are towels and bed linens in the closet. We just had the place cleaned after the last headliner got hammered, screwed two fans, and puked all over the couch. Fucking asshole. He asked for a hotel, but I talked him into staying here, which was my first mistake. So we burned the couch and bought a new one from Ikea. Don't puke on it."

"I promise, I won't," said Jake.

"You're the only one there until Saturday night but you'll be gone by Sunday morning, I suppose. Do you need Gavin to show you where it is?" Sherri asked.

Jake remembered what had happened when Randie in Milwaukee showed him to the club apartment,[2] so he politely declined. Instead, he found the place on his own—it was just a few blocks from the club—and he unpacked and took a shower, lay down for a short nap, and woke up to his phone's alarm. He did a bunch of pushups and sit-ups until his muscles ached, then got ready to meet Bianca for dinner. He stroked his cock in the shower, dreaming of her large breasts, and imagined sliding his cock in between them.

---

[2] Also *Stand Up, Lie Down #1: Molly in Milwaukee*

CHAPTER 2

It was a cool May evening, so Jake walked back to Cool Beans. He was wearing his work clothes, which he usually wore on stage: jeans, tan Oxford shoes, tailored dress shirt, and a light-gray sport coat. As he neared the shop, he spotted Bianca standing outside, wearing a deep-green, full-length cotton sundress that matched her eyes (He still didn't know if they were contacts), black Doc Marten boots, and a light denim jacket. She had undone her braid and tied it into a ponytail, her long, black hair reaching the middle of her back.

"Hi," she said, smiling at him.

"Hi," Jake answered. He wasn't sure how he should greet her, so he stuck out his hand as she went to hug him and ended up poking her in the belly. "Oops," he said.

"Sorry," laughed Bianca. "Let me try again." She went in and gave him a bigger squeeze, and Jake could feel her full breasts pressing against him, which caused his dick to stir a little. "Are you ready?"

She started walking and Jake noticed her dress was split up the left side, nearly to her hip. Jake tried to admire the view without being caught. The two chatted about Jake's work, the coffee shop ("Best coffee in Indianapolis, and we roast it ourselves!"), and the city. Jake learned Bianca was a former college volleyball player who still played in beach volleyball leagues on the weekends.

They soon reached Wasabi's Sushi Bar, a small restaurant with an outdoor patio. Bianca greeted the woman working at the hostess stand; apparently Bianca was a regular, because they knew each other and Bianca knew which booth to ask for: *the one tucked in the corner farthest from the door and the kitchen.* Jake counted only fourteen tables and booths, most of them with very long white tablecloths nearly reaching the floor.

Bianca took the seat against the wall, then patted the spot next to her. "This way, we can watch everyone else."

"There is no one else," said Jake. *Well, almost no one else*; there were a few people sitting outside and an older couple sitting at the sushi bar talking with the chefs. As he sat down, Bianca scooted very close to him and slid the tablecloth away from them a little so it hung longer on the other side.

"Your server's name is Lena, and she'll be with you in just a moment," said the hostess.

A few minutes later, Lena appeared. She was Asian-American, slender, and stood a few inches over five feet with her hair worn short. They chatted for a few minutes and Lena shared the evening's specials and recommended a couple of her favorites.

Drinks were ordered, menus were perused, more drinks were ordered, sushi rolls were ordered and delivered, and even more drinks were ordered. Jake and Bianca continued their conversations from the walk, even as she pressed her leg firmly against his. At one point, she fed him one of her pieces of volcano shrimp, getting some volcano sauce on the corner of his mouth.

"Oh, you missed some," she murmured, wiping it off with her thumb, dragging it lightly along his lower lip, then licking it herself.

"Let me try one of yours," she said.

Jake held up a piece of his spicy tuna roll and she guided his hand, catching his forefinger in her lips and sucking it into her mouth. His cock swelled, and so did Bianca when she reached over and ran her hand up his thigh. She rubbed his member through his jeans and hissed a little intake of breath when she felt its thickness.

"Can I get you anything else?" asked Lena.

Bianca never moved her hand but turned and smiled at the young woman. "Maybe another round of drinks."

Lena glanced down and smiled back, returning a few minutes later with the drinks and the little black folder with the check. Bianca's hand rubbed Jake's cock and Lena stole a second and third glance.

"I'll just leave this here, but you can take all the time you need," she said.

After she left, Bianca whispered in Jake's ear, "My pussy is so wet right now."

"Let me see," said Jake.

He slid his hand on her thigh and thanked the unknown fashion designer who designed a dress that was split so high. He slid his hand up and found her mound, almost coming in his jeans when he discovered she wasn't wearing any panties.

"Mmmmmmm," he growled in the back of his throat. Bianca spread her legs slightly, and Jake slid his middle finger down her pink folds.

"Mmmmmmm," she answered as he gently pried her pussy lips apart and slid his middle finger inside her. She gasped a little at his invading digit.

"Oh God, that's so good." He crooked his finger inside her. "And thank you for trimming your nails," she said wrapping her arms around his so it would only look like she was holding his arm, not that he was buried up to the second knuckle inside her wet cunt.

"Thank you," he said, gazing into her green eyes. *They have to be contacts!* "I had an old girlfriend teach me about trimming my nails and not keeping them cut square."

"Well, I'm glad you figured it out with her and not me—oh!" Jake slid his finger back out, over her clit, and back in, this time with two fingers. "Holy fuck!" she gasped, gripping his arm even tighter. Jake continued to slide his fingers in and out of her pussy, gliding over her clit.

"Oh God, this is so fucking dirty," she said in his ear. "I can't believe you're finger fucking me in public." Bianca breathed harder, in time with Jake's rhythm. "Oh, fuck," she whimpered. "I'm going to cum."

Bianca had long ago decided she preferred the spelling of "cum" to "come," especially if she was being finger banged in a restaurant with a guy she had only met five hours earlier. She loved "cum," both the word and the fluid.

"Then cum," he whispered back, using her spelling. "Cum on my hand."

"Oh God," she murmured quietly, scrunching up her face, but trying not to be too obvious. "I'm going to take you back to my place and ride that horse cock of yours. I can't wait to feel that big prick inside my pu—ooohhhhhhh," and she tensed up, nearly crushing his hand between her thighs, and gripped his arm as she shuddered through her orgasm.

He removed his finger from her pussy as she tried to catch her breath, still clutching his arm. Bianca looked around to see if anyone had noticed and saw nobody had. Nobody except Lena standing in a nearby corner behind the servers' station and computer. She had been watching Jake and Bianca, her hand down her shorts, rubbing her clit, and keeping an eye out for anyone coming that way.

Bianca smiled at her, and Lena realized she had been spotted. She yanked her hand out of her shorts and darted into the women's bathroom.

"Quick, come with me," said Bianca.

Jake left enough cash to cover the bill plus another $20 tip. But instead of leaving, Bianca led him to the men's room. Taking a quick peek over her shoulder, she pulled him inside and locked the door.

"Now let me see that cock up close," she said, undoing his zipper.

Jake pulled down his pants and lifted up his shirt. Bianca looked down in wonder. First at his cock, then up at his face, then back down to his eight-and-a-half-inch meat, then up at his face again. She ran her hands over his washboard abs and stroked the V muscles that directed her gaze to his shaved pubic region.

"It must be my birthday," she said, stroking his prick with her long fingers, a drop of pre-cum forming on the tip.

Bianca dropped to her knees and licked his pre-cum off, kissed the head, and *schlurped* his rod into her mouth, sucking in several inches.

Jake's knees nearly buckled, and he groaned, "Oh shit, that feels amazing."

Bianca slid his veiny prick in and out of her mouth, grabbing his ass, pulling and pushing to fuck her mouth with his cock. Jake could hear the squishy pops and bubbles as her tongue and lips engulfed him, squeezing and forming around every contour of his shaft. If there was one thing he loved, it was hearing the sounds a woman made while she sucked him off.

Bianca eagerly pumped the base of his shaft with her fist while she sucked him. This was not a slow, sensuous blowjob; Bianca was turned on, and sucking Jake off in a restaurant bathroom was driving her wild.

"Oh God, I'm gonna come," groaned Jake, slipping into the other spelling to see if she noticed. (*She didn't.*) "I'm gonna come."

Bianca popped his dick out of her mouth and kept pumping. "Cum in my mouth," she demanded. "Shoot it right in my mouth."

Jake nodded and guided her head back to its previous position. "Here it comes! Here it—aaahhhhh!" Jake moaned quietly as he pumped his load.

Two shots, three shots, *four* shots of his man-juice filled her eager mouth, and she swallowed every spurt. She swallowed deeply and sucked a few stray drops that continued to ooze out.

"Holy fuck, you're amazing," said Jake.

"Oh, I'm not done with you yet, tiger," said Bianca, standing up and wiping the corners of her mouth with her fingers. "I meant what I said earlier: I'm taking you back to my place and I'm gonna ride you like I stole you."

They left the bathroom and passed Lena as she was clearing the table. Lena smiled and looked down as they walked past. Bianca stopped, put her hand on Lena's lower back and whispered something in her ear. Lena's eyes widened and she smiled shyly at Jake, then whispered something back to Bianca.

Jake waited until they were back outside then asked: "What did you say to her?"

"I said, 'he just came in my mouth and now I'm going to fuck him.'"

"What did she say?"

"'I'll think about you both when I masturbate tonight.'"

Chapter 3

Jake woke up the next morning to the sounds of a shower. He didn't recognize his surroundings, but that wasn't uncommon. Most road warriors had their fair share of "where am I?" moments, waking up in a new city every few nights.

He looked over and saw his phone on the nightstand, then glanced over on the other side and saw an empty side of the bed with the covers kicked back. Laying back, He stared at the ceiling and remembered coming home with Bianca after dinner at that sushi place, and realized he was still at her apartment. He smiled and remembered what had happened after they got back. Looking on the floor next to the bed, he found three empty condom wrappers.

He checked his phone for the time: 7:30. *Fuck, it's still early*, especially since they had been up until after 2:00 enjoying each other. He heard the shower turn off and a few minutes later, Bianca emerged naked, drying herself off with a towel. Her breasts shook as she dried under her arms, and he watched her hips jiggle as she walked.

"Hey," said Jake, propping himself up on one elbow.

"Don't stare at my ass," said Bianca. "I don't like my ass."

"Really? Because I loved rubbing your ass last night. It's so sexy."

She blushed, not sure what to say, so she changed the subject. "Did I wake you?"

"No, I just woke up. What are you doing up so early?"

"I have to be at work at 9:00."

"Don't you have to be there early to open up?" Jake asked.

"Not today. I get to sleep in a couple mornings each week."

"Sleep in? Shit, I don't get up until nine or ten. I typically don't go to bed until 2:00 when I'm on the road."

"Then I did wake you."

"No, I had to pee."

"So that's not because you're happy to see me?" she said, gesturing to his erection and smiling.

"'Do I have to pee, or am I just happy to see you?' Is that what you're saying?" He patted her side of the bed, so she wrapped her hair into the towel and sat down.

"You don't mind if we skip a repeat of last night, do you?" she said. "I'm a little sore."

He grinned sheepishly, "I was kind of hoping the same thing. I've got a bit of a bang-over."

Bianca threw her head back and laughed like she had done less than eighteen hours earlier. Bang-over or not, Jake did like the way her breasts looked when she laughed. Or dried herself off. Or did nothing at all.

She stroked his arm with her fingers and looked down, unable to look into his eyes. "So, um, listen, I've got…"

"An early meeting?" Jake finished.

"Something like that."

"So, you don't need a second night?" Jake lifted her chin and looked directly in her eyes. He began to stroke her other arm.

"Something like that." Bianca crossed her arms and covered her chest. "Don't get me wrong. I loved everything we did last night, and I must have cum five or six times. But I just had an itch that needed scratching, and I hadn't scratched it in a while."

"And you're not itchy anymore?"

"No, but it burns a little when I pee now. Is that normal?"

Jake snort-laughed, "That's hilarious!" He reached out to her for a hug, and she uncovered her chest and leaned into his embrace.

She gazed deeply into his eyes then kissed him fully. "Well, I do have one more little itch that needs scratching."

Jake put his hands on her ass and began to squeeze her beautiful flesh. He said, "I think I can help you with that."

CHAPTER 4

Jake came into Cool Beans on Wednesday afternoon and found Bianca and another guy, Gerald, working behind the counter.

"Hey, big boy," she said.

"Hey, yourself," he said, smiling. They had spent the previous night apart, agreeing that they could be friends with benefits and promising each other that it wouldn't be weird if he continued hanging out there.

"You joined the loyalty club, remember?" Bianca had said. "That binds you, heart and soul, to our coffee shop."

"Wow, you guys take your loyalty club pretty seriously," Jake said.

"I'm thinking about rebranding it as a fealty club," said Bianca. "What can I get you? Your usual?"

"Sure, that would be great."

"What's that?" asked Gerald. "Do you want almond milk or soy milk?"

Jake made a face.

"I'll make it," said Bianca, "I know exactly what he likes."

She winked at him and moved over to the espresso station. Jake followed and stood on the other side of the counter; Gerald helped another customer.

"He's a bit of a goober, but he's a good kid," she said.

"Are you doing okay?" Jake asked.

"Oh shit, this isn't one of those pity visits, is it?" asked Bianca, rolling her eyes.

Jake looked at them deeply again. They were the same color, so he wasn't sure if she was wearing the same contacts or if—*no, they couldn't be that color naturally, could they?*

"No, no, not at all." Jake leaned in closer and spoke a little more quietly. "I, uh, I hurt my back. I wanted to see if you were in any pain yourself."

"When, yesterday?"

"No." He looked around to see if anyone could hear him. "No, it was, uhh, Monday night. When, you know—"

"Oh my God," laughed Bianca a little loudly. Jake shushed her. "Are you embarrassed?" she asked.

He stood up straight and puffed out his chest a bit. "No, not at all. No, that's—why should I—I mean, no, of course not. Shut up, you're embarrassed!"

Bianca laughed again as she steamed his milk. She leaned over the counter to him and murmured. "Look, anyone who slaps my ass when he's riding me doggy style should not be embarrassed about injuring himself during sex."

"I, uh, I just don't— Look, I'm from small-town Minnesota, okay! We just don't talk about—" He looked around again. "—*that.* At least not outside the moment."

"For someone who doesn't like to talk about it, you sure are good at it."

"I read about it, *a lot.*"

"Uh-huh." Bianca handed him his latte.

"But seriously, my back does hurt. I think our *sex* and the shitty club bed did a number on me. I was wondering if you know where I can get a massage."

"I don't, but I think you might get some good benefits from yoga."

Jake made a face. "I just told you, I'm from small-town Minnesota. We don't do eastern mystical stretchy exercises either."

"God, you're such a farmer," she said with a smile. "Look, those stretchy exercises can do wonders for your muscles, especially your back. I had a couple of nagging volleyball injuries and I started doing yoga and they've mostly cleared up. I can still aggravate them once in a while, but that usually happens if I haven't practiced yoga for a few weeks."

"Is there any place in particular I should go?"

"My instructor, Irene, usually comes in here on Wednesday afternoons after her class. She owns the studio over that way." Bianca pointed out the big window and across the parking lot. She looked up at the clock on the wall. "She should be here in about 30 minutes. You should talk to her."

"How will I recognize her?"

"She looks like a lollipop with tits."

Jake laughed at the image, not quite sure what she meant. He thanked her for the latte and sat down, pulling a book out of his jacket pocket. Reading, not paying attention to people who were coming and going, the bell on the door chimed every few minutes. He didn't even look up until Bianca was standing in front of him with two more lattes with a shortish woman standing next to her.

"Jake, this is Irene Jennings," said Bianca.

Jake stood up and Irene stuck out a small hand. She was in her late-40s and stood about six inches over five feet, although Jake realized that's because she was wearing three-inch clogs. Irene was wearing gray, cotton yoga pants and a black top that was form-fitted to her body, and Jake could also see why Bianca had called her a *lollipop with tits.*

Not only was she very skinny—built like a long-distance runner—but her breasts were a lot bigger than one might expect on a 5'3" runner. Not to mention her lips were full and lush, maybe a little too lush, probably another gift to herself from her plastic surgeon. And her hair was artificially blond, tightly curled, and hung down to her shoulders. She reminded Jake of one of those artsy-hippy types who married rich and had some work done, which is exactly what she was. Irene had been a yoga instructor for several years, then married a rich pharmaceutical executive—her first, his third—and started getting some work done when she turned 42.

Irene stuck out her hand and Jake shook it. "It's nice to meet you," said Irene. "What's your name?"

"Jake Nilsen."

"Nilsson?"

"No, Nilsen. And it's good to meet you too."

"Bianca was telling me that you were having some back problems." She smiled and winked at Bianca. "Why don't you tell me about how you hurt yourself, and the types of exercise you typically get."

Bianca set down the lattes and Jake gestured to the other seat. "Well," he said, "I typically run a few miles a day and I try to swim two or three times a week. I used to be a swimmer in college and still enjoy my time in the water."

"And how did you hurt your back this time?"

"That? Oh, uh—I, uh, we were—I mean, I pulled something when I was running."

"Well, someone pulled something, sport, and from what I heard, you weren't running."

Jake blushed deeply and stared at his latte.

Irene laughed softly. "Aww, don't be embarrassed, honey. Bianca told me about it yesterday after our yoga class. She needed some extra work after "running" too. From what I heard, you two ran for quite a while."

"Yes, well."

She laughed louder. "I can't believe you're shy about this. For one thing, she told me you had nothing to be shy about. For another, she said you know your way around a woman's body. So hold your head up high, stud."

Jake looked up at Irene and locked onto her hazel eyes. "So, Bianca said yoga can help my back," he said, desperately trying to change the subject.

"I think so. I can teach you some stretches that will bring you some relief and help you avoid further "running" injuries in the future. And she said she didn't mind if I gave you some private lessons. Are you up for it?"

"Sure, when do you have time?"

"What time do you have to be on stage?" Irene asked.

"Well, I've got an 8:00 and a 10:00 tonight and tomorrow night."

Irene looked at her watch and Jake noticed the wedding band on her left ring finger. "It's 3:30 now. I don't have any classes until 6:00 when all the lonely housewives start showing up. Do you have your workout clothes?"

"They're back at the club apartment. I can get changed and meet you back at your studio at 4:00."

"Excellent. Wear whatever you like. I'll have a yoga mat you can use."

Jake arrived one minute early at the yoga studio, which was just across the parking lot from Cool Beans and a couple doors down from Cracker's. He entered the yoga studio and found Irene at the front counter. The studio was basically just a large open space with a couple of bathrooms, a counter, an office, and a few plants to provide some greenery. There were some shelves behind the counter with mats for sale, bottles of water, and some essential oil diffusers and bottles. The windows had some bamboo shutters that were pulled down for privacy. Jake left his shoes in one of the cubbies near the door and took off his t-shirt. He was wearing a tank top that clung to his pectoral muscles and slim trunk, and was wearing bike shorts under his running shorts. Irene could see Jake had cannonballs for shoulders and her eyes lingered on his biceps for a few seconds.

"Great, just wonderful," said Irene, admiring the view. *Bianca wasn't kidding*, she thought.

Irene had changed into some black yoga shorts and a light purple sports bra with a zipper up the front, leaving her taut midriff bare. Right before he arrived, she had bent over and readjusted herself to push up her grapefruit-sized tits, then unzipped the zipper a third of the way to give Jake a mouth-watering glimpse of her cleavage.

"We'll set up over here." She locked the studio door, then walked over to a couple of mats already laid out. "First, show me where it hurts."

Jake reached around and gestured at the painful area, trying to indicate his entire lower back.

"Tell you what, show me on me," said Irene. She stood with her back to Jake and said, "Just use your hands and show me about where you're hurting."

Jake put his large hands on Irene's tiny waist. He placed the heels of his hands together at the lowest part of her waist and reached his fingers around toward her sides. She breathed in slowly as she felt the heat from his hands on her bare skin.

"Is the pain radiating down your legs at all?" Irene asked, sliding one of his hands down her leg.

"A bit. I had to sleep on my side to try to alleviate it."

"Well, you should sleep on your side anyway, or at least on your back. Not on your stomach. Now, can you touch your toes?"

Irene bent over and touched her toes so quickly that Jake, who hadn't taken his hands off her was surprised by her sudden movement. Her ass bumped into his crotch, and he jumped back.

"Sorry," she said, *not actually sorry*. She was able to touch her head to her knees and looked up at Jake through the gap between her thighs. "How far down can you go?"

Jake turned around and repeated the movement. He couldn't quite make it down to his knees, but he was able to see her between his own legs; he smiled at her. Irene slowly raised up and Jake did the same but had a little difficulty with it.

"Okay, so you're pretty flexible. Hold still for a minute" She came up behind Jake and began probing his lower back with her thumbs. "Oh, oh, yeah, you're really tense right here. I can feel it— yeah, yeah, this spot right here. Here, lie down face first on that mat."

Jake lowered himself onto the mat, and Irene kneeled next to him.

"How's this?" she said, kneading his sore spots.

"Amazing," he groaned. "I need to get a massage one of these days. This is wonderful."

"Thank you," said Irene. "You're a little tighter over here, so let me switch." She stepped over him and resumed her firm ministrations on his lower lumbar. "I think I'm getting you loosened up, now I want to try something a chiropractor friend of mine showed me. Do you mind if I sit on you for a minute?"

Jake almost popped his head up in surprise but managed to control himself. "Sure, whatever you need to do is fine."

Irene slowly positioned herself on Jake's firm butt but avoided grinding on him like she wanted to do. Instead, she placed her fists on either side of Jake's spine and pressed firmly, locking her elbows, and raising herself up a few inches. Jake felt something pop in his back and wiggled his toes just to make sure she hadn't broken something.

"What was that?" he said. "Did that do it?"

"Probably not," said Irene. "Your back joints are like your knuckles. If you've ever cracked a knuckle, that's just a gaseous bubble being popped in the synovial fluid in your joint. Basically, I just popped a bubble in your back." She walked her fists up Jake's back a little further and heard a couple more pops. "See? Like that."

Irene stood up again. "Okay, I'm going to show you a few exercises that should help alleviate some of your pain and maybe even straighten you back out. First, roll onto your back."

Jake did as he was told.

"Okay, bring your left leg up, but keep your foot on the floor, and keep your right leg straight. Now, spread your arms straight out at a 90-degree angle with your palms on the floor. Now cross your left leg over your right and touch your knee to the right side but keep your back on the floor."

Irene put her hand on Jake's knee and lightly pushed on it. She slid her other hand along his thigh and said, "You'll start feeling it pull here." She rubbed his thigh several times to illustrate where he would feel the stretch.

I think I know where I'd like to feel some pulling, thought Jake, trying not to smile.

She continued, "Go as far as you can. Hold it. Good. Now, switch your leg positions and bring your right leg over your left and touch your knee to the left side with your back on the floor. As far as you can and hold. Excellent. Next, we'll try a supine twist. Bring both knees up and then twist to one side and hold for ten seconds. Excellent, now the other side."

Irene led Jake through several poses—Child Pose, Cobra, Downward-Facing Dog, Bridge—none of which seemed too hard, but Jake was surprised to find he wasn't as flexible as he thought he was. As he did them, Irene would kneel next to Jake and press an area with her hand, whether it was to gently stroke it and say "are you feeling the stretch here?" or "Hold this position like this, and raise this up here."

There were more than a few stretches where it involved her rubbing her hand high up on his thigh, including poses that didn't actually affect his legs at all. Irene's face reddened and her breathing became a little labored as she was helping Jake with his different poses. He was getting harder at Irene's gentle touch, and he was thankful he was wearing his bike shorts, which kept his cock from tent poling the front of his shorts.

"Okay, now I want to show you one called Happy Baby. It's a little difficult, but it's a great way to open up your hips and relax your spine. Lay on your back and bring your knees back to your chest but bring your arms up through the insides of your knees and grab the outside edge of each foot. Keep your feet flat like you're walking on the ceiling."

Irene knelt down directly in front of Jake between his legs. "Now hold this pose. You should feel some stretching here—" she ran her hands on the backs of his thighs "—and here—" she began rubbing inside his thighs, moving down to his rock-hard prick.

"Oh, Bianca wasn't kidding," she said, rubbing her hand over Jake's cock.

She reached under his running shorts and continued. Jake slowly lowered his feet to the floor but kept his legs apart so Irene could continue what she was doing. She continued stroking his dick and began rubbing her pussy through her pants. The two locked eyes but said nothing as Irene rubbed her pussy and his cock.

"There's something special about these yoga pants," she said after a few minutes.

"What's that?" said Jake.

"They're called Sriracha pants. They have a special flap in them so you can have sex with them still on. Come and see."

Irene lay on her back on the other mat and asked Jake to kneel in front of her. "Just don't look at my feet," she said.

"That's going to be hard now that you told me not to. That's like saying 'don't think of elephants right now.'"

"I've got dancer's feet," she said.

Jake tenderly lifted her legs and put her feet on his shoulders. He turned his head and began kissing her ankle and working his way slowly up her calf and back to her ankle, then turned and repeated the motion on her other foot. Pressing her feet together, he kissed her arches, rubbing the tops of her feet as he did so, gently kissing her toes then taking a couple in his mouth and giving them a little suck. Irene moaned a little in response.

She lowered her knees and held them, spreading her legs; Jake could see a sort of gusset in the crotch of Irene's pants that was already getting wet. He ran his hand over her mound and could feel her heat.

"Open that with your fingers," she whispered. He opened the flap, which was like the Y-front on a pair of men's underwear and exposed her pink pussy lips plus a few hairs peeking out from the top.

"Beautiful," he whispered.

He stroked her labia with his middle finger, from top to bottom, and slowly, carefully opened up her slit, exposing her clit. He rubbed the tip of his finger on it and she raised her hips.

"That feels so good. I haven't been touched like that in months."

Jake leaned down and flicked his tongue on her clitoris a few times which made her gasp and her cunt got even wetter. He slid his finger into her folds like a cock and fucked her with it. She moaned and bucked her hips to meet his hand.

"Ahhhh... ahhhh... ahhh..."

He reached up with his other hand and massaged Irene's round tits through her sports bra. They were firm, but not hard. Jake had experienced both fake and natural breasts, and he wasn't about to complain. Tits were two of his favorite things in the world, and he considered himself to be fortunate to fondle, suck, squeeze, and fuck them in any form or size. Jake turned his hand slightly so he could fuck Irene with his middle and index fingers and rub his thumb on her clit every time he slid his fingers in deeper.

"Ahhhh!" she groaned louder. "Oh, fuck, that's it! I'm gonna come! Make me come with your hand! That's it that's it that's it that's—OOHHHHHHH!"

She dropped her pelvis down to the mat and grabbed his wrist with both hands, jamming his fingers into her as deeply as he could manage. After a few seconds, her quaking subsided and she slowed her breathing.

"Ohh, fuck. That was amazing. Oh, my God! I haven't come like that in so long. It's been a while since a man made me come with his mouth. My husband never does; he says he doesn't like the taste."

Irene sat up as Jake licked his two fingers and his thumb and said, "I think your pussy tastes like honey."

She gave a little sob and held him tightly.

"I think you get a turn," she said after several seconds, cupping his cock with her hand.

They heard someone try to open the door and turned to look, but the shades were down.

"We don't open for another hour. They'll be back," said Irene. Then they heard a key in the door. "Fuck," said Irene. "It's Dakota."

"Who's that?"

"One of my instructors. He's got a bit of a crush on me, but he's such a pantywaist."

A young man walked in wearing black yoga pants and a sleeveless t-shirt with the name of a local food co-op on it.

"Namaste, Irene," said Dakota, placing his hands together and bowing slightly.

He had a man bun and a scraggly beard, and Jake had to fight not to roll his eyes. In his mind, Jake started calling him *Dick-ota*.

"What's going on here?" Dakota asked.

Jake and Irene were still kneeling and facing each other. "Oh, I was giving Jake some private lessons to help his back."

"I see," said Dakota, narrowing his eyes.

Jake stood up and held his hand out to Irene, helping her to rise.

"Thank you, I do feel great. My back doesn't hurt anymore and that tingling down my leg has gone away."

"Let's hope that's the only thing down your leg that's gone away," Irene said with a sly smile, leaning forward and pressing her breasts into Jake.

Dakota cleared his throat.

"Well, I should probably go," said Jake. "I have to be on stage in a couple hours." Irene walked to the front counter and grabbed a pen and notepad.

"Oh yeah? What do you do?" asked Dakota.

"I'm a standup comic."

"Huh. So, you're probably on the road a lot, right? Never stay in one city too long? Bet that makes it hard to form a relationship."

"Actually, I get to meet a lot of wonderful people and form some excellent friendships," said Jake.

Irene reached over the counter and handed a slip of paper to Jake. "Here's my cell number. I want to come to your show tomorrow, but if you need any extra lessons in the meantime, let me know."

"I'll take you up on that. I'll text you about the show, and I may need some more lessons tomorrow afternoon."

Irene smiled sweetly at Jake, while Dakota stared daggers.

Jake waved at Irene. "Bye."

Dakota followed him outside. "Hey, man, Irene doesn't need anyone sniffing around her right now, especially some road warrior who can't stay in one city for more than a few days."

Jake turned slowly. "How do you know what she needs, *Dick-ota*?"

"I know she doesn't need you. She's having a lot of problems with her husband and the last thing she needs is some muscled-up lunkhead confusing her and making it worse."

"It sounds like you don't actually know what she needs, and even if you did, you can't give it to her. If you could, she would have asked you for it by now."

Dakota's face darkened. "Oh, yeah, lunkhead? Why don't you just get the fuck out of here before I make you."

"*Dick-ota*, you couldn't make a religious man pray. Now go back inside and diddle your chakras before I swing you around by that silly-ass man bun." Jake flexed his pecs and made them bounce.

Dakota's eyes widened, and he took a step back. Jake turned on his heel and walked back to the apartment to get ready for the show.

CHAPTER 5

A chime sounded on Irene's phone on Friday morning.

It was Jake. *Hey, do you still want to come to the show tonight?*

Absolutely, she replied. *Was hoping to finish what we started yesterday too.*

That was my next question. Any chance of another private lesson this afternoon?

Yes. I can be there at 2:00.

Jake texted her the address and grabbed a quick shower before she arrived. He wasn't sure how serious she was about actual lessons, so he put on some basketball shorts and the tank top from yesterday but left off the bike shorts.

There was a knock on the door at the appropriate time and Jake welcomed Irene into the apartment. She was carrying two yoga mats and was wearing wine-colored yoga shorts and a black sports bra similar to the one she had on yesterday. She had plumped up her breasts again and drew the zipper more than halfway down. Jake wondered; *how does the zipper even have the strength to contain her wondrous globes?*

He closed the door and she set the yoga mats on the floor.

"I think I need your help today too," said Irene, stepping up close to him. "I need you to stretch me out."

"Why, are you tight?" He gathered her into his muscular arms and held her closely.

Her tits came up to his rib cage and he could feel their firmness against him. He kissed her once.

"I'm very tight. And wet too." She pulled his head back to her and kissed him. With her other hand, she reached for his cock and began stroking it through his shorts. "Oh God, that's a fucking monster." She slipped her hand down the waistband and took hold of his meat, gasping at its size. "I don't know if I'll be able to handle all this."

"I'll be gentle," he promised. Jake picked her up and she wrapped her legs around his waist as they continued to kiss, and he carried her to the bedroom.

Jake turned and sat on the foot of the bed, still holding Irene and she positioned herself so she was sitting right on top of his thick cock. She kissed him deeply. Sliding her tongue into his mouth, Jake sucked on it lightly before slipping his own into her mouth, and she returned the favor.

Irene broke away. "I've been dreaming about your dick ever since Bianca told me about it. I have to see it for myself."

She climbed off Jake's lap and pulled at his waistband. He raised his hips and she yanked his shorts off and he took his tank top off.

"Holy fuck!" she said when his erection sprang free. "Oh, this is wonderful." She wrapped one hand around it and marveled at its size. "It's so thick. Oh, I've got to get this thing inside me, but I'm so small, I may break."

Jerking him off with both hands, she knelt down to gaze at his prick. She kissed his cock head a few times, gliding her tongue up and down it like a sucker, before licking up and down the sides. Irene cradled him in her hands and slid her tongue from the base of his shaft to the head. She slid his dickhead into her eager mouth and tried to slide down his shaft as far as she could. At first, she could only get a couple inches in between her overly plump lips, but she was determined.

Irene bobbed her head up and down, working Jake's cock with her mouth and her fists, occasionally going deeper, and fitting more in. Pretty soon, she was up to three inches then four. She jacked him off, using her saliva that ran down the sides of his shaft as lubrication.

When Jake had first met Irene, he wondered how her full, bee-stung lips would feel on his manhood and now he had his answer: *Fucking amazing!* He hadn't felt such soft and supple suction as with Irene's beautiful mouth. She sucked him so hard when she pulled back, her lips stretched a little and her cheeks hollowed. Then she slid her head back down, stopping just before her gag reflex, then sucking hard as she slid him back out. It was like being sucked off by a vacuum cleaner with thick lips, and he loved every second of it! Then he remembered something else he had been fantasizing about.

"Your tits," he gasped. "Let me fuck your gorgeous tits."

Irene smiled. "You don't sound so shy now." She raised up and squeezed her tits together with her hands, deepening her cleavage. "Beg for it."

"Oh, please, Irene. Please let me fuck your beautiful tits. I want to feel those luscious breasts wrapped around my hard cock and watch it slide in and out of your deep cleavage."

"With pleasure, stud."

Irene placed Jake's cock against her stomach below her sports bra then pulled on the lower elastic band and guided him into her awaiting cleft. The sports bra, which had been squeezing her globes together already, kept his dick from popping out. She put her hands on his hips and raised up and down, sliding on his eight-and-a-half-inch meat still wet from her mouth.

"That's better than I imagined," he said.

"Have you imagined it a lot?"

"Ever since I met you. I've jacked off thinking about this three times since then."

"And now?"

"Nothing can ever be as good as this."

He pumped his hips up, meeting her downward thrusts. Irene lowered her head and kissed his cock head every time it reached her lips. Jake began groaning and thrusting faster.

"Oh fuck, I'm going to come," he said. "Your beautiful tits are making me come."

"Not yet," said Irene.

She raised up and slid his dick from between her tits and resumed her sucking, this time much faster and more vigorously, using both hands to stroke his shaft.

"Oh, fuck! I'm gonna—I'm gonna—I'm AAHHHHHHHH!"

Jake jettisoned five shots of hot spunk into Irene's mouth as she struggled to keep it all inside. Some of it escaped from her mouth and began to trickle down Jake's shaft and her fingers. She licked the come off his cock like it was an ice cream cone then licked her fingers clean. Jake collapsed back onto the bed.

"That was amazing," he said, as his cock began to deflate.

Irene stood up and took off her sports bra and her tits sprang free. Jake slid fully onto the bed and watched in amazement, not sure which was more impressive: the size of her tits or the apparent strength of her sports bra to contain all that wondrous flesh. Next, Irene stepped out of her yoga shorts and put one foot on the bed. Jake noticed that her pubic hair was trimmed short, but not shaved completely clean.

He raised himself up on his elbows as she began to finger her pussy, tugging softly on her pink, engorged lips. Irene spread them with one hand and used the other to slide a finger in and out of her wetness.

"I fucked myself and thought about you when I got home last night," she moaned as she fingered her cunt. "I used a vibrator and came two times. They weren't as strong as the orgasm you gave me though, so I'm hoping you can repeat the magic today."

"I want to taste you," said Jake. "I want to eat your delicious cunt and taste your honey."

"Oh, fuck," moaned Irene. "How do you want me?"

"Sit on my face," Jake commanded.

Irene rubbed her clit a few more seconds and climbed onto Jake's bed, straddling his mouth with her wet pussy, positioning herself so she could look down at him. Jake began to lick her wet lips, driving his tongue deeply into her snatch. He grabbed her hips and pulled her down tighter to him so he could suck her lips into his mouth even as he slid his tongue inside her.

"Oohhhhhhhhh," she groaned. "Oohhhhhhhhh."

Jake began to flick his tongue on her clit, which made her squirm with delight. Jake reached up and began to squeeze her tits, first one then the other.

"That's so good. Keep doing that."

Jake decided to be a little more creative and began tracing the letters of the alphabet on her clit with his tongue, which made her squeal even louder. *A, B, C, D, E, F, G.*

Jake got as far as *O*, which Irene showed her appreciation for by screaming, "Oh God, keep doing that," so he continued to trace the letter *O* on her pink pearl, swirling and swirling. "Oh, fuck. That's it. Oh shit, you're going to make me come. I'm going to come! I'm—AAHHHHHHHH!"

Irene looked down as she came, watching Jake's blue eyes. (*Is he wearing blue contacts?* she thought.) Her orgasm wracked her body so deeply, that she ejaculated a little, shooting her pussy juice in Jake's mouth. He groaned in appreciation and continued to lick at her, cleaning up her own come, until she had to make him stop.

"Ooh, ooh, hold on. My pussy is super sensitive right now, at least for a few minutes."

She lay down next to him, pressing her tits on his chest and resting her leg on his stomach and cock.

She kissed him on the mouth a few times and said, "Where did you learn to eat a woman out like that?"

"I read about it a lot," he said and winked at her.

"What were you even doing?" Jake explained his technique and she asked, "So what letter did I get up to?"

"*O*," said Jake.

"Oh," said Irene with a smile. "Do any of your partners make it past that?"

"I got up to *S* once, but no, no one else has ever made it past *O*. *Q* is always a bit difficult."

Irene felt Jake's cock stirring under her leg, and she moved it and started stroking it with her hand.

She watched it grow and harden, "I think I'm ready to take the challenge."

"Do you want me to wear—?"

"No, I'm on the pill." She sucked his cock head for a few seconds to get it nice and wet. "Let me control this," she said. "I don't want to suffer death by dick."

Jake chuckled but promised to be careful. She stroked him further and rubbed him on her tits to make sure it was at its hardest then rose up and straddled his cock, guiding it to her pussy lips, still sopping wet from his earlier oral efforts.

Irene lowered herself tenderly onto his shaft, opening her mouth in a wide-but-silent scream as his head parted her lips and pushed into her pink snatch. She got it a few inches inside herself, keeping a firm grip on it with her hand. Jake massaged her tight and tiny ass with one hand and one of her tits with the other. He pinched her nipple which made her smile even as she groaned at her new invader.

She raised up, nearly pulling completely off his cock then slowly lowered back again, helping another inch find its way in. She repeated this process and worked nearly two-thirds of Jake's dick into her waiting cunt. She fell forward onto Jake's chest so now she only had to slide back and forth on his cock. This let her control his penetration and she rocked herself back and forth on his massive member, enjoying the stretching he was giving her.

Irene raised up a bit and dragged her nipples along his chest as she fucked him, pushing even as she did, reaching five inches, six inches, almost seven.

"Fuck, your dick is so big. I've never had anything this big inside my pussy before."

"Your pussy is so tight," said Jake. "It's wet and warm and feels like a glove. Good God, I love fucking you."

Irene grinned. "No, I'm fucking you at the moment. But in a few minutes, once I can fit you all the way in, you're going to fuck me until I can't see straight." Irene sat up straighter, pressing her hands on Jake's chest and groaned as she tried to fit the final inch or two of his cock into her. She sat and let her pussy adjust to his thickness then started grinding and rubbing her clit on his pubic bone.

"Okay, I can't push anymore," she said. "I want you to turn me—WHOA!"

Irene shrieked as Jake suddenly flipped over with his prick still inside her and laid her on her back. He raised himself up on his arms and Irene raised her feet up until her ankles were on his shoulders, which had the added bonus of opening her up and driving him in a little deeper.

"OH, FUCK!" she screamed. "Oh, fuck, hold on a minute. Let me—let me catch my breath."

Jake waited until she nodded and pulled out a little and gently glided back in. She arched her back when he pushed, then he slid back out until only an inch of his dick was inside her lips. She arched her back again and he pushed in again. Every time he withdrew a little, she relaxed, every time he thrust forward, she arched up to meet him. With a final thrust from him and a shriek from her, Jake bottomed out and filled her cunt entirely.

"I'm all the way inside you," said Jake, kissing her forehead. "I'm filling up your beautiful pussy."

"Yes, you are," she said. "God, I need this so bad. Fuck me hard. Now you can fuck me hard."

Jake eagerly complied, withdrawing his cock to its purple head before pushing himself forward. Irene clawed his back. He thrust again a little faster for a few strokes, and sped up a little more. Soon, he was withdrawing completely and slamming back into her tunnel.

"Yes! Yes! Yes! Yes!" Irene whimpered each time Jake shoved his cock inside her. Then she stopped him and said, "Let me show you something else that yoga is good for." She pulled her arms in front of her legs and pulled them back so she was nearly doubled up and her feet were near her ears. This repositioned Jake's cock inside her so it was stroking against the upper wall inside her pussy.

"OH FUCK!" screamed Irene when she felt the new friction. "Oh, that's it! Keep fucking me like that." Jake was more than happy to keep fucking, and he raised up and plunged home as Irene yipped with each stroke.

"Oh, this is it. I'm going to come again! I'm going to come all over your big prick!" she screamed.

"I'm going to come too. I'm going to come in your beautiful pussy."

"Fill me up! Fill up my cunt with your hot come. Ooh, here I come! I'm… COMING!"

At hearing her groans, Jake shoved his cock as deeply as he could and unleashed a torrent of hot sperm, flooding her cunt with his seed. He resumed thrusting and his come began to spill out and run down to her ass.

"Let me have it," she said. "I want to taste us together." Jake quickly pulled out and fell onto his back as Irene shoved his cock into her mouth as deeply as it would go, licking the head for a few seconds and being rewarded with a final spurt. Then she licked off the rest of his meat, tasting her juices mingled with his.

"Oh, holy fuck, that was incredible," gasped Jake, his body slick with sweat.

Irene, who was just as sweaty, collapsed back onto his chest, and the two lay together, chests heaving.

"For me too, babe," murmured Irene. "I haven't been fucked that deep or that hard in a long, long time."

"I've never been inside anyone so tight. It was like warm velvet."

"God, my pussy is going to be so sore for a few days. You sure stretched me out."

"I told you I'd be able to help you with that."

"You sure did. I don't know if I'll be able to walk tomorrow."

"Really? I know a couple exercises that can help you."

"Smartass," Irene laughed, smacking Jake on the chest. Then she kissed the spot where she whacked him, licked his nipple a few times, and patted his cock. "I may need it though, because I plan on riding this a couple more times before you leave."

Two days later, as Jake was driving to his next gig in Louisville, Kentucky, he smacked his truck steering wheel as he realized he'd forgotten something very important.

"Shit! I never found out what color Bianca's eyes are!"

Jake punched his cell phone on its dashboard display.

THE END

Chastity Veldt

Lydia in Louisville

Stand Up, Lie Down Collection

TABLE OF CONTENTS

CHAPTER 1

Jake put a Bluetooth earbud into his ear and punched the screen of his mobile phone. "Call Bianca," he said out loud.

"Hey, big boy. What's up?" said Bianca Garrett, a barista at Cool Beans coffee shop in Indianapolis. She and Jake had spent a steamy night together last week while he was in the Circle City.[3] It was Tuesday afternoon, and he was in his truck driving down I-65 toward Louisville. He had just finished up a run at Cracker's Comedy Club in Indianapolis then spent two more days with a yoga instructor, Irene, whom he had met and bedded at Bianca's urging.

"I kept meaning to ask you, but I always forgot: What color are your eyes? Are they really that green?"

"Absolutely," said Bianca. "My mom had green eyes."

"Well, they're gorgeous. I sort of wondered if they were contacts."

---

[3] See *Stand Up, Lie Down: Irene in Indianapolis*

"I get that a lot, but I promise they're real. Just like my tits," she added.

There was an awkward pause and Jake froze up, wondering how he should respond to that. Before he could say anything, Bianca asked, "So where are you now?"

"Heading to Louisville. I'm headlining at Peanut's Comedy Club for four nights."

Jake Nielsen was on a standup comic tour through the Midwest and Southeast in his pickup truck. Standing at 6'2", had light blond hair, and gold wire-frame glasses; people often said he looked like Tony, the first terrorist killed in *Die Hard*. Jake had been a swimmer at the University of Minnesota, and still maintained his swimmer's build thanks to his fitness obsession and frequent workouts.

"Where are you?" Jake asked.

"Taking a break in the office. Gerald is working out front."

"Cool, cool," said Jake, still unsure of what to say.

"So what are you wearing?" Bianca asked in a sultry voice.

"Uhh, jeans and a University of Minnesota sweatshirt."

"Do you know what I'm wearing?"

"I would guess jeans, shirt, and your barista apron."

"Jesus, dude, you suck at this," laughed Bianca.

"What? That's not a good guess?"

"Well, it's right, but I'm trying to have phone sex with you."

"Ohhhhhhh. So how does that work?"

"Well, I talk dirty about what I'm doing to myself so you get turned on, then you talk—"

"No, I mean, I know how phone sex works. I just thought—I don't know, I should be lying in bed or something, not going eighty down the interstate."

Jake could hear the smile in her voice. "Why? What would you be doing if you were in bed?" Bianca asked.

He hesitated. As long as he could remember, he'd been very inventive, vigorous, and even thoroughly descriptive when it came to actually having sex. On the other hand, he hated talking about it outside of the actual act. Jake usually stammered and turned red before trying to change the subject to something less awkward, like the time he walked in on his Grandma while she was peeing.

"Um, you know. Just, uh, just holding ... myself."

"Oh. Just holding ... yourself?"

"Fine. My dick. I'd be holding my dick."

"Okay, and what would you be doing with it?"

Oh, God, this is embarrassing, thought Jake. *Fucking conservative Minnesota upbringing.* He cleared his throat and continued. "Stroking it, thinking of you sucking on it, sliding your lips up and down the shaft and leaving it nice and wet."

"Ooh, that's nice. I do love sucking on a hard, thick—okay, I'll be right there."

"What?"

"Sorry, Gerald just said we're getting slammed. Do you want to try this again later?"

"Sure, just maybe when I can actually use my hands for something other than driving."

"By the way, here's something for you to think about until then. Remember Lena, our server at that sushi place?"

Jake flashed back to his and Bianca's first and only date. Jake had been sliding his long, thick fingers in and out of Bianca's pussy in their booth. As he made her come, they noticed Lena hiding behind the cashier station, watching them and fingering herself.[4] He smiled at the memory, especially the part where Bianca took him into the bathroom and sucked his cock until he erupted in her mouth.

"Yeah, what about her?"

"I hooked up with her last night, and I'll tell you all about it when you call me tonight."

"Can you give me a preview?"

"Well, I went back to Wasabi's last night and stayed for two hours, getting drunk, and flirting with her. I snuck her into the bathroom and we were kissing—goddammit, Gerald! I'll be right there!—sorry, big boy, I'll talk to you tonight. Bye."

"Well, fuck," said Jake as the call ended. He looked down at his hard cock straining to break through his zipper. "Just a few more hours, buddy."

An hour later, Jake was at Peanut's Comedy Club in downtown Louisville and had been shown to the back office. He found Sherrie,

---

4   Also *Stand Up, Lie Down: Irene in Indianapolis*

the club owner, working on her laptop, a small plate of French fries within easy reach.

"Hi, I'm Jake Nilsen."

"Nielsen?"

"No, Nilsen."

"Hi, I'm Sherrie." She stood up and shook Jake's hand. "We're looking forward to having you. You're performing one show Thursday night, two on Friday, two on Saturday, and one on Sunday, right?"

"That's what my agent told me," agreed Jake.

Sherrie offered up her plate. "Do you want a French fry?"

"No, thank you," said Jake. "I ate on the road."

"Well, I'll give you the key to the club apartment. It's down by the University of Louisville, and I can give you directions on how to get there. You're sharing with our middle, Curtis Sanders. The opener is a local woman who's been doing the Bourbon Trail circuit for a year."

"Oh, I know Curtis. We've performed together a few times. He knows his shit."

"Oh, yeah. He's been here a couple of days already, and the audience loves him. He's hosting the open mic tonight and Wednesday. You can come if you want, but he was here first, so I volun-told him he was the host." Sherrie winked at him.

Sometimes middles and openers would host the open mic nights on the early weeknights when crowds were small. It was a way to keep the club open and to find new talent. Every comedian got their start by going to open mic nights. It was the successful ones who kept going back until they were invited by a club owner to open.

"No problem. I emceed one in Indianapolis last week."

Jake thanked Sherrie and drove to the club apartment. It was located in a complex that looked like it was filled with a lot of students. He could hear music blaring from a few open windows. It wasn't great, but it was free, and free beat a quiet hotel any night.

"Hey, Jakey Nilsen! I heard you were my follow-up act this weekend." Curtis hollered when Jake walked in.

"Hey, Curtis, I think you mean I'm batting cleanup." Curtis stood up and the two embraced in that back-thumping, bear-hugging way men do.

Curtis was Black, skinny, and stood nearly as tall as Jake. He had long, gangly arms and legs making him look more like an awkward, teenage nerd than a 28-year-old man, which he used as part of his act.

Curtis sat back down and turned off the TV show he was watching. "I've got to tell you about this waitress I hooked up with in Cincinnati last week."

"Cool, I need to tell you about this bookstore owner I was with in Milwaukee.[5] She was fucking amazing!"

"Go grab a beer and let's see who's got the better story."

Jake and Curtis' tradition was to share stories about their sexual exploits on the road. They had a standing wager that whenever they reconnected, each would try to outdo the other with his best story, and the loser had to buy dinner. One story per person and the only rule was no exaggerating or lying.

---

[5] See *Molly in Milwaukee.*

Jake dropped his bag in the second bedroom, grabbed a beer from the refrigerator, and sat on the other end of the couch.

"Let's see," said Curtis, "I think you went first last time, so it's my turn."

CHAPTER 2

CURTIS IN CINCINNATI

"**Y**ou ready, Jakey? Here's my story:

"Two weeks ago, I was middling at this club in Cincinnati called The Big Laugh Machine on a four-night gig. I had been talking to this waitress named Anna whose parents were from Mexico. She grew up in Cincinnati and was studying to be a nurse.

"Well, this woman was almost as tall as me, and she was kinda heavy. She had some big titties and a nice big butt. You know how I love a big ass. For two days, she had been flirting with me and pressing her tits on me. Like, on my first night, I was sitting at the bar after my set, and she'd come up behind me and reach for a straw, but press her tits on me while she did it. Fuck, man, her tits were huge and meaty, and she did that to me five or six times that first night.

"After that, it was on. I'd squeeze behind her between tables and slide my cock across her ass, or we'd pass in the hallway which was kind of small, so we'd have to turn sideways a bit and she'd lean forward and drag her tits across my chest.

"Or I'd hug her good-bye and hello, and I could feel her pulling me in tighter, squeezing me on her tits. Then she'd do this thing where she would loosen her grip on me and keep me from stepping away so she could leave her tits pressed on me. We'd stand like that for a bit and just say hello and shit.

"So on day three of us rubbing up on each other, she was doing that loose hug thing and I decided to go for it. We were in the club office, and the owner wasn't due in for a few hours, so I kissed her.

"She kissed me back for a few seconds and then said, "About fucking time," then she plunged her tongue into my mouth. I grabbed that big beautiful ass of hers and pulled her against my cock, which by then, I was rock hard. I massaged her ass and we slid our tongues in and out of each other's mouths before I started licking her neck and her ear. I could hear her breathing hard and she moaned a little when I found a really sensitive spot on her neck.

"Anna squeezed my cock and rubbed me like she was trying to rip it out of my jeans. I unbuttoned her blouse and, I gotta tell you, Jakey, she had some of the biggest melons I've ever seen in my life. I undid the hooks on her bra, and there were four of them. Four, man! That bra strap was industrial strength.

"I sneaked a look at the tag and she had H cups. Her tits were big and round, and they sagged some, but they were real naturals, like that one porn star from the 1980s you told me about, Christy Canyon. Man, I loved that chick's tits. Anna's were way bigger, but they hung like Christy Canyon's.

"I bent down and sucked on her nipple while she's rubbing my head with her hands, mashing my face into her titty meat. I must have sucked and played with her tits for five minutes, and she was moaning and groaning and her nipples were sticking out like little brown erasers.

"When I stood up and kissed her again, she grabbed my belt and said, "Now it's my turn." She dropped to her knees and undid my pants. When she pulled down my pants and my shorts, my cock sprang out and hit her on the cheek. There was a little drop of pre-cum on the tip so she kissed it off and rubbed my cock on her face where it had hit her.

"Anna took my cock between her lips and sucked hard on the head, until her cheeks sucked in. That shit drives me crazy; I love it when a woman sucks my dick so hard her cheeks suck in like that, so I pushed my cock forward and she sucked me in about halfway, and she slid her head back off until my dick went POP out of her mouth.

"Then she looked back up at me with those big brown eyes and did it again. She sucked hard going in, and sucked hard going out. Each time she did it, she managed to get a little more in there. Now, my dick is about 7.5 inches long, and each time she sucked me back in, she managed to get a little more in there. After about ten or so times, she was able to get her nose right on my pubes and I could feel my cockhead tickling the back of her throat.

"After that, she raised right up and wrapped her big tits around my wet cock, squeezed them, and fucked my cock with them. Oh, my god! It was heaven, and she had gotten my cock so wet, it was like being in her pussy. She would fuck my cock with her tits then she would suck me, doing ten strokes of each.

"She called it *cum roulette* and said I could either come in her mouth or on her tits.

"I know! I know, man! It was hot as fuck.

"I tried to hold on as long as I could, and I think she got me four times with her tits and five times with her mouth. I could feel the pressure building in my nuts just as she was finishing up with her tits so I hurried and stuffed my cock in her mouth and just got to fucking. I held her head so I wouldn't give her whiplash and she opened her mouth and let me fuck her that way.

"I was grunting—'Uhh! Uhh! Uhh!'—and I fired right into the back of her throat. Her eyes were watering but she grabbed my ass and held on. Once I finished cumming, she went back to that sucking thing again and got a few extra drops out, then she showed me my cum in her mouth, like in a porno. She swallowed hard and opened her mouth and it was gone.

"Jake, I tell you, I fell in love at that moment.

"I stood her up, helped her out of her panties and lifted up her skirt, and put her on the desk. Then it was my turn to kneel before her and worship her beautiful pussy. She had this thick tangle of black pubic hair, so I ran my fingers through it and would grab a handful and tug on it gently. I spread her pussy lips and slid my tongue up and down her slit, and flicked her clit with my tongue. Then I slipped my finger inside her pussy and I could feel her muscles gripping my finger so tight I thought I might not get it back. Then you and I would be sitting here talking with this woman hanging off my finger.

"Yeah, I thought you'd like that joke.

"Anyway, I did that trick you told me about, and I licked the alphabet on her clit while I finger-banged her. I was working two fingers inside her and just kept licking. I actually managed to get all the way to the letter S and she was bucking her hips and grabbed my hair. So I just kept doing letter S on her until she came. I thought she was going to crush my head with those meaty thighs, but I made her cum twice before she pulled me up by my hair and begged me to stop.

"I was already hard again, so I stepped out of my pants and lifted Anna's legs, and put her feet on my shoulders. I started sliding the tip of my cock up and down her lips, rubbing it on her clit. She was moaning again, and I was worried someone was going to hear us, but the office is downstairs and there were only a couple people upstairs for lunch.

"So I kept rubbing her clit with my cockhead and she begs me to fuck her. *Please, baby, please put that fucking thing in me. Fuck me with that big cock of yours.* Well, I was horny, but I'm not an idiot. I had a condom in my pocket—you know I always carry one in case I get lucky—so I skinned it on and kept sliding my dick against her pussy so I could get it lubed up.

"She was still moaning, *'Oh, please, fuck me, Curtis. Fill me with that dick.'* I didn't need any more urging, so I glided right on in there. She covered her mouth with her hands and screamed.

"I said, *'Do you need me to stop?'*

"She said, *'No, no baby. I just wasn't expecting it to be that big.'*

"I'm serious, Jakey, that's what she said. Seriously, *'I wasn't expecting it to be that big.'*

"I gave her a few seconds to get used to me, then I pushed in real slow, sliding my cock in and out a few inches at a time. I could feel her relax a little and she's moving with me and moaning with every thrust. My balls were slapping her on her big butt and she was moaning every time I pushed inside her.

"She moaned more when I got inside her and she goes *'Deeper— unh! Deeper—unh!'* So I grabbed her forearms and she grabbed mine, and every time I pushed into her, I would pull on her arms so I could drive myself in farther. Then she's going *'Oh—God! Oh—God!'* as I go out and back in. She was trying not to yell, but she was still pretty vocal. *'Oh—God! Oh—God!'*

"I wanted to try a new position, so I had her climb down, turn around and bend over the desk. Licking my lips, I stared at her big beautiful ass, and her cunt, right there waiting for me. I rubbed her ass, kissing it all over when she demanded I put my cock back inside her. I quickly obliged and pumped her from behind. Grabbing onto her hips and pounding her as hard as I could. Pulling her back toward me as I thrust, which got her big tits swinging in rhythm, and they're swinging around in circles in opposite directions. I'd only ever seen that in those 1990s pornos, but that shit drove me crazy. I'm fucking her faster and driving my cock in as deep as I could go and her H cups were slapping together every time they would swing around.

"I thought about spanking her ass a few times, just to watch it jiggle but it was all I could do to hold on and keep up that pace.

"I was grunting every time I thrust, and I could feel my cum building up. I said, *I'm gonna cum, baby. Where do you want me to cum?'* and she said *'I want you to cum on me. Cum on my tits.'*

"I almost came right there when she said that. I thrust in her a bunch more times and then said, *'Okay, get ready.'* I pulled out and yanked off the condom while she turned around and dropped to her knees.

"I put the head of my cock in her mouth again and she's fucking me with her mouth again. She kept her mouth open instead of sucking on me, and she was making this noise whenever my cock hit the back of her throat—*'Gluck gluck gluck'*—and that did it for me.

"I said, '*Here we go,*' and I slid my cock out of her mouth and jacked off for her. She held her tits like she was offering them up to me, and I kept jacking until the cum boiled in my balls and erupted. My first shot went a little high and hit her in the chin, so I re-aimed and my next four splashed right on her beautiful tits and she moaned every time she felt my hot spunk land on her.

"Finally, I couldn't produce any more and she sucked my cockhead to get the rest of it out. I grabbed a clean bar towel off a shelf and wiped my cum off her tits—you're goddamn right I'm chivalrous—and then buried it in the trash can next to the desk. Just then we heard someone calling for her at the top of the stairs, so we hurried and got dressed and that's it."

CHAPTER 3

"Holy fuck, that's an amazing story," said Jake, trying nonchalantly to cover his boner with a throw pillow. "Did you keep up with her after that night?"

"Oh, yeah," said Curtis. "I took her to my hotel room and we spent the next two nights fucking like rabbits. And Cincinnati's not even 100 miles from here, so she said she's going to come down this weekend, so you'll get to meet her."

"Jesus, man, I don't think I'll be able to look her in the eye after that story."

"So how about you, man? Tell me about this bookstore lady in—where'd you say she was?"

"Milwaukee. Her name's Molly."

"All right, let's hear what you got."

So Jake related the story of his night of wild monkey sex with Molly, and gave a word-by-word recitation of everything that happened in Chapter 5 of *Stand Up, Lie Down: Molly in Milwaukee* (now available on Amazon).

When Jake finished his story, it was Curtis's turn to nonchalantly cover his boner with a throw pillow.

"Fuck, man, that's a good story. I liked the part where you had her look you in the eyes when you came. That's fucking hot. I'll do that with Anna when I see her on Friday."

"Thank you and you're welcome."

"I think I owe you dinner then."

"About fucking time," said Jake. "I've had to buy the last three times. Do you mind if I shower before we go? I want to wash off the road funk."

A couple of hours later, after each guy had secretly jerked off, and they'd eaten dinner before walking along Bardstown Road. Curtis had a little while before he had to be at Peanut's for the open mic night, so they were killing time. They spotted an art gallery with the lights on and a large number of people milling about. A chalkboard sidewalk sign announced an art exhibit featuring several local artists, so Jake and Curtis walked in.

"Welcome, gentlemen," said a young woman behind a table.

"Gentlemen? I think she means you," said Jake.

He was dressed in his "work clothes:" jeans, black t-shirt, gray sport coat, and tan Oxfords; Curtis was dressed in a mauve, wool suit with a stylish cut, tight-fitting pants, and a three-button coat. He wasn't wearing a tie, and his white shirt had the top two buttons open.

The woman laughed. "Welcome to the Bardstown Art Gallery," she said. "We're featuring twelve local artists for a month, and tonight's the opening night. If you'd like to talk to any of the artists, they're here to answer questions. If you'd like to buy any of the work, we can certainly make those arrangements."

They thanked her and slowly meandered around the gallery, retrieving glasses of red wine off a caterer's tray. The two were full from dinner at Cockles & Mussels, an Irish place just up the road, which served great fish and chips and Scotch eggs the size of a baseball.

The two men chatted, making the occasional comment about the art, asking the artists questions, learning more about the kind of work they did, and answering questions about being a standup comic.

Jake wandered around and lost track of Curtis, so he looked at the different pieces on the wall and display stands. He glanced over a few displays—he wasn't big into abstract expressionism, so he slowly passed those by without a second glance. He almost tripped over a table filled with several wine glasses and a couple hors d'oeuvres trays on it. Glaring at it, he wasn't sure if it was art or if they had shitty caterers.

He looked up and was Immediately captivated by a post-impressionist painting that looked like a fall in a neighborhood street on an 18-inch x 24-inch canvas. The card below it said the artist's name: *Lydia Woodruff*. He looked around for the artist and his heart began pounding. There stood a woman with fiery red hair and hazel eyes; Jake had a thing for redheads, and he just knew this *had to be* the artist.

Only 5'6", she stood ramrod straight while holding a glass of white wine, feet arranged in what ballet dancers call first position. She was built like a dancer, lithe and willowy, with small breasts and narrow hips. Jake tried imagining her slender legs wrapped around his waist as he thrust his stiff cock into her. One of his fantasies had always been to sleep with a redhead, but he was truly smitten with the painting.

"I love this piece," said Jake, not taking his eyes off the painting as it stirred up unsuspected pangs of homesickness. "Is it a real place?"

"Yes," said the woman, eyes traveling up and down at Jake's swimmer's physique.

Lydia liked what she saw, and she unconsciously licked her lips. Unbidden images leapt into her mind of this tall Viking thrusting himself into her from below, as she rode him like she stole him. She took a large drink of her wine. Those kinds of images usually didn't just pop into her head, especially of a stranger, no matter how handsome he was. She looked at his fingers and knew if what they said about the size of a man's fingers and his cock was true, she wanted to get to know him better.

"It's actually a street here in the Highlands, just a block over," she said. "I painted it last fall because I love the color of the leaves and the late Victorian architecture."

"It reminds me of home a little bit."

"Where are you from?" Lydia quickly drained her wine glass and grabbed another from a passing server.

"Mankato, Minnesota. My family owns a farm on the outskirts, but my mom and dad used to drive us around the Washington Park District in the fall when I was a kid to look at all the Victorian houses."

"I've been to Mankato before. I know the area you're talking about. I did an architectural restoration project for one of my classes in college. One summer, we went up and worked on an old Victorian with the architectural restoration department. I even painted the house while I was there." She touched his forearm lightly; Jake didn't pull away.

"Painted as in artist painted, or house painted?"

She laughed and Jake smiled at the sound. "Artist painted. In fact, that's what gave me the idea for this piece. I painted it two years ago in the fall."

"And so you're an artist here in town?" asked Jake.

"Well, I also manage this gallery and work as an art buyer for some wealthy patrons in the region, but I paint in my spare time. I'm Lydia, by the way."

"Jake Nilsen." She offered her hand, and he took it lightly, not wanting to crush her thin, delicate fingers.

"Nielsen?"

"No, Nilsen."

"What do you do, Jake?"

"I'm a comic," said Jake. "I'm on tour for a few weeks and have a long weekend show at Peanuts starting tomorrow. I took a few art classes in college and always loved doing it, but never had the talent to do what you do."

"Maybe you should have been a sculptor," she said, turning his hand over and examining his palm and wonderfully long fingers. "You certainly have the strong hands for it."

Jake looked into her hazel eyes even as she held onto his hand, and she gazed back into his ice-blue eyes, not letting go. She parted her lips slightly, licking them a little.

"Do you have anything else I might like to see?"

"Yes. Yes, I do," said Lydia, her voice a little husky.

"Can you show it to me," said Jake.

Lydia's face flushed and her breathing grew a little shallow. She took a small step closer, eyes still locked on Jake's. A couple glasses clinked somewhere nearby and broke the spell.

"Oh, you mean paintings," said Lydia. "I mean, yes. Yes, I have a couple more. Here." She stepped back and turned, sweeping her other arm to gesture at two other paintings, equally as vivid and reminiscent of the first one. One was of the Ohio River, complete with a bridge, and another was a horse racing park, both done in the same post-impressionist style as before.

The two stepped over toward the other paintings, Lydia unconsciously switching hands so she could guide Jake. He noticed she had not let go of his hand, but he wasn't about to say anything.

"This is the Big Four Bridge, which is a pedestrian and bicycle bridge between Waterfront Park and Jeffersonville, Indiana. I painted it this spring. And this is the Churchill Downs, where they run the Kentucky Derby. I did this one early last fall before it got too chilly to paint outdoors."

"They're all beautiful, but I especially love the first one of the Highlands. I love fall colors, especially orange." Jake could feel Lydia's palm get a little sweaty as she turned back to him. "I think it's one of my favorite colors. I could look at it all day," he said.

Lydia's heart thumped so loudly she thought Jake might hear it. She felt her chest and neck flushing deeper. Biting her lower lip she looked up at Jake. She stared at his red lips, and wanted to kiss them, but there were too many people milling around. Dropping her gaze, she wanted his strong hands cupping her breasts while he slid his cock into her and moved slowly in and out. She could feel her pussy getting wet, so she made up her mind.

"Come with me," she said. She set both of their glasses down on a table with other plates, taking Jake's hand again and began to guide him toward the back of the gallery.

"Hey, that's my installation, Lydia," complained a guy behind her.

"I told you you should do the cityscape, not the hors d'oeuvres, Tristan," she said over her shoulder.

She pulled Jake down a hallway and to a door marked *Staff Only*, punched a code on a keypad, and pulled him inside. They were inside an office with all kinds of paintings hanging on the walls, many of which were better than what Jake had been seeing out in the gallery. She still hadn't let go of his hand when she pushed the door closed behind him.

"First, you have to know that I never, ever do this, especially with someone I just met."

"Do what?" asked Jake.

Lydia pulled Jake's head down toward her and she kissed him. Jake gathered her in his strong arms and pulled her close, but not too tightly; *I might break her if I squeeze too tight*. She slid her tongue into his mouth and he groaned lightly in appreciation as they explored each other. Sucking his tongue into her mouth, and she felt it sliding over hers, his saliva mixing with hers.

Jake stood up straight, lifting Lydia with him. She sprang up and wrapped her legs around his trim waist. He carried her over to the desk and set her down on a coffee table book of Jean-Michel Basquiat. She squeezed his powerful arms and ran her hands over his chest, feeling his powerful pectoral muscles.

"Oh, my, you're pretty strong, aren't you?"

Jake smiled. "Yeah, well. I was a swimmer in college, and I still try to keep fit."

"Too much talking," she said and pulled him down to her again.

The two kissed deeply and Lydia ran her hands over Jake's torso, arms, and back, squeezing and feeling his muscles. Jake tentatively cupped his hand over Lydia's breast, questioning. She grabbed his hand and pressed it hard against her chest, her answer clear. He massaged her globe through her white peasant blouse and realized she wasn't wearing a bra, only a camisole. He felt her nipple spring to life underneath his tender fingers and he slipped his hand up her shirt. Returning to her now-naked breast, he gently squeezed and tweaked her nipple with his fingers. She began breathing harder and moaning into his mouth.

Lydia began rubbing his cock through his jeans and gasped at its hardness. "Oh, my," she said, squeezing it, trying to determine how big it was. "That's ... impressive."

Jake lifted up her shirt and massaged both tits with his fingers, getting her nipples equally hard. He leaned down and sucked one nipple into his mouth then the other, lightly pulling them with his lips and gently grazing them with his teeth.

"Oh God, what are you doing to me?" she moaned.

"Do you want me to stop?" Jake murmured, her nipple still between his lips.

"Don't you dare, I fucking love this."

Lydia pushed on Jake's chest, standing him up before undoing his belt and unzipping his pants, reaching in and slipping his cock out. Her eyes widened at what she found. "Oh, fuck, that's huge." She looked up at him. "I don't know if I can get all this inside me."

"We'll go slow and I'll stop when it's too much," said Jake.

Lydia wrapped her long, thin fingers around his cock, which were still cold, and Jake shuddered as she lightly stroked his shaft.

As Lydia jacked him off, Jake reached under her skirt, sliding his hands up her hips. He found the edge of her underwear and began to slide it off. She raised and he pulled it down to her thighs, then slowly around her knees, down her smooth, shapely calves. He saw in the low light that she was wearing tiny emerald-green panties, which he knew would look gorgeous against her red pubic hair. Lydia was still stroking his cock, so he used his foot to pull her panties off her feet.

She opened her legs wide and pulled Jake by his cock, guiding it toward her wet pussy. She rubbed the head on her clit for several seconds, breathing harder and moaning as she masturbated herself with his cockhead. She rubbed it up and down her pink pearl, using the friction to pleasure herself. She threw her head back while Jake supported her back with one hand. Lydia moaned quietly as she felt an orgasm building up.

"Ohh ohh ohh ohh," she groaned.

Jake desperately wanted to shove his cock deep into her pussy, but he held back. He could see she'd shaved most of her pussy, leaving a ginger landing strip to guide him to her beautiful slit where her engorged labia invited him to join himself with her. Lydia moaned quietly as her orgasm built up, prepared to shove Jake's prick inside her when it began.

"I'm going to cum," she said. "I'm going to cum and I want you to fuck me when I start." As a long-time aficionado of erotica, Lydia preferred the spelling of "cum," as well as the taste and feel of it, over the word "come," which she thought was too clinical and passionless. "Oh God, oh God, I'm nearly there. I'm going to—"

There was a loud knock at the door. "Lydia, are you in there?" said a woman's voice.

"I'm cum—I mean, yes, I am," called Lydia, she let go of Jake's hard prick and sat up. "What do you need, Nancy?"

"We're out of red wine and a big group of people just came," said Nancy.

"At least someone got to," mumbled Lydia, and Jake stifled a laugh.

"What was that," asked Nancy.

"Nothing. I'll go get some. I'll be back in ten minutes."

"Okay, great." They heard Nancy walk back down the hall.

"Shit, I'm sorry," said Lydia. "I really wanted that fucking thing inside me." Jake's dick had gotten softer even with Lydia's tender stroking. She looked up at him. "What are you doing tomorrow?"

"Whatever you want. I don't work until Thursday night."

"Great, come with me to get some wine and we'll make plans for tomorrow. I'd have you do me tonight, but it's going to be awfully late and I'll be wiped out. Still, you're not leaving town until you've fucked me good and proper."

Jake pulled Lydia close to him and planted a kiss firmly on her full lips, then flicked the tip of her tongue with his. "As you wish."

CHAPTER 4

Jake arrived at the restaurant a few minutes before 1:00 and seated when Lydia arrived. She looked stunning in olive green shorts and a white t-shirt that clung to her slender frame. On her head sat a wide-brimmed felt hat, which she took off as she approached the table. Jake stood up, gave her a quick kiss on the lips, and held her hand as she slid into the booth.

Sliding back into his seat across from her, he complimented, "You look great. It's good to see you again. And I really like your big hat."

"Thank you. I've already got a lot of freckles, but I'll get more if I don't protect myself from the sun."

She brushed her hand over her arm and Jake looked closely at her freckles. He adored redheads and he especially adored their freckles. He hadn't noticed them the night before because Lydia was wearing a long sleeve blouse, and it was too dark to see them in her office as he was teasing her nipples with his lips.

"I love freckles," he said. "I'm too fair-skinned to really tan, and I don't get anything as interesting as freckles. I just turn pink and then it goes away."

"Surely, you get darker in the sun. Everyone does."

"Well, it's true, I did have a farmer's tan growing up because we would spend every day outside in the summer, but even then, I wasn't nearly as dark as my brown-haired friends."

"Yeah, gingers are the same," said Lydia. "We only turn pink or get freckles."

"So a tanned redhead really just has one giant freckle?"

Lydia laughed. "Pretty much, although I don't think it's that bad."

The server stopped by with two glasses of water and took their order: Caesar salad, hold the croutons for Lydia, and a buffalo chicken sandwich and coleslaw for Jake.

The two chatted about their childhoods and growing up. Jake was a son of the soil, working on a farm until he went to college. He talked about his years in 4-H, raising cows and turkeys, even while he swam in high school, making it to the state swimming championship, winning the 1500-meter freestyle at the state competition, and winning third at Nationals.

"Shit, that's nearly a mile," said Lydia. "What made you pick that distance?"

"I hated farming. No, seriously," he said as she laughed. "When I was a freshman in high school, I started taking swimming more seriously and found that I could miss a lot of the farm work if I focused more on swimming. I was already good at it, and I liked it, so I picked the longest distance there was because it meant I had to practice more and longer and miss most of the chores. I would get to the pool at 6:00 each morning and swim until right before school, then we would have swim practice after school until about 6:00. All the short distance guys were doing sprints over and over, and the coach just had me swimming back and forth to build up endurance."

"Didn't that bug the other swimmers?"

"No, because they knew I needed that kind of work, and I could always be relied on to win my events."

"Wow, that's pretty cocky," she said with a wink.

"Maybe, but I was the best in the state. I only ever lost twice."

"That's impressive! Why didn't you stick with it? Did you try out for the Olympics?"

"Well, being the best swimmer in Minnesota is like being the best opera singer in Mississippi. I swam at the University of Minnesota all four years, but by the time I was at that level, there were 20 other guys in the country better than me, so there was no chance of going to the Olympics at that point.

"Besides, I found something I loved doing better. I joined a sketch comedy troupe in my sophomore year of college because I liked this girl who was in it. I had always been pretty funny and had written some comedy sketches in high school. That was enough to get me in and I found I was pretty good at it. I made the switch to stand-up after I graduated from college and got good enough to go on tour a few years later."

"Whatever happened to the girl you liked?"

"She got a job at the dining hall and had to drop out. Besides, she wasn't that funny."

Lydia laughed. "And look at what she launched," she said. "Does she know what she created?"

"I think I told her once. I was the middle at a comedy club in St. Paul—that's the second comic in a three-act night—and she was in the audience with her husband. I bought them a drink and thanked her for getting me started."

"Do you ever get any hecklers?"

"From time to time," said Jake. "It's usually just someone offering up a comment because they had a little too much to drink and they decided they wanted to contribute. I've been able to handle them pretty well."

The food arrived, and the pair dug into their meals. They continued to talk about Lydia's art career, how she went to a university in small-town Ohio, majored in art, and made jewelry and painted before moving to Louisville and working at the art gallery. She spent five years doing Nancy's job, finally becoming the manager and a part-owner.

After they finished, and Lydia had paid the bill—she called it a business expense—they stood outside on the sidewalk.

"So would you like to pick up where we left off last night?" asked Jake.

Lydia tilted her face up and leaned into Jake. "I absolutely do, but I have to meet with a client to talk about some art she wants me to buy for her. You don't work tonight, do you?"

"No," said Jake. "My first show isn't until tomorrow night."

"Great, take me to dinner and take me home, then we'll finish what we started. I'm aching to get that big cock of yours deep inside me."

Jake was feeling nervous. He'd had a quick phone sex session with Bianca last night after he'd returned, and told her about Lydia. Bianca had moaned, fingering herself, as she listened to Jake describe how Lydia had rubbed his head on her clit, and she told him about eating Lena's pussy two nights earlier.

Oh, fuck, I'm supposed to say something dirty in Lydia's ear here, like Bianca told me to do, he thought. *Don't fuck it up.* "I really want to feel your ... hot pussy wrapped around my shaft," he whispered in her ear. His cock hardened and he pulled her tightly to him so she could feel it pressing against her.

"I can't wait. My pussy is already wet right now. I'm going to go back to the office and finger myself thinking about you."

"I'm going to stroke ... my cock and imagine your beautiful cunt."

"Save some of that hot spunk for me, okay?"

"As much as you want."

The two kissed deeply, and a car beeped at them as it drove past.

"Stop by the gallery at 6:00 and we'll get dinner, then you can fuck my brains out," said Lydia.

She pulled on his bottom lip with her teeth and then turned and glided away. Jake watched her narrow hips and perfect ass as she walked back toward the gallery. She looked over her shoulder, smiled and waved, and continued on.

CHAPTER 5

"You live above the gallery?" Jake asked as Lydia opened the door to her apartment. They had just finished dinner at a Korean barbecue restaurant a few blocks away, and Jake had insisted on paying, saying lunch may have been business, but dinner was a date.

"Yes, which makes it both really convenient and a pain in the ass," said Lydia. "The gallery owner owns the building, and he lets me live up here for reduced rent in exchange for me managing the gallery. It's also convenient in case there are any emergencies or I have to work late."

"What, like an art emergency? Do you have many of those?"

"Oh, a few times a year. We'll get art riots where the sculptors talk shit to the painters, or the interpretive dancers want to throw down with the writers."

"Meh, I've seen interpretive dancers fight. It's like a bad West Side Story knock-off."

Lydia snorted and said, "I used to be a dancer in college."

"I could tell," said Jake. "Last night, when I saw you at the opening, I noticed you were standing in first position. Plus you stand up very straight, and you move like a dancer. Very graceful and smooth." He moved closer to Lydia and put his hands on her waist. "Are you flexible as well?"

"I can still put my feet behind my head if that's what you mean," Lydia said, tilting her face up to kiss him. Jake pulled her close and kissed her hard, their tongues writhing together.

"Excuse me one second," she said. "I want to freshen up a bit. Why don't you pour some wine? Glasses are next to the sink."

Lydia grabbed something in her bedroom and went into the bathroom where she brushed her teeth and rinsed with mouthwash. Jake rinsed his mouth as best he could in the kitchen sink and popped a couple of mouthwash tablets he always carried with him for just such an occasion.

His phone pinged with a text from Curtis: "Hey, Jakey, Anna is coming into town tomorrow night for the weekend. Bring your redhead to the show, we can go out after."

Shit, thought Jake. *They'll be fucking all weekend.*

He selected a nice white wine, found two glasses, and by the time he had set everything up on her coffee table and sat down on the couch, Lydia returned from her ministrations wearing a knee-length deep blue negligee. The sexy outfit set off her beautiful red hair, which she'd combed back into a ponytail. Jake gasped.

"You like?" Lydia said with a smile.

"Very much," said Jake, his dick hardening. "You look beautiful. Blue is definitely your color."

"Thank you. Now, there's something I've very much been wanting to do to you all day."

"Oh, yeah?" It was Jake's turn to smile. "What's that?"

"It's better if I just show you." Lydia picked up a glass of wine, took a sip, and smiled. "Nice choice, that's my favorite. I always keep a few bottles on hand." She set the glass back on her coffee table and straddled Jake, who scooted his butt out a little bit so she could rest directly on his hardness.

"Mmmmmm, I can tell you really like this negligee," she whispered.

"Well, not by itself. You make it look fantastic. But you'd look great without anything on too," Jake said with a smile.

Lydia laughed, the spellbinding sound that Jake loved. He liked making her laugh.

"Let's see if I'd look good with you on me."

Lydia crushed her mouth to his and thrust her tongue between his teeth. Jake realized she had brushed her teeth and was glad he had used those mouthwash tablets—Korean barbecue is merciless in times of shared intimacy. He placed his hand on the small of her back and pressed her closer to him.

She began grinding her pussy on his hard cock and Jake slid his hands, slowly, sensuously up her narrow hips, cupping her cheeks with his strong hands, kneading her flesh with his fingers. He felt around and realized she wasn't wearing any panties, so he slid his hands back around her hips, slid his thumb between the two of them, and found her clitoris.

"Oh," she gasped, as Jake rubbed her hard clit even as she continued grinding on him. "Oh, fuck," she breathed into his ear. "That's so wonderful. That's—OH! I'm going to cum! I didn't get to cum last night, but this time I'm going to cum for you. I'm going to—oh God! I'm—this is—ohhhhh—ohhhhh—ohhhhh—I'M CUMMING!"

Lydia shuddered and shook as her orgasm wracked her body and she kept grinding until she came a second, then a third, time. She clamped her mouth down on Jake's and moaned into his mouth over and over, screaming as each wave took her. When she stopped grinding, Jake pulled out his thumb, and stuck it in his mouth, savoring the taste of her sweet pussy juices.

"Holy fuck, that was amazing," said Jake.

"That was intense," Lydia agreed. "I don't think I've ever cum like that. That definitely deserves a thank you."

She lay on his chest, slowly kissing him and catching her breath for a few minutes. She stood up, knees still a little shaky, and slid her coffee table back a few feet.

Lydia kneeled down between Jake's legs and said, "I want to get reacquainted with this thing."

She undid Jake's pants and fished his hard member out of his pants.

"Fuck, it's even more beautiful up close," she said.

Jake's dick was eight-and-a-half inches long, and thick, and it looked even bigger as Lydia wrapped her slender fingers around his shaft and slowly stroked it. She licked a drop of pre-cum off the head and savored the taste before sliding her mouth down his cock. Lydia was only able to take in a few inches, her lips barely reaching halfway, so she settled into a rhythm of taking him in as far as she could, using her hand to stroke Jake's shaft at the same time. Occasionally, she would lick the underside of his dick, from his freshly-shaved ball sack to the head of his cock, before sliding it back into her mouth for a few strokes, then licking up one side of the shaft and down the other, and returning it to her mouth.

Lydia gently squeezed and massaged Jake's balls with her other hand and felt them tighten as he grew closer to his own orgasm. He groaned as she coated his thick cock with her saliva, sucking and jacking him off. He was glad she was wearing a ponytail because he loved seeing his cock slide into her mouth.

"Ohhhhh. That's so amazing. I'm going to cum," he said, deferring to her spelling. *After all, when in Rome...* he thought.

Lydia pistoned his cock in her mouth, sucking and jacking him faster.

"Oh, get ready, baby. Get ready," warned Jake. "This is for you. I'm going to—GAAAHHHHH!"

Lydia shoved Jake's cock in as far as she could take it as he rocketed out rope after rope of hot, salty cum into her eager mouth. She tried swallowing after each spurt but still couldn't keep up with the three, four, FIVE spasms that sent streams of Jake Jizz between her lips. Jake watched some of his milky cum slip out of her mouth and dribble over her fingers and down his shaft. Lydia raised her head, and looked Jake in the eye and swallowed her last mouthful. He shuddered as she rubbed her finger over his sensitive dickhead.

"Holy fuck, that was amazing," he said.

"That was tasty," she said, licking her fingertips, getting every yummy drop. She took a few swallows of wine, and said, "What's next? I still want to feel that thing inside my pussy."

"Right now, there is nowhere I'd rather be, but I do need a little time to recover. I have an idea in the meantime."

Jake stood up and reached his hand out, helping Lydia to her feet. The two kissed, and she helped Jake take off his shirt then knelt back down and helped him step out of his pants and socks before kissing his soft cock once on her way back up. Jake helped her remove her negligee, slowly gathering it up at her waist, and sliding it up and over her head. He realized this was the first time he was actually seeing her breasts in full light, freckles and all. Lifting her up, he had her stand on the coffee table as he savored her small breasts. They were round, perfect globes that he lovingly sucked and licked, tweaking and gently twisting her nipples with his fingers, feeling them harden and grow. Lydia breathed hard as he flicked his tongue over her buds, biting them oh-so-lightly with his teeth.

"Oh shit, lover, that's wonderful. I hope you eat my pussy this good."

Well, thought Jake, *eat your pussy well*, but knew better than to say that out loud.

"I'm going to lick your pussy until you're about to cum, then I'm going to shove my cock inside you, just like you wanted last night." *Why can't I talk like this on the phone?* he thought.

Lydia gasped and she felt as if her knees were about to buckle.

"Do you want me to wear a condom?" he asked.

"No, I have an IUD, plus I just finished my period, so I want to feel as much of your hot cum gushing inside me as I can."

Now it was Jake's knees that nearly buckled. "I can't wait, but I want to do something else first. Do you have a scarf?"

"Uh, you're not going to tie me up, are you?"

"Not unless you want me to," said Jake. "But I'd like to blindfold you. Is that okay?"

Lydia jumped off the coffee table into Jake's arms and wrapped her legs around his narrow waist, like she did last night. "As long as you fuck me with that magnificent prick of yours, I'm open to anything."

Jake carried Lydia through the kitchen to her bedroom, grabbing a new two-inch artist's paintbrush off her kitchen table on the way. "Where's your scarf? he asked.

"The closet," she said. He carried her over to the closet and she grabbed a purple scarf out of her closet and he carried her to the bed, gently laying her across it. He kissed her again, lying on top of her and she opened her legs. Jake felt himself getting harder, but he wanted to make her cum first. He rolled up her scarf and tied it gently around her head, covering her eyes, but not pulling too tightly.

"Is that okay? Not too tight?" he asked.

"No, it feels fine."

"And are you still comfortable with this? If you want to take it off or want me to stop, you just have to say so, and I'll stop."

"No, I'm fine. I trust you. But why did you grab my paintbrush?"

Jake smiled. "You'll see." He gently pushed Lydia onto her back and stayed kneeling over her. He picked up the paintbrush and flicked it lightly over Lydia's nipple.

"Ohh," she gasped.

He flicked it over the other nipple, the soft bristles barely touching her stiffening buds.

"Mmmmmmmmm," moaned Lydia, as Jake began gently painting over Lydia's sensitive nipples. "Oh, holy shit, that feels great." Lydia's hands drifted down to her pussy and she began to rub her clit.

"Ah-ah," said Jake. "This is for me."

"Oh, God, then please touch my pussy." Jake was still kneeling between her legs, so he set his hardening prick on her pubic hair landing strip.

"Oooh," squeaked Lydia, raising her hips to rub her clit on his meat.

"Not yet, baby. I'll give you what you want in due time." He continued brushing her nipples and slid his cock back and forth over her public hair but not on her clit, which made her groan even louder.

"Oh, fuck," said Lydia. "Oh, this is driving me crazy. You should have tied me up because I want to grab your cock and shove it in my pussy. Touch my clit and fuck me, goddammit."

"Uh-uh. I want you to beg me for it."

"Please, please, PLEASE fuck me with that cock, Jake."

"Trust me, not yet."

"But I can't—OH MY GOD!"

Jake had stopped brushing her nipples and was now using her paintbrush on her clit. He pulled his hips back far enough so the head of his cock was now nesting between her inner pussy lips. Lydia tried to buck her hips forward to slide her cunt over his cock, but he had positioned his knees to block her.

"Ohh fuck! What are you doing? That feels amazing! Please don't stop!" Lydia reached down and rubbed Jake's cockhead between her lips again in a repeat of last night, even while he delicately brushed her clitoris, like a treasure hunter carefully uncovering his prize.

"Ohhhh, God. That's so good. I'm getting close, Jakey, I'm getting close. Please fuck me with your monster cock. Fill me up with that big fucking thing!"

Jake dropped the paintbrush on the floor and grabbed his thick cock, pressing the underside of his shaft against her clitoris and moved his hips to slide his shaft along her clit.

"Ooohhhhhh! Ooohhhhhh! Ooohhhhhh!" Lydia cried. "I'm going to—I'm going to—I'm go—HOOOLY FUCK!" Lydia howled as Jake plunged his cock into her waiting pussy, gliding it in on her wetness, driving his thickness as deep as it would go.

The surprise invasion of his thick meat made her cum immediately and she slammed her arms down on the bed, grabbing handfuls of her quilt as she stiffened in throes of pleasure. He continued pumping her and she screamed as he brought her to a second orgasm, fucking her and rubbing her clit with his thumb.

"FUUUUUUUUUCKKKKK!" she shrieked, now covering her mouth with her hands.

He pulled back and plunged in again and again. "OH—FUCK! OH—FUCK! Let me see it. Let me see you fuck me." Lydia pulled off her scarf and looked down at the beautiful sight of Jake's eight-and-a-half inches sliding in and out of her pink pussy lips. She watched him thrust into her for several strokes before falling back, panting.

"Wrap your legs around me," Jake commanded, and Lydia happily complied, putting her heels on his back and pulling him down to her. He slowed down some to give her a rest after her two orgasms.

As he slid out, she pulled him back each time, using her dancer's leg muscles to drive his powerful cock into her wet snatch. Jake propped himself up on his elbows to watch her facial expressions each time he sank into her folds. She kissed him and moaned into his mouth as he did so, "Mmmmf! Mmmmf! Mmmmf!"

"Do you want me to take you from behind?" Jake panted.

"Take me any way you want," Lydia panted in return. "Just get back in me quick."

Jake wrapped his arms around her and raised up quickly, his dick slipping out of her satiny box. He stood on the floor, spun her around to face the bed, and bent her over at the waist. He grabbed his slippery shaft, repositioned himself at her velvety entrance, and drove into her again.

"Aaaggghhh!" they groaned together.

This put Jake's cock at a new angle in Lydia's cunt, and she loved it. He grabbed her slender hips and thrust himself into her, his hips slapping into her pert little ass.

"Unnh unnh unnh," he grunted. He reached around and cupped her breasts with both hands, momentarily stopping his rhythmic pumping.

She dropped to her elbows and looked back at her Viking lover. "Cum inside me, Jake," she demanded. "Fill me up with your hot cum."

Jake grabbed her hips and began pulling her back into him, driving his hips forward at the same time. Their bodies continued to slap together—*WHAP! WHAP! WHAP!*—as he plowed her dripping cunt. Jake lifted up her legs and she wrapped them around his ass in reverse of what she had been doing earlier.

"Fuck! Fuck! Fuck! Fuck!" she shrieked.

Lydia had pinned her arm underneath herself so she could rub her clit. Jake jammed his cock into her pussy, even as she sprawled facedown on the bedspread, sliding to and fro as he pulled and pushed her onto his cock.

Jake could feel himself getting closer, his ball sack began to tighten and that familiar sensation traveled up his cock.

"I'm going to cum. Oh, fuck, Lydia, I'm going to cum for you."

"Fill me up, Jake. Say my name when you do it. Say my name!"

"Oh, fuck, Lydia. Here we go. It's all for you, Lydia! Lydia! Lydia! LYDIAAAUUUGGGHHH!"

Lydia could feel a hot torrent of Jake's sperm fill her swollen cunt, and she used her inner muscles to grip him tightly when he began to flood inside her.

"GAAAAHHH!" shouted Jake as her velvety muscles squeezed him while he spasmed and fired out shot after shot after shot of sticky, milky cum. He stayed inside her as his spasms died down and he finally slipped out of her pussy.

"Oh, my God," he said and crawled onto the bed, flopping onto his back. "I'm spent."

Lydia crawled up next to him and nestled into the crook of his arm, her cheek resting against his chest. Both were gasping and covered in sweat.

"That was fucking amazing," said Jake. "I don't think I've ever come so hard."

"I don't think I've ever come five times in one weekend," said Lydia, "let alone in one night. You have a magic cock."

"Your pussy is pretty amazing too. Good Lord, that was incredible."

"Do you think you have it in you to go again?"

"Absolutely," said Jake. "Whenever you want. Just, maybe let me catch my breath for a few minutes first."

"You? Hell, I need many more minutes to catch my breath."

"Good, I was hoping you'd say that," said Jake.

"We could take a shower in a little bit, and maybe have some dessert. I've got some Derby pie in the fridge, and I could make some coffee. When we're done, I've got something I want to do with that paintbrush and some whipped cream."

"You're on," said Jake, kissing her on the forehead, and brushing her sweaty bangs off her forehead.

"Do you think you could spend the night?" asked Lydia. "I think I'm enjoying laying here, and I'd love to cozy up to you after you roger me one more time."

"Roger you?" Jake laughed. "I will roger you vigorously. And I'll stay as long as you want. Especially since my roommate's freaky new girlfriend is coming to visit him this weekend, and I'll have to listen to them fucking like rabbits the whole time."

"Great, stay all weekend. Now let's get that shower because your cum is starting to leak out of me and I can feel it running down my ass." Lydia popped off the bed, careful not to drag her cum-covered ass cheek across her bedspread, and Jake followed her into the bathroom.

"Hey, is that a detachable showerhead?" said Jake. "I've got another idea."

THE END

CHASTITY VELDT
Natasha
in Nashville
STAND UP, LIE DOWN COLLECTION

TABLE OF CONTENTS

Chapter 1

Jake closed the door to his hotel room, dropped his suitcase on the chair, and pulled the comforter off the king-size bed. He folded it up and stuck it by the door before picking up the phone and pressing 0 for the front desk.

"Hi, this is Jake Nilsen in room 615. I was wondering if I could get a fresh comforter, please."

"Nelsan?" asked the front desk clerk

"No, Nilsen," said Jake. "I just want to make sure it's fresh and clean."

"We'll make sure it's freshly laundered," the clerk promised.

Jake unpacked his suitcase, carefully unfolding and hanging up his only sport coat, followed by his shirts and jeans. As a standup comic, Jake made sure to always take good care of his "work clothes," which meant unpacking as soon as he arrived in a new city, and hanging everything up, including his jeans.

He also always requested a new comforter as soon as he arrived, because he had heard the horror stories about how infrequently the housekeeping staff changed the comforters, so he wanted to be sure there weren't any unexplained dried fluids on his quilt.

It was early Tuesday afternoon, and Jake was in Nashville for a rare five-night gig at a comedy club called Fries. The club had put him up in a hotel on Broadway, just a few blocks from the club and the downtown Nashville bar scene.

Jake had been in Louisville two weeks ago, and this past week had spent a rare week off visiting an old friend from college in Bowling Green, Kentucky.

Rob and Jake had been on the University of Minnesota swim team together, and Rob was now a high school social studies teacher in Bowling Green and the school's swim coach. Jake helped Rob coach the young swimmers during the afternoon and spent his mornings at a coffee shop near Fountain Square Park writing new material, or the evenings going to Bowling Green Hot Rod baseball games at the ballpark.

Jake's week in Louisville had been spent in the bed of Lydia Woodruff, the manager of an art gallery as well as an outstanding artist. He bought one of her post-impressionist paintings, which was now crated up and secured in the back of his pickup. She had also sketched and painted a few nudes of Jake featuring his swimmer's physique and toned abs, as well as his eight-and-a-half-inch dick. Most of them were only half-finished and seriously wrinkled since Jake and Lydia usually ended up doing it on top of her sketch pad when she was half-finished with a sketch.

This week, Jake was supposed to middle at Fries as well as emcee the open mic nights on Tuesday and Wednesday nights. He hated emceeing open mics, but he preferred longer stays than just the one-and-dones he had as an opener, so he asked his manager to book longer stays in cities, even if it meant emceeing the open mics. Plus they paid $50 per night, and he wasn't too proud to listen to shitty comics for 100 bucks.

Jake had just finished putting his underwear and socks away when there was a knock at the door and one of the housekeeping staff delivered his new quilt. Jake tipped her a few dollars and closed the door. He remade his bed and decided to lie down for a quick nap before he checked in at the club to let them know he was there.

Two hours later, Jake was at Fries, knocking on the manager's door, which was already open.

"Hey there," said the woman sitting at the desk. She stood up and offered her hand. "I'm Cheri."

"Hi, Jake Nilsen."

"Nelsan?" said Cheri.

"No, Nilsen."

"Popcorn?" asked Cheri, holding up what looked like a tub of movie popcorn.

Jake held up his hand and shook his head. "No, thanks."

"We have a popcorn machine at the bar and I'm on this damn diet where I can only eat popcorn for lunch and dinner."

"Wow, I'll bet that gets boring after a while," said Jake.

"Yeah, and my farts smell like butter."

Jake laughed and said, "That's pretty good. Did you ever do comedy?"

"For a while, but I got tired of life on the road. My husband and I decided to buy this place when the owner was sick and looking to sell. We got divorced a few years later. He got the dog, and I got the club."

"Wow, that worked out pretty well for you."

"Maybe. The dog may constantly lick his balls, but he isn't a self-entitled dickhead who demands his own dressing room."

"I knew a comic like that."

"A self-entitled dickhead? There's lots of those."

"No, he could lick his own balls."

Cheri threw her head back and laughed. She high-fived Jake and said, "You win. That was good."

"By the way, thanks for the hotel room. I managed to get a quick nap before I got here."

"You're welcome. I appreciate your flexibility. The headliner is a woman and I just don't feel right forcing co-ed housing on you both. Besides, my cousin is the manager at the hotel, and she gives me free nights if they're not overbooked."

"Not a problem. I appreciate it."

"Besides, between you and me, the apartment's a bit of a shithole and I'm having it fumigated before she gets here. Plus, she's really obnoxious and I don't like her that much, so I stuck her in there and gave you the hotel. But she draws a big crowd, so I keep having her back."

"I've seen her work. She's really funny."

"And...?"

"And yeah, she's really obnoxious."

The two chatted for a few more minutes before Jake asked for some dinner recommendations.

"There's The Distillery Bar & Grill just around the corner, and they have some of the best burgers in town. Plus they've got live music in the afternoons."

"Seriously, that early?"

"Well, it's like our open mics. Young musicians can get their start at these bars, playing for free to tiny crowds. If the manager likes them, they'll have them back for an opening act later in the evening."

"That makes sense. So it's a real hodge-podge of acts?"

"Yeah, and it's a Tuesday, so who knows what you're going to find."

Jake thanked Cheri and left to get dinner.

"Here you go, hun," said the server, setting a hamburger and fries before Jake. "There's ketchup on the table, and the music's about to start."

"Who's playing?"

"I don't know, some new girl. They're usually only here for a day or two and then we never see them again."

"Hi, I'm Natasha Blake and this is my first time here," said a woman from the small stage, her voice quavering. "I'll be performing, uh, a few songs for y'all. Or, well, just you." Natasha smiled at Jake and the server.

Jake was the only one in the club, and he was seated right in front of the stage. He smiled at her. She was clearly nervous, so he tried to project an image of reassuring calm.

Natasha slid onto a tall wooden bar stool and adjusted her guitar. Her hands shook a little as she played. She strummed a few chords and began to sing: *"He said 'I'll love you till I die,' she told him 'You'll forget in time.'"*

Jake stopped, his hamburger halfway up to his mouth, and forgot to close it. Natasha may not have been as confident in her playing, but her gorgeous voice arrested him. Jake was not a country music fan, but his mother was, and he immediately recognized George Jones' *"He Stopped Loving Her Today,"* a song that sometimes made her cry. He set down his hamburger and listened, trying to hold back a tear or two of his own. He clapped wildly when she was finished.

Natasha smiled and said, "Thank you."

He finished his hamburger as she ran through "I Saw the Light," "Mama Tried," and Tammy Wynette's "D-I-V-O-R-C-E." Her voice cracked when she sang *"Our D-I-V-O-R-C-E becomes final today,"* and Jake saw a tear fall down her cheek as she reached the end.

When she finished, she stood up, wiped her eyes, and said, "Thank you very much."

Jake stood up and applauded as loud as he could, and Natasha smiled and looked down at her feet.

"Bravo!" shouted Jake.

Natasha stepped off the stage and walked over to his table. She was average height, around five-and-a-half feet tall. Her hair was chestnut brown, with highlights and big curls. She had thick thighs and hips, curvy all around, and her jeans and shirt were a little tight. She smiled even as she blushed brightly at Jake's applause.

"My first standing ovation," she said when she reached his table.

"But definitely not your last," said Jake. "That was great. My mom loves country music and I recognized all those songs from her CD collection. We'd be driving down the road and she'd put on 'He Stopped Loving Her Today' and just cry and cry."

"Oh, it's definitely a sad song. It's about a guy who stops loving his wife only because he died. He made a promise to love her for as long as he lived, which he did even though she left him for another man. I'm Natasha Blake, by the way."

"Jake Nilsen."

"Nelsan?"

"No, Nilsen."

"Ah. So is this your first time here?"

"Well, the first time at the Distillery. I've been to Nashville a few times. I'm here for a few days, and someone recommended this place for dinner."

"It's my first time at the Distillery too," said Natasha. "I started playing music a few months ago, and I thought I would try performing in public. I called around to a few places, and they were good enough to give me a try here. I'll do a couple sets today, and then I get to put the Distillery on my resumé."

"Would you like to sit down?" asked Jake.

"Sure, let me put my guitar in the green room."

As Natasha returned and settled in, the server brought Jake the bill. "Can I get you anything else, hon?"

"I'm good. Do you want anything?" he asked Natasha.

"No, I'm good."

"No special dessert to celebrate your first show?"

"I'd better not."

"Well, I'll take some banana cream pie, and we'll take two forks." The server left, and Jake said to Natasha, "You can have a bite or two if you change your mind."

"Oh, maybe one bite. I need to lose some weight." She patted her thighs and said, "My husband—my nearly ex-husband—used to say I was 'Rubenesque,' like in those paintings by that artist, Ruben. You know, the ones with the fat women?"

"I know the paintings, but I don't agree with your husband's assessment."

"Ex-husband. And that was one of the nicer terms he used for me."

"Wow, he sounds like a real asshole."

"He was, and that's why I'm divorcing him. That, and he was sleeping with his secretary, Katrina. Best day of my life was when I threw him out. He called me every foul name he could think of, and I threatened to brain him with a frying pan. Grabbed some clothes and he left."

"Wow, that must have been some frying pan," said Jake.

"Yeah, it was my Mama's old cast-iron pan, but he's a skinny little pansy too. I mean, he's this scrawny little accountant type who can only make himself feel better by tearing other people down. So I kicked him out, started working out, and took up the guitar again. I gave it up when I married him, but I've been playing every day ever since."

"So when was all this?"

"Just three months ago. I called an attorney a couple weeks ago who said he can help me and will file the papers in a few weeks. In fact, I did this show to celebrate my new freedom."

"So that's why you sang the D-I-V-O-R-C-E song."

"Yep. I learned it just for this day."

Their server brought the banana cream pie and Jake urged Natasha to have a few bites. "An important accomplishment deserves a celebration, even if it's a little one."

The two talked about their lives, Jake's work, Natasha's work (she ran the accounts payable department for one of the local manufacturers), and working out. Natasha was pleased to hear that Jake was an exercise fanatic, and had been eyeing his chest and biceps since she sat down.

Jake offered to work out with her one day this week, if she was interested, and the two made plans for lunch in two days. Natasha explained that work had given her the week off to deal with her divorce and to let her concentrate on her show. So she was taking the time to focus on herself and to do some self-care.

After Jake settled the bill, the two hugged each other tightly, exchanged mobile numbers, and Natasha got ready for her next set as a few new diners started coming in for the dinner hour.

Chapter 2

Most open mic nights at a comedy club were pretty tame—and lame—affairs. Every professional comedian started there, but for every professional comedian there were a hundred open mic first-nighters who never had a second night.

Tonight, however, was a little more fun. A group of six women had all come to the club in the hopes of a fun night out, and to try comedy. They were all a little drunk, and they were laughing at everything they said at the table. When one of them got up for their set, it was usually just rehashing the jokes they had been telling at the table.

Jake was a good host too. He encouraged the audience to applaud wildly after each performer. As the night went on, the table of women laughed harder at everything, so as the other comics performed, the women screamed with laughter, which was an ego boost to all the baby comics.

Even Jake had to admit it felt great as he told a few jokes and the group howled at everything. When it was all over, Jake approached the table and thanked them for coming.

"It was our pleasure," said one.

"It was more than our pleasure," said a woman with short, platinum-blonde hair, eyeing Jake up and down.

The other women burst out laughing again.

"I don't think that came out the way you meant it," said the first one.

"Probably not, but I'll bet it goes in the way I meant it," said the woman, and Jake thought the others were going to pee themselves. "Excuse me for a minute." She tottered unsteadily toward the bathroom on cherry red high heels.

"I think it's time we all went," said another, and the five remaining women thanked Jake, each giving him a hug that lasted for several seconds, or squeezing his biceps.

"Where's Mandy?" said one of the women.

"I think she's outside. Come on, the Lyft is here. I got us an SUV."

They all scurried out, laughing, and the place was finally empty, except for Jake and the bartender, who was putting chairs on the tables. Jake helped him put up some chairs and they chatted for a few minutes as they worked.

"Shit, where did my friends go?" said a woman behind Jake.

"Uh-oh," said Jake. "Are you Mandy?"

"Yes. Did those bitches leave without me? I was in the bathroom!"

"They thought you were outside. Maybe if you hurry, you can catch them."

Mandy was back in a few seconds later. "Nope, they're gone, and April was my ride."

"They all caught a Lyft."

"Well, fuck," said Mandy. "I don't even have the Lyft app."

"I can give you a ride," said Jake. "Where do you live?"

"I live in Forest Hills."

"Well, I don't know where it is, but we can find it on GPS."

Mandy was in her mid- to late-40s, slender and looked like she worked out. She reminded Jake a little of Irene, the yoga instructor from Indianapolis,[6] maybe because she was wearing yoga pants and an off-the-shoulder top, with no obvious bra straps showing. Slim and trim, including her chest and butt, Mandy was built more like a runner than a yogi. *But she looked sexy in yoga pants.* Her platinum hair was cut short up the back and longer on the sides, and gave her a little air of *"I'd like to speak to your manager."*

Jake helped her step into his truck and he admired the view as she climbed unsteadily up into the cab. He and Mandy chatted as Jake drove to her house. She touched his forearm quite a bit as they talked, and she told him how her husband was on a business trip overseas for a few weeks.

When they pulled into the driveway, Mandy said, "I hate to sound like the helpless woman, but could you check for intruders? Whenever my husband travels, I hate leaving the house because I'm afraid someone is going to be waiting for me in there."

---

[6] See *Stand Up, Lie Down: Irene in Indianpolis.*

"No problem," he said.

"My hero," she smiled squeezing his thigh.

Mandy unlocked the door and crossed over to the alarm panel, and entered the code. Jake made a quick tour of the house, looking in the bathrooms, bedroom, and guest rooms.

"Looks all clear to me," he said. "Do you need anything else?"

"Do you want a drink?" asked Mandy.

"No, I'm fine. I had a few at the club," said Jake.

"Well, sit with me for a bit. My husband has been away for ten days and I've been lonely for some company. Tonight was the first night I've done anything with anyone outside of work, and you saw how well that went."

"I thought your friends were great, other than leaving you behind. They certainly made me feel good on stage."

"Yeah, they're some crazy bitches and we have fun. I just get overlooked once in a while, like tonight. And it happens here at home more than once in a while."

Jake sat down on one end of the couch and put his arm on the back. Mandy took that as an invitation and she sat next to him, leaning into him, resting her hand on his thigh.

She closed her eyes and murmured, "This feels nice."

Jake could feel a familiar tingling in his groin, and he put his arm around Mandy. She took a deep breath and scooched closer to him as he pulled her tighter. They stayed that way for several minutes, making small talk, as Mandy stroked his thigh, squeezing it gently as her hand slid up and down his leg. Each time she slid her hand up, she got a little closer to the bulge in Jake's pants until she grazed it with her finger, and slid away. The next time, she touched it a little harder, and slid away. Then she brushed his shaft with her fingers, and slid away. Then she squeezed it and this time, her hand did not move away.

"Hey," said Jake, the word barely a whisper.

She looked up and Jake kissed her. Mandy returned the kiss, sliding her tongue into his mouth, and squeezing his cock through his jeans. Jake began kneading her ass and pulled her onto his lap where she faced him and straddled one of his legs. Mandy shoved her thigh against his cock, even as she ground her pussy onto his powerful thigh.

She broke off the kiss and pressed her body against Jake, breathing heavily into his ear. "Oh, God, this feels so good," she moaned. "I need this."

Jake cupped a hand on Mandy's small breast and realized she definitely wasn't wearing a bra. Mandy's nipples hardened under his touch, and he pinched her nipple through her shirt. As Mandy continued to grind against his thigh, he lifted the hem of her shirt slowly, almost as if he were asking for permission. She answered for him by raising up and lifting her shirt over her head. As she leaned back, Jake tenderly took one of her nipples into his mouth while he played with her other breast. Mandy groaned out loud and continued the grinding friction on his leg.

"Take your shirt off," whispered Mandy, unbuttoning his shirt.

He quickly complied and Mandy gave a little "oh" when she saw Jake's washboard abs and large pectorals. She played with his nipples and ran her hands over his chest before leaning back into him. Shuddering as she felt their skin together, reveling in the warm embrace of another person.

"I've missed feeling this," she said. "I've missed just feeling someone against my body."

"You feel great against me," said Jake, feathering his fingers up and down her spine. He felt goosebumps form on her back and she shuddered.

"Oh, fuck, I'm going to come," Mandy groaned in his ear, still rubbing her pussy on his thigh. "Oh... Ohh... Ohhh... fu-u-u-uck!" Her thighs clamped down on his and she squeezed her arms around him as she shuddered with her first orgasm. "Holy... shit..." she breathed. "That was great. I haven't had one of those in a few months."

"I'm glad I could help," said Jake.

"Oh, we're not finished. That's just a warm-up. I want to feel you inside me. And I want a couple more of those."

"I think I can help you with that too." Jake lifted her off of him and slid her yoga pants down around her ankles. She wasn't wearing any panties and had shaved her entire pubic region so her pussy was smooth and bare. Jake kissed her belly and slid his thumb across her clit.

She winced and said, "Ooh, I may need a few minutes. I'm still sensitive." She pulled him up and kneeled down before him, working at his belt and unzipping his pants. "Now, let's see what Santa has brought me tonight."

Mandy gasped as Jake's eight-and-a-half-inch cock sprang free and nearly hit her in the face. Jake kept his own manly region as smooth and hairless as his torso, even his scrotum, and Mandy admired its size and smoothness.

"Oh, my, you're a big one, aren't you." She wrapped her slender fingers around his thick shaft. "It's so ... goddamn ... thick. You're a lot bigger than my husband." She stroked him a few times. "I hope you fit inside me, because you're not going home until you do."

Jake took off the rest of his clothes and tossed them aside and Mandy returned her attention to Jake's tool. She wrapped her hand around it and stroked as she studied his cock head. She licked the tip a few times, cleaning off the pre-cum. Popping the head into her mouth, she sucked hard like she was trying to get something out of it. As she stroked, she tried to fit more of his dick into her mouth, but could only manage a few inches. Still, Jake appreciated the effort and was happy any time a woman was willing to suck his cock.

Mandy stopped her sucking and licked underneath Jake's shaft from base to tip. She returned and licked his ball sack, gently taking each one into her mouth then licking back up to the tip of his cock again. Jake shuddered at the sensation and groaned his appreciation.

She pushed Jake back onto the couch and resumed sucking, taking another inch of his meat into her mouth until it hit the back of her throat. She nearly gagged a couple times, but was undeterred. She used her saliva as lubrication, and jacked him off as she sucked.

Mandy paused in her sucking and held Jake's cock between her small tits, pistoning herself up and down so his dick slid between them. Jake moaned and she returned to sucking and licking the head of his cock.

"I'm going to come," said Jake, using his preferred spelling. "Oh, fuck, I'm going to come."

"Not yet," said Mandy, squeezing Jake's cock head between her finger and thumb. "I want you to cum somewhere else," she corrected, using her preferred spelling.

Ah, well, thought Jake, *when in Rome... Or is that, Rum?*

Mandy settled onto the couch next to Jake and lifted her legs, grabbing them behind her knees. "Fuck me with that thing and I'll tell you where to cum."

Jake didn't wait to be told twice. He knelt before Mandy again, grabbing his thick cock and guiding it toward her folds. He slid the head on her labia, swollen from her grinding, then used it to guide him where to gently part her lips. Her pussy was wet and slick and he slid his head up and down between her lips, lubricating it on her juices.

"Oh, please! Please don't make me wait. Please, fuck me, Jake!" she begged. "Stick that monster—OOHHHHHH FUCK!"

Jake slowly pushed his hips forward, introducing his cock into her folds, spreading her pussy apart with his shaft.

"Oh, fuck, that's so goddamn big!" Mandy shrieked as Jake drove forward even more.

She put her hand on his stomach to stop him from penetrating any further and he waited a few minutes to let her get used to the new invader.

He made his cock throb and she jumped and giggled. "Oh, fuck, what was that?"

"Kegels," said Jake. He did it again.

"Ho, shit! Fuck! That's a weird—oh!"

Jake carefully slid forward some more and was able to bury himself completely. Mandy wrapped her ankles around his shoulders. "Fuck me, please. No kegels, just pound me."

Jake wrapped his arms around Mandy's thighs and drove home, pumping slowly and pulling Mandy's thighs toward him so he could drive as deeply as he could. He squeezed his tight ass and pushed himself, hoping to squeeze even a millimeter more than before.

"OH! OH! OH! OH!" cried Mandy with each powerful thrust. "OH! OH! OH! OH!"

She grabbed onto Jake's forearms and pulled herself forward to meet his pistoning, trying to pull more of him into herself. After a few minutes of pounding, Jake felt the familiar tingle returning in his scrotum.

"Oh, God, I'm going to cum," Jake said, smoothly switching spellings without Mandy noticing. "Where do you want me to cum?"

"I want you to come on me," said Mandy, playing with her clit. "Cum on me, Jakey."

Jake slowed down a bit. "What, like on your face?"

"God, no. What is this, a smut book? Just cum on my stomach. Shoot your hot cum on my stomach and say my name when you do."

Jake drove himself into her a few more times and quickly withdrew, raising himself up slightly and started jerking off, pointing at her smooth, flat stomach. Mandy started groaning as her own orgasm began to build.

"Ohh, get ready, Mandy. Get ready for my cum. This is for you, baby. Here you go, MAHHHHHHHHHH. "

"OH, FUCK!" Mandy shouted, cumming just as Jake's hot seed spattered on her stomach.

His first shot landed right on her belly, the second one had a little more ambition and reached up to between her breasts, and with his third and fourth landing back around her navel. Mandy held onto his arm with her other hand as his spasms reduced and she was sure he wasn't going to give her any surprises. She ran her fingers through his semen, lightly tracing little shapes with her finger.

"Holy fuck, that was amazing," said Jake. "That was great."

"I haven't had anyone cum on me like that in a while," said Mandy. "Not since college."

"Not even your husband?"

"No. It makes him squeamish. And he won't even go down on me."

"So when's the last time anyone licked your pussy?" asked Jake.

Mandy thought for a minute. "Five or six years ago."

"How long have you been married?" Jake said.

"Eighteen years." Mandy smiled. "Remember one of the women in my group with black hair?" Jake nodded. "We hooked up a few years ago when my husband was out of town. It was a one-time thing, and we haven't done it since."

"Well, let's break your dry spell tonight, because I want to return the favor."

"That's fine, honey, but first I need a towel, because I just don't feel like having dried cum on me all night. But I will want some more fresh stuff."

CHAPTER 3

The air was a little chilly as Jake was out for a run in the Germantown neighborhood near downtown Nashville. He loved running through old historic neighborhoods in the cities he visited, and he often thought back to the days when his parents would drive him around the old historic neighborhoods in his hometown of Mankato, Minnesota.

He was getting in his regular run this Thursday morning when his mobile phone rang, interrupting the song he was listening to. He looked at his phone before answering, tempted to let it go to voicemail, but saw that it was Natasha.

"Hey," said Jake. "What's going on?"

"Jake, I'm so sorry, but I have to cancel our lunch today." Jake heard her choke up and sniff a little on the other line.

"Are you okay?" he asked.

"Yes," she said. "No. I just— I don't—" and she started to cry. "I'm sorry."

"Hey, it's okay. What's wrong?"

"I don't know what to do."

"What's the matter? What can't you do?"

"It's my husband, Richard," said Natasha. "He's coming over here and said he wants to file for divorce."

"But that's what you wanted, isn't it?"

"Yes, but he's got some hot shit attorney and now he's going to take the house and throw me out."

"What? How?"

"He said he's entitled to it because he's paid for the upkeep all these years, and he said it's too big for just me. But it was my house before we got married, and when we got married, I put it in both our names. Now he's trying to take my house. He said he'll pay for half of it, but this was my house before I ever met him. And get this, he said he and his secretary are going to start a family, and they need the space!" She started to cry again.

Jake waited until she used up most of her tears. "So how did you find this out?"

"He said he was coming over to settle on the price and have his attorney draw up the agreement. And now I can't find my shitty attorney and I don't know what to do. So I'm going to have to cancel lunch and figure this out."

Jake started jogging back in the direction of his hotel. "Where are you? I'll come over."

"Wow, you must really want lunch," Natasha laughed between sobs.

Jake chuckled. "Yeah, it's not that. I just don't like bullies, so I'll come over and help."

"You really don't have to," said Natasha. "I'll be alright. This just has me so flustered."

"I know I don't have to, but I want to. Besides, your husband sounds like a dick, and you need someone to back you up. Where do you live?"

"I live in East Nashville, in the Porter Heights area. I'll text you the address."

"I'll be there as soon as I can."

"Thank you so much. I appreciate you."

"I'm glad to do it," he said, and tapped his phone to end the call.

Forty-five minutes later, Jake pulled up to Natasha's home, a dark blue house that looked like it had recently been re-sided. He was wearing an Under Armour t-shirt that stretched across his chest and enhanced his pectorals. His biceps stretched at the sleeves too. Jake called it his "Dude Bro Douchebag" shirt and he only wore it when he was lifting weights, but he thought it might make a memorable impression in this situation.

A large tree in the front yard had not yet changed color for autumn, but the days were getting closer. Jake was sorry to be missing the fall this year, because he knew Nashville could be gorgeous when the leaves turned.

He parked on the street and rang the doorbell. A woman Jake didn't recognize opened the door.

"Hi, I'm looking for Natasha," he said.

The woman looked him up and down with a slightly confused, but appreciative gaze. Her nostrils flared as if she had caught Jake's musk on the wind.

"She's in the kitchen with her husband," said the woman. "Ex-husband. I'm Katrina, by the way."

"Hi, Katrina, how do you know Natasha?"

"I don't. I, uh, I work for her husband."

"Oh, the secretary," said Jake. Katrina blushed and turned away.

"Because it's not yours," they heard Natasha shout from the kitchen.

"The hell it's not!" came a man's thin voice, pitched a little high. "Who do you think paid for the fucking siding."

Jake followed the sound of the raised voices into the kitchen.

"Hey, Natasha," said Jake from the doorway.

"Oh, Jake, thank you for coming," she said, sitting at the kitchen table, tears streaming down her face.

She held a crumpled tissue in her hands and twisted it around her fingers. A small wiry man with glasses who reminded Jake of Kip from *Napoleon Dynamite* stood over Natasha, hands on his hips. Jake recognized the Napoleon Syndrome instantly.

"Who the fuck are you?" demanded the man. Jake guessed that this was Richard.

"I'm Jake. Who the fuck are you?"

"I'm her husband, and this is my house, so get the fuck out."

Jake ignored him and looked at Natasha. "Are you alright?"

"I'm fine now," said Natasha.

"It's none of your concern how she is," said Richard.

Jake stepped in front of Richard and knelt down to look at Natasha on her level. "Do you need some help?" he asked quietly. She nodded and wiped at the tears on her face.

"Who the fuck do you think you are?" demanded Richard. Jake pointedly ignored him and stayed where he was, patting Natasha's hand.

"Hey, I'm talking to you," Richard said.

"I know. I was ignoring you."

"Listen, she doesn't want your help, you dumb fucking Swede!" Richard tried to grab Jake around his bicep, but Jake's bicep was too big for the little man's short fingers.

Jake stood up and whirled around quickly which startled Richard, who stepped back. He puffed his chest up and flexed his back muscles the way he had seen bodybuilders do in bodybuilding competitions to make themselves look bigger.

"First of all, *Dick*, I'm Norwegian," growled Jake, taking another step toward Richard. Richard's eyes widened and he took another step back. "Second, you don't get to say what she wants or needs. Third, I'm clearly smarter than you because you're the one who grabbed me when you're barely as big as my arm."

"This is not your fucking house and it's not your fucking problem," said Richard, who had all the sense of a tiny dog trying to pick a fight with a big dog.

"From what I hear, it's not your fucking house, either. And it hasn't been since Natasha kicked you out for sleeping with Katherine out there." Jake flexed his bicep as he pointed toward the living room.

"Katrina," called Katrina helpfully.

"Sorry Katrina," called Jake.

"No problem, Jake."

"And since you were the one to have an affair, I'll bet any divorce lawyer in this city is not only going to see that you do not get this house, you'll end up buying her a second one just to store your tiny balls."

Katrina snorted from the living room.

"So if you don't get out of here. Right. Now—" Jake made his pecs bounce with those two words. "—I'm going to whip you around by your fawn-like ankles and throw you across the street—" he paused "—Dick."

Richard's face flushed deep red, and Jake wondered if he was going to have a stroke. He pointed his finger at Jake and opened his mouth to speak so Jake bounced his pecs again.

"Oh, my," Katrina breathed from the kitchen door. Jake winked at her, and she blushed.

"You'd better go before she does something you'll regret," said Jake.

Richard closed his mouth, looked at Katrina, looked back at Jake, then back at Katrina. He grabbed her by the hand and stormed out of the house. "This isn't over!" he shouted over his shoulder.

"It's totally over," said Jake to Natasha.

"Oh my God," said Natasha, running over and putting her arms around Jake, wrapping them around his chest. He could feel her full breasts pressing against him and he put his arms around her too, enjoying the sensation. "That was amazing. Richard is such an emotional bully; he makes everyone cave. How did you make him leave?"

Jake turned and moved away from Natasha. "Like this," he said, and bounced his pecs again. "Either I intimidated him or he realized Katrina was about to dry hump me."

"Yeah, well I can't blame her," said Natasha as she stared at Jake's chest. She clapped her hand over her mouth and turned bright red. "I didn't mean to say that out loud."

Jake laughed, "Look, if you're not happy with your attorney, I know someone who can help you. One of my friends from college is a divorce attorney here in town. I was going to meet her before my show tonight for dinner, and if you'd like I can call her and set up a meeting for you this week."

"Is she any good?"

"Oh, yeah. She's told me about some of the women she's helped and how much she got from their husbands. I know it doesn't go well if the husband had an affair, so she'll probably be able to get you a good settlement without ever having to go to court."

Jake made a quick call on his cell phone, stepping out into the living room for a little privacy. After a few minutes, he walked back in and handed the phone to Natasha. They chatted for a few minutes until Natasha finally sobbed with what sounded like relief.

"That sounds wonderful, thank you," said Natasha. She hung up and handed the phone back to Jake.

"She said she can help me file papers, and she'll get him served tomorrow afternoon. She said that there was no way Richard was getting my house. Even if I put it in our name when we got married, the fact that it was mine first weighs in my favor, especially since he was the one who had the affair. Oh, and she said she's doing it for no charge. Why would she do that?"

"I don't know. She sometimes helps people who really need it."

"Well, whatever she's doing, it sounds like she's good at it. She's drawing up the papers and will have them for me when we meet tonight and she'll file them tomorrow and have him served at his work. Oh, and she wants to meet with me at 5:00 at her office downtown."

"Excellent," said Jake.

"Wait, you were supposed to have dinner with her. I don't want to mess up your date."

"Oh, it's not a date. Her wife doesn't like her dating men. Besides, we're meeting at 6:30, which is early for her. She usually works later than that."

"I don't have anything decent to wear to meet with her though. I've been working out for a few months and my good clothes don't fit me anymore. Just some old clothes I've had for several years. That blouse I wore at The Distillery was a little tight because it was six years old."

"Well," said Jake, "I don't have anything going on right now. Let's go get some lunch and we'll pick up a couple shirts for you."

"Blouses," said Natasha. "Women's shirts are called blouses. And you must really want lunch."

Jake laughed again. "I'm really in the mood for tacos," he said.

"I know just the place."

CHAPTER 4

As the two browsed a women's clothing boutique on 12th Avenue near the Melrose neighborhood, Natasha spotted a few blouses she liked and took them into the dressing room to try them on. She came out and modeled each one for Jake, who appreciated how they accentuated her curves and made her look elegant, even in jeans.

One of the blouses was dark blue and showed off her deep cleavage between her plump breasts. Natasha wore a necklace with a small charm that settled just at the top where her cleavage began, drawing Jake's eyes to the cleft. He pictured sliding his cock between them and started giving himself a boner. He shifted in his seat to keep the bulge of his eight-and-a-half inches from becoming too noticeable.

"What did you think?" Natasha asked when she was finally finished. She held up the four shirts she had tried on.

"I liked the dark blue one, because it set off your, uh, highlights," said Jake.

"Uh-huh," she said with a smile. "I saw you checking out my 'highlights.'"

Jake blushed, "And I liked the burgundy one because it looked like something you'd wear to the opera."

"Well, maybe the Opry around here, but thank you. Those were my favorites too. The green one and the polka dotted one, not so much."

"So are you going to get them?"

"Oh, I can't. They're pretty expensive. I can't spend that kind of money right now. I just want to look and dream."

Jake looked around and grabbed a few items off a rack. He said, "Here, try these on and I'll put the others back for you."

He handed her a couple dresses and a pair of jeans. She handed him the shirts (*excuse me, blouses*) and went back into the dressing room.

Jake walked over to the cashier and put the blouses up on the counter. "We'll take the blue one and the burgundy one. Could you wrap them up like a gift, please?"

"Oh, your girlfriend will look great in these," said the cashier, swiping Jake's credit card. She wrapped up the two he selected and placed the other two on a rack behind the counter.

Several minutes later, Natasha came out of the dressing room and returned the clothes she had been trying on, and Jake hid the box behind his back.

"Yeah, I didn't like any of those. What do you have behind your back?"

"Nothing," said Jake with a mischievous grin. "We should go. I'm famished."

"Okay, but what do you—you're not shoplifting, are you?"

Jake laughed. "No, they don't have anything that fits me. I'll show you when we get to the restaurant."

"Well, it's just two doors down, so let's go."

As they sat down, he handed her the box and said, "Here, congratulations on, well, everything."

Natasha looked puzzled as she opened the box. "What did you—oh my God, Jake! What did you do?"

"Well, you looked so good in them that I wanted to make sure you got them."

"Thank you so much. I don't know what to say, except thank you!"

Jake put his hand on hers. "That's all you have to say."

"But they're so expensive. You're just a comic—well, not *just* a comic, but comics don't make that much money, do they?"

"No, standup comics don't make much money."

"Then why are you spending this kind of money on me? You barely know me."

"Can I tell you a secret that I don't share with many people?"

"Sure." She leaned in close. "You're not a hit-man for the mob, are you?"

"No, not really. I, uh, I made some good investments when I was first starting out. I had an uncle who died and left me a lot of money.

Instead of just blowing it like most college kids, I learned how to invest in real estate. I bought a couple cheap houses, fixed them up, and started renting them out. I was able to leverage that into a few more houses. Now I own twelve different rental properties near a couple colleges in Minnesota and that's how I make my money.

"A buddy of mine does the maintenance and I pay him, but I handle the payments and business aspect of it. So I'm not rich, but I make enough that I can be a comic for fun. And if I can become successful, then that's all the better. So now I—what's wrong?"

Natasha's eyes filled with tears and she said, "I've had such a shit day and someone I barely know has just made it one of the best days I've had in a long time."

Jake grabbed both her hands and squeezed them. The server set their tacos down and quickly left, thinking she was witnessing a breakup.

"I mean it," Natasha continued. "Nothing has gone right for me for the last several months. My debut night audience was sparse. You were my only audience for my first-ever show. My stupid husband and his stupid slut secretary want to take my house. And I don't have anything to wear because I'm too small for my good clothes and too big for my old ones." She blew her nose into her napkin. "And here you come, this buff Viking with your improbably-blond hair and your big muscles, and your bulldog lawyer friend, and you just—well, today has been an amazing day, even though it started out so shitty because of Richard."

"Dick," said Jake.

She laughed and wiped her eyes. "Yes, because of that ... shrimp, Dick. Which if I had known about *that* before we got married, things might have turned out differently."

"What, you mean…?"

"Oh, yeah. You know how they say *'big feet, big dick?'*"

"Yeah."

"Well, Richard and I have the same shoe size."

Jake snorted. "Wow, that's, uhh…"

"Disappointing? You're telling me."

"Didn't you know beforehand?"

"Oh, no. We met in college at the Student Baptist Association at the University of Tennessee. Richard and I were virgins when we met. And he was so serious about waiting until we were married that he wouldn't do anything more than kiss while we dated. One time, when we were going hot and heavy, I put my hand on his crotch and he came instantly."

"No shit?" Jake laughed.

"No shit. Jizzed right in his pants. He was so embarrassed and he kept stammering about how he was just nervous and that it was my fault because that had never happened to him before."

"What, that no one had ever touched him before?"

"Well, that too. And it should have been a red flag that he blamed me. It didn't get much better after we got married either. Richard was just not very adventurous in bed and he didn't last very long. He only ever let me go down on him once and he never did it for me, and his performance was … 'efficient'—" she made air quotes with her fingers "—to say the least. He would finish in a few minutes. My private joke was that he could go from horny to finished in *'Dixty seconds.'*"

Jake laughed.

They ate quietly for a few minutes before resuming their conversation.

"Anyway, his slutty secretary must have showed him a few tricks because she's apparently happy with his performance, which is why he left me for her. And all I have is internet porn and my—um, little friend."

Jake's face turned red. He was bad at dirty talk when he wasn't having sex. Phone sex was the second worst for him, behind actually talking about it face-to-face with another woman. He could describe past experiences to a guy friend with no problem. But any phone call that started with "So what are you wearing?" was about as awkward as taking your sister to the prom and kissing her afterward.

"Well, you're better off without him just based on what I've seen," Jake said, trying to skim past her implications. "The guy is a bully and you deserve better."

"Yeah, but I have a hard time believing that. He was such a shit to me that sometimes I hear his voice when I go do things like work out or play music."

"So how do you ignore it?"

"That's just it. I ignore it. I tell myself that I was clearly wrong about him in the first place, so whatever I hear his voice telling me, I do the opposite of it."

"Well, he's certainly a moron, and I think Kate is going to get you a great deal that keeps him out of your hair forever."

"Wait, are you paying for her too?"

"Hey, finish your tacos. They'll get cold."

"Jake?"

"Umm, I can't answer that." He took a big bite of taco and said with his mouth full, "Attorney-client privilege." It came out *"Attoy-cwient pwivi-wij"* along with a few crumbs.

Natasha smiled. "Thank you, Jake. You're a good friend. I've only known you for a few days, but you've been so generous." She took a drink of her sweet tea. "And I'd like to, um, repay you ... for everything ... any way I can." She lowered her head and looked up at him, her face burning bright red.

"You don't have to," said Jake. "It's my pleasure to do this for you."

"Yes, but I want to. I just don't know if I should. I've always been pretty conservative about sex, and Richard and I were each other's firsts. I, uh, I haven't ... *had* it for a couple years. Other than what I, uh, said earlier."

"What, seriously?"

Natasha buried her face in her hands. "Oh God, this is so embarrassing." She rubbed her face for a few seconds before looking up at him. "No. Richard had been having an affair for months and always made up some excuse about why he didn't want to. Before that, he made me feel like I was too ... big for him. And he's such a skinny little stick anyway, that I couldn't bring myself to try anything because I thought he was right." Natasha began to cry and she buried her face in her hands again.

Jake got up and moved to the chair next to her, putting his arm around her shoulders. "Hey, hey, you're very beautiful, and I like you as you are. If we did end up together, I would want it to be because we like each other and want to be together, not because you 'owe' me. In fact, I'm telling you right now, you don't owe me anything. The blouses were a birthday gift."

Natasha sniffed. "My birthday is in April."

"Well, that's my fault for missing it. That's why there are two."

Natasha laughed.

"And the thing with Kate—not that I'm admitting to anything—just pay it forward to someone else someday. You'll meet someone who just needs a friend or a favor, and you'll be able to help them out. So don't pay me back anything, help the next person, and ask them to help someone after that."

"Okay," said Natasha, and she put her arms around Jake and he squeezed her tightly to him.

"I'll tell you what. Why don't you come see my Friday night show and we'll go out and go dancing or something. Wear one of your new blouses, and we'll show you off to the city."

"I think I'll wear the blue one," she said shyly. "You can appreciate my highlights some more."

"I'd love to see more of your highlights, as long as you're comfortable with it."

"Well, I think so. Let's see how the night goes."

They hugged again, Jake paid the bill, and they headed back outside.

CHAPTER 5

Jake pulled his truck into Natasha's driveway late Friday night. They'd been out for a late, late dinner after Jake's final show ended, catching one of the late-night acts at one of the honky-tonk bars on Broadway. Jake wasn't a big fan of country music, but anytime he was in Nashville, he found himself appreciating it more than when he was in any other city.

"Do you want to come in for some coffee? I have decaf," said Natasha.

"Sure, that would be great."

They walked inside and Natasha flipped on a few of the lights and they went back into the kitchen. Jake couldn't believe it had just been thirty-six short hours when he had rescued her from her shitty nearly-ex-husband in this very room. She made some French press coffee while the two chatted about the night, Jake's work, her work, and how she had grown up in Nashville playing music with friends. Apparently, she had stopped after she graduated from college. Cups of decaf in hand, the two moved out to the couch, both of them sitting on opposite ends of the couch.

Natasha said, "So, do you want to, uh...you know?"

"Uh, do I know what?" said Jake.

"I'm sorry, I'm just, you know, uncomfortable talking about ... *it*."

"Oh, I am too. I just get really awkward."

"Well, I wore your favorite blouse because I knew you'd like to see my, uh, highlights."

"Believe me, I've been checking out your ... highlights."

"I just, I'm shy talking about it because I've only ever done it with one other person. I grew up really conservative and sex was frowned upon. Even Richard made it seem shameful and he didn't like to do much. Everything I know, other than the missionary position, I learned from watching porn online."

"What did you learn?"

"There are a few things I want to try, but I don't know if I should do them or not. I still hear my mother's voice telling me what good girls don't do."

"Rule number one: bringing up one's mother during a discussion about sex? Real mood killer."

Natasha laughed and said, "Oh, I've seen some videos where moms are in on it, too. Like, I know what a MILF is."

Jake laughed and said, "So ... what are you comfortable with?"

"I don't know. I feel guilty even trying anything. I know I'm getting a divorce, but it feels like I'm cheating."

"I don't want to pressure you. If you don't want to do something, we won't do it."

"So what do you suggest?"

"Well," Jake thought for a few seconds, "how about masturbating? You said yesterday that you enjoyed that."

Natasha smiled shyly. "I think I would. God, that sounds hot. I'll masturbate for you, and you can masturbate for me." She rubbed her crotch through her jeans. "I love that idea. Holy fuck, mutual masturbation." She continued to rub herself then said, "I don't think I'm dressed for it though. I'm going to put on something more accessible." She walked back to her bedroom and called over her shoulder, "And you can make yourself comfortable too."

Jake stood up and quickly took off all his clothes. There was a laundry basket with a few towels in it on a chair, so he grabbed a towel, sat back down and covered himself with it. He thought for a second, put his underwear back on, and recovered himself with the towel. Then he thought for a few more seconds, took it back off, and sat back down again.

He was about to put it back on for a second time when Natasha reappeared, wearing a filmy negligee and robe. It suited her curves perfectly, accentuating them and calling attention to her full breasts and luscious hips. He could see her hard nipples underneath the black fabric, and he felt himself get hard as she swished to the couch. She stopped and slid the dimmer switch on the lights so they could mostly see each other, but couldn't make out how much either of them might have been blushing.

Natasha sat down on the other end of the couch and said, "Okay, tell me what you want."

"I want to see your breasts," he said, rubbing his hardening cock under the towel.

She slowly took off her robe then slid the spaghetti straps of the negligee off her shoulders one at a time, holding the material over her breasts as she did so. Then she let the fabric glide down, exposing her breasts, which were full and heavy as she cradled them under her arm.

"Pinch your nipples," he said, and she did so, pinching her nipples, first one then the other. She gave a tiny moan.

"Show me your cock," she said, and Jake handed her a corner of the towel.

She pulled it off and unveiled his semi-hard tool. She sucked in her breath.

"Oh, my," she said.

"There's more," he said, stroking it lightly.

"Show me," she whispered.

Natasha slid one hand inside her panties and ran her fingers over her moist pussy and breathed heavily as she stroked. Jake wrapped his hand around his shaft and began to pump, his cock growing even as he did so.

"Take off your panties," he half-whispered.

Natasha slid her panties off and her negligee as well. Her bush was trimmed closely and as she stood; Jake could see her body in the low light. Full hips, thick thighs, and heavy breasts that hung down, with nipples that stuck out from her playing.

"Don't sit down yet," he commanded. "Put one foot up on the couch and play with yourself."

She put her right foot on the couch and Jake could see her pussy lips and swollen labia. She slid her middle finger down her slit and into her cunt two, three, four times.

"Stand up and keep jerking off," she said. "Put your foot up too."

Jake did as he was told and continued to stroke his cock. "You're so beautiful," he groaned. "I love looking at you."

"My gorgeous man," she answered. "You make me wet. I love seeing your big hand wrapped around your dick."

"It's so hard because of you," he said.

"Ohh," she gasped. "Ohh, this feels so good. I'm going to come soon."

"Let me help you. I want to masturbate you. I want to make you come." Jake was secretly pleased that she said "come" instead of "cum," and he almost did so himself when she said it.

"Ohh, fuck," she said and her knee nearly buckled. "Yess, I want you to masturbate me." She sat back down in the middle of the couch, legs spread, and showed her wet pussy to Jake. "Masturbate me, make me come."

Jake knelt before Mandy and rested his hands on her thighs, his prick standing full at attention. He used his thumbs to slowly spread her lips apart and slid one of them up over her clitoris. Natasha gasped, and he did it again.

"Oohhhhhhh," she moaned. "That's so good."

Jake slid a finger into her cunt, even as he rubbed her clit.

"OHHH," she moaned louder. "Oh fuck, keep masturbating me." Jake slid a second finger into her wetness and continued rubbing her clit with his thumb. "Ohh! Ohh! That's it! Right there, like that. Oh, masturbate me, Jake! That's it, I'm going to—OH, FUUUUUCK!"

Natasha grabbed his forearms and arched her back as she came hard, her inner muscles convulsing around Jake's fingers. He removed them and put his hands back on her thighs so she could recover. Natasha panted for several seconds, sweat beading on her forehead. As she finally came down from her post-orgasm high, Jake pulled her up to him and kissed her deeply, pressing her naked globes against his chest, his cock pressed down against the front of the couch so he didn't stab her with its hardness.

"Do you know that's the first time you've kissed me?" she said when they broke apart. "You made me come then you kissed me. That's so fucking hot."

He kissed her again and said, "I hope I can do both a few more times."

"Oh, I want that very much. But now it's your turn. I'm going to masturbate you."

She made him sit down on the couch and she knelt down, taking his throbbing prick in her hand and gazed at it, studied it, before she stroked it a few times.

Jake shuddered a breath and said, "Your hands are so soft. I love feeling your hand on my dick."

Natasha smiled and kissed him before returning her attention to his thick member. She slid her hand up and down the entire length of his cock before circling just her index finger and thumb around it. She stroked the entire length of his dick, sliding it through the hole she had made, watching it throb as she traveled her hand up and down.

"Do you like it when I masturbate you?" she asked, smiling.

He had never tried mutual masturbation, and he had certainly never referred to hand jobs in that way, but hearing her say it turned him on. His dick was so hard by now, it could have pounded nails, and hearing her say *when I masturbate you* made the blood pound in his ears.

"Oh, yes. I love your fingers on my cock," he groaned. "I love watching you stroke my cock like that. I love seeing you masturbate me."

Natasha cupped Jake's balls gently and massaged them with her other hand. Jake groaned his appreciation.

"You can also masturbate me with your tits," said Jake. "Squeeze my cock between your tits and rock up and down, and masturbate me that way."

"Like this?" she said, doing as he asked. She wrapped her breasts around his dick and moved slowly up and down, squeezing her tits together with her hands. "Is this still masturbating you? Or are you just tit fucking me?" she asked with a sly smile.

"Let's call it masturbating," he answered. "It's so hot if we call it masturbating."

"Then I'll keep masturbating you with my tits. I won't feel so guilty if we're only masturbating," she said with a wink. She continued her rocking motion as Jake lay his head back and enjoyed the experience.

After a few minutes, she asked. "Is there anything else you want me to masturbate you with?"

"You could masturbate me with your mouth," Jake suggested. They were both caught up in the moment now and shivered with the naughtiness of their "masturbation" pushing the boundaries.

"Ohh, fuck, that is hot," she said. "Yes, I would love to masturbate this monster with my mouth." She leaned down and held the base of his prick in her hands and tentatively put her mouth on the head. Natasha slid her mouth over his cock a few times, but could only manage a couple of inches. She scraped his shaft with her teeth and Jake worried this was not going to be a great, uh, mouth masturbation.

"Like this? I've never done this before. Tell me if I'm doing it right."

"Maybe not with your teeth so much," he said gently. "Open your mouth wider and use your lips like a vacuum."

She tried his suggestion and Jake immediately felt much better. "Mmmmm," hummed Natasha with understanding.

"Oooooh," responded Jake. "Keep moving your hand too."

Natasha stroked his hard cock in time with her bobbing head, and Jake could feel himself getting ready to come.

"Ohh, baby, I'm going to come. I'm going to come for you."

"Not in my mouth," she said. "What should I do?"

"Point it at your tits and keep jerking me off," said Jake.

"I love those videos where the guy shoots on the girl's tits," she said, and gave him one last suck on his dickhead.

"Then keep masturbating me until I come on your tits."

Natasha pointed his cock at her tits and continued stroking him until he grunted and shot one, two, three ropes of come onto her bountiful chest. "Ahh! Ahh! Ahh!" Jake half-shouted with each convulsion that sent his seed splashing onto Natasha's tits.

"Ohhh, fuck, that's so hot. Your come is so hot on my skin," she said. "That feels so good." She ran a finger through it like it was a finger paint then tasted it. "That's, um— Another taste. That's not too bad. You taste kind of sweet."

"Some women like the taste of come, some don't," he said, breathing hard.

"Maybe I'll let you come in my mouth later," she said.

"I would love that," said Jake. He pulled her into a sitting position next to him on the couch and knelt in front of her. "But first I'm going to masturbate you with *my* mouth."

"Oh, you shouldn't," said Natasha, trying to close her legs.

"Why not?"

"Because it's dirty. Richard used to tell me women smelled bad down there."

Jake pushed her legs apart gently, and rubbed her clit with his thumb, like he had two orgasms ago.

"I love your scent," he said, lowering his head and taking a deep whiff. "It smells wonderful." He went in the rest of the way and licked up her slit. "You taste like honey."

Natasha gave a little cry that sounded like both a sob and a moan, and he licked her again. And a second time. And a third. Natasha moaned with each lick as his tongue stroked between her cunt lips and over her clit.

"Oh, good Lord!" she cried. "What have I been missing all my life?" She pulled Jake's head down to her pussy. "Lick my honey pussy, Jake! Fuck me with your tongue."

Jake quickly complied, grabbing her thighs and pulling her toward him, jamming his tongue into her cunt and sliding it up and down her slit, darting it in and out. He licked her clit and ran the length of his tongue over her pink pearl. After six or seven licks, she began to buck her hips.

"Jake, I'm going to come. I'm going to come, you'd better stop."

"Why?" he asked, not looking up.

"I'm going to come in your mouth."

"Good," he said and licked faster, flicking her clit with his tongue and slipping a finger inside her.

"Ohmigod, ohmigod, ohmigod! I'm coming, Jake, I'm coming! YEEEESSSS!"

Jake held onto her hips as Natasha's orgasm crashed over her and he slowed his flicking tongue as she recovered from what the French call *la petit mort, "the little death."*

"Oh, my," She breathed hard several times and used Jake's towel to wipe her face. "Masturbation is a lot of fun, don't you think?" she finally said.

"I agree," said Jake. "And if you'd like, in a few minutes we can masturbate each other."

"We just did," Natasha said looking a little confused.

"*With* each other. I'll masturbate your pussy with my cock, and you'll masturbate me in return."

"I love the sound of that," Natasha said, leaning in for another kiss and reaching for Jake's stiffening cock.

Jake woke up Saturday morning to a rebel yell and a naked Natasha bouncing in her bed.

"What's up, babe?" he said, rubbing the sleep out of his eyes.

"Kate just texted me." She showed him her phone up then read it. "'Served Dick yesterday at work and called his attorney and told him what we had on Dick. Atty persuaded him to settle. Has agreed to split marital assets, but house is still yours.'"

"Hey, congratulations!" Jake hugged her close and felt her breasts against his skin, which got his cock stirring. "I told you Kate was great."

"Yes, and you're great too. I think I'd like another mutual masturbation session to show you how much I appreciate you. Only this time, I want you to masturbate my pussy from behind."

"Gotta love masturbation," said Jake. "I just hope I don't go blind."

"We'll quit when we need glasses," giggled Natasha.

THE END

Chastity Veldt

Alyssa in Atlanta

Stand Up, Lie Down Collection

TABLE OF CONTENTS

CHAPTER 1

"Fucking traffic," growled Jake. "God save me from Atlanta traffic. Why is there so much traffic in the middle of the afternoon?"

Jake Nilsen was sitting in his pickup at the parking lot known as the I-75/I-85 merger, just north of Midtown Atlanta. It was 2:30 on Wednesday, and Jake was in town for a four-day show.

"What was that?" a woman's voice said over his stereo speaker.

"Sorry," said Jake. "We're completely stopped right where 75 and 85 come together on the north side of town."

"I've been there a few times. Yeah, that's pretty terrible down there," said the voice. Jake was talking with Molly Moser, a bookstore owner from Milwaukee. He had spent a few days with Molly while he was doing his standup in her hometown.[7] "Hey, did you ever finish those Rex Stout books?"

---

[7] See *Stand Up, Lie Down: Molly in Milwaukee*

"Oh, sure," said Jake. "I even bought a few on my Kindle, and I've been going through about one every two days."

"Kindle, Jake? Jesus, you sure know how to hurt a girl."

"Sorry I haven't been able to find a good bookstore. At least, not one with all the great service yours offered."

"Best servicing you've ever had," corrected Molly. Jake could hear her smile.

"I still get turned on thinking about it," he said.

"Maybe you can tell me all about it. What was your favorite part?"

Jake realized this was the time where she was expecting him to talk dirty, and he felt his face grow hot. He hated talking dirty when he wasn't actually having sex. It made him very self-conscious, like everyone else on I-75 would know he was doing it. He loved talking dirty while having actual sex because it made everything hotter. But if he was expected to perform on the phone, he froze up.

"Ding-a-ling!" He heard the one in Molly's store clang. *Saved by the bell!*

"I've got to go," she said.

"New customer, or did Prudie Judy come in?"

"Uh-huh," said Molly. "Talk to you later. Bye." She hung up quickly.

"Fuuuuuuuuuuuck," said Jake casting his gaze over the miles of slow-crawling cars. "Hey Siri, how far is it to the Popcorn Comedy Club?"

"The Popcorn Comedy Club is four miles away. Take exit 249D in two miles."

Jake spotted exit 250 just ahead and knew if he could make it onto the surface streets, it'd be faster than if he stayed on the highway. Besides, he wanted to stop for lunch before he checked in, and he knew he could get there from here. He zipped off onto the shoulder and started heading up to the exit, whipping past a semi-truck that had tried to pull over to keep him from doing just that. Jake never understood why semi drivers thought they were the enforcers of the road rules, so he raised his arm out the window, middle finger fully extended, and drove up the ramp. The semi driver yanked on his horn in frustration that someone was getting away with something.

"Die mad about it, asshole," Jake mumbled as he continued on the ramp. "Hey Siri, take me to The Varsity."

"Turn left on 14th Street NW, then turn right on Spring Street NW," said the GPS.

The Varsity is a beloved Atlanta institution serving some of the best hot dogs in the entire Southeast, and Jake made it a point to stop by anytime he passed through town. And he got the same thing every time: two slaw dogs, a chili dog, and a Coke. He had worked out extra hard for the last few days just for this and figured he would have to double his run tonight because he was in the mood for fries.

"Turn right on North Avenue NE, and your destination will be on the right," said the GPS.

"What'll ya have, what'll ya have, what'll ya have?" the cashiers called as he opened the door and the smell of the best hot dogs in the Southeast beckoned to him.

Oh, yeah, thought Jake. *Tonight's the night to be bad.*

An hour later, Jake climbed back into his truck and recalibrated his GPS to get him to the Popcorn Comedy Club, where he was performing as the middle act for a three-day weekend. He needed to check in with the owner and get the keys to the club apartment. Many comedy clubs had a small apartment where they put up traveling comics since they normally didn't pay enough for the comic to stay in a hotel. Apartments actually helped clubs save money and protected their cash flow.

He parked behind the club near a large shopping plaza and wandered in. A blonde woman behind the bar was facing away and stocking the refrigerator.

"Hi, I'm Jake Nilsen. I'm the middle this weekend."

"Hey," said the blonde woman, turning around. "Did you say Neleson?"

"No, Nilsen."

"Oh. I'm Alyssa Dupont. I'm the bar manager."

"Nice to meet you." Jake reached out and shook her hand.

She had long fingers and a strong grip. A low-cut t-shirt clung to her large breasts and flat stomach, over some cutoff denim shorts, and hiking boots that added an inch to her already statuesque 5'11" frame. Her hair was a dishwater blonde, cut into a spiky blonde pixie crop.

Alyssa's eyes widened a little bit as she took in Jake's features. Jake stood 6'2" and was built like a swimmer with a tight waist and wide shoulders. He had very light blond hair, piercing blue eyes, and wore round glasses. Wearing a Modest Mouse t-shirt, it was a little tight in the chest and sleeves, showing off his physique. He would have cut a more impressive figure if he didn't have a chili stain on his shirt.

Alyssa turned back around and returned to filling up the lower refrigerators. "You'd better not be looking at my ass," she said.

Jake quickly snapped his eyes back to the top-shelf bottles. "No, ma'am," he said. "That would be wrong." To be fair, it was a nice ass, pert and well-toned, and her thighs were shapely and muscular. Jake could see the quad muscles shift as she crouched down to her task.

"I'm just kidding," said Alyssa, popping up and facing Jake again. "I have a nice ass."

"I wouldn't know," said Jake. "I'm a perfect gentleman."

"Then you're probably not a real comic. All the guy comics I know are real pigs."

"#NotAllComics," said Jake. "Where can I find the manager?"

"Oh, all business, huh, Mr. Middle?" Alyssa crossed her arms in front of her, squeezing her impressive breasts together, causing them to swell and accentuate her cleavage. She bit her lower lip suggestively, and Jake fought to maintain eye contact.

Jake smiled at her. "It's important to be a professional, especially with the person who's making your drinks."

"Well, I won't be making them tonight, Mr. Middle. I'm off until tomorrow. I'm just restocking and doing inventory."

"That's alright. I don't do my A material until the weekend anyway. I just make shit up in the middle of the week to see if anyone notices."

"Really? That doesn't seem very professional."

"No, I'm kidding," laughed Jake. "I try to do the same show every night. But if I add new material, I do try it out during the week rather than when I've got a big crowd."

"Well, we've got some pretty big crowds on the weeknights. All the college kids come in during the week because it's cheaper than the weekends. You'll probably have a sizable crowd tomorrow."

"Oh, really? That'll be a nice change. Most places are half-dead in the middle of the week."

"Yeah, not here. We get a pretty strong showing Wednesday through Saturday. Our open mics even get some decent crowds." Alyssa raised a part of the bar on a hinge and stepped out. "Come on, I'll take you to Sherie's office."

She started walking in front of Jake. "You can look at my ass now," Alyssa said.

She looked over her shoulder to see if he was, but Jake had already snapped his eyes back up before she noticed. She glanced down at Jake's crotch and bit her lip again. Alyssa put a little extra wiggle in her hips as she continued looking back at—

"Ow, fuck!" She slammed her hip into a table corner. Stopping, she rubbed at the pained area. "Motherfucker, I got myself pretty good."

"You okay?" Jake said.

"Yeah, I'll be fine. That'll probably turn into a bruise."

"Do you need anything? Can I help you?"

"Oh, so you're going to carry me like I'm some damsel in distress?"

"What? No. I was going to get you some ice and a towel."

"I'm just fucking with you, Mr. Middle. No, I'll be fine. I do this all the time. Fucking tables. I had to work at a place that has square tables. My last gig had all round tables and this never happened."

"Fascinating," said Jake.

"Yes. Yes, I am," said Alyssa. "Just support me like when they help a football player off the field."

"Uh, okay," said Jake as he stooped to put her arm over his shoulder.

"Jesus, I'm fucking with you!" Alyssa laughed. "Get the fuck out of here with that white knight shit." She laughed and pushed his arm, feeling the hard muscles.

"Oh my," she said. She reached out and squeezed it a few more times appreciatively. "On second thought, I'm badly injured. I need you to carry me."

"Yeah, whatever," said Jake walking toward the back leaving Alyssa behind. He stopped and turned. "And don't look at my ass."

Alyssa bit her lip a third time and followed him down the hall past the bathrooms and into the manager's office.

"Sherie, the middle's here," called Alyssa. "And I'm terribly injured and he left me behind."

Jake tried not to roll his eyes. "Hey, I'm Jake Nilsen," he said, extending his hand.

Sherie stood up and shook his hand. "Neleson?" she asked.

"No, Nilsen."

"You'll always be Mr. Middle to me," said Alyssa from behind him where she had been staring at his ass. Jake tightened his glutes a couple of times, and he could hear her gasp quietly. He stepped further into the office to make room for her.

Sherie held out a plastic bag to him. "Chips?" she offered.

"Just a few," said Alyssa, reaching into the can.

"No, thanks, I just ate," said Jake.

"The Varsity?"

"Yeah, I stop there every time I'm in town. How'd you guess?"

"You got chili sauce on your shirt," said Sherie. She touched just below the spot on his shirt and let her finger linger on his hard pectoral muscle.

"Ah, shit," said Jake. "Oh, well. It's an old shirt, and I carry a Tide pen with me anyway."

"I don't blame you. I love their chili dogs." Sherie popped a cashew in her mouth. "So you need the keys to the club apartment?"

"Yes, please."

"We do have a washer and dryer there if you need to do some laundry." She poked his chest again.

"That would be great, thank you."

"Oh, and the headliner's already there. You'll be sharing with him. Hope you don't mind."

"No problem," Jake said. "Curtis and I are good friends."

Curtis Sanders was another comic who had been in standup nearly as long as Jake, and the two often appeared together as the middle and headliner, often changing roles depending on the city. He and Jake had a standing wager every time they met up to exchange stories of their latest sexploits on the road. Whoever had the hotter story, the loser had to buy dinner. The last time Curtis and Jake were together was in Louisville,[8] and Jake had won with his story about Molly Moser, the bookstore owner in Milwaukee.[9]

Jake thanked Sherie and Alyssa and headed back to his car. Alyssa hurried after him.

"So, Mr. Middle, you look like you work out. Do you need a gym while you're here?"

"Actually, yes. I was going to go for a run today, but I haven't lifted in a few days. Do you know a good gym?"

"Well, I can bring a guest to my gym. I'm usually there five days a week. If you wanted to go, we could work out together."

"That would be great. When are you going again?"

"I go in the mornings, usually around ten or so. Text me your number, and I'll give you the address."

Jake sent his contact information to Alyssa's phone, and she sent back the address to her gym.

"I'd love to meet you there around 10:00," Jake said. "And if you'd like, we can go to lunch afterward."

"Why, Mr. Middle, are you trying to pick me up?" Alyssa folded her hands in front of her and shrugged her shoulders, digging the toe of her hiking boot into the ground, looking every bit the shy girl.

"What? No, I was just—"

---

[8] See *Stand Up, Lie Down: Lydia in Louisville*

[9] Check out *Stand Up, Lie Down: Molly in Milwaukee*

"Jesus, lighten up. I'm just fucking with you again." Alyssa threw her head back and laughed. "You Midwestern boys are all the same. So shy and gentlemanly. These Southern boys could take a lesson or two from you. They're all about trucks and tramps—pickups and hookups—and wouldn't know good manners if it slapped them on the ass."

"Shit, you need to stop doing that. I never know if you're being serious or not."

"I'm almost never serious. You'll know when I'm being serious. And yes, lunch would be great. I know a good tapas place on 5th Street."

"Great. We can take my, er, vehicle. I'll see you tomorrow."

"Sounds good, Mr. Middle." She reached in for a quick hug, making sure to press her breasts against him and to feel his back and arm muscles.

Ten minutes later, Jake was unlocking the door to the comics' apartment, just a couple blocks from the club.

"Is that you, Jakey Nilsen?" called a voice from the living room.

Curtis Sanders was sitting on the couch, watching a video on his phone when Jake arrived. He set down his phone and stood up to give Jake a hug. While Jake unpacked and changed his shirt, the two caught each other up on their own news, how the road had been treating them, and future shows coming up.

"You got any stories to trade, Jakey?" said Curtis. "I'm pretty hungry, and I think I've got a winner today."

CHAPTER 2

CURTIS IN CINCINNATI

"Alright, here's my story:

"You remember the last time we were together, and I told you about that waitress from Cincinnati, Anna? Well, we've been sort of seeing each other. Nothing serious, but you remember she came to the apartment in Louisville.[10] Of course, you hooked up with that redhead, what's-her-name—Lydia, yeah—and spent most of your time over there, but Anna and I were together for a couple days, fucking like rabbits.

"Anyway, I had a couple shows down in Tennessee then headed back up to Cleveland to middle at their big club up there, Major Laughs. Anna said she had a few days off, so she was bringing her best friend with her to hang out. I was going to be staying at a hotel because the club apartment was being redecorated, and I managed

---

207

to get an upgrade to a suite. So I said sure, bring her up. I figured me and Anna could sleep in one bed and the friend could sleep in the other.

"So Anna and her friend, Debi, show up that first afternoon, and we go sightseeing around Cleveland. Visited the Rock and Roll Hall of Fame and had lunch at some burger joint. Both girls are being flirty, making sly comments when they think I don't hear, and sometimes when I do. A couple of times I think I feel Anna grab my ass, only when I grab the hand, it's Debi's.

"Debi's this short blond girl with great tits. Like, nice big tits for such a skinny girl. And she's about 5-foot-three or so, and with great legs and hazel eyes. She's a server at one of the restaurants downtown so she's in pretty good shape from hustling all the time.

"Anyway, they come see my show that night, and Debi drives back to the hotel, which is about half an hour away. Anna and I are in the backseat, and she's rubbing on my dick, getting me all hard and shit. She unzips my pants, pulls my dick out, and starts sucking my cock right there.

"She starts licking it like an ice cream cone and she's moaning while she does it. 'Mmmm. Mmmmm. Mmmmmmm.' And her humming is vibrating my dickhead which is making me crazy. Anna's not even trying to keep it a secret what we're doing. She's slurping it real loud, jerking off my shaft, and moaning on my cock. Debi turns off the radio so she can hear, and Anna just starts doing it louder. I wasn't sure if Anna was doing it on purpose or what Debi was going to think about Anna sucking my cock in the back seat.

"That's when Debi adjusts the mirror so she can see my eyes. Like, we're making eye contact in the mirror and I can see her smile and lick her lips at me. Then she says, 'Make sure you save me some.'

"And Anna says, 'Trust me, he'll have plenty for both of us.' That's when I knew Debi wasn't going to be sleeping in the other bed all weekend.

"Debi started sucking on one of her fingers and turned her head so I could see, and that made me come right there in Anna's mouth. I looked at Debi's eyes in the rearview mirror the entire time that I unloaded in her friend's mouth.

"Anna actually choked and sputtered a little bit when I shot my load, but she held it together like a champ and clamped down on my cock, so every drop ended up in her mouth. She sat up, swallowed hard, and opened her mouth to show Debi and me that it was all gone. Thirty seconds later, we arrived at the hotel.

"No, that's not the end of the story, man. Do you think I'm a One-Pump Chump? There's plenty more.

"Anyway, we get upstairs, and the girls push me back on one of the beds while I recover. They start making out and running their hands all over each other. Anna's about five-nine, and Debi's a few inches shorter, so when Anna gets her top and bra off, Debi leans over and starts sucking on Anna's nipple. Anna's got those big tits, and Debi's just working on them like it's her job. Anna's caressing the back of her friend's head, pulling her close as Debi sucks on one nipple, then the other, then back to the first one, then the second one again.

"So I stand up behind Anna, reach around and unbutton her jeans and slide them off her, and Anna starts rubbing her clit. Then I get behind Debi and undress her. Neither woman says anything, although I kiss Anna a few times.

"Once they're both undressed, I reach around Debi and take both her tits in my hands. They were about the size of grapefruits, all-natural and really firm. I'm still amazed at how big they were for such a tiny girl. Anyway, she pushes her ass back, so she's rubbing against my cock, which is getting hard again. Then she steps back from Anna, sits on the edge of the bed, lays back, spreads her legs, and says, 'Okay, you two, eat my pussy.'

"Anna gets down and starts lapping at her pussy while Debi is tweaking her own nipples. I get undressed while Debi's watching me, and she gives a little gasp when she sees my hard cock for the first time."

"Fuck you, Jakey. I have a nice cock. Oh, it's bigger than your little Norwegian sausage.

"Anyway, I get down next to Anna and start licking Debi's slit with her. She's got that big meaty labia and I'm pulling on it gently and licking where I can. We take turns lapping at her pussy, and when I'm not licking it, I'm rubbing Anna's melons and playing with her nipples.

"Then Anna says, 'Why don't you suck on her tits? I'm going to make her come.' (Yes, she said it C-O-M-E. Why does that matter?)

"So I get up on the bed and suck on Debi's grapefruits. Her nipples are already hard from her playing with them, and I just lick and suck them like I've been poisoned and the antidote's in them. Pretty soon, she's bucking because Anna's sliding a couple fingers in and out of her slit, and she's grabbing the back of my head so I'll suck her tits harder. Well, it's a good thing I got us a suite at the end of the hall, because Debi's screaming, 'OHH, FUCK! EAT ME, YOU BITCH! EAT MY WET CUNT!' until she shudders like she just died and just lies there for a few seconds catching her breath.

"No, I'm not done yet.

"While Debi's recovering, Anna has me stand up so I'm in

front of Debi and she starts stroking my dick. Then she says, 'Don't either of you do anything, let me guide you.' She guides my dick toward Debi's snatch and puts my head on her pubic hair. She lifts Debi's legs and puts her ankles on my shoulders. Now her pussy's lifted up toward me, and my cock is resting right on her lips.

"Anna presses right up against me from behind and starts humping and pushing me so I'm humping Debi, running my cock over her pussy. I push her legs together to close the gap. That pushes my dick right against her clit and Debi starts moaning again and says 'Fuck me, Curtis. Fuck me with your big cock.'

"Anna opens Debi's legs, takes my cock, and drags the head up and down her wet slit, getting my dickhead wet with her juices. She flicks it over Debi's clit a few times and Debi's moaning, 'Please, Anna, put it in. Put his dick in me.' So Anna puts the tip right inside her entrance and tells me not to move. She gets up behind me and grabs Debi's legs again and says, 'Beg me to fuck you, bitch.'

"Debi moans, 'Please fuck me, Anna. Fuck me hard.' And Anna pulls on Debi's legs and shoves forward so it buries my cock into Debi's cunt. Then she pulls my hips back with one hand and drives forward again. Soon we're both fucking Debi in tandem, I push back so Anna lets me move, then she pushes forward and I let her move me, so now Anna and I are fucking her together.

"Oh, man, it was so fucking hot.

"After a few minutes of this, Anna wants her turn, so she has Debi get up and makes me lay on the bed. Anna straddles me and impales herself on my dick and now she's riding me. I reach up and play with her tits while she grinds back and forth on my cock, rubbing her clit on my pubic bone. I look over and see Debi with one leg up on the bed while she's playing with her pussy. I pull her onto the bed and tell her to sit on my face.

"She hangs those meaty labia over my face and I'm lapping them up, flicking her clit with my tongue and pushing it in as far as I can. Meanwhile, the girls are making out and fondling each other's tits and moaning into each other's mouths.

"Pretty soon, Anna starts coming and moaning into Debi's mouth. Debi says, 'kiss me when you come. I want to taste your moans.' Sounds weird now, but I was fucking two women, so I wasn't going to complain. Anna starts moaning and Debi's moaning from that and from me eating her pussy. I can feel Anna's cunt clench on my shaft and squeeze it real tight when she comes as she's moaning real loud into Debi's mouth. All I could hear was "MMMM! MMMM! MMMM!" from both of them.

"When she finishes, she rolls off of me to rest. I keep eating Debi's pussy while my cock is unattended. I needed the break anyway because I was close to coming myself.

"After I was calmed down, I had Anna lay up at the head of the bed, put Debi down between Anna's legs to eat her pussy, then started fucking Debi doggy style. Debi was moaning while she was eating Anna's cunt and the vibrations set Anna off because she started coming again.

"I was pounding Debi pretty hard, and the motion kept driving her forward, so she just stuck her tongue out and let my pounding make her tongue slide up and down Anna's pussy. Her tits were swinging like a pendulum and I reached around and squeezed them, using them to pull her back into me, then I'd slam forward with my hips to send her forward again. She was doing a lot of the motion herself too. She was moaning, Anna was moaning, and I said, 'Oh fuck, girls. I'm gonna come. I'm gonna shoot my load.'

"That's when Debi spins around end-for-end and she gobbles my cock into her mouth. I keep up the fucking motion and she's slurping up my dick as it's hitting the back of her throat. She's going *'Gulk! Gulk! Gulk!'* every time I thrust forward, and I feel my ball sack start to tighten. I shout, 'Here it comes, baby. Take my load.' Debi clamps her lips around my cock and keeps moving her head as I blast four or five shots of spunk into her mouth. She holds on while I spasm a few times, and she sucks the last couple of drops out of my dickhead.

"Then she lays down on top of Anna and kisses her, and they share my come. They're moaning and kissing and sliding their tongues out of each other's mouths. I just stayed back there massaging Debi's ass and sliding a finger in and out of Anna's pussy for a few minutes before I sat on the other bed and watched the two of them make out and get each other off for another ten minutes.

"After that, the three of us fell asleep together for a couple of hours until one of them woke up to pee. They woke me up with another blowjob, and we more or less had a repeat performance, but Anna got to be in the middle that time.

"So, what did you think of that, Jakey? Think you can do better?"

Chapter 3

"Fuck, that's hot," said Jake, who had hidden his erection by untucking his shirt, which he'd changed into when he arrived. "How long did they visit?"

"They were there the whole weekend and left on Monday morning," said Curtis. "We fucked every night and even during the day. Anna said the next time I'm within a few hours, I should call her and the two of them will meet me."

"Sounds like you're getting serious."

"Serious about fucking. I don't know if this will go anywhere, but I'm going to enjoy the shit out of both of them while I can. I'm going to be in Indianapolis next month, and they're talking about coming over for an overnight."

"Maybe you can tell that story next time we're together."

"Deal. Now tell me about that girl you hooked up with in Louisville. I didn't see much of you after that night."

"That was Lydia. Yeah, she was pretty awesome. We nearly had sex in her office that night, but we finally did have sex the next night."

"All right, let's hear what you got."

So Jake related the story of his night of wild fucking and gave a word-by-word recitation of everything that happened (including the part about the blindfold and the paintbrush in Chapter 5 of *Stand Up, Lie Down: Lydia in Louisville* (now available on Amazon).

When Jake finished his story, he reluctantly agreed that Curtis's was the hotter story—"Sounds like I'm going to have to get three women next time," he said—and the two went out for dinner, Jake's treat. They visited a taqueria not too far from the apartment and ate taco after taco until it was time to report to the club for that night's show.

That night, as Jake was walking back to the club—Curtis was staying behind to see if he could hook up with one of the Georgia Tech and SCAD students—he popped in a Bluetooth earbud and dialed Molly's number. She answered after a few rings.

"Hey, Jake, what's up?" she said upon answering.

"Not much. Just got finished with my set at the club, and I'm heading back to the apartment."

"Alone, I'm guessing?"

"What makes you say that? I do all right!"

"Well, you're calling me at 9:30 on a Wednesday night, so I can't imagine your latest conquest would be interested in a phone sex three-way with someone 800 miles away."

"I think I resent the term 'conquest.' I'm not some sex-addled halfwit interested in pickups and hookups."

"In what?" asked Molly.

"Oh, something a friend said to me. She said the guys down here were only interested in trucks and tramps, or pickups and hookups."

Molly laughed. "Well, you do own a pickup truck."

"So what does that make you?"

Molly stopped laughing. "Not funny, Nilsen."

"That's what I'm saying. That's why I don't think of you as a conquest." Jake was standing outside the apartment, pacing back and forth. The night was a bit chilly, but nothing a farm boy from Mankato, Minnesota couldn't handle. This was still t-shirt weather as far as he was concerned, but he was dressed in his work clothes: a button-down shirt, blue jeans, gray sport coat, and a pair of tan Allen Edmonds cap-toe oxfords, so he was warm.

"So what would you call me?" teased Molly.

"A lover," said Jake.

"Eww, fuck! That sounds awful. Don't say that word."

"What, lover?"

"Ewww!" Molly laughed.

"What's wrong with calling you my lov-ahhh," Jake said, pronouncing it like the old skit on Saturday Night Live.

Molly laughed louder. "Oh God, what the fuck is wrong with you?"

"Okay, if you don't like lov-ahhh, how about partner?"

"Um, no."

"Intimate partner? Bedmate? Friends with benefits? Bedfellow? Paramour?"

"God, those all sound terrible," said Molly.

"Lov-ahh it is!" Jake bellowed, holding one arm high in the air as if he were making a royal proclamation. "Hey, how ya doing?"

"What?" said Molly.

"Nothing. A couple was walking by just as I said that. Now I'm embarrassed."

"You should be, bellowing a shitty word like that at those poor Atlanteans. Is it Atlanteans or Atlantans?"

"I think Atlanteans are the people at the bottom of the ocean. I should probably go inside before I embarrass myself any further. Good night, lov-ahh." Jake opened the door and walked up the flight of stairs to the comics' apartment.

"Ew, stop that. Wait, before you go, I should tell you I'm dating someone."

"Wow, really?"

"What do you mean, wow, really? Don't you think I could get someone? Did you think you ruined me for all other men?"

"No, that's not what I meant. It was supposed to be a supportive 'wow, really.'" Jake let himself in and took off his shirt and jacket. "I meant it more as a 'hey, that's great.'"

"You probably should have led with that."

"I know. But I'm happy for you, really."

"Aren't you going to ask me who he is?"

"Do I want to know?"

"His name is Tad, Tad Ackroyd. My Aunt Judy set me up with him. I've been out with him a few times, and he's actually kind of nice. It's nothing serious, but we've gone out for a couple months."

"Wait, is this that tax attorney you told me about."

Molly sighed. "Yeahhhhh. Prudie Judy wouldn't shut up until I went out with him at least once. We had a good time and just kept going out. He's really nice; you'd like him. He loves murder mysteries almost as much as you do."

"That *is* great. I'm happy for you," said Jake, feeling a little sad. "I really mean it."

"Thank you. I appreciate it. Oh, by the way, there's a used bookstore there you should visit called Bookish Atlanta. I was in there a few years ago on a road trip with a couple girlfriends, and they've got a huge selection."

"I'll check it out tomorrow," said Jake. "I'll talk to you later."

After the two said their good-byes, Jake turned off his phone and tossed it on the bed. He wasn't sure how to feel about Molly's news. He knew they weren't dating; they certainly weren't even in any kind of relationship. They had texted a few times after their amazing time together when he was last in Milwaukee. And he certainly never expected her to wait for him to return, just like he never assumed he wasn't free to sleep with other women. But it still made him a little sad that he could never hook up with her again when he passed back through Milwaukee.

Jake took off his clothes and stepped into the shower, soaping his rock-hard abs and bulging pectorals. He took pride in his body and worked hard to keep it sculpted and in shape. It was so easy to let himself go to seed with life on the road. Being a standup comic actually meant a lot more sitting down than standing, driving from city to city, with only fast food as his food options in many cases.

To avoid the temptation, he usually bought road food at grocery stores, making sandwiches or eating ready-made salads or even baked chicken from a store's deli counter. He also tried to eat at healthy restaurants whenever he could, usually getting fish or chicken and a lot of salad.

He knew that if he stuck with that as his diet, he could afford to cheat at a place like The Varsity or a pizza place once in a while. Of course, he would work extra hard the next day, running five more miles or swimming an additional 30 minutes to make sure he kept his physique.

As Jake soaped himself up, he spent some extra time on his groin, stroking his dick with his soapy hand. He thought about Molly and how they had fucked on her couch with her straddling his lap and staring deeply into his eyes as she clenched his cock with her velvety pussy lips until he came, jetting several globs of hot come inside her.

Jake's cock hardened, and he continued stroking it, remembering how Molly had sucked his eight-and-a-half-inch prick hard, using her small fist to jack him off even as she slid his cock in and out of her mouth. Jake grunted quietly as his own fist stroked the entire length of his clean-shaven manhood.

As he continued jerking himself off, the vision in his mind changed from Molly sucking his cock to Alyssa Dupont riding him much in the same way Molly had. Jake stopped and shook his head.

What the fuck is she doing in my head? She was kind of irritating, and the only reason he was meeting up with her tomorrow was so they could work out at her gym together. *Isn't it?*

He recalled her tight ass and strong thighs, seeing her cleavage bulge when she folded her hands in front of her waist and squeezed her arms together. Jake continued to imagine Alyssa's lithe, slender form lifting up and sinking back down on his cock, gliding up and down. He wondered whether she was a moaner, a dirty talker, or was she fairly quiet? *She probably talks constantly*, he thought. He jacked faster as he imagined Alyssa's ample tits bouncing in front of his face as she bounced on his dick.

"Ohh, fuck, Alyssa. You've got a hot pussy," Jake whispered.

He continued stroking his shaft, adding a little more shampoo to his hand to lessen the friction and feel more like Alyssa's tight, wet cunt. He imagined sucking her hard nipples while she shifted direction and started grinding back and forth, rubbing her clit on his pubic bone.

"You're so fucking annoying and gorgeous, and your pussy feels like velvet on my dick."

In his mind, Jake switched positions and was now driving into Alyssa from behind as he grabbed her waist and pulled her back toward him while he thrust his hips forward. He could feel himself getting ready to unload his wad for his imaginary lov-ahhh—excuse me, lover.

"This is for you, baby. This is for you. I'm gonna fill your pussy with my ... COOOME!"

Jake jetted his jizz toward the shower drain, groaning quietly as the water rinsed his seed down the drain. He stood, water beating down on his chest and head as he inhaled a few deep breaths and felt a sense of calm envelop him.

As he stepped out of the shower, Jake heard voices outside his bedroom. Curtis must have met someone at the club, so he figured he had twenty minutes tops before they would be grunting and groaning in the bedroom next to his. He quickly toweled off, slipped into some boxer briefs, put in one earbud, and crawled into bed, looking for a lo-fi radio station on his phone's radio app. He set his alarm for 9:00 AM and tried to fall asleep before Curtis and his new lov-ahh—excuse me, intimate partner—started banging away.

"Uhh! Uhh! Uhh! You're so wet, baby. What'd you say your name was?"

"Huh! Huh! Huh! Celeste! Huh! Huh! Oh! GOD! Oh! Fuck! Oh! Wait, already?"

Jake chuckled to himself as he fell asleep. He was going to give Curtis so much shit tomorrow morning.

CHAPTER 4

"Hey, Mr. Middle, you ready to get your sweat on?"

They met inside Alyssa's gym, which was nearly empty at that time of day. The early morning exercisers had come and gone, the lunchtime crowd was a couple of hours away, and a small yoga class was using the studio upstairs. They almost had the place to themselves, other than a few solitary treadmill and exercise bike users.

Alyssa was bright and chipper this morning. She was wearing short spandex shorts and a runner's tank top that clung to her slender frame and stretched over her ample breasts. Jake realized he was going to have a hard time not staring at her ass or her tits today. Maybe once they started working out, he would be too focused on not injuring himself that he could control himself.

Jake was wearing spandex bike shorts and a tank top that was just a little bigger than his frame, so he wouldn't wear something too clingy. When he was going to lift weights, he preferred something looser than the usual skin-tight tanks he wore when he was out for a run.

"Sure, what do you want to do?" Jake asked.

"Today is leg day for me," she said. "You can do whatever you need to. You only need me to get in as a guest, but you don't have to be with me the whole time."

"Okay, today is chest and shoulders for me."

"Cool, I may ask you for a spot if that's alright."

"Absolutely, just say the word. I may need you to help me with the bench press too."

The two high-fived and Jake went off in search of the free weights. He started with some overhead presses, lifting 30-pound dumbbells over his head as he sat on a bench. He looked over and saw Alyssa in the leg extension machine, cranking out rep after rep, defining the muscles at the top and sides of her thighs. Jake tried not to stare in appreciation as he realized just how strong her thighs were, and he imagined them wrapped around his waist as he pumped himself into her. His dick got harder, and Jake was glad he was wearing a jockstrap to keep it in place. Jake wrenched his attention back to what he was doing and started another set of overhead presses.

As she rested between sets, Alyssa looked over at Jake, and her eyes widened a little as she saw him pressing the dumbbells over his head, seeing the definition in his shoulders and triceps with each rep. She visualized his strong hands massaging her firm breasts, gripping her waist, lifting her up and down as she straddled his cock. Alyssa could feel her pussy tingling as these thoughts entered her mind, unbidden. Yesterday, she had been flirting with Jake, but seeing how he was built, and she was thinking about more than just flirting.

The two continued moving to different stations, completing different exercises, stealing glances, imagining the things they would do, each getting harder or wetter as appropriate. After nearly an hour, they were both getting tired.

Jake found Alyssa and said, "I just need to do the bench press, then I'll be done. How about you?"

"I just need to do squats. That's where I could use your help."

"Same here. If you can spot me on the bench and make sure I don't crush my windpipe, I'd appreciate it."

"Okay, but if I do end up lifting the weight for you, I'm telling everyone I saved your life."

Jake snorted, "That's a deal. Do you want to go first?"

"Sure, that would be fine." She set the weight bar for the right height and racked a few weights onto the bar. "I like to do this last because I want to work all the smaller muscles first before I do this. I can get more action with lighter weights and do more reps, so I keep my muscles toned."

"If I had ever looked at your ass, I would have noticed that. But I haven't because that wouldn't be gentlemanly."

"Uh-huh. Whatever, sport. I just need you to stand behind me and keep your hands on my waist so I can maintain my form. You don't have to lift, just make sure I don't stick my ass too far out. Otherwise, I could injure my back."

"Yep, I can manage that."

Alyssa stood under the bar, knees bent, then straightened up and lifted the bar off the stops. She took a few steps back to clear them. "Okay, put your hands on my waist and hold it kind of tight. I'm doing 25 reps."

She lowered herself down, so her thighs were parallel with the floor, held it for two seconds, and then raised herself back up.

"One," she huffed and lowered herself again. Her butt started to shift backward toward Jake, so he stepped forward and pushed back against her hips to keep her back and butt properly aligned. "Two. That's good, keep doing that."

She lowered again, and this time she felt her ass rub against Jake's cock. She raised herself a little slower that time, so she could rub against it on the way up. Alyssa looked down at Jake's feet and noticed he hadn't moved, so she did it again, a little harder this time. She realized his cock had gotten even harder.

"Get closer," she said. "Move with me." Alyssa felt Jake press his hard-on against her taut ass. She began to lower again, which pressed her even harder into Jake's hard shaft and she gave a little groan of appreciation. They continued moving that way, up and down, Jake pressing his boner into Alyssa's ass cheeks. He even stopped a little short so she could slide her ass up and down the full length of his cock.

Jake tried to concentrate more on Alyssa's form so she wouldn't get injured, but he was a little relieved when she reached 25. He was especially worried because a few more reps and he would have come in his shorts.

Alyssa put the bar back into place and turned to face Jake, standing close and looking at him. She was tall enough that she didn't even have to turn her head. "Thanks for the spot, Coach. This was my favorite workout of the year." She patted his hard-on with the back of her hand.

"Do you mind helping me finish?" said Jake.

"What, here?" said Alyssa. "Why, Mr. Middle, I didn't know you were into public nasties."

"No, I meant—! Jesus, why do you do that?" Jake smiled. "I meant on the bench press."

"Ooh, even better. Do you think it will support us both?"

Jake snorted, "As long as we stay near the support arms."

They walked over to the bench press station, and Jake racked on 175 pounds.

"Is that all you can do?" asked Alyssa. "Big macho man like you; I figured you could move a lot more than that."

"I do the same kind of workout as you. Work the smaller muscles first so I can get a better workout with lighter weights later. Plus, I have a feeling I might be distracted a bit."

Alyssa bit her bottom lip, and Jake realized that must be her habit. A very sexy, sultry habit.

"You might be," she purred.

Jake assumed the position on the bench, gripped the bar, adjusted a few times, breathing in and out.

"Twenty reps," he said as he raised the bar and began lifting.

Alyssa stepped forward a bit and spread her legs so Jake was looking right up at her spandex-clad crotch and noticed a small wet spot there in the middle. As he breathed in and out with each lift, he began to catch a whiff of her wet pussy and he smiled slightly.

"What are you grinning at, Mr. Middle?" said Alyssa.

"Nothing."

He breathed deep as he pushed out several more reps, and Alyssa noticed his cock hardening in his shorts. While his jockstrap kept everything under control, she could still see the bulge grow as he breathed in her musky aroma.

Jake paused at the top of his last rep and said, "I may have a little trouble with this, so you'll have to lower yourself and help lift the last few inches."

Alyssa smiled and lowered her crotch so it was a few tantalizing inches from Jake's face. He breathed deep as he lowered and easily raised the bar for one last rep.

"I do declare, Mr. Middle," said Alyssa, adding a little more twang to her mild Southern accent, "you are quite the scoundrel."

Jake sat up. "And you are quite the Southern bell."

"Belle," corrected Alyssa.

"What'd I say?"

"Bell."

"What's the difference?"

"A silent E and a whole lot of judgment from our mommas."

Jake laughed and grabbed his towel. He sprayed down the bench with a bottle of spray near the station and said, "That's it for me. Do you need to do anything else?"

"No, I'm good. Sometimes I'll go sit in the sauna, but if you still want to go to lunch, we may want to skip that until another day."

"That's a good idea," said Jake. "I skipped breakfast so I could eat tapas with you. I've been looking forward to that."

Jake and Alyssa walked out to his truck so they could ride to the restaurant together.

"So, Midwestern boys drive pickups, huh? Does that mean I'm a hookup?"

"Not yet," said Jake, a mischievous smile tugging at his mouth.

"Wow, somebody's pretty sure of himself."

"Yeah, I'm a little cocky sometimes."

"Not as far as I could tell," said Alyssa, opening the door.

Jake laughed and climbed in.

CHAPTER 5

After lunch, Alyssa offered to take him back to her place so he could shower. Jake had brought a change of clothes and planned to visit the Bookish Atlanta bookstore after a shower. But if things went the way he hoped, he may have to visit it tomorrow.

Throughout the entire lunch, the two talked about their past and how they got into comedy. Jake talked about his career and how he had worked his way up to become a reliable middle in big cities and a headliner in the smaller ones. He talked about how his agent had booked him on a tour of the Southeast, and he was making his way from Milwaukee all the way to Jacksonville, Florida, with a stop at Abraxus Tasker College on the way.

Alyssa talked about how she had played soccer in college but quit after two years when she injured her knee. During her recovery, she discovered acting and improv, and focused her attention on that. She decided she liked comedy and wanted to be an actor, so she started working as a bartender in a comedy club in order to network, meet other comics, and pursue acting as Atlanta was such a hotbed of TV and film production. She even had an agent and went on a few auditions each week, securing a few small commercials and bit parts in independent films.

They squeezed next to each other in the half-circle, purple-upholstered booth, chatting and trying different dishes. They turned to face each other and fed each other bites of their favorites, licking each other's fingers supposedly to get any stray juices.

While they ate, Alyssa rubbed her hand up and down Jake's thigh, occasionally flicking his cock with a fingernail, and Jake stroked the inside of her thigh, reaching higher up her thigh and nearly touching her eager pussy with his pinky. Whenever he came within a hair's breadth of touching her aching cunt, Alyssa would tighten her buns to push herself forward just a little bit to get him to touch her. As she did, he would smile, slide his hand back just a little bit, and caress the crease where her thigh and pelvis joined.

After a few near misses, Alyssa leaned forward and breathed in Jake's ear, "Touch my pussy right now, or this is as close as you'll ever get." Jake quickly complied, feeding her a small potato with his left hand, stroking her pussy through her spandex shorts with his right. She moaned quietly in his ear and said, "That's so good. I need you to take me home and give my pussy a good workout."

"Let's go right now," said Jake, reaching into his wallet and dropping $100 on the table. That was more than enough to cover the bill and a generous tip, but he didn't want to wait any longer. She climbed into the truck with him, neither wanting to lose the momentum they had built up. Jake punched Alyssa's address into his GPS and saw that it was only ten miles away. As Jake navigated his way out of the parking lot, she rubbed his cock through his shorts. "How big is this thing anyway?" she gasped.

"Eight-and-a-half inches," he said.

"That's rather specific," she said. "How do you even know? Did you measure it?"

"Every guy measures it. Anyone who tells you they didn't is a fucking liar."

"Well, it's nice and hard, and I'm going to make it fit me, no matter how long it takes. Do you ever have a hard time fitting it into other girls?"

Jake thought back to all the women he'd been with over the last few months. The ones who'd had the most trouble with it were the smaller women—Molly in Milwaukee, Irene in Indianapolis—but they had persevered with a little patience and a lot of stubbornness and were eventually able to fit his entire shaft inside them.

"I've never had anyone who wasn't able to take it all," said Jake, smiling.

Alyssa pulled his steely hard-on out of his shorts, and her eyes popped. "Fuck, it's bigger than I thought. Yeah, I'm going to have some fun fitting it inside me."

She looked around to see if there were any cars nearby, and when she didn't spot any, she quickly darted down and sucked his shaft into her mouth, sliding her lips up and down on his veiny prick, managing to get a little over half of it in her mouth. She made a wet slurping sound as she withdrew his cock with each stroke and lowered herself until she felt his cock head nearly reach her gag limit.

"Ohhhh, fuck," Jake groaned.

Alyssa released her grip and sat up, "There's plenty more where that came from, but it's hard to take so much when I'm riding side-saddle like that," she said. "Plus, I don't think I can wait for you to recover. I want you inside me right away."

"Fuck, you're irritating!" Jake growled and pressed harder on the gas. Alyssa laughed and sucked on her finger at him. Jake reached over and began rubbing Alyssa's pussy through her shorts. She raised up her hips and lowered her shorts past her well-toned ass cheeks to give her new lover better access to her swollen lips. Jake slid a thick finger in and out of her cunt, sliding up to her hard clitoris, dragging the length of his finger over it and back, dipping into her pussy before sliding back over her pink pearl again.

"Oh, fuck," she breathed. "Oh, that's it, just like that. Oh, God, that's it. Right there, right there, right—what the hell, man?"

Jake pulled his finger away from her pussy, a devilish grin spread over his face. He licked his finger clean of her juices and said. "I can't wait for you to recover either."

"Motherfucker!" Alyssa said, smiling. She continued rubbing her own slit and Jake slowly stroked his cock. "Turn right here," she said. "Third building on the right. Park here." She pointed at a visitor's spot in front of the building and the two quickly pulled up their shorts, scrambled out of the truck, and ran all the way to Alyssa's apartment.

Alyssa locked the door, faced Jake, and pantsed him, jockstrap and all. His dick was still mostly hard so she slipped it into her mouth for a few pumps to get it hard and wet again. She stripped off her own shorts and leaned against the back of the couch, which was facing the entryway of her apartment. Jake admired her long legs, her tight ass, and the meat of her engorged labia. He gazed at the wetness that was running out of her cunt, and slid his cock along her wet lips.

"Fuck me with that thing right now," she commanded. "Don't wait, don't tease me with it, just shove—OH FUCK!" Jake did as he was ordered and jammed his eight-and-a-half-inch prick into her eager pussy without hesitation, driving all the way home in a single thrust. He waited for a few seconds so Alyssa could adjust to the concrete-hard invader suddenly inside her, and when he felt her relax a bit, he withdrew so only his dickhead was nestled between her lips then slammed back inside again.

"Ohhhhhh," moaned Alyssa. "That's the ticket. Just keep doing that. Don't go slow, pound the shit out of me."

Jake eagerly complied and drove a steady pile-driving rhythm, gripping her slender hips, and thrusting himself into her. "Ungh. Ungh. Ungh. Ungh."

"Oh. Oh. Oh. Oh." grunted Alyssa in time. "Fuck my wet pussy. My pussy is so wet for your big cock." Jake had his answer from when he was masturbating and fantasizing about her: *She's a dirty talker and a moaner.*

Jake reached around and cupped her still-covered breasts as he fucked the tall, leggy blonde. She lifted her sports bra, letting her heavy tits fill his hands, and he continued plowing her wet cunt, both of them grunting and breathing hard.

Alyssa reached down to her pussy with a free hand and began to rub her own clit even as Jake slid himself in and out.

"I'm gonna come," she said, and Jake was secretly thrilled that she used the right spelling; it nearly made him come himself. "Oh fuck, I'm going to come all over your big cock. That thing's going to fuck me to death, and I'm going to come before I die."

Jake released her bountiful tits and grabbed her hips once more. He slammed into her dripping cunt as hard as he could, pushing Alyssa's tight slit apart.

"More, more, more. Fuck me more, Mr. Middle. Shove that prick inside me and don't stop!" she begged. "That's it, that's it, I'm coming… I'm coming… I'm—OH, MY GOOOOODDDDDDDDDDD!!!"

Alyssa wailed as her orgasm washed over her and her knees buckled. Jake slowed his rhythm and held her up. "Oh, fuck, Jake. That was incredible. No, don't stop. Come for me, Jakey Nilsen. I want you to come for me."

"I'm getting close," he growled. "Where do you want it?"

"In. My. Mouth," she answered between his powerful pumps.

"Then get ready."

Alyssa pulled away from him, spun around, and kneeled before him, slurping his cock back into her mouth. She grabbed his hips and pulled him toward her, fucking her mouth with his shaft. He grabbed handfuls of her blonde hair.

"Ohhhhh, fuck. I'm going to come," he said, making sure to use his preferred spelling.

"Mm-hmm, mm-hmm." Alyssa agreed that proper spelling is important, even in the throes of sexual ecstasy. At least, that's what he thought she was saying.

"Ohh! Ohh! Here it is. Get ready. I'm gonna come for you. You're making me … COOOOOOMMMMMMEEEEE!" Jake's thick seed spurted from his cock and quickly filled Alyssa's awaiting mouth.

She barely had a chance to savor the first mouthful when another erupted, eager to join its friend. Alyssa swallowed them both down when a third burst shot out to find out what had happened to the first two, then a fourth came to offer moral support. Alyssa swallowed those just in time for a fifth and final load to bring up the rear and wander off in search of its mates.

Alyssa let that last spurt sit on her tongue while she enjoyed Jake's sweet-salty taste and ran her tongue over his sensitive cockhead. He shuddered once, twice, while she licked off any remaining spooge. She finally clamped down and pulled her mouth off while exerting strong suction, making sure to get every drop of his white gold. Jake's knees buckled and he doubled over as she teased his now-sensitive head.

"Fuck, now that's what I call an orgasm," said Jake.

"Oh, God, me too. Thank you, sir."

"No, thank you, m'lady. You fuck divinely."

Alyssa walked to her refrigerator, kicking off her shoes and socks along the way, and pulled her sports bra off, dropping it on the floor. She grabbed two sports drinks out of the refrigerator and returned to the living room. She sat down on the couch and patted the seat next to her. Jake stripped off his shirt and removed his shorts, which had been down around his ankles the entire time, as well as his shoes.

They snuggled up closely, enjoying the post-coital bliss and feeling each other's skin. They talked for a few minutes, giving a blow-by-blow replay of their first fuck session, telling what they each liked best.

"You got some nice abs there, Mr. Middle," said Alyssa, running her hands over Jake's washboard abs. "If I had known that, I might have taken you on my back so I could admire the view."

"We still have time for more," he answered. "Besides, I loved looking at your tight little ass. I may want to get you from behind again just so I can appreciate it."

"Oh, no, I don't think I could handle that thing in my ass. Getting it inside my pussy was hard enough."

"No, I didn't mean that. I just want to fuck you from behind so I can see that beautiful ass."

Jake marveled at how easily he could talk dirty to a woman when they weren't on the phone. He realized he was going to have to get over that reluctance one of these days.

He pulled her on top of him so she was facing him, her pussy resting on his still-soft dick. They kissed deeply, and Jake massaged her tits, squeezing her nipples between his index fingers and thumbs.

"Mmmmmm," moaned Alyssa as they were kissing. "Let's take a shower and clean each other up before we try round two." She sprang off Jake, who looked down at his hardening cock.

"Soon, buddy," he said, patting his cock.

Alyssa snickered and led him by his cock to the bathroom. They kissed again as they waited for the water to warm up then stepped inside. They began running their hands all over each other under the pretense of applying soap. The result was Jake's dick and balls, and Alyssa's tits had never been cleaner. He also spent some attention rubbing her shower sponge on her pussy, making Alyssa gasp and grab his arm. After they were cleaned and had toweled off, she led him to her bedroom.

"I want you to eat my pussy," she said. "Taste my cunt and make me come."

Jake excused himself and ran back to the kitchen, his semi-hard cock flopping against his belly and thigh. He came back with a glass and something in his mouth.

"What's that for?" she said.

"You'll see," he said, his mouth full of some mystery object.

Jake pushed gently down on Alyssa's shoulder, perching her shapely ass a few inches back from the edge. He knelt in front of her and parted her legs with his hands. Then he picked up the glass and spit out an ice cube, mostly melted.

He blew cold air over her pussy lips, and she shuddered. Then he leaned in and ran his cold tongue up her slit and over her pink pearl.

"Oh fuck, that's cold," she said.

He licked her a few more times then put the ice cube back in his mouth and sucked on it some more, letting it melt completely in his mouth, and returned to his ministrations on her wet cunt, licking and sucking her lips, flicking her clit with his tongue.

"Oh, holy shit, that's so good. Keep licking me, Jake. Run your tongue up my pussy. Oh, fuck, that's it. Oh, yes, that's—oooohhhhhhhh!"

Jake slid a finger and then a second into her pussy, and continued to lap at her even as he probed her with his fingers.

"Ohhh, that's it, Jakey. Oooooh! Oooooh! I'm going to come again. Here I... Here I... I'M COOMMMMING!" She grabbed his hair with both hands and shoved his face into her pussy, while he licked, sucked, and finger-fucked her to two orgasms.

"Holy shit, that was awesome," she panted. Jake waited for her, giving light kisses to her pussy lips and clit, gently sucking on her lips.

"And now I want to make you come again," Alyssa said, moving into a new position. "Go over to the foot of the bed." He did as she asked. standing up as she was lying down—*hey, that's the name of this series!*—face up, upside down on the bed, her head lined up with his stiff cock.

Alyssa slid toward the foot of her bed until her head was hanging over the edge. "Feed that to me," she ordered, and Jake eagerly complied.

Alyssa parted her lips, and Jake slid his cock into her eager mouth. He pushed forward gently until he felt some resistance and pulled back out. He pushed again to the same depth, then slid back out. He repeated his gentle motions, and Alyssa provided the suction, pulling him in and resisting his withdrawals. Her suction hollowed out her cheeks and extended her lips as he pulled out each time.

He pushed in a little further and heard it when he hit the back of her throat.

"*Gluk,*" said Alyssa. Jake slid back in and hit the spot again. "*Gluk.*"

"Oh, fuck, I love that sound," Jake moaned.

"I love making it," said Alyssa. "Fuck my face and hit my throat with that cock."

Jake was only too happy to give her what she wanted. So he continued fucking her mouth, making sure not to push too deeply.

"*Gluk. Gluk. Gluk. Gluk. Gluk. Gluk,*" said Alyssa. She played with her clit with one hand while holding the base of Jake's shaft with the other, all while letting him stuff his cock in her mouth. "*Gluk. Gluk. Gluk. Gluk.*"

As Jake pumped, he could feel his balls boiling again, and he knew he was close. "I don't want to come again too soon," he said. "Let's change up."

She released Jake's dick with a "POP" and said, "Fuck my tits."

Jake climbed onto the bed as she slid back on. He straddled his athletic lover, laying his thick meat between her firm tits. She held them together and put her hand over her cleavage as Jake slid his slippery dick inside it. He stared deeply into her eyes, and she looked back at him as he rocked back and forth for a few more minutes. She occasionally lifted her chin to suck on his cock head whenever it reached her lips.

"This is amazing," said Jake. "Your tits feel wonderful wrapped around my cock."

"I want you back inside me now," she said. "Take me from behind like you wanted."

Jake quickly climbed off while Alyssa flipped onto her stomach and spread her legs slightly, even as Jake straddled them. "Take me like this." She raised her hips slightly, and Jake pointed his dick right at her pussy, zeroing in on her heavenly opening.

As he entered her, she opened her mouth in a silent moan until he bottomed out. Jake slid in and out a few more times as Alyssa groaned with each push.

"Unh. Unh. Unh. Fuck, that's good," she moaned. "Unh. Unh. Unh."

Jake grabbed her ass cheeks with both hands and massaged them deeply, even as he pushed into her wet cunt. "Your pussy feels like velvet on my dick," he said, remembering his masturbation session in Chapter 3.

Jake leaned forward and lay on top of Alyssa. He reached one hand around and cupped her breast even as he continued fucking her from behind. The two lay that way as Jake slowly slid his cock in and out of her warm wetness for several minutes.

"Oh, this is amazing," she said. "But now I want you to fuck me doggy style."

Jake raised back up, pulling out of her for a minute. Alyssa followed suit and rose up to her hands and knees.

"Please get that back in me," Alyssa gasped. "I need it."

Jake pushed back into her in a repeat performance of the living room just a half-hour earlier. He held still and grabbed her waist, pushing and pulling her onto his cock, slamming her ass hard against him, rocking her heavy tits with each thrust. Soon, he began meeting her halfway, so each was moving half as far as they needed. Jake pounded her faster and faster, getting her pendulous tits to swing as they slapped together, ass to front.

"Oh, fuck, baby! This is so good!" screamed Alyssa. "Fuck me with that monster cock!"

Jack began pumping her furiously, slamming his cock into her even as her pussy juices trickled down her legs.

"Oh fuck, I'm going to come," he moaned.

"Ooh, yeah. That's it, baby. Fill me up with your hot come. It tasted delicious, and now I want your hot come in my pussy. Ohh! Ohh! Fill me with that hot come."

"This is for you, baby. This is for you. I'm gonna fill your pussy with my ... COOOME!" Four jizz jets shot out of Jake's dick and filled Alyssa's hole. He continued fucking until the friction on his sensitive cock head was too much for him. He lay down with her next to him, still inside her. As his cock began to shrink, it slipped out of her, and Alyssa could feel his hot spunk slipping out of her.

The two lay next to each other, breathing heavily, covered in sweat again. Jake kissed her neck and cheek, and she turned back and kissed him on the mouth.

"I've dreamed of this since the first time I met you," he said.

"Ah-ha! You *were* looking at my ass."

"No, I was fantasizing about it," he said, reaching down and giving it an appreciative squeeze.

"Oh, yeah? What about?"

"Exactly this."

"So, do you want to work out tomorrow together?" Alyssa asked.

"We could, but they say you burn 150 calories with every orgasm, so maybe we could just skip it and stay in and burn our own calories."

"I'd be alright with that. Maybe we could burn off enough calories that hot dogs for lunch might be in order."

"You're a woman after my own heart, Alyssa DuPont."

"No, I'm after your dick, Jake Nilsen. And for the next few days, I plan on screwing the hell out of it."

"That sounds like a great plan," said Jake. "Do you like riding cowgirl?"

THE END

Chastity Veldt

Betty in Birmingham

Stand Up, Lie Down Collection

TABLE OF CONTENTS

CHAPTER 1

"Is there anything else I can get you, hon?" Jake Nilsen looked up from his book at the woman standing next to his table holding a pitcher. It was a Wednesday afternoon, and Jake was reading an old Rex Stout paperback novel. Finished with his lunch at a smallIe called French's, he decided it was time to move on.

"I'm sorry," said Jake. "Do you have a to-go cup by chance? I'd love to take some sweet tea with me. And maybe the check?"

The woman—her name tag reading "Kellie"—returned with a Styrofoam cup. "That's good tea, isn't it?" she asked. "We make some of the best sweet tea in the city."

"Well, this is my first time in Birmingham, and it's definitely the best tea I've had."

"I could tell you were a first-timer," said Kellie.

"Really? How so?"

"'Cause you said Birming-am like you're British. We say Birming-Ham."

"Ah, okay," said Jake.

"So where are you from?"

"I grew up in Minnesota, but now I'm a stand-up comic and I travel a lot."

"Are you in town for a show?"

"Yep, I'm headlining for three nights at Chip's Comedy Club."

Kellie pulled a black folder from her apron pocket and set it on the table. "I know Chip's. My cousin, Jerry, is the bartender there. I may have to come see the show. Are you performing tonight?"

"No, just tomorrow night, Friday, and Saturday. I just came into town a day early because I didn't have anything booked for tonight. So I thought I'd come hang out and check out a couple of bookstores."

"Have you been to Reed Books yet?"

Jake held up his Rex Stout novel. "You bet! That was the first place I went to and I got a few Rex Stout novels. A friend of mine owns a bookstore in Milwaukee, and she made me promise to stop in there as soon as I got into town."

Jake flashed back to last week's phone conversation with Molly Moser, a friend and lover from Milwaukee, Wisconsin.[11] The two had discussed her new relationship with Tad Ackroyd, a tax attorney she had started dating at the insistence of her Aunt Judy. As they talked, Jake mentioned where he was heading for his next gig, and Molly half-shouted in his ear.

---

[11] Check out *Stand Up, Lie Down: Molly in Milwaukee*

"Oh! You have to check out Reed Books! That's an amazing bookstore!"

"Jesus, do you know every bookstore in the country?"

"Maybe," Molly mumbled. "I always like to go on little vacations with my book-nerd friends and we check out bookstores. Besides, Tad says I can call it a buying trip and write it off on my taxes."

Jake snapped his attention back to Kellie. "So anyway, my friend turned me on to Rex Stout and I found a few novels I hadn't read yet."

"I've heard of him, I think," said Kellie. "What's he write?"

"He wrote the Nero Wolfe mysteries in the 1930s and 1940s."

"Ah, okay. That's how I know him. I prefer Stephen King and Erika Lance myself," said Kellie. "Horror stuff."

Jake grimaced. "I can't stand horror novels," he said, shuddering. "They give me nightmares and I jump at every little noise in the room. It's worse when I'm on the road and staying in some apartment I've never been to before. Every noise is some kind of killer clown coming to kill me."

Kellie laughed. "Yeah, I can see that. They're not for everyone. Well, I've got customers to serve, but I hope I can make it to your show, Jake. Thanks for coming in."

"Thank you," said Jake. He stuck $30 into the check folder and handed it back to Kellie. "Keep the change."

"Thank you, honey. Come back soon."

Jake climbed into his pickup and drove the few miles to Chip's and parked in the parking lot behind the club. He climbed out of the truck and locked it, stopping to double-check the lock on the bed lid too. He had an aluminum weather-tight lid installed so he could carry his luggage and a few favorite items, like a plastic tub filled with books. Locking it with the same key fob that locked his truck, he headed into the club.

In his "day job," Jake was a real estate investor who'd made quite a lot of money buying dilapidated homes and turning them into rental properties for college students. He did standup comedy as a hobby because it gave him a chance to drive around the country and do what he really loved: *Making people happy*. It also meant he could afford high-tech security for a seven-year-old Toyota Tacoma pickup.

"Hi, I'm looking for the owner," said Jake.

"She's in the office back there," said the guy, pointing across the room at a door marked Private. He went back to drying a glass and didn't look up from his task.

"Are you Jerry?" asked Jake.

"Who wants to know?" The bartender looked up. He was short and wiry, and had tattoos on both arms.

Jake looked around to see if there was anyone else in the room. "Well, I ... do?"

"Yeah, and who are you?"

Jake leaned in conspiratorially. "Who wants to know?"

"Jesus Christ!" exclaimed the bartender.

"Whoa, seriously? You know Jesus? And he was asking about me?"

"Goddammit, everyone's gotta be a damn comedian."

"Actually, I am a comedian. I'm the headliner this weekend. I'm just checking in."

"So why do you want to know who I am?" demanded the bartender, glaring at Jake

"If you're Jerry, I met your cousin, Kellie, at her restaurant."

"And if I'm not." The bartender had been drying the same glass for over a minute now.

"Then I met a woman named Kellie."

The bartender busted out laughing. "Yeah, I'm Jerry. I'm sorry, I was just messing with you. Curtis Sanders says 'hi.'"

Jake roared with laughter at Curtis's name, and he shook Jerry's hand. "Holy shit, man, you got me. That was awesome. Curtis put you up to that?"

"Yeah, he was in here a couple of weeks ago and he saw that you were on the schedule. He said when you got here, I was supposed to fuck with you somehow."

The two men laughed and chattered, replaying the gag and breaking it down like they were football analysts discussing a great play. They even took a selfie on Jake's phone, both of them flipping off the camera.

"I'm sending this to Curtis," said Jake. "I'd better check in with the owner. Is that Chip?"

"No, Shari runs the place now. Chip was the last owner; we just never changed the name."

Jake and Jerry shook hands again, and Jake headed through the door Jerry had pointed at. He walked down a short hallway to the office and knocked on the door frame.

"Hi. Shari?"

"Who wants to know?" said the woman, popping a fried brown disc into her mouth and chomping on it.

"I'm Jake Nilsen."

"Knellson?"

"No, Nilsen."

"Well, what'dya want. I'm busy here." She ate another fried brown thing.

"Did Curtis tell you to fuck with me too?"

The woman laughed. "Yeah, he did."

"I just got it from Jerry," Jake said. He related the story to her and Shari cried with laughter. "Yeah, Curtis is a good friend, but he pranks me pretty hard sometimes."

"He can be a handful, but we love having him here," Shari said. She stood up and shook Jake's hand. "Nice to meet you. I'm Shari Tucker."

"Thank you for having me. I appreciate you letting me show up a day early. I usually come into town the day of a show, but I didn't have anything booked, so I thought I'd visit some bookstores and see what I could find."

"You picked a great day for it. Have you been to Reed Books yet?"

"I was there this morning. Picked up a couple Rex Stouts I hadn't read yet."

"Excellent. I'm more of a Tami Hoag fan myself. You want a fried pickle?" She offered up a plate of the chips she had been munching on.

"No, thanks, I just had lunch at French's."

"Oh, I love French's. Jerry's cousin works there."

"I know. I actually met her and we chatted for a bit."

"Kellie's a peach. And they have the best sweet tea in the city, too." Shari ate another fried... *pickle chip! That's what she's eating.* "So you probably need the keys to the apartment, right? It's not too far from here. We have another comic who's finishing up tonight and she's staying there until tomorrow morning. You don't have a problem sharing a place with a woman, do you?"

"Not if she doesn't," said Jake.

"Great. Her name is Kayla Baker, and she was our middle over the weekend. She said she'd stick around and run our open mics during the week before she left for Mobile. She's middling down there too."

"I've met Kayla a couple of times. We were on the same stage at a couple comedy festivals in Charleston and Asheville. She's a lot of fun, but I don't know her that well."

"Oh, excellent. She knows you're coming, and I've got the key right here." Shari texted the address to Jake, and he looked it up on Waze. He thanked her, said his good-byes to Shari and Jerry, and headed to his apartment.

Chapter 2

Several hours later, Jake was awakened by pounding on the door of the apartment. He had fallen asleep on the couch after going on a long run and a visit to a chain of 24-hour gyms where he had a membership. Jake was a former swimmer and had an athletic build that he worked hard to maintain, even while he was on the road. In his dream, he was being chased by Tad Ackroyd wielding a shotgun and wearing a bright-red bowtie that pulsed whenever he was about to pull the trigger.

There was another pounding on the door. Jake got up and crept over, senses on high alert. He stood off to the side, visions of jealous boyfriends with shotguns dancing in his head.

"Who is it?" he demanded, lowering his voice to sound more intimidating.

"It's me, Kayla. I forgot my key."

Jake looked through the peephole to be sure Tad wasn't cleverly disguising his voice and saw it was indeed Kayla.

Kayla Baker was a tall Black woman with gorgeous curves and dark umber skin that glowed in the bright porch light. She waved at the moths fluttering around the bare bulb. Her long hair had been relaxed, straightened, and hung down to her shoulders. Her black slacks hugged her curvy hips and her sleeveless, cherry-red blouse strained against her large breasts. Jake noticed the top two buttons were undone and he imagined getting lost in her deep cleavage.

He opened it and stepped aside to let her in.

She looked Jake up and down, still wearing his running shorts and a tank top. "Well, well, this is a nice way to be greeted when I come home; a nice hot man to open the door for me. If you had a drink on a silver tray, that might be even better. I'd have to call you Jeeves though." Kayla laughed and put her hand on Jake's shoulder to steady herself.

The two comics had a history of flirting heavily with each other whenever they'd met, although Jake got the impression she would have gone further if he'd made the attempt. Actually, he got the impression she would have fucked his brains out, but the timing had never been right. *Would tonight be the night?*[12]

"Ohh, my," she purred, caressing Jake's shoulder and bicep. "I wouldn't make you wear the funny little butler's outfit though. This would be just fine."

Jake's heart was still beating after being jolted awake from a nightmare and still a little groggy. The two embraced and Jake savored feeling Kayla's large breasts pressed against him.

"Hey, Kayla, how was the open mic?"

---

[12] You're reading book 6 of an erotica series. What do you think?

"Shitty, as always. But Jerry gives me free drinks and Shari gives me 50 bucks, so I won't complain."

"How'd you get home then?"

"Took an Uber. I left my car here because I knew I was going to be drinking a bit."

"Sounds like more than a bit," said Jake, smiling.

"You getting all judgy on me, Jakey Knellson?"

"Nilsen."

"What?"

"Nilsen, not Knellson."

"What's the difference?" said Kayla.

"Knellson has a silent K in it."

"I don't hear it."

"That's why it's silent," Jake said with a smile. "Don't worry about it. Most people can't hear it. But when you have a name like mine, you learn to hear the silent K."

Kayla slowly walked into the living room and Jake admired her butt as she sashayed away from him. She sat on the couch where Jake had been sitting.

"Mmmm, it's nice and warm. It was getting chilly out there tonight. I may just sleep right here." Kayla closed her eyes and crossed her arms under her breasts, squeezing them together to deepen her cleavage.

"Okay, I'm going to take a shower and go to bed."

"Or you could snuggle up next to me and keep me warm," said Kayla.

"I had a run earlier so I don't imagine I smell too good," Jake said.

"So come out here when you're done," Kayla hollered. "I'm lonely, Jakey Nilsen!"

"Er, okay." Jake was pretty sure she wasn't serious and would forget all about him in two minutes, especially as she had closed her eyes and seemed to be going to sleep.

Still, he studied her for a few seconds. Her breasts were pushed together under her arms, deepening the cleft, and he imagined sliding his cock between them.

Jake shook his head and padded off to the bedroom. He stripped off his clothes and stuffed them in a laundry bag. Looking at himself in the bedroom mirror: bulging pectorals, narrow waist, and a ripped abdomen with those little V muscles[13] that directed the eye downward. Not that Jake had anything to be ashamed of, as his cock was eight-and-a-half inches when he was hard. He wasn't fully hard now, but he was getting there after imagining him and Kayla on the couch. She was straddling his lap and grinding her pussy on top of his thick—

"Hurry up, Jake, I'm still waiting," called Kayla.

Holy shit, was she serious? "Uh, okay," he called.

He wrapped a towel around his tapered waist and walked back to the bathroom. Turning on the water, he waited for it to warm up before stepping in. Jake quickly soaped himself down and shampooed his hair. Running his hands over his dick and the public

____

[13] It's called an Adonis belt. *Rowr!*

region above it, feeling the stubble from where he had shaved a few days earlier. Jake liked to keep clean-shaven there, and it felt like he could go another day or two without shaving again. He continued soaping his cock and balls thinking about Kayla. Stroking himself, he knew nothing would happen with her, but he could at least enjoy a few fantasies about her.

The bathroom door opened, and Jake froze, hand still on his hard member. Kayla yanked the shower curtain back and Jake tried to cover himself with his hands.

"I got tired of waiting for you," said Kayla before looking down at his hard shaft. "Is that for me? Were you thinking about me and rubbing one out? That's sweet, but I think I can give you something better."

Kayla unbuttoned her blouse and let it slide from her shoulders. She unhooked her bra from the front and let it fall to the floor as well, her voluminous tits defied gravity—Kayla looked like she was getting some doctor-provided assistance there, but Jake had always firmly believed that "tits is tits," and was never one to turn his nose up at a pair of tits, no matter how big or small, perky or heavy.

Jake removed his hands and let the shower rinse over him to get rid of the last of the soap. Kayla slipped out of her slacks and panties and stepped into the shower. She wrapped her arms around Jake's neck and kissed him deeply. The water rained down Jake's back, their tongues sliding over each other, exploring each other's mouths. He pulled Kayla close to him and felt her luscious tits crush against his torso, his cock trapped between their legs.

Kayla shifted a little and spread her legs, and Jake's thickness sprang up between her legs and nested against her bare pussy. Jake was pleased to discover she was a shaver as well. He loved having sex with women who shaved because the sensation was not only more pleasurable, but neither of them would inadvertently pull a hair during sex, or get a hair in their mouth while going down on the other.

Jake reached a hand up and palmed Kayla's large breast, massaging and squeezing it, pinching her dark nipple, and feeling it harden. He bent down and sucked on one nipple then turned his attention to her other one, feeling them stiffen between his lips. Sucking on one then the other before returning to her mouth, roiling his tongue with hers. Jake cupped Kayla's curvy ass and pulled her back to him. She squeezed her legs together which pushed Jake's cock firmer against her pussy lips, and she slid her hips so it would rub against her.

When Jake realized what she was doing, he drew his hips back so he could push forward in time. Kayla moaned into his mouth as he continued grinding his cock against her hot pussy.

Suddenly, Kayla stopped and backed away, but before Jake could say anything she knelt down and slipped Jake's dickhead into her mouth. She sucked it between her lips and slid it back out. She slid it in again, back out, then in again further. She repeated the process, taking a little more of Jake's cock with each push until she reached about halfway down his eight-and-a-half inches. She circled her thumb and forefinger around his shaft and jacked off the lower half as she sucked off the upper half.

Kayla slid her mouth onto his cock, using the heavy suction to pull her mouth over his meat. She continued to stroke his other half, using the water and her saliva as lubrication. It felt like two pussies that could each apply pressure on only one half of his prick and give him a double-dick workout. He groaned his appreciation.

"Don't hold back, lover," Kayla said, popping his shaft out of her mouth for a second. "Just give me that hot jizz."

"It's all for you, baby," Jake moaned. "H-h-holy fuck," he said as she sucked her way back down to her limit. "Oh, I'm close," he murmured after a few minutes of her ministrations. "I'm going to cum for you, Kayla."

"That's it, come for me, baby," she corrected, and he swooned when she used his favorite pronunciation. "Just jerk off and aim it at my mouth."

"What if I miss?"

"Don't," she said with a sexy grin. Kayla settled back on her heels and tilted her face up to Jake. "Stroke that thick cock. I haven't had something that big in my mouth in a long time. And when we're done here, I'm going to ride you like a horse and you're going to fill me up with that giant prick."

Kayla's sexy talk and Jake's rapid strokes built up the pressure in his balls and he could feel the come building up. "This is it," he groaned. "This is it; I'm coming."

"Give it to me, Jake. Give your seed to Kayla. Look at me when you come in my mouth."

"Oh, fuck, here I ... COOMMMMME!" Jake shouted as the first rope of jizz flew from his cock, landing in her open mouth, followed by a second and a third.

She swallowed quickly and kept her mouth open as Jake shot his fourth and fifth shots back into her waiting mouth. When he finished, Kayla slid Jake's cock back into her mouth and sucked any remaining jizz out of the head. Jake doubled over as the pressure on his now-sensitive dickhead was too great.

"Holy shit, that was hot," he groaned, wiping off a bit of come that had landed on her chin. She caught his hand and sucked it off his thumb.

"I can tell you take good care of yourself. Your come is very sweet and a little salty."

Jake helped Kayla stand up and she stepped past him to rinse her face off. "I need a shower too," she said after a minute. "I may need your help soaping up, and then you're going to take me to the bedroom and fuck me with that big prick of yours."

"Whatever you want, I'm up for it."

"Well, maybe not at the moment," said Kayla, giving a sly grin at Jake's deflating cock. "I'll give you some time to recover. Do you like to eat pussy?"

"There's almost nothing I'd rather do than eat your pussy," said Jake.

"Almost nothing?" said Kayla.

"Well, I do want to fuck you," He pulled her to him and kissed her again.

After soaping each other off, and paying special attention to each other's erogenous zones, plus Jake nearly slipping his cock into Kayla's wet cunt from behind, they toweled each other off and Kayla led Jake to his bedroom, both still naked. She sat on the edge of his bed and lay back, propping herself up on her elbows.

"I've been dreaming of watching you eat my pussy since the day we were at Charleston together. I just never had the chance to get you alone to myself," said Kayla. "And now I get to feel your tongue all up in me before you fill me up with that monster dick."

"Your wish is my command," said Jake as he knelt down and put her strong legs over his shoulders.

He kissed her thighs and licked them, giving little nibbles and sucks as he approached her shaved slit. Continuing to lick and nibble, bite and suck, Jake did this first on one thigh, then the other. As he switched sides, he blew a cool breath over her pussy lips. Kissing up her thigh, turn and blow, kiss up her other thigh, turn and blow, until finally, he was able to lick the crevice where her leg met her public bone.

Jake kissed her pussy a few times and inhaled deeply, smelling her musk. Her pussy was wet with anticipation, and he enjoyed the smell of her slit. Jake slid his tongue into her crevice and slid from bottom to top, sliding his tongue over her clit. Kayla gave a little shudder, so he did it again. She whimpered with delight as he continued sliding his tongue over her moist lips. Jake continued to probe Kayla's pussy, slipping his tongue between her folds.

As Kayla's labia engorged with desire, he gently sucked one of her lips into his mouth then the other before gently suctioning her clit between his own lips and sliding a finger into her dripping cunt.

"Oh, fuck, Jakey, where did you learn to eat pussy like that? That's going to make me fucking—OH!" Jake sucked harder on Kayla's clit and flicked his tongue on it. "Do that again! Do that— OH! Holy fuck, if you make me come that way, you're gonna be my new boyfriend I will fuck you whatever way you—OH!"

Jake looked up at Kayla with a twinkle in his eye, and she flopped flat onto her back. He loved that she pronounced it "come" and not "cum," so he was going to give her her heart's and cunt's desire.

"Eat my pussy, Jake! Keep doing that to me! OH GOD, YES! I'M GOING TO COME! THAT'S IT! THAT'S IT! FLICK MY CLIT! THAT'S—OH GOD, I'M COMIIIIIINNNNNNGGGGGG!"

Kayla bucked her hips and pulled Jake's face deeper into her wet snatch as he licked, flicked, and sucked for all he was worth. She rode a first wave, followed by a second wave, of a blissful orgasm.

"Fuck me now, Jake. Fuck me right fucking now!" Kayla demanded. "I want you to stick that thing in me and fuck the shit out of me."

Jake hopped up to his feet, positioned his throbbing shaft at her dark pussy, and slid the head of his cock inside her. He watched carefully as her lips and folds spread and contoured around his fleshy invader.

Kayla gave one long, continuous moan as Jake pushed his thick cock deep into her wet gash. Thanks to his attention, she was sopping wet and Jake slid into her without any resistance, until he was crushing his pubic bone against hers.

"Holy fuck, that's a lot," she said. "Keep it in there for a minute until I get used to—AH, FUCK, WHAT WAS THAT?"

Jake snorted a laugh. "I bounced my cock in you. Guys can do Kegels too and I did one."

Kayla laughed. "Jesus, it felt like it was alive."

"That's because it is." He twitched again.

"Fuck! Cut it out!" Kayla kept laughing. "Stop making me laugh. We're supposed to be fucking."

"We're comics. We're already fucking funny."

Kayla snorted. "Just fuck me with your big cock and save the jokes for later."

Jake gladly complied and slid his dick almost completely out, leaving only his head between her lips, hesitating for a few seconds. Kayla gave a little whimper at the new emptiness, so Jake pushed deep inside her one more time, and she moaned again. He pulled out one more time and quickly pushed himself inside her again.

"Let me see," said Kayla. "Let me see it go inside me." She propped herself on her elbows again and watched as Jake slid his thick shaft in and out of her eager cunt.

"That thing's inside me," she murmured breathlessly. "I love watching it just go up inside me, it's so big. That looks beautiful."

Jake was holding onto Kayla's calves as he drove inside of her, but he pulled out and quickly grabbed the pillows at the head of the bed.

"What are you doing?" said Kayla

"Put these behind you." She raised up and Jake stacked the pillows behind her back so she could prop herself up and watch his monstrous cock slide in and out of her wetness. He grabbed her ankles and put them on his shoulders, and with one hand, guided his stiff prick back into her hot pussy.

"H-h-hooo, fuck! That got it in deeper," she said. "That's amazing."

Jake held onto Kayla's thighs and reached down with his thumb and rubbed her clit as he pumped himself into her.

"Ungh! Ungh! Ungh!" Jake grunted with each thrust, and Kayla matched him each time he pulled out. "Ohh! Ohh! Ohh!" So it was a little symphony of "Ungh! Ohh! Ungh! Ohh! Ungh! Ohh!" which both of them stored away to laugh about later.

"I'm gonna come in a minute, baby," said Jake. "Oh, fuck, I'm going to come for you. Where do you want it? Where do you want my hot come?"

"On me," moaned Kayla. "I want you to come on me." She played her fingers over her chest and stomach. "Right here. I want you to come on me here."

"I know just the thing," said Jake, smiling. He pulled his cock out of Kayla's pussy one more time and she whimpered at its absence. He opened her legs up and spread his feet apart a little more so he could rest his cock right on her labia. Then he squeezed her legs back together, the pressure holding his cock right against her pussy. He then fucked her thigh gap, rubbing the underside of his cock on her clit, her firm breasts swaying from the motion.

"Ohh, that's new," said Kayla. "I like that a lot!"

"Holy shit, I didn't know how great this would be!" said Jake. "Your pussy is like silk. I'm gonna do it, Kayla. I'm going to come for you."

"Say my name, baby. Say my name."

"Ohh, Kayla, I'm going to come for you, Kayla." Jake began thrusting harder and faster. "Kayla, this is it. Get ready for me."

"Shoot it on me, baby! Shoot that hot jizz on me!"

"Here we go! Here we go, Kay-LAAAAAAAA!" Jake thrust his cock forward one more time, poking its purple head out from between her thighs.

A hot white stream spurted out of the tip and nearly reached Kayla's full mounds. A second rope of come landed between her tits, nearly to her neck. A third jet landed just at her ribs, and the fourth reached a few inches above her belly button. Jake grabbed his cock and jacked off to get a few ghost spurts out and he shuddered as his orgasm subsided.

"Oh, fuck, that was amazing," he groaned. "That was great."

"God, your come is so hot, baby. I can feel the heat from your jizz." She ran her fingers through it, tracing it onto her skin, then stuck her fingers into her mouth. "It's still sweet, too. That was amazing, baby. Thank you so much."

"The pleasure was all mine," said Jake. He went back to holding her legs against his chest, running his fingers over her thighs and calves.

"Well, I hope you don't have anywhere to be tomorrow morning, because I've got a couple more ideas for you to try," said Kayla.

"Anything you want," said Jake. "I've got you covered."

"Yeah, you do," said Kayla, running her fingers in his seed one more time.

CHAPTER 3

"Turn left and you have arrived at your destination," said Jake's phone, mounted to the dashboard.

It was Friday afternoon, two days after Jake and Kayla had fucked. They had tried a few other positions, and the two agreed they had waited too long to hook up and promised to do it again the next time they were working the same venues.

Kayla left the following morning, after the two had fucked in the kitchenette, Jake entering her from behind as she bent over the counter. Before he came, she stopped, knelt down, and slurped Jake's cock into her mouth just as he blew his entire load into her eager mouth. She swallowed every drop and thanked Jake for a mind-blowing night. She said she was never going to be able to finish an open mic without dreaming of "getting fucked by a hot white boy" again.

That next night just before Jake was going to start his second set, he received a text from an old teammate from high school. Alan and Jake had been swimmers together in high school, with

Jake continuing on through college. Meanwhile, Alan had gone to Northwestern University, gotten a degree in Finance, and was now a "wealth advisor" (a polite term for "financial advisor for rich people") in Birmingham. He also handed a few of Jake's non-real estate investments, like part ownership in a small strip mall in the tourist section of Savannah, Georgia, and two high-end car washes in Miami that Jake had never seen.

Jake was actually doing very well financially, thanks to his rentals and other investments. Nowadays, he was earning mid-six figures in a good year, and he did stand-up comedy because it was his passion. He wasn't good enough to earn a full-time living, but he managed to do okay for himself. Jake figured it was a good month if he could support himself with what he earned in standup without touching his investment earnings.

Alan was one of three financial advisors Jake used to keep his portfolio healthy. He had learned long ago never to put all his eggs in a single basket, so if one ever stole from him, they didn't have access to everything. None of them ever had, but Jake's grandfather had once been fairly rich and lost a lot of it when his financial advisor turned out to be "crookeder than a duck's dick"[14] and stole nearly half of Grandpa Johnsen's fortune.

Jake texted Alan he was going to be in Birmingham, so Alan suggested they meet for lunch at his country club. Jake climbed out and pressed the button on his key fob. He surveyed the surroundings. This was a swanky club with plenty of BMWs, Mercedes, and more than a few Teslas parked on the spotless parking lot. The grass was a lush green, and there were enough flowers to make a master gardener cream her tan slacks.

---

[14] A duck's penis is actually corkscrew-shaped.

"Excuse me, but contractors have their own parking in the back," said a voice.

Jake looked around and spotted a woman standing next to a white Mercedes in the next row. She was not very tall, about 5'3", slender, and wearing a white sleeveless designer blouse, black skirt, and black Jimmy Choos, with a chunky gold necklace around her neck.

"I'm sorry?" said Jake.

"That's not a problem. You didn't know," said the woman with a thick Southern accent.

As Jake stepped a little closer, he could see she was in her late 40s, and her hair was a white-blonde, short, sculpted, and sprayed so it looked like she could play football.

"No, I mean, I'm not sure what you said," said Jake.

"I said contractors have their own parking in the back," repeated the woman. "If you're here to work on something or fix something, you have to park in the back."

Jake smiled. "Thank you for letting me know," he said, then turned and walked into the club.

Jake was wearing jeans and a polo shirt, plus a pair of tan leather boat shoes, so he didn't know exactly how he could be mistaken for a contractor. He thought he heard the faint *clip-clop, clip-clop* of angry Jimmy Choos skittering after him, and he increased his pace just a little. He heard the skittering try to keep up and he smiled.

Jake walked to the restaurant entrance and said to the hostess, "Hi, I'm here to meet Alan Johansen."

"Okay, he's already here," said the hostess. "I can take you back to his table. Oh, hi, Mrs. Abernathy."

Jake turned to see the blonde woman who had accosted him in the parking lot. She looked a little surprised and embarrassed to see Jake come to the club's restaurant and ask to meet with someone.

"Can I help you with something?" Jake asked.

Mrs. Abernathy looked up at him. "Er, that is, I was, I mean, I'm meeting someone here."

Jake smiled, his eyes twinkling. "What a coincidence, so am I." Mrs. Abernathy blushed and pretended to look into the restaurant to find her companion.

"I can take you back to your table too, Mrs. Abernathy. Your party isn't here yet," said the hostess. "If you would each follow me."

She turned and walked into the dining area, and Jake held his hand out and gestured for Mrs. Abernathy to walk ahead of him. She mumbled her thanks and followed the hostess.

Jake noticed her ass was toned and pert like she spent hours each week sculpting it in the gym and yoga studio, which she did. She reminded him a bit of Irene Jennings, the yoga instructor he had spent three passionate days with in Indianapolis.[15] Irene was flexible and adventurous, and she had struggled to fit Jake's entire prick inside her, but she took it slow and managed to accommodate his thickness. They occasionally texted dirty pictures to each other, and she would regale him with stories about her man-bunned studio assistant, Dakota, who kept trying to get into her yoga pants without any success.

---

[15] See *Stand Up, Lie Down: Irene in Indianapolis.*

Jake snapped back from his memory as Mrs. Abernathy and the hostess stopped at a table near the middle of the room.

"Your party is here, Mr. Johanssen," said the hostess.

"Johansen," said Alan.

"What?" said the hostess

"Johansen," said Alan.

"What'd I say?" asked the hostess.

"Johanssen," said Alan.

The hostess rolled her eyes and smiled flirtatiously at Alan. "And here you go, Mrs. Abernathy. Mrs. Beauregard should be here any minute."

"Hey buddy, good to see you," said Alan, standing up and wrapping Jake in a bear hug, thumping his back as men do to assure bystanders that this was a non-romantic embrace.

"Great seeing you too," said Jake, settling into his chair.

"How are you doing, Betty?" said Alan to the woman at the next table.

"I'm fine," said Betty Abernathy. "I'm a bit embarrassed, however, because I thought your friend was a contractor and I suggested that he park his truck in the construction parking in the back."

Alan roared with laughter. "He is a bit scruffy-looking, I'll grant you," he said, "but this is Jake Nilsen. We've known each other for almost 15 years. We were on the swim team together in middle school and high school. And now he's a client, too."

"Knellson?" asked Betty.

"No, Nilsen," said Jake.

"Ah. Well, it's a pleasure to meet you, Jake."

"It's nice to meet you, too, Betty," said Jake, raising a hand in greeting.

Alan and Jake ordered drinks and perused the menu as they caught up since their last visit, chatting about old teammates, their families, and Jake's latest tour. Heavily censored, of course. Alan was a conservative Christian Republican who would have been shocked at Jake's sexual adventures.

"Well, shoot," said Betty, looking up from her phone. She gestured for the server. "It looks like Mrs. Beauregard won't be able to make it, I'm afraid. Can I just settle my bill?"

"Is Clarice not coming?" Alan said to Betty.

"No, her husband got called away to New Orleans on business and she's going with him. She doesn't like it when she's home alone for more than a day, so I guess I'm just going to go home."

"Well, you could join us," said Jake. "If that's alright with you, Alan."

"Sure, that would be fine," said Alan, looking a little pleased. He had been hoping to snag Betty and Gene Abernathy as clients, and this was a good first step. When their server returned, Alan said, "Mrs. Abernathy will be joining us instead." Then he silently mouthed and gestured to put her lunch on his bill.

"So what brings you to Birmingham, Jake," asked Betty, once she was settled in and they had placed their orders.

"Oh, well, I'm a standup comic, and I'm on tour in the eastern United States. But Alan is also one of my financial advisors, so I thought I would meet with him and discuss a few options while I was in town."

"How exciting," said Betty. "You must meet some interesting people in your travels."

Jake thought of Irene Jennings again and how he had once lifted her up and impaled her on his dick while she wrapped her legs around his narrow waist. By flexing her legs, and with a little help from Jake, she was able to fuck him as he stood and held her up.

Jake snapped back to reality again as he realized Betty had asked him a question about his standup career. "Oh, I've been doing this for a few years now, and I'm starting to headline in smaller cities. My agent thinks that in a few more years, I could be a regular headliner at the big clubs."

Lunch arrived, and the three of them talked about Jake's work, their respective schooling, and their athletic past. Jake and Alan had been swimmers, although Jake had continued swimming in college. Betty played golf and was in a sorority at Samford University in suburban Birmingham, which is where she had met her husband, Gene.

"We graduated in 1996 and were married six months later," said Betty. "Four years after that, our daughter, Bethany, was born. Now she's in her junior year at Auburn University, studying theater, of all things."

Betty gestured to their server for another white wine, which arrived promptly. The three continued to talk about their exercise regimes—Jake lifting weights and running, Alan running triathlons, and Betty with a strict regimen of yoga and weights—the drinks mellowing them out and relaxing them, Betty getting a little more relaxed than the other two. Soon, the three were laughing and joking like they were old friends reliving hilarious memories.

"And then," said Alan, gasping, "Jake comes out of the showers with a towel around his head and shaving cream on his nipples, and he says—"

Jake interrupted and they said in unison, "There is chartreuse goose juice coming out of Lucy's caboose!"[16]

The three laughed so hard, the older people at the other tables gave them stern looks of "Well, I never," while some of the younger women considered asking to speak to a manager.

"Well, folks, I have to go," said Alan. "Jake, I've got a proposal for you for a tech startup I wanted you to look at. These people are making some new app that they're calling 'Airbnb for cars.' It looks pretty exciting. Betty, if you'd like to take a look at it too, I can forward it to you and Gene as well, if you're interested. Otherwise, I have a 2:00 I have to get to."

"I'd love to see it," said Jake. "And I'll get the bill."

"No, no, it's on me," said Alan.

"You've made me quite a bit of money," said Jake. "I'm happy to cover this one."

"But you're the client, so I'm supposed to pay," protested Alan.

Neither of them noticed Betty slipping the server her Platinum American Express when she brought another glass of wine. "Boys, boys!" she said loudly, "it's covered."

---

[16] This joke actually isn't that funny. I just wanted to make the audio book reader say something that sounded utterly ludicrous. —C.V.

Jake and Alan thanked Betty profusely, and Alan left for his next appointment.

"Thank you again, Betty," said Jake. "I'm glad you were able to join us today."

"I am, too. I wasn't looking forward to lunch with Clarice Beauregard. She may be a friend, but she is so tiresome. She's a member of the Ladies' Auxiliary, Daughters of the Confederacy, Daughters of Alabama, the Women's Society, the Cotillion Beau Monde, Order of the Eastern Star, advisor to the Rainbow Girls, and Birmingham Loves Bach, and I have to hear about the same high school drama bullshit about each group because all the same women are in the same groups."

"Are you involved in any of them?"

"Sadly, I am. I dropped out of the Daughters of the Confederacy five years ago after my daughter loudly pointed out their racist roots to some of the ladies who had come over for tea."

"Ouch."

"It was decided that I would drop out to save everyone the embarrassment of having to remove me or rebuke me publicly."

"But that didn't affect your standing in the other groups?"

"Oh, no, my husband is very wealthy, and you're given a lot more grace when you have money. People will overlook all kinds of flaws and problems if you've got enough money."

"So they didn't let you back into the Daughters of the Confederacy?"

"Well, they asked after an appropriate amount of time passed, but I had realized they actually were a bunch of racist bitches, so I politely declined."

Jake threw his head back and laughed again. "Good for you," he said.

"I'm having quite a nice time with you, Jake. I'm so, so sorry I thought you were a contractor. That really was quite rude of me. You must think I'm quite the stuck-up bitch," said Betty, slurring her words a bit.

"No, not at all. I've enjoyed our time together, and it will be a funny story we can tell the next time we're together."

"When will that be?" Betty blurted out.

Jake was caught off guard. "Oh, whenever you'd like," he said

"Soon, I think," said Betty. "I'd like to do it soon. Hey, do you do yoga?"

"Actually, I do," said Jake. "A friend got me into it a few months ago, and it's done wonders for my back."

"Well, I have a dear friend from college who runs a yoga studio in the Highland Park area. I usually go to her 11:00 class, and then we have lunch afterward. I would love it if you would join us tomorrow. That is if you want to. I'm sorry, I'm rambling. I'm a bit drunk, and it's been a while since I've had a man actually pay attention to me."

"But aren't you married?"

"Yes, I am. And my statement still stands, I haven't had a man pay any kind of attention to me for quite a while. So sometimes I feel a bit lonely."

"Well, I don't see why, because you're fascinating," said Jake, leaning on his elbows. "And I love your accent. It makes me melt."

"Aww, you're making me blush," said Betty, whose neck and chest were also flushed.

"Well, count me in for yoga tomorrow. I'd be happy to join you," said Jake.

"Great, I'll text you the address, and maybe you could join us afterward. Her name's Sheila Goodwin and she's a lot of fun."

CHAPTER 4

"I guess I'd better get home. My husband is leaving for a conference tomorrow, and I should probably make a show of being at home." Betty started to rise then sat back down. "Ooh. Maybe I should call an Uber. I've had a bit too much to drink to drive."

"I'd be happy to drive you home, Betty," said Jake. "That's no problem at all."

"Oh, no Jake, I can't let you do that. I don't want to impose."

"It's really no imposition, Betty. I've enjoyed your company, and anything I can do to extend our time together would make me happy."

Betty teared up again at that. "Why, Jake, that is so sweet. Gene always seems to want to be someplace else."

"Then he's making a big mistake because you're amazing."

"I wish he thought so, because I think he's using this conference as an excuse to sleep with his marketing manager again. He thinks I don't know, but they've been going to a lot of conferences together for the last sixteen months, at least once a month. And there are little indications whenever he comes back home."

"Maybe you need to find someone who can appreciate you for who you are."

"Oh, I could never divorce Gene. One does not do such things in our social circles."

"Who said anything about divorcing him? He found someone to 'appreciate' him." Jake made air quotes. "Maybe you need to be appreciated, too."

"I haven't been properly appreciated for three years," said Betty, smiling through her tears. "I tried self-appreciation, but it's not the same."

"Well, if I were in his shoes, I'd make sure you felt appreciated several times a week."

Betty blushed even further as Jake stood behind her chair and helped her slide it back to stand up. He offered his arm, and Betty slipped her hand through the crook of his elbow, leaning on him to avoid tipping over. Most of the club members had left and the staff was cleaning up to get ready for the dinner service as the two strolled out into the nearly empty parking lot.

"We can take your car, and then I'll just Uber back here to get my truck," said Jake.

"That sounds like a splendid idea," said Betty, leaning her head on Jake's bicep and squeezing his forearm.

She handed him the keys, and he held her hand and lowered her into the car before closing the door. Jake climbed in, adjusted the seat, and began to ease out of the parking space. Betty clipped her phone into the dashboard holder, fired up Waze, and hit the button to guide them back to her home. As Jake drove, he rested his right hand on the shifter between the two of them. Betty rested her hand on his and gave a gentle squeeze. She looked up at Jake and smiled before removing his hand from the shifter and resting it on her bare thigh.

Betty began pushing his hand to indicate she wanted him to rub her thigh, which he did, slowly. She reached up and unbuttoned one of her blouse buttons, exposing her cleavage. While her breasts weren't as big as Kayla's had been two nights ago, they were still a handful. He remembered the description about Irene—"a lollipop with tits"—and thought that was an apt description for Betty. She was small, muscular, and tight, and her breasts were bigger than he had realized. They were full and round, about the size of softballs. She had clearly had some work done as well, but Jake was an aficionado of women's breasts, and he appreciated all shapes, sizes, and configurations.

He ran his hand up and down Betty's thigh, sliding her skirt a little higher. Betty raised up and pulled her skirt up so there were only a few inches covering her lap. Jake rested his hand on her skin and he felt her get goosebumps under his gentle stroking.

"I'm so much older than you, Jake," said Betty. "Why would you want an old woman like me?"

"First of all, you're not an old woman. You may be older than me, but I think you're gorgeous. Besides, I'm older than you think."

"How old are you?"

"I'm 27."

Betty laughed. "I'm nearly old enough to be your mother."

"Yes, but I'm old enough to appreciate you several times in one night." Betty breathed in sharply as Jake slid his hand up toward her heavenly mound. "Besides, you look way, way younger. I would have guessed you were old enough to be my hot aunt. You know, the one who never got married and flirts shamelessly with her nephews."

Betty laughed again. "Hot aunt it is. Only not really, because that does sound a bit creepy."

"Agreed."

They drove on quietly, Jake kneading Betty's upper thigh.

"You have such gentle hands for someone so strong," she said. "Oh, turn right here."

"But that's the opposite way from your house," said Jake, nodding at the directions on Waze.

"I know. If you turn right, it will take ten minutes to get home. If you turn left, it will take two."

"Ah," said Jake.

He pushed her skirt up higher, pausing in case she wanted him to stop, but she said nothing. Instead, she pushed his hand the rest of the way up until he was touching her pussy through her panties.

"Oohhhhhhhhh," moaned Betty. "That's it. Touch me there." Jake stroked his finger between her legs, feeling her silken panties get wetter with each stroke. "Mmmmmmmmmm," she moaned again. "I haven't been touched there in a long time, Jake. Touch me. Touch me on my … vagina." Betty seemed reluctant to say the actual words like she wasn't used to talking dirty.

Jake could sympathize since he was often too embarrassed to talk dirty on the phone. He could only do it when he was physically with a woman, then his inhibitions dropped.

"You mean your pussy?" he said. "Do you want me to touch your wet pussy?"

"Yes, Jake, please. Touch my hot, wet pussy. Slip your finger into my pussy."

Jake slid her panties to the side—they were red and silky, he noticed—and found her folds and her clit. He gently stroked up her lips, dragging his finger over her clit. As Jake drove, the GPS rerouted them through a quiet neighborhood and he followed the new directions, even as he fingered her wetness.

"Ooooohhhhhh," she moaned, spreading her legs further apart. "More, Jake, please."

Jake obliged, slipping his digit inside her sweet slit and she groaned even louder. "Oh, God, yes. Ho, fuck. Finger my pussy and rub my pearl."

Jake slid his finger in up to his second knuckle and slid it back out again, pulling it across her clit. "How do you taste?" he asked.

"Oh, don't," said Betty. "Gene said I don't taste good. He only ever went down on me once and he said he didn't like it."

Jake pulled his finger out of her folds and licked it like a popsicle. "Mmmmm," he said. He licked another side. "You taste wonderful. I want to get my tongue inside you." He slid his finger back into Betty's wetness and she moaned and half-sobbed when he did. Jake continued sliding his middle finger into her cunt.

"Ooohhhh!" moaned Betty, even louder. "More, do that some more."

Jake complied and picked up the pace a little bit, but still inserted his finger gently.

"Oh, fuck. I think I'm going to come," she declared, a little surprised. "I think I'm going to—oh God, I'm going to—oh yes! Yes! Yes! I'm—OH, FFFUUUCCCKKK!"

Betty grabbed onto Jake's forearm and shuddered, as he slid his finger on her clit a couple more times, stopping when her shudders did.

"Oh, shit," she said. "I don't think I've ever come like that. Gene has never done that to me. I certainly do feel appreciated now." She gasped for breath, inhaling deeply as Jake slid his finger out of her pussy a final time. He put his finger in his mouth, tasting her wetness.

"You taste like honey," he said. "I definitely want to lick your pussy when we get to your house."

At a stop sign, he leaned over and quickly kissed Betty, darting his tongue into her mouth so she could taste herself a little.

"Mmm. Maybe I'll be able to go down on you too," she said. "I know how to do that very well. Most of us sorority girls know how to suck a cock. Gene certainly doesn't mind it, but he just won't do it for me."

"You're a gorgeous woman, Betty Abernathy. You deserve to be loved and appreciated. And right now, I actually do appreciate you, truly. Just sitting with you, making you happy? That makes me happy."

Betty swallowed hard a few times and blinked back tears. "Thank you, Jake. I want you and to be with you. Maybe we can tomorrow, and you can appreciate me a few more times?"

"Count on it. Wherever and whenever you'll have me, I want to enjoy and appreciate you as much as we both can handle."

Betty straightened herself up, pulled her skirt back down, and opened up the windows so the car didn't smell like her sex. She checked her makeup in the mirror and straightened her hair. Then she reached over and gave Jake's hard cock a few squeezes.

"If that's as big as I think it is, we're going to have a hell of a time making it fit." She squeezed it again. "But we're going to have a lot of fun trying."

The GPS announced, "You have arrived at your destination" and Jake pulled into the driveway.

"Oh, fuck," said Betty. "Gene's home already."

The front door opened and a tall, balding man with a paunch came outside, looking a little confused. *Who was this young man driving his wife's car? And why was she in the passenger seat?*

Jake and Betty got out of the car, and Jake introduced himself. "Hi, Mr. Abernathy, my name is Blake Schenectady. I work at the country club. Mrs. Abernathy wasn't feeling well, so I offered to take her home in her car." Betty carefully walked around the car and stood next to her husband without touching him.

Gene looked confused for a moment then broke into a big smile. "Oh, that's wonderful, just wonderful. Thank you, er, Drake. That's a fine thing." He pulled out his wallet and said, "Here, let me get you something."

"No, thank you. It's no problem at all, sir."

"How are you going to get back though?" asked Gene.

"I thought I would just call an Uber and head back there."

"I certainly can pay for your Uber though." He opened his wallet and pulled out a $100 bill. "Here you go, I hope that covers it."

"Oh, that's plenty. Thank you very much."

"Excellent. Well, thank you again. I'd better get Mrs. Abernathy inside and put her to bed." He turned around and walked toward the house ahead of Betty.

Betty turned back, even as Gene kept walking. "Goodbye, Blake," she called, winking. Then she mouthed the words, "Text me" and made the texting motion with her thumbs. Jake nodded, blew her a kiss, and pulled out his phone to call for an Uber.

Then he sent a quick text. "Looking forward to tomorrow.

CHAPTER 5

"Okay, now into Reclined Goddess and hold for 20..." Sheila called gently over the Eastern-influenced yoga music.

Jake and Betty were two of 12 students in the Highland Park yoga studio at that time of day, and Jake was the only man. It certainly attracted a lot of attention from the women in the group, and it was all Betty could do to keep from snarling at the women to keep their claws off her new boyfriend, but she knew better. Besides, she had plans for him later on.

Jake and Betty had met in the parking lot behind the studio and exchanged a brief hug, but couldn't let anyone else know about their intentions since a few of Betty's friends also did yoga with her. She did tell him she had some special plans and a surprise for him for lunch.

"Now, feet up into Happy Baby. This is good for your back, right Jake?" said Sheila.

Betty had introduced her to Jake before they started, and he told her about how he was introduced to yoga a few months ago as a cure for back pain. He didn't tell them about the hot sex with Irene, of course, but he did say she had managed to straighten him out and solve his back issues.

Sheila made an adjustment to the direction Jake's ankle was turned and ran her hand down the back of his thigh nearly to his butt.

"You should feel something right here." She slid her hand around the inside of his thigh, letting her fingers run across his cock, and gave his thigh a squeeze. "I know I want to," she whispered.

Jake was in the back of the room next to Betty, he popped his head up and looked over at Betty, who was watching them and smiling. She gave Jake a wink and puckered a kiss at him. He realized what the surprise was going to be, and he nodded and smiled.

Sheila was about Betty's size—5'3", built like a dancer or a serious yogi, but hadn't had the same work done as Betty. Where Betty was built up to be beautiful—and she was very beautiful—Sheila was a natural beauty whose strawberry blonde hair and freckles would turn a lot of heads. She was slender and willowy, her legs and arms showed serious muscle, and her butt was tight and her shoulders were like little cannonballs. Sheila glided gracefully around the room, giving small directions to her students as they moved through the flow. Her sandy blond hair was pulled back into a ponytail and when she smiled, smile lines appeared around her eyes and mouth.

As a comic, Jake could tell who the laughers were in a crowd by their smile lines. The more they had, or the deeper they were, he knew they would be a good audience and he would target them with his jokes, calling on them during audience interactions. Sheila looked like a woman who loved to laugh, and he liked her for it.

"Finally, lower yourself slowly into savasana, or the corpse pose. Don't fall asleep, Helen." The others chuckled quietly.

After class ended, and the others were filing out, Betty and Jake stayed behind to continue chatting with Sheila as she locked the door. "So, this is the president of the Betty Abernathy Appreciation Society?" Sheila asked.

"He is, and he made me feel very appreciated on the ride home yesterday," said Betty, putting her arm through his. "Would you like to join our little society?"

"Well, I was just thinking after our phone call last night that I hadn't felt appreciated in a while either. And from the way you described your new friend, I wondered if he would be able to appreciate the both of us."

Betty looked up at Jake and smiled. "And I said he probably could. What do you say, Jake? Do you think you can handle two old ladies?"

"Do you even want to?" said Sheila.

"Well," said Jake, putting his arm around Betty's waist then Sheila's, "if I see any old ladies, I'll let you know. But until they show up, I'd love to show my appreciation for both of you." He leaned down and kissed Betty deeply, crushing her to him. Then he pulled Sheila to him and kissed her as well, his tongue sliding between her teeth and caressing her tongue. "Do you have any place special in mind? Or should we just be on the floor here?"

"I have a small apartment upstairs that I let friends use sometimes, but it's empty. The bed is even made."

"Then lead the way," said Jake.

They followed Sheila to a door and up a long flight of stairs.

"The studio is closed until our next class at 5:00, so we've got a few hours to ourselves," she said.

When they reached the top of the stairs, Jake lifted Betty into his arms. She held onto his neck and gazed up at him, smiling at his attention. He carried Betty across the threshold and kissed her again before setting her down.

"I'm going to shower first because I've taught three classes today. Do you want to join me?" offered Sheila.

"Sure, that would be lovely," said Betty.

She looked straight into Jake's eyes and peeled off her tank top and unzipped her sports bra, exposing her softball-sized globes. They were firm and did not sag and they were a physical contrast to her flat, trim belly.

Jake took his t-shirt off and pulled Betty back to him so he could feel her skin against his. He kissed her again, rubbing his strong hands up and down her back. Sheila put her hands on both of their backs, her shirt now off as well. Jake pivoted a little and welcomed Sheila into their embrace. He kissed Sheila deeply again then raised up and put a tiny bit of pressure on both Betty's and Sheila's backs to get them to move closer together.

Betty got the hint and kissed Sheila on the mouth. Sheila wasn't shy and returned the kiss, sliding her tongue in and out of Betty's mouth. The two women gave each other long, wet kisses as Jake leaned down and sucked one of Betty's nipples then Sheila's.

He inched his way behind Betty and cupped her mounds in his hands, gently squeezing and massaging them, playing with her nipples, and causing her to moan into Sheila's mouth. Jake stuck his thumbs into Betty's waistband and slid her yoga pants down to her ankles. He stepped on them and Betty stepped out of her pants, all while still kissing Sheila.

Next, he stepped behind Sheila in the same way. He cupped her breasts which were smaller and hung a little lower, but years of yoga had kept her firm and supple. Jake pinched her large nipples until they were like pencil erasers, and she moaned with delight. He slid Sheila's yoga pants down as well, then cupped one of her breasts in his large hand and slid the other down to her mound. Her pubic hair was short and neatly trimmed, with only a thin strip of hair guiding the way down to her heavenly folds. He slipped a finger slightly into her pussy and pulled her back into him, letting her feel his hard cock against her.

"Ohh," she cooed. "I definitely think we need that shower now." She reluctantly broke away from Betty and Jake and walked to the bathroom.

Jake held Betty's hand and felt her trembling. "Are you okay?" he asked.

Betty smiled, eyes watering. "I haven't felt this appreciated in years," she said. "And I mean that in the real sense of the word. Whatever else we do, thank you."

"No, thank you," said Jake. "I'm honored that you trust me enough for this, and I'm looking forward to showering you with attention."

"Heh, don't get any ideas that this is going to be flowers and love making though. I want you to fuck me 'til I can't walk straight."

"Me too," said Sheila, turning on the shower.

It was a walk-in shower big enough for the three of them, with large slate-gray tiles and a shower head big enough for two of them directly overhead.

"I wanted a luxury apartment in case I ever left my husband and moved in here," she said. "He's at the same conference as Gene, probably for the same reason, so I think we're going to use it for the next few days."

"Now, let's see what you've been saving for me since yesterday," said Betty. She knelt down before Jake and pulled at his shorts. "Ho-o-o-oly shit!" she said as his meaty cock sprang out and nearly slapped her in the face. "That thing's thick enough to choke an Alabama Belle. Or even two of us." She and Sheila stroked it with their small hands and thin fingers, which made Jake's cock look even bigger.

The three lovers stepped into the shower and began soaping each other's bodies, paying special attention to their erogenous zones. When Betty and Sheila were soaping Jake's cock for the third time, he warned, "I'm going to come if you keep doing that."

"Mmmm, I want that, but I don't want to waste it on a soap handy," said Sheila. She took a removable shower wand off the wall and rinsed Jake's dick and balls, making him spread his legs so she could clean his undercarriage.

"Looks like someone's a shaver," said Sheila.

"It's been a while since I've sucked off a shaver," said Betty.

"Me too," said Sheila.

"I think it was the same guy in college," said Betty.

"Same night, too," said Sheila, kissing Betty one more time before turning and sucking Jake deep into her mouth.

As Sheila bobbed up and down on Jake's dick, Betty shifted her attention to his balls, gently sucking one then the other into her mouth. She jacked off the lower half of Jake's cock for several seconds, while Sheila took as much of Jake into her mouth as she could.

"My turn," Betty said eventually. As Sheila moved aside, Betty vacuumed up Jake's massive prick and hit the back of her throat with it.

"*Gulk*," she gagged. "*Gulk. Gulk. Gulk. Gulk.*"

Betty repeated the gagging sound as she bobbed her own head up and down on Jake's member. The two women took turns sucking Jake, while the other suckled his balls and jacked off the lower half of his shaft.

After several minutes of their ministrations, Jake could feel the boiling sensation in his nut sack beginning. "Ohh, this is it, ladies, I'm going to come," he said, pronouncing it his favorite way. "You're going to make me come. Who wants it in their mouth?"

"You're Betty's new boyfriend, I think she should get the honor of the first load."

"Agreed," said Jake.

"You would have agreed if I said Sheila could have it," said Betty smiling, still stroking his dick.

"As long as I can come in someone's mouth, I'll be happy," said Jake. He stroked his cock, using his other hand to position Betty's head for optimal aim.

"Ooh, let me," said Sheila. She stood behind Jake and wrapped her fingers around his hard shaft and gently massaged his balls. She stroked it slowly at first but picked up speed slightly as Jake's thighs tensed up.

"Oh, that's good. That's going to make me come, Sheila. Make me come for Betty. Open your mouth, baby, I'm going to come in your mouth."

Betty moved into position as Sheila guided Jake's cock so the head was resting on Betty's bottom lip. "Look at me when you do it," she said.

"Ohhhhh," moaned Jake. "I'm going to come. I'm going to—AHHHHHHHHHHH!!!" Sheila jacked his cock furiously as his hot jizz spurted into Betty's waiting mouth and Jake fought to maintain eye contact.

"Unnh," she moaned with her mouth open, as each sweet-salty shot landed in her mouth. "Unnh. Unnh. Unnh. Unnh." Five blasts of come filled Betty's mouth as Sheila knelt down next to her and kissed her deeply, her tongue swirling into the come. She broke away and smacked her lips, even as Betty made a big show of swallowing every drop of white gold Jake had given her.

Jake turned off the water to the shower and reached for a towel.

"We're not done, are we?" whined Betty.

"Oh, no," said Jake. "I want to eat your sweet pussy, and I want to eat Sheila's pussy, and I want you each to help me do that, but I want to do it on the bed. That will give me time to recover, and then I can fuck both of your hot cunts as much as you want."

If both women hadn't been on their knees already, they would have buckled at Jake's plans. They toweled each other off and they filed out of the bathroom to the bedroom and a queen-sized bed with a navy-blue bedspread.

"Sheila, will you help me lick Betty's pussy?" he said, holding out his hand.

"I can't wait," said Sheila. Betty lay back on the bed, propping herself up on her elbows.

"Wait, I know a trick for that," said Jake, propping up the pillows behind her. He knelt down before Betty and spread her legs apart with his strong hands. He kneaded her thighs, massaging her in a way no one had done for years, then flicked his tongue over her pussy once, twice, thrice.

"Mmmm, I was right. You do taste like honey," he said.

"Ooh, let me try," said Sheila. She lapped up Betty's slit and groaned in appreciation as Betty moaned under her touch.

"Oh, that's lovely," Betty mumbled. "Yes, more of that please."

Jake and Sheila were only too happy to oblige, each taking turns licking up Betty's slit and flicking their tongues over her clitoris as she gripped the bed covers tightly. Jake slid one finger into Betty's wet pussy, slowly sliding it in and out as he licked her pink pearl. With his other hand, he reached up and kneaded Betty's beautiful tits, squeezing them and pinching her nipples even as he slurped at her folds.

"Now it's your turn," he said to Sheila.

Jake moved aside, and Sheila took his place. She slid her finger into Betty's dripping cunt and licked it several times, before putting her mouth over Betty's mound and alternating between sucking her lips and sliding her tongue into Betty's heavenly folds. As Jake retook his place and ate Betty's wet slit, she moaned with each new finger that was introduced and was huffing in time with every thrust of their fingers. Sheila also massaged one of Betty's wonderful tits as Jake sucked the other nipple.

"Now both of us," grunted Jake, and Sheila slid her finger in with his, while the two of them both groped her firm mounds.

"Oohhhh!" said Betty. "Ohh fuck, that's so tight. I can't believe you're both finger fucking my cunt." Sheila and Jake fell into a rhythm of finger fucking her together and licking a few times each on her hard clit until she moaned louder. "Ohh, fuck! That's it, right there. Right there. Don't stop, just keep doing that. Keep doing—oh GOD, OH FUUUUCKK!!!!"

Betty threw her head back onto the pillows, yelling and trembling as her orgasm overtook her. She didn't quite pass out, but she closed her eyes to recover briefly. Jake and Sheila withdrew their fingers from between Betty's sopping lips. Jake held Sheila's wrist and put her finger, still wet with Betty's cunt juice, in his mouth, sucking it clean. Sheila took Jake's finger and did the same.

"Do you want some of that, too?"

Sheila's eyes widened. "You know I do!" She climbed up on the bed next to Betty, briefly sucked on one of Betty's nipples, then lay back and spread her legs wide. A few drops of moisture glistened on Sheila's fat cunt lips and Jake licked them off as if he were cleaning off an ice cream cone. Several heavy licks up her engorged labia, darting it between her folds and over her clit, and Sheila was groaning almost as loudly as Betty had.

As Jake continued to munch on Sheila's pink snatch, Betty had sufficiently recovered to raise up and suck one of Sheila's hard nipples into her mouth, pinching the other one with her fingers. Jake ran his fingers up Betty's leg and cupped her still hot mound under his palm, massaging it gently.

"Betty, come eat Sheila's pussy with me," Jake said gently, and both women moaned at hearing him say their names with something so dirty.

"Yes, please eat my pussy, Betty," groaned Sheila.

"I would love to eat your beautiful cunt," purred Betty, and she and Jake lapped at Sheila's lips until she was breathing heavily and moaning their names.

Betty slipped her finger into Sheila's lips and sucked on her clit, like Jake and Sheila had done for her. Jake flicked his tongue on Sheila's clit, even as Betty finger-banged her. Every few seconds, she would withdraw her finger and Jake would put his mouth over Sheila's wet hole and drive his tongue in as deeply as he could. Then Betty slid two fingers inside Sheila while licking her pearl.

"Ohh, sweet fuck, Betty. That's so good. Keep doing that because I'm going to—I'm gonna—I'm gonna … COOOMMMMMEE!!! AAAAAAHHHHHHHH!!" Sheila's body tensed up and she jerked three times like electricity was coursing through her body. A small amount of fluid shot from her pussy onto Betty's face as she screamed a final time. "FUUUUUUCCCKK!!"

She fell back, panting heavily. "I squirted. Holy shit, Betty, you made me squirt. I actually came on your face." Betty licked her lips and used her fingers to delicately wipe Sheila's fluid from her cheeks. Jake helped lick the juices from Betty's face and they kissed, wildly intertwining their tongues, tasting Sheila's come in each other's mouths.

"Fuck, that's hot," said Jake. "I've never seen a woman actually squirt before. I've always wanted to because I wanted to taste it."

Sheila said, "I've only ever done it once before, and that was at a college party when I fucked two guys for hours. At one point, I was on my back and one guy was buried in my cunt up to the hilt, and the other was shoving his cock in my mouth while my head hung over the bed. It was so hot, plus I was on Ecstasy at the time, and I squirted when I came."

"That does sound hot," said Betty, rubbing her pussy again. She looked up at Jake. "And now I want you inside me, Jake." Betty climbed back onto the bed again, next to Sheila. "Please, Jake. My pussy is aching for your big prick. Oh, please put it inside me."

"As you wish." Jake smiled. "I've been thinking about this since I met you."

"You mean at lunch?" she asked.

"No, in the parking lot," he said. "I saw you there in your tight skirt and your fuck-me shoes, and your pearl necklace, and I imagined bending you over your car and filling your cunt."

"Then do it, lover. Fill my cunt with your meat and then with your come."

"I told you that would be a great story," he said with a smile.

"I want to see this," said Sheila, raising up.

Jake stood up and positioned himself between Betty's thin, muscular legs. Sheila grabbed Jake's hard cock and guided it toward Betty's waiting snatch. He let himself be guided and pushed himself in until Betty put her hand on his chest; Sheila watched Betty's lips shift and move around Jake's thick shaft.

"Ohhhhh, fuck it's so big. I need a minute to adjust." Jake was about three inches inside her and he could feel her muscles clenching and trying to accommodate this new sensation. "Okay, go slow," she said. Jake eased himself deeper until Betty put her hand on his chest again. She gazed up at him intently, her blue eyes searching his, conveying so much more than her words could. "I love this, Jake. I love how you make me feel. You feel so good inside me. I just haven't had anyone inside me in a while. And definitely never this big."

"I'm here for whatever you need," said Jake, smiling. "You're beautiful—you're both beautiful—and I'm enjoying every second with you. This is all about you, so use my cock however you need it."

Betty blinked back tears again and Sheila scooted up to kiss her deeply, fondling one of her round breasts as she did. Jake pulled his cock back out partly and slid inside once again to where he had stopped before. He slid out one more time and slid back in, out again and in again, each time, returning to six inches of depth.

On the third push, Jake slowly eased himself further and Betty opened her mouth as if she were screaming, but she didn't make a sound or stop him. Once Jake had buried himself to the hilt, he waited for a few seconds.

"How is it? Are you okay?"

"I'm better than okay. My pussy is full and I feel loved." She kissed Sheila one more time and Jake leaned down and kissed her.

He pulled out once more and slid his full eight-and-a-half inches all the way back in, and Betty was able to handle it without any discomfort, so he pulled out and pushed in again. Several more times and Jake was able to build up a good rhythm as Betty's cunt stretched and lubricated to handle the fleshy invader as it plumbed depths Betty hadn't felt in nearly 28 years.

"Oohhh. Oohhh. Oohhh." Betty sighed with each deep thrust. "Oohhh. Oohhh. Oohhh."

Jake kept up a slow-but-steady rhythm for several minutes, holding Betty's calves at his waist, and pushing himself into Betty.

He looked down at his new lover, and they gazed deeply into each other's eyes as he glided in and out of her welcoming folds.

Sheila lay on her back, next to Betty, legs apart, and fingered her pussy. "I'm ready for that cock, too, big boy. Can I borrow him for a few minutes, Betty?"

"Sure, I just want his first load."

"Deal. As long as I can get the ne—OH, WOW! SHIT!" Sheila grabbed Betty's wrist as Jake pushed his dick into Sheila's wet snatch.

She was looser than Betty, but not by much. Jake was able to get himself in halfway before he stopped. He repeated the same slow, easy thrusting, returning to his stopping point until he felt Sheila relax enough that he could continue in until he bottomed out again, and he held onto her knees to keep her pelvis tilted up to receive him.

"Sweet holy fucker," panted Sheila. "That's so huge. Betty, you just had this thing in your pussy and now it's in mine. I'm so turned on right now just thinking about that. This cock was in your cunt and now it's in my cunt. H-h-hoooo, fuck, this is so great. Fuck me with that thing, Jake. Fuck Betty and me with the same prick."

Betty leaned over Sheila and kissed her deeply now, fondling her smaller tits and occasionally sucking her nipples. Sheila pulled her legs away from Jake. "Watch this," she said and spread her legs until they were nearly in horizontal splits. Jake grabbed her forearms for leverage to pull himself deeper.

"Hunh! Hunh! Hunh!" grunted Sheila. "Fuck, that's deep. You're so deep in me right now, Jake!"

Betty climbed above Sheila, hovering her head over Sheila's tits, and leaving her own tits hanging over Sheila's mouth. The two women sucked each other's nipples for several minutes as Jake slowly slid in and out of Sheila's pussy. Then Betty got up and stood behind Jake. She gripped Sheila's thighs and pulled so both she and Jake could fuck her harder.

"That's it, lover," said Betty. "Let's fuck my new girlfriend with your fat prick. I'm going to help you fuck her." She shoved Jake's ass with each forward thrust, slamming him into Sheila's hungry snatch.

"OH! OH! OH! OH!" barked Sheila. "Oh, fuck me, you bitches. Both of you fuck me!" Jake and Betty continued to hammer Sheila's beautiful muff before Jake felt the familiar tingling in his balls. He needed to stall before he blew his load and he wanted his first one to be for Betty.

"I'm getting close. Betty, get on your hands and knees," said Jake. Betty quickly got back onto the bed and presented her ass to Jake.

"Like this, lover," she purred. "Are you going to fuck me from behind? Oh, take me from behind, Jake. I haven't been fucked like this since college. Make me feel young again, Jake."

"I keep telling you, you ... *are* ... young!" Jake grunted as he thrust himself back inside Betty's wet honeypot. "Young and beautiful. I love being inside you."

He slid right in, burying himself again without any resistance and Betty smiled as she shrieked. "Oooooh. Oh, you're so big, lover! Oh, I love the feeling of that big cock. Isn't he wonderful, Sheila?"

"Oh, yes, we're going to wear you out before you leave town, Jake," said Sheila. She slid under Betty's body until her head was directly under her friend's pussy and she could watch Jake's massive prick sliding in and out of her friend's canal.

Sheila reached up and gently fondled Jake's ball sack and rubbed Betty's clit. Jake moaned as Sheila slid her tongue on the underneath side of his shaft. He slowed his thrusting so he could feel her tongue more as he pulled out and pushed in. With a free hand, Sheila was also fingering her own pussy and rubbing her clit, keeping up with the pace of Jake's fucking.

"Oh, Betty, you've got such a wonderful pussy. It's so wet and tight and it feels like a velvet glove wrapped around my cock. I'm going to come in a minute, so tell me where you want it. Do you want me to fill up your pussy, Betty, or do you want a mouthful of come, Sheila?"

"Come inside me," said Betty. "I want you to come inside me, Jake. I want you to fill up my wet, MILF pussy with your hot, hot jizz."

Betty's sexy talk made Jake's blood boil and he grabbed onto her hips and drove deep pile-driving thrusts into her cunt as Sheila lay back, eyes wide open, to watch every slap of his body against Betty's ass, watching his giant dick disappear into her tiny love hole.

Jake grunted with each pounding, "Nngh! Nngh! Nngh! Nngh! Nngh!" He pulled Betty back toward him and their bodies crashed together, Betty's toned ass jiggling with each impact until Jake roared. "This is it, Betty! I'm going to come for you, Betty!"

"Ohh, I'm coming too, Jake! Fill me up! Fill up my wet pussy with your hot come. I'm coming for you! Oh, Jake, I love yoooooooouuuu!"

"I love you too, Betty! I love—GAAAAAAAHHHHHH!!!!"

Underneath both of them, Sheila moaned through her own orgasm—"Hhhunnnnnhhhhhhhhh"—brought about by her own adept fingers and hearing Jake and Betty's moaned declarations.

Jake blasted a rocket load of hot come that painted Betty's insides, a second blast recoated them, and a third one filled her completely. The fourth and fifth ones were just showing off, so Jake pulled out to share them with Sheila who sucked them out of Jake's cock and felt them trickling down her throat. She slurped as much of Jake into her mouth as she could to clean him off then raised up and sucked some of Jake's still-hot come out of Betty's pussy.

The three lovers were soaked in sweat and trembling from their efforts. Jake climbed into bed and the two women lay on either side of him. He pulled them close and kissed each of them, savoring their naked skin pressed against his.

"Holy fuck, that was intense," said Jake. "That was amazing. Don't ever let anyone tell you you're too old, because that was maybe the most intense sex I've ever had."

"Oh God, for me too," said Sheila. "I was only frigging my button, but listening to you two, that put me over the edge. I came right when you two did."

"That was the deepest orgasm I've ever felt, and I think your come reached my liver, Jake. I can feel it inside my pussy."

"I know I haven't come that hard. And I've never done it with two women."

"I've never been in a threesome before either," said Betty.

"This wasn't my first, but it's by far my favorite," said Sheila.

"I'm sorry for what I said though, Jake," said Betty. "I was caught up in the heat of the moment. I didn't mean to say it. It doesn't count and I don't want to scare you away."

"Oh, no, don't apologize," said Jake. "I was caught up too, and I said it too. I know we said something that we maybe won't feel tomorrow, but we felt it today. This was very special, and it stirred up some emotions in both of us.

"So for right now, for as long as I'm here and you'll both have me, we can feel this way, and we can say it this weekend, even if it doesn't last. We'll be a temporary couple—well, a throuple—and say it whenever we feel like it, and it'll be true. It will be true for us for as long as we're with each other. And when I leave, we'll go back to the way we were before. But for the next three days, I love you, Betty Abernathy."

"I love you too, Jake Nilsen." The two kissed deeply.

"What about me?" asked Sheila.

Jake kissed Sheila, and then Betty kissed her. "I love you as well, Sheila Goodwin," said Jake.

"And I love you, Jake Knellson."

"Nilsen," corrected Betty, smiling.

Chastity Veldt

Carrie on Campus

Stand Up, Lie Down Collection

TABLE OF CONTENTS

Chapter 1

"Welcome to Abraxus Tasker College," read the formal-looking sign with raised letters on a steel background supported between two brick bases.

Jake Nilsen drove his truck past the sign that marked the official entrance to Abraxus Tasker College and welcomed him to this seat of higher learning.

"What's the Deal With the XTC Comedy Weekend?" read a 20-foot vinyl banner stretched across the main street. Jake rolled his eyes at the tired old comic's phrase and hoped they were using it ironically.

"Get Ali Whippe's XTC erotica books from 4 Horsemen Publishing on Amazon!" read a spray-painted bedsheet hastily yanked into place by book-loving hooligans and ne'er-do-wells.

Jake thought, *Wait, am I in some kind of crossover?*

'No, that's weird,' said the author. 'Just focus on your driving.'

Jake decided that sounded weird, and he focused on his driving.

His GPS told him to make his final turn to the visitor parking next to the XTC student center and the signs directed him to the check-in. A few minutes later, he was at the registration table.

On this Tuesday morning, Jake was in town for the Abraxus Tasker Comedy Conference and Festival, a five-day, well, comedy conference and festival where young comics from around the country could perform sets in the evening at different venues around campus, as well as take workshops on comedy writing, improv, performing, and the business of comedy.

Jake had been contacted by his agent, telling him the Abraxus Tasker organizers had specifically asked for him and a few other comics to attend to teach some workshops and perform a set or two on Saturday night. He managed to arrive in town the day before the conference started because he wanted to relax and recover from his gig in Birmingham.[17]

The festival was one of the leading college comedy conferences in the country; Jake had originally attended many years ago when he first started learning comedy during his college years. It felt weird to be coming back as an instructor and performer nearly eight years later.

A lot had changed for Jake since then. He had been a swimmer on the University of Minnesota swim team and had nearly earned a spot on the U.S. Olympic team but missed it by two-tenths of a second. After he graduated, he threw himself into comedy and improv, living off some smart real estate investments he had made while still an undergraduate, buying up dilapidated houses, fixing them up, and renting them to college students. With a real estate

---

[17] See *Stand Up, Lie Down: Betty in Birmingham*

portfolio of nearly twenty rentals, as well as some car washes in Miami that he had never seen, he wasn't quite rich, but he could see rich from his house.

He continued swimming and working out, making sure he stayed in shape. Jake had toyed with the idea of making a comeback but was having too much fun as a standup comic.

Maybe in another year, he thought.

Jake had been performing standup comedy professionally for five years and was actually able to live on his earnings from comedy, even as his investments continued to grow and pile up. His former U-of-M teammate, Alan Johansen, was now his wealth advisor, and he continued to grow Jake's investments to nearly seven figures.[18]

"Hi, I'm Jake Nilsen, I'm here to check-in for the festival."

The young man sitting behind the table looked up. "Hi, I'm Justin Cooper." He clattered a few keys on his laptop. "Let's see, you've got your own check-in station down there."

"Really?" said Jake. "Why?"

Justin just held up his hands and shrugged. His muscular arms filled out a Stallions Football t-shirt, arms that looked like they were capable of holding a tall redhead upside down for several minutes,[19] and said, "Sorry, I'm just filling in a friend—I mean, filling in for a friend—I wasn't really supposed to be here today."

---

[18] See *Stand Up, Lie Down: Betty In Birmingham*

[19] See *Extra Credit (Abraxus Tasker College Book 4)* by Ali Whippe. BECAUSE THIS *IS* A CROSSOVER!

Jake thanked him and walked to the other end of the row of tables and found a blonde co-ed with a bright smile. Her name tag said, *Cheree.*

"Cherry?" asked Jake.

"No, not since my fresh—er, that is, it rhymes with 'Sherry.'" said Cheree, looking Jake up and down and liking what she saw.

"I'm Jake Nilsen."

"Nilsin?" said Cheree, looking down at her laptop.

"No, Nilsen."

"Ah. Here you are," said Cheree. "Welcome to our fair city of—" She was interrupted when a table of steel travel coffee mugs collapsed.

"Sorry about that. That's the second time that's happened today. Anyway, you're our VIP talent." She waved her hand at a small plate of jalapeño poppers. "Would you like a popper?"

"No, thank you. What do you mean I'm your VIP talent?" asked Jake.

"You're the headliner for the main night in the Pickles venue, plus you're one of the celebrity judges, so that makes you a VIP. *The* VIP, in fact. Out of all our IPs, you're the Vee-est." Cheree laughed at her little joke.

"Wait, hold on. Celebrity judges? VIP? My agent didn't tell me anything about this."

"Really? I'm so sorry. Yes, we specifically wanted you to be our headliner and one of our celebrity judges."

"Sorry, it's just hard to think of myself as a 'celebrity'" said Jake, making air quotes. "I'm just a guy who tells jokes."

"Really? That's a shame."

"Yeah, my parents weren't really happy with my career choice either."

Cheree laughed. "No, sorry. I meant it's a shame that you don't think of yourself as a celebrity."

"Oh," said Jake with a laugh. "I'm from Minnesota. We're a very modest people."

Cheree held out a canvas tote bag already filled with several booklets, pamphlets, and other convention tchotchkes, baubles, gewgaws, bibelots, and knickknacks. "This is your welcome kit, plus a few thank you gifts from Abraxus Tasker College. Your hotel reservation is also in there. You're staying at the Tophat Executive Suites just a few miles north. There's a list of some of the great restaurants in town, as well as any of the bars if you're so inclined."

"Do you have a favorite?" asked Jake.

"I recommend St. Andrew's Tavern, because it's quiet, and it's like an English pub, I guess. That's where the graduate students go. Chugly's is an undergrad bar where all the kids with fake IDs get blitzed, and it's loud and obnoxious."

"I remember St. Andrews! I attended this conference several years ago, and spent my free evenings at St. Andrew's. Are there any good bookstores in town?"

"Well, there's the student bookstore, but you probably don't want that. There are a couple chain bookstores downtown, and there's an old used bookstore on Clinton Street."

"That's perfect, that's what I'm looking for. Is there anything else I should know?"

"Yes, there's a reception tomorrow night for all the out-of-town talent. Our faculty advisors will be there, and I know Professor Caine wanted to meet you."

Jake thanked Cheree once again and decided he would take a quick tour of the venues before he headed to the hotel and the bookstore.

CHAPTER 2

"Is that book any good?"

Jake snapped back to reality. "Hmm?" he said, looking up. "I'm sorry?"

Jake had been reading one of his purchases from the bookstore, an old mystery from the 1940s, *The Weird Sisters*, by Charlotte Armstrong.

"Is that book any good?" asked a young woman.

"It is so far," said Jake. "I'm only about a fourth of the way into it, but it's pretty riveting."

"It must be good," said the woman, "because my friend and I have been watching you for the last 30 minutes and you haven't looked up from it the entire time."

"Sorry," said Jake, smiling. "It really is very good. Would you and your friend like to join me?" Jake moved a couple of empty glasses and his dinner plate aside and made some room at his booth.

"Sure, that would be great," said the woman before turning and gesturing at her friend. She motioned for Jake to scoot over so she could sit next to him. "I'm Lynn, and that's Krissi."

Lynn was about 5'5", curvy, and her hair was brown and slightly curly, hanging straight to the nape of her neck. She was wearing a denim miniskirt and tank top with a pushup bra that added a lot of lift and volume to her plump breasts. Jake imagined sliding between them but made sure he didn't let his gaze linger too long over her cleavage because a gentleman never stares.

As Lynn slid into place, Krissi walked over to their table. She was a few inches taller, nearly six feet, had straight blonde hair and was fairly skinny, like she regularly did yoga. Jake was still aching over his recent love affair with Betty the Southern Belle and her yoga instructor friend[20]—*a real love affair. We said 'I love you' and everything*, thought Jake, interspersing his internal dialogue with the narrative, which is annoying because it's hard to punctuate the sentences.

Oh, boo hoo. You're the writer, so deal with it. Jake thought.

Jake felt a sudden rumbling in his stomach and realized tonight's fish and chips weren't sitting well with him, and he was going to explosively shit his pants in exactly five seconds... four... three...

Alright, alright, I'll stop! I'm sorry!

The feeling disappeared as quickly as it came on, and Jake felt healthy and refreshed. He smiled at Krissi. "Hi, won't you sit down?"

"Thank you, I'd love to," said Krissi.

---

[20] Also *Stand Up, Lie Down: Betty In Birmingham*

"I'm Lynn Robertson," said Lynn, "and this is my dearest friend, Krissi Gavinson. She works at the Bursar's office, and I'm a graduate student in English literature." Lynn held her hand out and Jake shook it, then shook Krissi's hand.

"I'm Jake Nilsen."

"Nilsin?" said Lynn.

"No, Nilsen."

"I don't hear the difference?"

"Are you from Minnesota?" asked Jake.

"No, Ohio."

"There's the problem. If you were from Minnesota, you would hear the difference."

"I'm from Wisconsin so I sort of hear it," said Krissi.

"So what do you do, Jake Nilsen of Minnesota?"

"I'm a standup comic. I'm here for the comedy festival this week."

"Oh, I heard that was going on," said Lynn. "Some of my friends are going to see some of the acts this weekend. Are you one of the participants?"

"Yeah," he nodded.

"Are you funny?" asked Krissi.

"I guess so. At least the organizers thought so because I'm one of the instructors and I'll be judging the big competition on Sunday night."

"Oooh, Mr. Big Shot," laughed Lynn. "Where did you go to school?"

"University of Minnesota. I was on the swim team through college."

Lynn pointed at herself. "Ohio State. Go Big Ten!" she said, referring to the college athletic conference both schools were in.

"University of Wisconsin," said Krissi, mentioning another school in the same conference.

"I didn't know that," said Lynn.

"I didn't know you were from Ohio State—" said Krissi

"THEE Ohio State," interrupted Lynn, making a well-known joke that every Ohio State University graduate makes, but which annoys the shit out of everyone else who didn't go to Ohio State.

Krissi just laughed and rolled her eyes. "Whatever. Our schools are playing football in a few weeks. Let's get hammered and watch the game at my house."

"Sounds like a plan," said Lynn, and the two ladies high-fived across the table.

They settled into an easy conversation, talking about their interests, their work, and Lynn's graduate program. As an English lit student, she was especially interested in female authors in the 20th century, so she was familiar with Charlotte Armstrong although she had never read any of her work.

Lynn flirted shamelessly with Jake, who flirted right back. She scooted closer to Jake and pressed her bare thigh against his leg, and occasionally picked at a piece of nonexistent fuzz on Jake's t-shirt.

Krissi tried flirting as well, but Jake was still trying to get over Betty, so he didn't respond to Krissi as warmly as he could have, which is why he missed out on another possible threesome so soon after his last one.

Look, I said I was sorry! thought Jake.

Uh-huh, and maybe next time you'll think before you sass back to the author. The author paused. *Fine, let me see what I can do,* she said.

Lynn, on the other hand, continued to capture Jake's attention, laughing at his jokes, pressing her breasts against him, and rubbing his thigh. Jake felt his dick swell with her attention and frequent breast-pressing.

At one point, when Krissi went to the bathroom and asked Lynn to go with her, she patted Jake's cock under the table before she left. Jake smiled up at her and spread his legs a little to show his erection through his jeans. Lynn gave a sharp intake of breath when she saw its outline down Jake's left leg through the fabric. Krissi looked over Lynn's shoulder and saw it as well. She nudged Lynn, winked at Jake, and they walked to the bathroom. Jake watched them go without being too obvious in his staring.

The two returned a few minutes later, and Lynn returned to her seat, but moved even closer to Jake and gently stroked her hand up and down his cock, while Krissi finished the last of her drink. Jake made no move to stop Lynn and shifted in his seat a little to give her better access.

Krissi said to Jake, "I have to go, because I have to be at work tomorrow. Would you be able to give Lynn a ride? Home, I mean." Lynn giggled, and Krissi winked at them both.

Jake faced Lynn and answered Krissi, "I'll take her as far as she needs to go."

The three walked out to the parking lot and stood next to Krissi's car parked under a tree in a dimly lit corner. There weren't many cars around because it was Tuesday night, so Krissi had managed to park well away from anyone else.

At her car, Krissi hugged Jake and pulled him close, putting her mouth close to his ear and licked it, before reaching down and cupping his hard cock under her hand.

"Please be gentle with my friend. That thing looks like it could break her," said Krissi.

"I promise I'll be gentle," Jake whispered back and licked her ear in return.

"She said I could get a sample of it before I left," she murmured. "You don't mind, do you? I'd join you, but I'm involved with someone. It's still new, but I'm hoping to see where it goes."

"Sample as much of it as you want."

Krissi looked around to make sure no one could see her and she crouched down in front of Jake. As she worked at his zipper, Jake pulled Lynn to him and leaned down to kiss her. She drove her tongue into his mouth and placed a hand on her breast, which he began to squeeze and knead. Lynn shuddered and gave a little moan into his mouth.

Meanwhile, Krissi freed his thick member from its denim prison and gazed appreciatively at his eight-and-a-half-inch prick. "Motherfucker! Oh, honey, he's going to fill you up tonight." Lynn looked down to see Krissi stroking Jake's cock with both hands, her face just a few inches away from his meat.

"That looks so hot," said Lynn. "Move your hands so I can see it."

Krissi released her grip, and Jake's dick continued pointing at Krissi's face. Lynn wrapped her much smaller hand around it, which made it look even bigger.

"Try it," said Lynn. "Put it in your mouth."

"Oh, I shouldn't," said Krissi.

"No, it's alright, I don't mind," croaked Jake. "Feel free. *Please.*"

Krissi looked up at him and winked. She opened her mouth and slid it over Jake's cockhead before removing it again with a pop. She returned it into her mouth, sliding it deeper, again and again, until she reached Lynn's fingers.

"Mmm. Mmm. Mmm," moaned Krissi as she pumped several inches of Jake's shaft into her eager mouth. Lynn held it in place for her so Krissi could grab Jake's ass and pull him into her mouth. She stopped for a moment, "Oh, Lynn honey, I'm sorry, I shouldn't use up your date like this."

"That's alright, it's a make-up for Brad last year," Lynn answered, sliding her hand under her skirt to rub her clit.

"I had my ginseng this morning so I should be good for a few rounds," Jake offered helpfully.

He stroked Krissi's hair as she continued gobbling his cock, and he returned to devouring Lynn with his mouth. He raised up her tank top and unclasped her bra, releasing her softball-sized breasts from their own captivity. Lynn moaned her approval as Jake leaned down and sucked one nipple then the other, tweaking the free one with his fingers; Lynn's nipples hardened and stood out in the warm night air.

Krissi bobbed her head up and down as Lynn jacked his cock with one hand and fingered her own pussy under her skirt with the other. Jake could feel that wonderful tingling pressure build up in his nutsack.

"I'm going to come," he announced. He figured that since he was on a college campus, he should use the correct pronunciation, instead of *cum*. "Krissi, I'm going to come in your mouth. Look at my eyes when I shoot in your mouth."

Krissi let go of his ass and held onto his powerful thighs for support, holding his dickhead in her mouth; Lynn continued jacking Jake off while he gazed deep into Krissi's blue eyes. Krissi could feel Jake's thighs tense up and she braced herself just as he shot his first load of hot jizz.

"Mmmph!" grunted Krissi.

"Aahh," groaned Jake. "Ungh," he groaned again as a second blast filled her mouth, followed by a third then a fourth. Lynn pulled Jake's cock out of Krissi's mouth and leaned down to take it into her own mouth, just in time to catch Jake's fifth spurt. It was a small one but gave Lynn a sample of what she would be getting later. She smacked her lips, savoring the sweet saltiness.

She shifted slightly and kissed Krissi, their tongues swirling, each tasting Jake's hot semen on their tongues. Krissi reached and played with Lynn's breasts.

Jake knelt behind Lynn and was delighted to discover that she wasn't wearing any panties. He wondered briefly if she had removed them earlier in the bathroom, but decided he didn't care. He slid his tongue up the length of her pussy, and Lynn jumped at the unexpected sensation. He lapped at Lynn's pussy while Krissi sucked her full tits.

"Ohh fuck, Jake, that's a magic tongue. You know how to eat pussy," said Lynn. "Krissi, you need to get some of this."

"I'd love some." She stood up, leaned against her car, raising her skirt to expose her clean-shaven cunt. Without missing a beat, Jake moved over and lapped at Krissi's slit. He held onto Lynn's hand and pulled her next to her friend, pulling her skirt back up.

After sampling Krissi's wet pussy, he scooted a few inches to his right and returned to Lynn, who had a Brazilian landing strip leading down to her sweet wetness. Lynn moaned a little louder when Krissi leaned in and sucked her nipple.

Jake returned his attention back to Krissi's wet cunt, slipping his tongue and a finger between her swollen labia. Lynn returned the favor to her friend and raised Krissi's blouse and sucked at one of her small breasts.

"More, sweetie, do it harder," Krissi moaned, clamping on the back of Lynn's head.

Jake grabbed Lynn's hips and returned her to her previous position and began lapping at her clit one more time, finger fucking her with two fingers. Lynn grabbed Krissi's head and made out with her before pulling Krissi's head back down to her breasts.

"Ohh, I'm going to come, you guys," groaned Lynn. "You two are going to make me come."

Krissi sucked her friend's nipple and flicked it with her tongue while she kneaded Lynn's other tit with her long, thin fingers. Jake continued thrusting his two fingers inside her, sucking on her clit as he did so.

"Ohh, this is it," moaned Lynn. "Ohh, Jake, I'm going to come in your mouth. Look up at me like Krissi did. Krissi, honey, you have to move your head." Krissi raised up and watched Lynn's face, still massaging her friend's breasts.

Jake looked up at Lynn, searching her brown eyes as he sucked her pink pearl and worked his thick fingers deep inside her.

Lynn shrieked as a deep orgasm washed over her, "Ohhhh! Oh yes! Yes! Yes! Yes! Oh, shiiiiiit!" She clamped on the back of Jake's head as she shuddered under his ministrations.

Lynn slumped back against the car, her knees shaking. Jake stood up and supported her with one strong arm. He pulled Krissi close to him.

"Taste your friend," he said and kissed her, sliding his tongue into her mouth. Krissi moaned as she tasted Lynn's tangy juices in his mouth.

"Now you," said Jake, kissing Lynn.

"Fuck, you taste good, sweetie," said Krissi.

"Yes, I do," said Lynn. "You taste pretty good yourself," she said to Jake.

"Yeah, you do," said Krissi. "And you come a lot. My God, that was a lot of come. You got any of that left?"

"I definitely do," answered Jake.

"Good, because I want some of it for myself," said Lynn. "Are you going to join us, sweetie?" she asked Krissi.

"You bet your sweet tits." Krissi gave Lynn's breast one more squeeze.

"What about what's his name?" said Lynn.

"Meh. We'll save that one for a different book," said Krissi.

Chapter 3

Jake approached the check-in table at the Wednesday night opening reception, where a young woman sat with an iPad and several name tags spread out in front of her. Her name tag said *Bree*, and she was wearing a t-shirt that said, "I'd rather be studying [with the] Stallion football team."[21]

"Hi," said Bree with a bright, satisfied smile. "Your name, please?"

"Hi, I'm Jake Nilsen." He was wearing what he called his work clothes: jeans, a light blue button-down shirt, gray sport coat, and tan Oxford dress shoes.

"Nilsin?" asked Bree.

"No, Nilsen."

"Ah, there you are. We've got your name tag right here, and I've got a note on my file that says Professor Caine wants to meet you."

---

[21] See *Athletics* (Abraxus Tasker College Book 3), available on Amazon. Holy shit, it's another crossover character!

"Oh, really? Sure, that would be great. Is she here?"

"Yes, she's right over there." Bree stood up and pointed to a woman in her 30s who was talking with a skinny bearded guy.

Jake ordered a beer from the small bar set up in the corner, then walked over and waved his fingers at her to get her attention.

"Hi, Jake," said the woman, recognizing him immediately.

She was about a foot shorter than he was, her body fleshy with voluptuous curves—ample breasts and hips. She had red, sensual lips, green eyes, and a wild mop of curly, light brown hair with blonde highlights that framed her face like a mane. She was wearing a tight-fitting, black, athletic-wear top with a plunging neckline that barely contained her beautiful breasts. She was also wearing an olive-green skirt that clung to her hips and reached mid-calf, and tan leather boots that came up to her knees. She looked like a very glamorous fitness instructor for the Army.

"Hi, I'm Carrie, faculty advisor for the Abraxus Tasker Comedy Festival Union—the XTC-FU, as we call it." She offered her hand which Jake shook gently in his large palm.

"Hi, Carrie, nice to meet you."

"Doctor Caine," said the guy.

He was an earnest young man with an earnest beard and an earnest man bun on his head. Jake was already fighting not to roll his eyes. He hated earnest young men and their earnest hairstyles, especially when they looked like a hairy balloon.

"Hi, Dr. Caine, I'm Jake." He shook the guy's hand.

"No, she's Dr. Caine. I'm Mr. Platt"

Oh, for fuck's sake, thought Jake. *He's one of* those *guys!*

Carrie sighed. "It's fine, Tristan."

"I'm sorry, I just think people need to use your professional title when they meet you. You earned it."

"If it helps, you can call me by my professional title," said Jake.

"You have a professional title?" asked Tristan.

"Sure, it's Vikomte, which is Norwegian for Viscount. It's more of a hereditary family title, but we still use it. So, you should actually call me Vikomte Nilsen." Carrie suppressed a smile.

"What, seriously?" demanded Tristan.

Jake hesitated for a few seconds. "Oh, I'm sorry, were you talking to me?"

"Yes, I was," said Tristan.

Carrie covered her mouth with her hand.

"Yes, you were... ?" Jake trailed off and looked at Tristan expectantly. "Vikomte Nilsen?" he whispered helpfully.

"I'm not calling you that," said Tristan.

"I'm not calling you that...?"

Carrie burst out laughing and Jake joined her. "Oh, shit, that's great. This is why I suggested you specifically for this event, Jake. I was at a show you did in Ann Arbor several months ago, and saw you take down this heckler so hard, I almost peed my pants." She turned to Tristan. "It was the funniest goddamn thing. Some drunk guy called Jake a 'liberal cuck,' and Jake said 'that's a mean thing to call the guy fucking your wife.' The whole place lost it and the guy stormed out in shame. That's when I knew I wanted him to be one of our instructors." She turned back to Jake. "I teach in the theatre department here," said Carrie, pronouncing it "theatre," not "theater."

"Tristan is ... a friend from the art department. Anyway, I'm teaching a class on improvisational theatre, and I was hoping I could persuade you to speak to my students on Friday about how to think on your feet and improvise during a performance."

"Oh, sure, I'd be happy to. What time is the class?"

"11:00 on Friday," said Carrie. "I made sure that we didn't book any workshops for you before 1:00 that day so you would have time in your schedule."

"That sounds great. I studied improv in college and was in an improv troupe for my last two years there."

"Oh, yeah? Where did you go to school?" asked Tristan.

He couldn't be sure, but Jake thought Tristan was challenging him somehow. He just wasn't sure how or why. Tristan was skinny, but not runner skinny. More like pale-and-tragic skinny. He reminded Jake of Dakota, that man-bunned little asshole from Indianapolis.[22] Jake wondered if they were related somehow. *Maybe they're in the Man Bun Club together*, he thought.

Jake didn't think Tristan would try to challenge him physically. The guy was about 5'7" to Jake's 6'2", and he weighed in around 130 pounds. Not to mention, he was wearing skinny jeans and a plaid shirt like a shitty lumberjack. Jake weighed 175 pounds, had a torso like a V, and his blonde hair and piercing blue eyes were the object

---

[22] See *Stand Up, Lie Down: Irene in Indianapolis*

of every eligible farm girl's masturbation fantasies in Mankato, Minnesota. And even a few of the guys.

Jake wondered if maybe Tristan and Carrie were in a relationship, and he was feeling threatened that someone was sniffing around. Jake knew never to engage with threatened tiny men because they were always more trouble than they were worth.

He figured Tristan might try to one-up him on the education front. Oh, well he'd played that game too, Like the time he got into a pissing match with a political science graduate student from Colorado at a friend's party. The guy was a staunch conservative, and Jake riffed so many Mitt Romney puns, the guy finally slammed down his glass and stormed out.

"University of Minnesota," answered Jake. "I graduated six years ago."

"Hey, no kidding. I was at University of Wisconsin finishing my PhD," said Carrie.

"Big Ten," said Jake, toasting her with his beer.

"Big Ten," she responded, clinking his bottle with her glass of red wine.

"I went to Oberlin College," said Tristan.

Jake looked blankly at Tristan.

"It's in Ohio."

"Ah," said Jake.

"Did you ever go to any of the football games?" asked Carrie.

"Only a couple. I was at the Wisconsin-Minnesota game in 2013. I usually didn't go to football games because the swim season was from September to March."

"I was at that game!" said Carrie, excited. "We kicked your ass that year!"

"That's not surprising. Minnesota always kind of sucks at football."

"Some friends and I went while I was in graduate school. I was dating a guy who wanted to take a road trip and check out the Minneapolis theatre scene, and we did that after we went to the game."

"I played Ultimate Frisbee for half a year," offered Tristan.

Jake looked at Tristan blankly again for a moment. "I tried that once," he said. "Way too much running for me."

"Well, you have to be in shape, you know," said Tristan, thinking he had found Jake's weakness. "It's not for everyone, but you certainly have to be in pretty good shape to do well."

"I was training for a spot on the Olympic team at the time," said Jake. Tristan turned beet red and Jake was sure he was grinding his teeth.

"I'm getting a drink," said Tristan, through a clenched jaw. "Does anyone want anything?" And he turned and left without waiting for an answer.

"I'm so sorry about him," said Carrie after he was gone. "We dated for a few weeks last year."

"Oh, should I—?"

"No, no, you don't need to do anything," said Carrie, putting a hand on his forearm and letting it linger for a few seconds. "We only went out for six weeks. We had sex a couple of times, but he just wasn't very good at it."

"Oh, my," said Jake, covering his mouth with his fingertips and batting his eyes like he was a high-society socialite hearing some juicy gossip. "That sounds like a special secret."

"Let's just say Ultimate Frisbee isn't the only thing he only did for a short while."

Jake roared with laughter and wiped his eyes.

"I'm glad I could make the comic laugh. Maybe I should attend a couple of your workshops."

"That would be great. I would love to have you. Uh, at the workshop," he said, his face turning red. "I would love to have you at the— I would love it if you would attend the workshop."

Carried laughed again at his embarrassment.

"Real smooth, Vikomte. Bet you're a hit with the ladies."

Jake's face grew even redder. "I have never been good at … discussing … intimate things," he stammered. "I just get really flustered and nervous."

"And your face gets really red." She rested the back of her hand on his cheek. "Good Lord, your face is hot. Er, I mean, I'd think you were running a fever if I didn't know any better." She patted his cheek a couple of times.

"Anyway, we stayed friends, and he's harmless even if he's irritating, like a jealous moth who keeps fluttering around after the light is off. He still gets all guard dog on any guy who comes near me at one of these functions. Earlier, he chased off one of the middles from the Friday night show, even though the guy was gay. Oh, and watch out, because he likes to flex on his private school education. He thinks that and his Master's degree makes him hot shit. Also, he minored in Gender Studies, which is why he insists people call me by my academic title, but I couldn't care less. Besides, I like it when you call me Carrie." She smiled and bit her lower lip.

"I'll keep an eye out for him." Jake smiled back. "Carrie."

Tristan returned, jaw still clenched, clutching a can of raspberry White Claw.

"I'm back," he mumbled.

"You didn't bring us anything?" said Carrie.

"I didn't know you wanted anything."

"That's because you sulked away. I'll go. Jake, can I get you something?" She rested her hand on his forearm again and let it stay, stroking it with her index finger.

"Sure, if you're offering. I'd like another beer." He held up his bottle to show what brand he was drinking. "Please and thank you." Carrie headed to the bar.

"So, Tristan, what do you teach?" Jake asked after several moments of awkward silence.

"I'm a ceramics instructor in the art department."

"Really? That's interesting. So, like, making pottery?"

"Well, ceramics has a rich and in-depth history, actually," Tristan sniffed, "but if that helps you understand, then yes, I make pottery."

Carrie returned with the drinks and handed Jake his new beer. "Thank you," he said.

"And you majored in it?" Jake asked. "I mean, you majored in pottery?"

"Ceramics, yes. I even have an advanced degree in it."

"What, you mean like a Ph.D. in pottery?"

"Ceramics. And no, you can only earn an MFA in it. That's the terminal degree," said Tristan.

Carrie said nothing and just watched what was going on. It was Ann Arbor all over again, and she was enjoying the show.

"Ah." Jake took a pull at his beer bottle and thought for a moment. "And what's an MFA?"

"A Master of Fine Arts," sneered Tristan.

"Oh!" said Jake with a start. "That's not what I was thinking. At all."

"Why, what did you think it meant?"

If a man can smile demurely, Jake did just that as he winked at Carrie. She snorted and stifled a laugh. It took Tristan a few seconds longer to get the joke.[23]

"Oh, ha, ha, Carrie. Real mature," said Tristan.

Bree from the reception table approached. "Excuse me, Professor Caine, the facilities manager is here and wants to speak to whoever was in charge. Something about AV arrangements for tomorrow."

---

[23] *Motherfucking asshole,* in case you were wondering.

Carrie sighed. "I'll be right back. Jake, maybe we can get some dinner after this?"

"That would be great," said Jake. "I'll be here with my pal, Tristan." He watched her over Tristan's shoulder and admired the view.

Carrie took a quick glance back at him.

"Listen, I'm not your fucking pal," said Tristan, snapping Jake's attention from Carrie's ass. "And I don't need some muscled-up meathead coming in here and sniffing around my girlfriend."

"Ex-girlfriend. And from what she said, you guys didn't last that long. Especially you."

Tristan turned redder than ever before. He wanted to lash out at Jake and hurt him somehow, but he was a self-proclaimed pacifist. So he selected the only tool in his toolbox.

"At least I've got an advanced degree and a respectable job. What are you, a college dropout, you fucking carny?"

"No," said Jake, "I have a degree in business. Also, I'm rich."

"With your daddy's money, no doubt."

"No, my daddy's a farmer. I just made smart investments." Jake took a drink of his beer and Tristan pounded the rest of his White Claw. "Does having your Master's degree help you make better ashtrays than all the other potters?" Jake asked. "Like, does your mom still have all the ashtrays you made in school?"

"Hey, fuck you, meathead," Tristan growled, stepping up like he was about to pound Jake, and not in the good way. "You fucking comedy clowns come in here and spew your hateful, sexist bullshit with your so-called comedy. We should be celebrating the arts, man. Not a bunch of misogynists telling crude jokes about women. You comics should be canceled because you can't do your job without denigrating other people."

"Whoa, whoa, Tristan, man, breathe," said Jake in a soothing tone. "Practice your ocean breathing. Come on, deep breath in through your nose."

"Wait, ocean breathing?" said Tristan, looking confused.

"Yeah, it's a yoga breathing technique. Come on, do it with me." He took a deep breath and motioned with his hand for Tristan to do the same thing.

"No, I know what ocean breathing is," said Tristan, confused. "I'm just surprised you know it." Jake's knowledge of a yoga term threw him for a loop, and he tried to find sense in the world again.

"Yeah, so am I. Now, breathe," Jake took another deep breath, and Tristan did the same. Jake repeated it two more times with Tristan following. "Okay, are you feeling better? Are you relaxed?"

"Yes," said Tristan, sulking. The wind was definitely out of his sails.

"Okay, good." Jake put his hand on Tristan's shoulder. It felt so slight and small under Jake's large hand. "You looked like you were about to take a swing at me, and that's not a good idea for any number of reasons."

"Why, because you would kick my ass?" He pushed Jake's hand away.

"No, but we both know I could. Because if you took a poke at one of your campus guests, you'd probably be fired."

"So? It's not like you care."

"Well, no. But that doesn't mean you should do it. Also, not all comics use sexism or racism for their comedy. You shouldn't lump us all together just because of some comic you saw in the 1990s."

"Yeah, well, I'm not sorry for what I said," said Tristan, still sulking.

"That's fine, I'm not either. I might want to buy one of your pots though."

"Maybe. Asshole," said Tristan.

"That's Vikomte Asshole," said Jake. He took another drink of his beer as Tristan fought to keep a small smile from breaking his angry demeanor. *Fucking Jake Nilsen*, he thought.

"You boys getting along better?" said Carrie, returning.

"Yes, Professor Caine," the two said in unison.

"Great, Jake, let's go to dinner," said Carrie. "'Bye, Tristan." As they walked, Carrie said, "I saw what you did. I really thought Tristan was going to try to punch you, so I thought I'd better get you out of there. What did you say to him?"

Tristan glared after the two of them as they walked out. *It isn't fair!* thought Tristan, *I'm the sensitive one! I'm the one who had watched out after Carrie and kept these sexist assholes from glomming all over her! And now she and that meathead are going to—*

"Excuse me, was that Jake Nilsen that just walked out?" said a woman next to him.

"Yes, it was," said Tristan, not turning to look at her.

"How do you do?" said the woman. "I'm Kayla Baker,[24] I'm one of the comics at the convention. I spotted you and my friend, Jake, and I thought, 'I just have to meet this gorgeous skinny man.' I'll talk to Jake later, but I wanted to get to know you better."

Tristan looked at Kayla and his eyes widened when he saw a tall Black woman with gorgeous curves and dark umber skin.

"Hi, I'm Tristan," he said, entranced, and he offered his hand. "And I just *love* comedians."

---

[24] See *Stand Up, Lie Down: Betty in Birmingham*

CHAPTER 4

"How was your first day of the conference?" Carrie asked, taking a sip from her cocktail. It was Friday night, and the two were on what could be called their third, or even fourth date depending on how you counted their other meals together. They had gone to dinner Wednesday and Thursday night, plus they had grabbed lunch after Jake spoke at Carrie's class. The two were at Mar-Tina's, one of the city's fancier restaurants.

"Great. I talked to a bunch of people, taught a breakout session on improvisation after your class, and another on structuring long-form stories. I also bumped into another comic friend, Kayla Baker, and she had a little gossip to share."

"Oh, I know Kayla," said Carrie. "I met her at the Funny Femmes of Florida Festival two years ago. She taught a session on Women In Comedy today. So how do you know her?"

Jake nearly choked on his martini. "Oh, we just know each other from the circuit."

"You've slept with her, I'm guessing."[25]

"Uh, well, that is—"

Carrie laughed, "Jake, I don't care. I've been with her too."

"Oh, really? I'll bet that was something to see."

"Oh, it was pretty hot. So what did she have to say?"

"Well, apparently, she and Tristan went home together last night and *'spent a magical night together.'*" He said the last bit in a sexy voice and made air quotes.

"Seriously, Tristan? Platt? Skinny guy with a man bun? I would not have taken him for her type. You're more her type."

"Yeah, Kayla said something about hot monkey love and that she was going to make him her boy-toy all weekend."

"Wow, that was rather unexpected. Maybe he'll get off my dick now," said Carrie.

Jake looked startled. "Um, Carrie, is there something you haven't told me?"

"What? Oh, no, no. I'm 100% female. This isn't that kind of book," said Carrie. "I just like to say that when people are getting on my nerves. It usually shocks them into backing off. I'm like most theatre people and just have a dirty-whore mouth."

"Yeah, you do," said Jake. As soon as he said that, he looked mortified. "Oh God, I mean, you talk dirty. Shit, no, I mean you're a filthy— Fuck! No, not a filthy fuck. Goddammit." He paused and

---

[25] He totally did! In *Stand Up, Lie Down: Betty in Birmingham.*

took a deep breath. "I have noticed you are a little more prone to swearing than most people I have met."

Carrie was laughing so hard, she was clutching her ribs and wiping tears from her eyes. "Holy fuck, Jake, you make me laugh even when you're not trying. I'll bet you're just a neurotic mess during phone sex."

"Oh, you have no idea. I can't do phone sex at all. It gets so awkward it makes that last little outburst sound like Marvin Gaye. I'm pretty good at it when I'm engaged in the real thing though."

"I think I'd like to hear that," said Carrie. Now it was her turn to blush and stammer. "Uh, that is, I mean, we don't—you don't have—I don't expect—"

"Why, Professor Caine," said Jake with a smile and a wink, "are you trying to court me?" He fanned himself with his menu and spoke like he was in Downton Abbey. "Father says one should not associate with theatre folk, but Mama said to follow my heart."

Carrie's laughter rang out across the restaurant. The waiter hurried over, looking nervous, with his little notepad and pen at the ready.

"Are you ready to order?" he asked, forcing a quivering smile. Apparently, loud, raucous laughter was frowned upon at Mar-Tina's.

"Sure, I think we're ready," said Jake as Carrie sipped her martini. Carrie ordered the salmon, and Jake ordered the same. He also ordered a course of oysters as an appetizer.

"Ooh, excellent choice, sir," said the waiter. "We're close enough to the ocean that the oysters are only a few hours old."

"Where exactly are we?" asked Jake. "I don't even think I know what city we're in."

"Why, sir, we're clearly in the city of—" A loud clatter rang out in the kitchen as a busboy and a server collided, spilling a tray of dinner orders. "Excuse me, please," said the waiter, and he scurried off.

"Anyway, you were stumbling over your pickup line," said Jake.

"I was not!"

"Oh, yeah, admit it, Carrie." Jake put his elbows on the table and rested his chin in his hands. "You're into me. You just can't get enough of the Big Dog."

Carrie laughed again, not so loud this time. "Fuck no, not if you refer to yourself as the Big Dog."

"Trust me, I won't," said Jake. "I know too many dude bro comedians who are like that. They're frat boys with a microphone, and they're not that funny. Their whole shtick is usually some variation on 'women be shopping,' or 'my girlfriend doesn't understand me.' It's like they lifted their act from old Andrew Dice Clay videos from the 1990s."

"Yeah, Tristan really hates those guys."

"I know, he told me. He said we were all misogynists and couldn't do comedy without making fun of other people."

"I've heard that lecture from him countless times. The only reason he agreed to be a faculty advisor was so he could make sure none of the conference faculty were objectionable."

"How did Kayla get in then? She's one of the filthiest comics I've heard. I mean, she's funny as shit and she's one of my favorites, but still."

"Oh, well Tristan is a die-hard feminist, and when he heard we were considering a Black female comic, he nearly accused the committee of being racist because we were only considering her."

"Yeah, well, if he wasn't before, he's her number one fan now."

The server showed up with the order of oysters, which the two tucked into and enjoyed, feeding each other the occasional bite. They chatted about comedy, Jake's life growing up on a farm, and Carrie's life growing up surrounded by theatre people because her parents were working actors. Once dinner arrived, they continued talking and flirting, enjoying the food, and once again, sharing bites of each other's dinner even though they were eating the same thing.

As they were sitting back and letting their food settle, Carrie leaned back and slid her foot up Jake's calf under the table, "So about hearing you do dirty talk," she said.

"Yes...?" Jake asked, arching one eyebrow.

"How would one ... arrange to hear a performance?" Carrie asked like a bad Shakespearean actor, a favorite game of the XTC theatre department.

"If one were so inclined," Jake replied in a similar manner, "one must understand this is a participatory performance. One does not simply *watch* from the comfort of one's seat. One must ... *encourage* the performance. Even *engage* the performer. Perhaps, if one may be so bold, to *actively participate* in the performance."

"Oh, one *is* so inclined," said Carrie.

"Then perhaps we should retire for the evening, and see how the second act plays out." Jake signaled the waiter for the check and slipped the cash and a generous tip into the little notebook after it arrived.

"Shall we?" Jake asked, holding out his hand and helping Carrie to her feet. The two walked out and stood out in the parking lot.

"Let's go for a little walk before we go," said Carrie. "It's a lovely night for a walk."

Jake bent down and kissed Carrie deeply, and she wrapped her arms around his neck. After a few seconds, they broke apart. "We should find a drugstore while we're out, because one of us will need a toothbrush," said Jake.

"Yeah, maybe salmon and oysters wasn't the smartest choice tonight," she agreed.

CHAPTER 5

"I've never been in the Tophat Executive Suites," said Carrie. "It's pretty nice in here. Plus, you've got a great view of the city. I've never seen it from this height, especially at night." The Tophat Executive Suites towered at fifteen stories, which was unusual for a city this size. Jake was on the fourteenth floor; it certainly paid to be a VIP, even in a city like this.

"Yes," agreed Jake, "the lights here are beautiful. Whoever thought I'd be back in the great city of—" A loud clatter rang out in the hallway as a bellhop and a server collided, spilling a tray of room service orders.

Jake had pulled the suite's loveseat around so they could sit with the balcony door open and the lights off, looking out at the night skyline. He was sitting on the right side, and Carrie was sitting on his lap as the two enjoyed the cooler temperatures of the summer night.

They had stopped by a drugstore, picked up a toothbrush for Carrie, and they returned to his room where they both brushed and rinsed vigorously. *Salmon and oysters really are a bad choice for a date that promises to end in sex.*

"I'm glad we skipped the garlic fries," Carrie had said through a mouthful of toothpaste.

Now they were enjoying the night from high atop the city. Carrie mindlessly stroked Jake's blonde hair and tickled his ear, while he massaged her neck.

"I'm really enjoying this," said Carrie.

"So am I."

"I can tell. I can feel your dick. God, that thing feels huge."

Carrie pulled on the back of Jake's head and kissed him deeply. Their tongues probed each other's mouths, sliding over one another, getting better acquainted.

"Mmm, minty fresh," said Jake.

"Mm-hmm," Carrie moaned into his mouth. She grabbed his left hand and placed it on her heavy breast, and Jake gently kneaded it. He unbuttoned her blouse and pulled the tails free from her skirt. A quick peek showed that her bra was a front-clasping model, which she helped him with, her tits loosed from their confinement.

"Do that some more," she said. "Harder."

Jake eagerly complied and kneaded her flesh, feeling her nipple harden under his palm.

"Ohh, that's it. Oh, I'm getting wet," she murmured. She began squirming on Jake's lap, trying to generate some friction on her pussy. "Oh, God, my pussy needs some attention too, but I don't want you to stop massaging my tits."

"Turn this way and put your back against me."

Carrie did as he said, and slipped off her blouse and bra. Her tits were heavy in Jake's large hands, and she ground her ass into his hard cock as he reached around and massaged her globes and played with her nipples. Jake nibbled at her earlobes and darted his tongue into her ear. He slid down to her neck and lightly sucked on it, being careful not to leave any telltale marks. Licking up the entire length of her long neck, he gave Carrie goosebumps and made her nipples harden even more.

"Ohh, fuck, that feels so good. Touch my pussy and see how wet you've made me," said Carrie. "Feel my wet pussy."

Jake lifted her skirt and discovered she wasn't wearing any panties. *Holy shit, was she going commando the whole night?* Jake wondered.

"I took them off when we got here," said Carrie, answering his unspoken thought.

Jake slid one hand up her thigh, even as he massaged her other breast and continued licking and kissing her neck and ear. Carrie's bush was neatly trimmed and short, and Jake found her slit. He slipped in a finger, and it slid inside of her easily.

"Ohhhhh, fuck, you're so wet," he murmured.

"You do that to me, Jake. You've made me this wet since I met you. I've masturbated to you every night this week, and once after lunch today. I've imagined your huge cock inside me and can't wait until you fill me up with that great big prick."

"I've been hard for you since that day I met you," said Jake. "I wanted to fuck you. As soon as I got back here that first night, I jacked off and imagined you riding my dick."

"And now we both get what we want."

"Turn around and face me," commanded Jake. "I want to do something I think you'll like."

"Let's undress first," said Carrie.

The two stood up and faced each other. Carrie unbuttoned Jake's shirt and kissed his chest as she undid each one. When she pulled his shirt off, she sucked at both his nipples and ran her hand over Jake's ripped abs, pausing to admire the V-muscles, his Adonis belt, guiding her down to his groin. She slowly pulled down his pants, revealing the rest of his V-muscles and exposing his hard prick. It sprang out, and she licked her lips.

"Fuck, that's a big one," she said. "I'm going to have fun getting this inside me."

She knelt down and slurped his meat into her mouth, bobbing her head on it a few times.

"I want that in my mouth again later, but I want to see what you have planned for me."

Jake stepped out of his jeans and underwear and stripped off his socks (*because men look completely ridiculous naked except for socks*).

"I think you'll like it."

He pulled at Carrie's skirt and slid it past her wide hips and the two were standing totally naked. She gripped his cock and stroked it lightly with her fingers. Jake bent over and sucked at one of her tits and then the other, sliding his finger in and out of her wet slit.

"Ohh, fuck, Jake, show me what you want to show me before I shove that thing inside me."

He smiled and said, "Okay, we're going to masturbate each other with each other. You're going to rub your wet pussy on my cock and we're going to get each other off."

"I like the sound of that."

Jake sat down in the center of the loveseat and held Carrie's hands as she straddled him. Jake's stiff dick stood at attention, and Carrie thought about just sliding down onto the shaft and fucking his brains out, but she wanted to see what he had planned. Carrie had not had sex for over a year and a half, her brief sessions with Tristan being just that: brief. She hardly counted it as actual sex. So Carrie was ready to get jammed and was looking forward to a deep plowing by the biggest cock on the college comedy circuit.

Jake pressed his cock down and Carrie rested her wet snatch on top of it. She wrapped her arms around his neck and the two resumed their passionate oral exploration once more. Jake wrapped his strong arms around Carrie's torso and held her tightly. She instinctively started grinding slightly and whimpered once, very lightly, as the two created friction between them. She could feel Jake's cock between her pussy lips without actually being inside her. The top of his shaft was rubbing against her clit and opening, and she understood why Jake liked this so much. It felt almost as good as fucking, and in some ways, it was better because it prolonged the pleasure.

"Ohh, shit, you're right, baby. This feels amazing," groaned Carrie. "Your cock feels good on my clit."

Jake put his hands on Carrie's hips and helped her rock back and forth. Her juices continued to flow as she slid her lips up and down Jake's prick. She leaned back, hands on Jake's shoulders, as he returned his attention to her tits, burying his face between them and licking her breastbone, then sucked and kissed his way around each breast. He even left a few hickeys on her side boob and under boob, knowing she could keep those covered in public.

"Ohh, fuck, Jake, I'm going to come," Carrie said, leaning her head back and grinding harder and faster. "Jake, I'm going to come on your cock." She pronounced it "come," what with being a college professor and all.

"Do it, baby, come for me. Come on my big cock." He laced his fingers behind her back so she could lean back without falling. She leaned back hard as she ground her clit on his cock, and Jake's biceps bulged as he held her in place.

"Ohhhhh. It's so good. It's so—Ohhhhh."

"That's it, Carrie. Fuck me and come. Come on me."

"OH, FUCK! OH, FUCK! IT'S SO FUCKING—AAAAAHHHHHHHH!" Carrie shuddered as her orgasm washed over her and she threw her head back. Jake held her in place and watched as Carrie's eyes fluttered. "Holy shit, Jake. I haven't come like that in a long time. What did you do to me?"

He smiled. "I only held you. You did all that beautiful work yourself." She slumped forward and Jake wrapped his powerful arms around her, reveling in the feeling of her naked flesh against his, enjoying their skin touching. The two lovers breathed hard and their bodies glistened in the cool night.

"But you still need a turn," said Carrie, rocking back and forth a couple of times on Jake's still-hard member. "Or rather, I still want your dick inside me."

"There's nowhere else I'd rather be at this moment."

Carrie slipped off Jake's lap and his cock sprang back up. Carrie knelt down and took it in her hand. She licked the underside of his shaft and then sucked one of his balls into her mouth, letting his member rest against her cheek. She took the other one into her mouth in turn, switching back and forth between the two. Then she slid her mouth back over Jake's schlong and worked as much of it in as she could.

"Oh, shit, that's amazing," Jake groaned, as Carrie managed to fit nearly six of Jake's eight-and-a-half inches into her mouth. "Holy fuck, where did you learn to do that?"

"I've always been able to do it," she said, and then sucked him back into her mouth to the same depth to prove it. "I have a deep gag reflex." She sucked him into her mouth as deep as she could take it and held it there for a few seconds before she started to gag. She withdrew Jake's meat with a loud, wet slurp, and a long string of saliva hung between his cock and her mouth. She wiped off her mouth and said, "Right now. I need you inside me right now."

Carrie stood back up and held Jake's member in place as she positioned her wet pussy over it. She slipped the tip inside and slowly lowered herself down, getting it inside a few inches. She raised back up until only the head was inside her then lowered herself again to a little more than the same position.

"I'm going to need a few minutes," she said. "I don't know if it's the length or the thickness that's going to break me."

"Take all the time you need," said Jake. "I'm enjoying the journey."

Carrie lowered herself once again, taking in even more. She raised up one last time and this time, let herself drop, completely taking Jake's tool inside her. She growled as it filled her up and took several short breaths.

"Hooooooly fuck, this is big." Carrie began raising up slowly and lowering herself gently as she got used to Jake's massive invader. "I'm getting used to it though. Oh yeah, it's so good." She picked up the pace, bouncing harder and faster. "Oh yeah, that's it. This is so good. You feel so good inside me, Jake honey." She kissed him deeply and ran her hands through his hair, her torso still pressed against his, her nipples getting more sensitive from all of Jake's attention and rubbing against his chest.

"Oh. Fuck. Oh. Fuck," Carrie said as she lifted up then dropped back with each word punctuating the motion. "Oh. Fuck. Oh. Fuck."

Jake could feel the pressure building in his ball sack and knew he was close to coming. "Oh, not yet, baby," he said in her ear. "I'm getting close, but I don't want to come yet."

He stood up off the loveseat. She didn't know how he had the strength, but he stood straight up and she wrapped her legs around his narrow waist. She squeezed her thighs together and raised herself up on his cock and lowered herself again by releasing them.

"Ooh, that's nice," he said and helped her raise up and re-impale herself several times.

"Take me from behind," she commanded. "Fuck me from behind standing up."

Jake lifted her off his cock and she could feel the emptiness in her cunt where he used to be. She stood on wobbly legs and walked out onto the balcony overlooking the city. She grabbed the railing and bent over, presenting her ass to him.

"You know, you never did tell me what city we're in," said Jake, stepping up behind her and guiding his dick toward her heavenly slit, her labia engorged and full. He slipped the head in between her lips.

"Oh, sure, we're in the city of—FUCK!" she cried as he rammed inside her tight cunt.

"Oh God, I love that place," said Jake.

He grabbed her hips and drove himself forward into her again and again, their bodies slapping together in the darkness. Carrie's large tits hung down and rocked back and forth with each pounding thrust. Jake leaned forward and grabbed her tits with both hands and she raised up to give him better access to them. This changed the angle of his cock and Jake bucked his hips in an upward motion to accommodate the new position.

Carrie rubbed her clit and moaned, "Oh, fuck, I might come again."

"Do it, baby, come for me again."

Carrie leaned forward again, held onto the balcony railing with one hand, rubbed her clit with the other, while she braced her feet against Jake's doggy-style pounding.

"Hunh, hunh, hunh," she groaned with each thrust, his pelvis slapping against her beautiful ass. He picked up his speed and Carrie knew he was getting close. "That's it, Jake. Fuck me and come for me."

"Where do you want me to come, baby?" He asked. "Do you want me to fill up your beautiful pussy? Or do you want me to come in your hot mouth?"

"Come in my mouth later. Right now, I want a pussy full of come. Let's make each other come."

Jake growled in response and grabbed Carrie's hips once more and drove his steel cock, over and over, deep into Carrie's cunt, grunting with each powerful thrust.

"Ungh! Ungh! Ungh!" grunted Jake. "Oh, God, I'm going to come, Carrie. I'm going to come in your beautiful cunt."

"That's it, Jake," moaned Carrie, frantically rubbing her swollen clit. "Oh fuck, Jake. I want your hot come in my pussy. Fill up my pussy, please. Oh, please fill up my pussy."

Jake's balls tensed as he fucked them both into wondrous bliss. "Here it comes, baby. Here it comes. It's all for your beautiful pussy. All my hot come is for your beautiful pussy."

Jake slowed down and pumped his cock into her one... two... three more times before he buried himself as deeply as he could go and released his first load of jizz into Carrie's eager pussy.

"OH, FUCK!" he shouted.

"Oh, fuck!" she echoed. "Ahhhhhh" Carrie came as soon as she felt Jake's load splash her inner walls, and her knees buckled.

Jake held onto her hips and kept himself buried as he unloaded a second then a third come blast. He pumped a couple more times and felt his fourth and fifth load fire as well.

"Oh, fuck," he breathed. "Oh, fuck. That was amazing."

"Oh, my God, you came so much," said Carrie. "I can feel it. Ohh, I can feel it in my pussy. There's so much come in my pussy."

Jake's dick began to soften, but he stayed inside her, leaning forward to wrap his arms around her.

"I certainly wasn't expecting to come this much tonight," said Carrie.

"Me either," said Jake. "This was mind-blowing."

He slipped his cock out and Carrie turned around. The two embraced, feeling the cool air on their glistening skin.

"I hope you're not done just yet, though," she said. "I want to ride you cowgirl-style. And I'd love to suck your cock some more. Plus, I want to hear more of your dirty talk. You're right, you are pretty good at it in person."

"We've got all weekend, if you're up for it," said Jake.

"Absolutely," said Carrie.

A faint sound floated up to them from a few floors below.

"Wait, shh," said Carrie. "Listen."

It was Kayla Baker caught in the throes of passion from her room three floors below them. Her balcony doors must have been open as well.

"Ohh, fuck! Tristan, you're a goddamn beast!" shouted Kayla. "Fuck me, you beast!"

Jake and Carrie stared at each other, astonished.

"I could have gone my whole life without hearing that," said Carrie. "At all."

"Maybe we should close the door," said Jake.

CHASTITY VELDT

Jackie in Jacksonville

STAND UP, LIE DOWN COLLECTION

TABLE OF CONTENTS

CHAPTER 1

Hello, Mankato South Grizzlies, Class of 2011! Can you believe it's been ten years? We're excited to see you again for the upcoming reunion at the Eagle Lake Yacht Club. Dinner is at 6:30, drinks and dancing in the ballroom at 9:00, and the memories will flow all night! Hope you can make it, fellow Grizzlies! Rawr, rawr!

Jake glared at the heavy cardstock invitation once more and sighed as he checked himself in the mirror. *Buttons straight? Yep. Shirt tucked? Also yep. Wallet? Yep, yep yep.*

He pulled on his jacket, grabbed his keys and the invitation. Walking out of the hotel, he couldn't remember what kind of car he had rented, so he took a few minutes to scan the lot before finally hitting the panic button. The alarm sounded off, and he found the car. He pulled out of the parking lot and headed toward his destination. Jake was not particularly looking forward to his reunion, but he was going because his parents had begged him to go.

He called home at least once a week, but he hadn't been back to Mankato since he left on his trip nearly eight months ago, making his first stop in Milwaukee, Wisconsin.[26] That's because Jake had been touring the Midwest and Southeast as a standup comic, working as the headliner in small venues and the middle in others. Jake had just finished a conference at Abraxus Tasker College,[27] and flew back home for the reunion. He planned to drive to Jacksonville, leave his truck at the airport, then fly home. When it was all over, he would return to Florida and do his show in Jacksonville that week.

"It'll be good to see you, Jakey," his mom had said as he drove to the airport. "We haven't seen you in months."

"It'll be good to see you and Dad, too. I've been a little homesick."

"You'll have to get a hotel room though," she said.

"What, really?" Jake asked. "What's wrong with my old room?"

"Well, your father and I have turned it into our meditation and yoga studio. We cleaned everything out, replaced the carpet with bamboo flooring and tatami mats, and now we sit in there and meditate or do yoga. It's very sensual."

"Mom—" Jake squirmed in his seat, uncomfortable at the direction this conversation had taken.

"Or is that sensuous? Whichever one means sexy."

---

[26] See *Stand Up, Lie Down #1: Molly in Milwaukee.* Now available on Kindle!

[27] See *Stand Up, Lie Down #7: Carrie on Campus.* Now available on Kindle!

"Mom, I don't like where this conversation is go—" Jake looked for a cliff he could drive over, but he was in Florida driving to the Jacksonville airport.

"Sometimes, we'll turn on a portable heater and do hot yoga."

"Mom, please."

"Ooh, and sometimes, on a special occasion, your father will want to do hot nude yoga, which always ends up with us—"

"MOM! Okay, I'll get a hotel room."

"Thank you, dear. I don't think you'd want to sleep in there with the state it's in."

"I don't think I want to sleep in there ever again."

At the mention of yoga, Jake's mind briefly flitted back to a torrid love affair he'd had with Betty and Sheila in Birmingham, Alabama.[28] Betty was a rich Southern belle and Sheila was her yoga instructor. His cock began to swell as he thought of the three-day threesome they'd had and their passionate declarations of love.

Then his thoughts shifted... At the mention of hot nude yoga, Jake accidentally thought of his parents doing what he and Betty had done, and his hard-on quickly vanished. And his cock hammered on his pelvic bone, begging to please be let back inside, *pretty please.*

His parents had always been rather open and frank about their personal lives, which drove Jake and his siblings crazy. "Seriously, Mom, you don't need to keep me apprised of your personal life. I only need to know that you and Dad love each other and that you remember each other's birthdays."

---

[28] See *Stand Up, Lie Down #6: Betty In Birmingham.* The last few pages are my favorite in the entire series. — C.V.

"Speaking of birthdays, did I tell you about the yoga session your father and I had on my last birthday?"

Jake dropped his phone in his lap. "Shit! Shit! Hold on, Mom. Are you still there?"

"I'm still here."

"Dammit," Jake whispered.

"Anyway, about my lovely birthday yoga session."

"What, Mom? I can't hear you. I'm going into a tunnel. My... breaking... call... later."

"Jakey, you're in Florida, there are no tunnels."

"kkkkkkkk... massive forest fire... kkkkkk... flames all around..."

"OK, Jakey, message received. I'll see you when you get here tomorrow. Bye-bye, Sweetie."

"Bye, Mom."

Now, after spending a few days with his family and avoiding eye contact with his parents whenever the subject of yoga came up, Jake was off to his ten-year reunion of the Grizzlies of Mankato South High.

He pulled into the Eagle Lake Yacht Club and tossed his car keys to the valet who handed him his ticket. He walked into the Club, buttoning his jacket and looking around for anyone he knew. The foyer was empty, but there were several dozen people in the dining room off to the right. The large room was decorated in Mankato South's colors, purple and cream, with the large purple grizzly bear statue the school was known for.

Jake recalled the time that the football team from Mankato North stole their purple grizzly before the city championships. He and some of his swim team buddies stole it back before the game started as well as stealing the school's state baseball trophy and drinking celebratory beers from it after the game. Mankato South had lost 21 – 20, so they consoled themselves by getting drunk out of the stolen trophy before returning it a week later.

This grizzly looked newer than the one they had ten years ago, and Jake wondered if the old one had been stolen again but never found.

He approached the registration table and said, "Hi, I'm here for the reunion."

"Jake Nellson?" asked the woman standing behind the table. She was slender and wore a black cocktail dress and a pearl necklace. Her hair reached down to her chin and curved around her face like a couple of parentheses. She looked like she fit right in at the Eagle Lake Yacht Club, and he recognized her as one of the "Mankato Elite" that he went to high school with.

"Nilsen," said Jake. "Is that Hatty Cooper?

"Hattie Kuper, actually," said Hattie, a touch of frost in her voice. "Kuper-Rasmussen."

"Sorry, I'll bet you get that a lot," said Jake.

"You have no idea," said Hattie.

"I can imagine. Sorry about that. It's been a while, and I've been away."

"So I hear. You're a big-time comic now, right?"

"Well, I wouldn't say big-time. How about you?"

"I'm married to Tad Rasmussen, and we have two wonderful children, Liam and Oliver. Tad is in real estate development and I lead the local group chapter and take my boys to soccer and dance lessons. Do you want to see some pictures?"

Jake flinched. He had always thought Hattie Kuper was insufferable in high school, and he was already reaching his limit with her now. "Ohhh, maybe in a little bit."

"Great, well most everyone is here for dinner, we're just waiting for a few stragglers. You can go in and grab a seat, and we'll get started soon."

"Thank you, Hattie. It's good to see you." Jake walked away and pinned his name tag to his lapel.

Jake wandered inside and looked around. There were over a hundred men and women in the room, nearly all of them white, which you would expect in rural Minnesota. He looked for someone he knew, but despite it only being ten years since they had all been together, Jake was having a hard time recognizing most of these people.

He began to wonder if he'd made a mistake and should just leave before anyone noticed him when he heard a voice call his name. He looked over and saw a guy stand up from a table and wave.

"Jake! Jake Nilsen! Over here!" shouted the guy.

"No, Jake Nilsen over here," Jake shouted back, pointing at himself.

"Come here, dumbass," called the guy.

Jake strode over, a grin splitting his face. "Leadweight Larsen," he said and embraced his friend in a bear hug. "How the hell are you?"

"Doing great now, buddy. Now the party can start." Ken "Leadweight" Larsen turned to a blonde woman standing next to him. "Babe, this is my buddy, Jake Nilsen. We were on the swim team together."

"Nilsen?" asked the woman.

"Er, yes?" said Jake, a bit surprised. No one ever said his name right the first time.

"Hi, I'm Alice Larson-Larsen," said Alice Larson-Larsen. She held out her hand, and Jake shook it. Alice was short, around 5'4", a true Minnesota blond with blue eyes and cannonball shoulders but a slender body like a runner's.

"Are you a swimmer too?" asked Jake.

"Triathlons, actually," said Alice. "I was a swimmer at University of Wisconsin, and I took up triathlons after I graduated."

"Badgers, eh? How'd you end up in Gopher territory?"

"That's where we met," said Ken. "I was swimming for Wisconsin and she was on the women's team."

"I thought you went to Minnesota, but I know you left," said Jake. "I never heard from you when you came back." Several of his swimming teammates all went to the University of Minnesota, although Jake was the only one good enough to make the school swim team. He was nearly on the 2016 Olympic team but missed it by a fraction of a second; he didn't like to talk about it.

"Actually, I didn't go back. I dropped out for a year and moved to Madison to work for my uncle at his company. I met the residency requirement and enrolled at UW and got on the swim team there. And that's where I met Alice. We got married a few years ago."

"And Larson-Larsen?" asked Jake.

"My maiden name is Larson, so I hyphenated."

"Ah." Jake leaned in a bit. "Do you ever get people who say your name wrong? Like, not terribly wrong, but just a tiny bit wrong?"

"Like the difference between Larson and Larsen?" asked Alice.

"Yes! Or like Nilsen and Nilssen. Or Nielsen. Or Nilsin."

"All the time! It's like people can't even hear the difference, which is weird. It's so obvious!"

"I know!" said Jake. "It's like I'm speaking a foreign language to them."

"Jeez, tell me about it," said Ken Larsen. "I don't know how many times people have asked me whether my Larsen or her Larson is first in her hyphenated name. I mean, it's pretty obvious, isn't it? It's mine, right, babe?"

"What? No! Are you kidding me right now? It's my name. Larson!"

Ken threw his head back and laughed. "Gotcha!"

Alice laughed and swatted him with her napkin. "Ass."

Jake felt a hand snake around his waist, and he turned around. "Rachel Hagen!" he exclaimed when he saw who was attached to the hand.

She squealed with excitement and leaped into his arms as he picked her up in a huge embrace. Rachel planted a big smooch on his lips and said, "Welcome home, big boy!"

Rachel was a few inches taller than Alice, a few pounds heavier, had dark brown curly hair in an upsweep hairdo that made her look like a 1940s film star. She wore a black satin dress that was cut low in the front, pushing her ample breasts together and showing cleavage so deep that, if a small child fell into it, it would prompt a national news story as rescuers tried to dig her out. Jake couldn't tell if they were natural or medically assisted, but he didn't care. They were spectacular. Her arterial-blood-spray-red lipstick shone in the lights, a little smeared after kissing Jake.

In high school, Rachel had been what your grandparents would have called "bawdy" and "brassy," or even "coarse" if your grandparents were uptight little prudes like they were in Mankato, Minnesota. She laughed loud, was raucous, loved to laugh, made inappropriate jokes, and everyone knew when she was in the room.

"You look amazing," Jake said. "Wow, I mean look at you. You look really wonderful."

"So do you," said Rachel. "The years have been most kind." She squeezed his biceps and let her eyes wander up and down his trim, muscular form a couple of times.

Jake turned and put his arm around Rachel's shoulders as he held onto her hand and pulled it around his waist. "Ken, do you remember Rachel Hagen?"

"Of course," said Ken. "You were one of the theater kids. I remember you and Jake were in The Drowsy Chaperone with Jake our senior year. You were Janet van de Graaff and Jake was—"

"I am ... Adolpho!" Jake declared, recalling his memorable line from the play. Rachel squealed and clapped her hands together, jumping up and down a little, which made her breasts jiggle.

"Hi. I'm Alice Larson-Larsen," said Alice, moving possessively closer to her husband and holding out her hand.

"Larsen-Larson?" said Rachel.

Alice rolled her eyes. "No, Lars—"

"I'm just kidding," said Rachel, winking. She shook Alice's hand and winced a little at the strength of Alice's grip. "With a name like Hagen, I get it all the time. Haugen, Hawgen, Haggen. I even convinced one guy my father was Mr. Häagen of the Häagen-Dasz ice cream company."

"What happened?" asked Alice.

"The dumbass ghosted me because he had Type 2 diabetes and didn't want to be tempted."

"So who are you here with," asked Jake.

"Nobody, how about you?" asked Rachel.

"Same as you."

"Fine, then you're my date tonight. Is that alright?" declared Rachel; Alice visibly relaxed but didn't release her grip on Ken's bicep.

"It's the only thing keeping me here," said Jake, smiling bigger than he had all week.

All throughout high school, Jake had harbored a secret crush on Rachel Hagen and had tried out for a play his sophomore year so that he could be near her. Even though Jake was one of the best swimmers in the state and fit in with the jock clique fairly well, they never quite accepted him because he was also a regular member of the theater department, appearing in any plays that didn't conflict with the swimming season or practice. He even started attending theater workshops and camps in the summer. But he never quite fit in with the theater kids either because he was a jock.

Jake never acted on his crush on Rachel, considering her out of his league. So he just gazed at her from afar until it was time to go to college. Jake went off to the University of Minnesota, Rachel went to Hamline University, and the two lost touch.

The four of them sat at their table and chattering happily about what they had been doing since they left high school. Ken and Alice lived in Milwaukee and worked for tech startup companies. Rachel was an account manager at a marketing agency in Minneapolis. And Jake had his stand-up comedy. He didn't discuss his real estate investment or recent investment in two high-end car washes in Miami or the strip mall in Savannah, Georgia, preferring to keep his small-but-growing fortune secret.

After dinner, the four moved to the ballroom for drinking and dancing, and despite several requests from other men and women, Rachel and Jake didn't share their dancing with anyone else. They sat in a corner on a couch and talked all night, pausing only to greet old classmates who stopped by. As the night wore on and the crowd thinned out, Ken and Alice said their goodbyes and headed out the door after promising to meet for dinner the next evening.

"We should probably get out of here too," said Jake, "otherwise they'll put us on the cleanup committee."

"Ooh, they totally will. Hattie Kuper already asked me if I wanted to help out when I got here. She said my marketing experience 'would be so helpful.' Bitch. And that's after she tried to get me to look at pictures of her damn kids," said Rachel. "I said I had plans afterward and couldn't stick around. God, she was always a stuck-up bitch in high school."

"Do you have plans after this?" asked Jake.

Rachel smiled. "I don't know. Are you staying at your parents' this weekend?"

"No, I'm at the Squire Arms downtown."

"Then, no, I don't have any plans. I hear the Squire Arms has very nice rooms. Is that right?"

"Well, my room is pretty nice. I upgraded to a suite and it's pretty elegant for Mankato."

"Oh, really? That's very nice. Maybe you could send me some cell phone photos of it," Rachel deadpanned.

"I mean, sure, but I figured you might want to come up and see for yourself."

Rachel swung her leg over Jake's lap and straddled him, her cocktail-length skirt covering her ass as she ground her crotch on his hardening cock and her cleavage pressed against his chin.

"I thought you'd never ask, Loverboy." She rubbed her pussy against his cock, and he could swear she wasn't wearing any panties.

"Oh, look at the time. We'd better go." Jake stood up suddenly, holding onto Rachel so she didn't fall backward before setting her down. Jake adjusted himself so his boner wouldn't show and hustled toward the parking lot.

"Are you two free to help with cleanup?" Hattie Kuper called after them.

"No, we have to leave urgently," said Jake.

"Sorry, Hatty Cooper," called Rachel.

"It's Hattie Kuper, goddammit," Hattie grumbled to herself. "Hattie Kuper-Rasmussen."

CHAPTER 2

"Wow, this *is* a nice suite," said Rachel, flipping on the lights. She ran over to Jake's bed and flung herself through the air and bounced when she landed on it. "Now, where were we?"

"Well, at the Yacht Club, you were straddling my lap on the couch," Jake said, gesturing to the couch several feet away.

"That's as good of a starting point as any," Rachel rolled off the bed taking Jake's hand, and guided him over to the couch. She pushed him down and straddled him once more. She kissed him deeply, grinding her pussy on his hard cock. Jake wrapped his arms around her waist and pulled her tightly to him. Rachel's breathing quickened as she continued to rock her hips and her sensitive nether regions responded to the friction.

Jake felt around on Rachel's back until his thick, strong fingers finally found the zipper, and he slowly pulled it down, opening it until he reached the end. Rachel raised up and slipped her arms out, then pulled it over her head. She was wearing a red lacy bra, and as Jake discovered, a matching red thong.

The bra looked like it was in need of a break as well as it had spent the entire night squeezing Rachel's bocce ball-sized breasts together.

"Do you like 'em? They were a gift to myself after I divorced my husband, Owen."

Jake showed his admiration for them by burying his face between them, kissing and licking Rachel's chest.

"Mmph mmm hmph hmm?" said Jake.

"What?"

Jake raised his head from the place where he hoped to die one day. "Why did you divorce him?"

"He was sleeping with my assistant."

"Ouch," said Jake. "That sucks."

"Tell me about it," said Rachel. "I haven't been able to find an assistant as good as Gary."

"Ah," said Jake. "Enough talking, more sexing."

Rachel laughed and shoved Jake's head back into her cleavage. "Agreed. Suck my big titties, Loverboy."

As Jake eagerly complied, Rachel fumbled with the buttons of his shirt, getting a few of them unbuttoned before she couldn't reach anymore. With his help and a few interruptions of his eager ministrations, she pulled his shirt over his head and gave a little gasp as she saw his rippling abs and huge pectorals.

"Oh my," she murmured. "If I had a dick, I would fuck those pecs."

"I know the feeling," said Jake, kneading her breasts with his powerful fingers.

"Oh, trust me, You're going to put your big cock between my tits. Stand up and let me see what I have to work with." She knelt and undid his belt and pants. "I hope it's not true that swimmers all have little—holy fuck, no it's not!"

As Rachel pulled down Jake's pants and underwear, his eight-and-a-half-inch prick sprang up and pointed itself at Rachel's face. "Oh my, no wonder you were popular with the girls in high school."

"Actually, I wasn't," said Jake. "I only ever wanted one girl in high school."

"Oh yeah? What happened to her?"

"Well, I'm hoping she's about to put my cock in her mouth and make a 13-year fantasy come true."

"Ewww, gross," Rachel said.

"Thirteen. YEAR. Fantasy! Not a 13-year-old's fantasy! C'mon, man!"

Rachel smiled and opened her mouth obligingly. Jake groaned as he watched his dick slip between her still-deep red lips. Rachel delicately held his shaft between a thumb and forefinger as she slowly fed herself, her mouth conforming itself to his cock as it slid, inch-by-inch, into her mouth.

Jake was mesmerized as he watched his dick nearly disappear, only two inches showing before she moved her head back and removed it from her warm mouth. When the tip of his cock reappeared, she looked up at him, smiled, and then repeated the process. She locked eyes with him as she once more returned his cock inside her mouth; Jake felt her relax her throat muscles and slide his member down her throat, her nose touching his pubic region, which he kept shaved smooth.

"Ahhhhhhh," Jake groaned as he heard all the little pops and squishes of her sucking action.

Rachel hummed her appreciation of his prick, and Jake felt the vibrations.

He nearly came right then when she did it. He thought about baseball as much as he could to hold off from jetting in her mouth.

Rachel withdrew it again, strings of thick saliva connecting her lips to his shaft, and she breathed deeply. She smiled, wrapped her long fingers around his cock, and jacked him slowly, using her honey-like saliva as lubrication, making his cock slippery. Jake could not have dreamed anything better than right now: His high school crush sucking his thick cock, taking it into her throat, and jacking him off, cupping his balls with her other hand.

As she felt his balls tighten, she stopped and said, "Not yet, I still have something I want your cum for." Rachel pronounced it "cum," instead of the right way. Jake thought, *Well, what do you expect from theatre girls?*

"That was so fucking hot," Jake said. "I love seeing you suck my cock. Your mouth is so hot and wet."

"Do you know what else is hot and wet?" she asked.

"I don't know, but I bet I'd love to taste it," said Jake.

"I'd love for you to taste it."

Rachel stood up and smiled, removing her tiny red thong. She glided over to the bed, lay back on it, and put her feet up on the bed, spreading her thighs as she did so. She exposed her nearly clean-shaven pussy, running her fingers through the closely-trimmed triangle shape cut into her pubic hair.

Jake knelt before her and lapped at her folds and the dew already emerging. He flicked his tongue on her clit and slid one of his thick fingers into her slit, noting the unintentional rhyme.

"Ooooohhh," moaned Rachel. "Yeah, baby, eat my pussy."

Jake eagerly complied, putting his mouth over her swollen labia and sucking her meaty lips into his mouth. He reached up and rubbed her clit with his thumb.

There was almost nothing Jake loved more about a woman's body than her pussy lips, swollen and red, and he loved nibbling and lightly sucking them, driving his tongue between them. Jake tended to Rachel that way, feasting on her wet snatch, lapping up her juices as she moaned and grabbed handfuls of his hair between her slender fingers. He alternated between sliding his tongue up her slit and flickering his tongue on her pink pearl. He slid two of his fingers inside her, and that's all it took to push her over the edge.

"Oh God, Jake! That's amazing. Fuck, where did you learn to eat pussy like that! Oh, don't answer, just eat me, goddammit. Eat my pussy. OH GOD OH GOD I'M CUMMING, JAKE! OH... GOD... AHHHHHHHHHHHHHHH!"

Rachel clamped her thighs around Jake's head as he continued to tongue-fuck her and rub her clit.

As the waves of her first orgasm crashed over her and subsided, Rachel released her death grip on Jake's head and pulled him up. "Oh, hold off a bit, Chief. My pussy's a little sensitive after I cum."

Jake raised his head and grinned, his face shiny with her juices. "No problem. I was hoping there was something else we could do."

Rachel grinned and squeezed her tits together with her hands. "Me too."

Jake climbed onto the bed and straddled her torso, resting his cock between her tits.

"I think you need a little lubrication first," she said, opening her mouth in invitation. Jake raised up and leaned forward, guiding his cock toward her mouth. She managed to suck in an inch or two, so Jake moved forward in a plank position, his cock directly over Rachel's head. He slid his cock into her mouth as if he were fucking her face, and she moaned in appreciation.

Jake slid his member in and out as she provided counter-suction, making it like no cunt he'd ever been inside.

"Oh fuck, that feels amazing," he groaned. "I want to do that again later." He reluctantly pulled out of her mouth and consoled himself by putting his thick shaft between her tits. Rachel squeezed them together, trapping his dick, and he slid his cock in and out of her cleavage. He went slowly, enjoying the feeling of her gorgeous tits on his cock.

"All night, the guys at the reunion kept staring at my tits," said Rachel. "Some of the women, too. But all night, I only wanted you to see them and to put your mouth on them."

"Is it everything you wanted?"

"It's amazing," she gasped. "And now I want you to cum on them. What do you say, Loverboy?"

"Let's see what we can do." Jake reached down and helped her squeeze her tits together. *OK,* maybe not so much helped as squeezed and played with them even as she held them for his pleasure. "Ohh, fuck, I've dreamed of this for years," he groaned. "I've wanted to have my cock and my hands on your tits."

"Wow, you *are* a dirty little perv," Rachel said, smiling. "That's why this is so much fun."

Jake stopped for a moment. "I need some more moisture," he said as he drove forward into her eager mouth. She opened up and accommodated his shaft, letting him fuck her mouth for several seconds. As he sat back down, he pulled a pillow with him. "Lift your head," he said. As she did so, he placed the pillow under her head. "I have an idea."

He resumed his position, placed his dick back between her tits, and drove forward far enough so that his dickhead reached her lips. She smiled at his idea and accepted his cock into her mouth, providing some suction on his head with each thrust so that her mouth popped each time he pulled it out.

Soon, Jake could feel the pressure beginning to build in his balls as he continued to thrust between her globes. Then he raised up, gripped his cock, and jerked off.

"Ahh! Ahh! Here you go, baby, this load is for you. Oh, Rachel, I've dreamed of this."

"Yes! Yes!" shrieked Rachel. "Give me your hot cum!"

"GAAAAHHHH!" Jake bellowed as a rope of white cum jetted out of his cock and splashed onto her tits.

A second burst landed on her tits and reached her neck just below her chin. The third one reached nearly as far, and the fourth and fifth ropes covered her wondrous tits like the glaze on a heavenly doughnut. Rachel propped herself up on her elbows and gave Jake's dick a few quick cleaning sucks to make sure she got every drop.

Then she used her fingers to scoop up some of Jake's cum frosting and popped it into her mouth. "Mmm, that's good cum. Next time, I'm going to want it all in my mouth."

"Just there?" Jake said, breathing heavily, his face and torso slick with sweat.

"Maybe in my pussy too."

"Wherever you want," he said. "I'll give you as much as you want."

"Excellent. Then get me a towel, let's clean up, and we can figure out how much and where."

CHAPTER 3

"Thank you for flying with us," said the voice over the PA, four days later. "We will be departing shortly as soon as the last of our passengers are aboard." Jake returned the safety placard to the seat pocket in front of him and settled in for the connecting flight from Atlanta to Jacksonville, laying back.

A boyfriend, thought Jake. *She has a fucking boyfriend!*

It was Wednesday morning, and Jake was sitting in Business Class on his flight back to Jacksonville, where he had left his pickup in long-term parking at the Jacksonville International Airport. He had a show in Jacksonville at the Poppers Comedy Club that weekend.

He settled in and closed his eyes as his thoughts drifted back to the previous week. He had reunited with the girl of his dreams and had the kind of sex he had fantasized about with her for the entire weekend. He had hoped this was the start of a wonderful new relationship, only to learn that she had a boyfriend.

"When can I see you again?" Jake asked Rachel as they were eating brunch in the Squire Arms restaurant Sunday morning. Both were more than a little tired—and sore and raw and fucked out—after an all-night lovemaking session where neither of them slept for more than a couple of hours. "If you'd like, I can fly you down south to one of my shows."

"Ohh, Loverboy, I wish I could. But I have a boyfriend," Rachel said, slipping a link sausage between her lips and biting down on it, severing the tube of meat in half in a ham-fisted metaphor on the part of the author.

"What, seriously? Why didn't you say anything?" Jake didn't actually have any qualms about sleeping with someone who was already married or had a boyfriend,[29] but he was hoping this could last beyond the weekend.

"Well, it's not serious," she said. "Plus, sleeping with you was something I've been wanting to do since high school. And I finally got to do it."

"Really? Because I had a crush on you in high school," said Jake.

"Yes, really. And I had a major crush on you in high school too."

"Why didn't you say anything?" said Jake.

"Why didn't you?" Rachel retorted.

"I don't know, I was really shy back then, and I was afraid that if you said no, then I wouldn't be able to hang out with you anymore."

---

[29] There was Randie in *Stand Up, Lie Down #1: Molly in Milwaukee*; Mandy in *Stand Up, Lie Down #4: Natasha in Nashville*; and Betty in *Stand Up, Lie Down #6: Betty in Birmingham*. Wow, Jake is a bit of a horndog, huh?

"You certainly didn't seem shy last night. Good God, where did you learn things like that?"

"Uhh, oh, books and Internet porn."

"Uh-huh." She leaned forward and lowered her voice. "That thing you did with your tongue is not something you learn by reading or watching." She leaned back and chomped down on the remaining half of the sausage link, completing the metaphor. "Regardless of where you learned it, I'm not complaining. I've never had that done to me before."

"Not even by what's-his-name?"

"Hoo-boy, especially not by what's-his-name. He's just some guy I latched onto. He just graduated from the U a couple years ago and works at another marketing agency in town. We started out as just fuck buddies, but I think it may get serious soon."

"Then why did you and I—"

"Because it's not serious yet."

Jake took a deep swig of his coffee and got a serious look on his face.

"Oh, come on, Loverboy. I don't have to be back in Minneapolis until tomorrow morning, and I want some more of that good fucking. What's-his-name's got nothing on you, and I need something to remember until I can teach him better. Or until the next reunion." She kicked off her shoe and rubbed her foot on Jake's crotch. She lowered her voice again. "Do you think you can fuck me a few more times before dinner with Ken and Alice?"

"That's not until seven, so I think I can manage once or twice."

"Great, because I want you to bend me over the desk and take me from behind."

Jake forked up another bite of eggs. "We're going to need some more protein then," he said, smiling.

Jake smiled as he felt for his earbuds in his jacket pocket. He may not have had a future with her, but he finally got to live out his high school fantasy with her. Several times.

"What's so funny?" said a voice next to him. Jake's eyes popped open, and a woman was sitting next to him. She was in her mid-thirties, lightly tanned, with green eyes and straight brown hair that curled near the ends and hung past her shoulders.

"Huh? Oh, uh, I was just working out a joke in my head," Jake stammered.

"Do you often laugh at your own jokes?" asked the woman.

"Only the good ones."

This made the woman smile, and he noticed the smile reached her eyes, which showed evidence of several years of joy and laughter. He smiled in return; he never trusted people who didn't have laugh lines.

"Hi, I'm Jake," said Jake.

"I'm Jackie," said Jackie. She held her hand out, and Jake took it in his and shook it. His hand was much larger than hers, but she had a strong grip that surprised him.

"Jackie from Jacksonville?" he mused.

"Yeah, my parents loved the alliteration."

"I know what you mean. I've, uh, met several people with those kinds of names over the last several months."

"Really? How do you manage that?"

"I'm a standup comic and I've been on tour for the last several months. I've got a gig in Jacksonville this weekend. How about you?"

"Ah, so that's why you laugh at your own jokes. I'm a sculptor and potter," she said, which accounted for her strong hands and forearms.

"What are your mediums? Other than clay, that is," he said.

"Well, I like to make outdoor sculptures, so for the last few years, I've worked with steel and welded pieces together, and I've done some blacksmithing. I also like working with stone, so I've done a lot with carving limestone and shaping concrete."

As Jake studied her, he could see that she was rather muscular and in great shape. She was wearing a fitted t-shirt with very short sleeves and a scoop neck. Jackie was also wearing a long skirt and a pair of sandals. Her shoulders were round and developed, her forearms were muscled, and she had strong biceps and a flat stomach.

"I'll bet moving all that iron and stone gives you a workout."

"Oh, absolutely. I really started getting in shape when I started working with outdoor sculptures. How about you? You look pretty toned up."

"I'm a swimmer," said Jake, "and I run when I can't find a pool."

"Well, there's a Y and a few gyms with pools near my studio if you need a place. Where are you staying?"

"I'm not sure yet. The comedy clubs usually have apartments, but this one doesn't for some reason. So they sometimes spring for a hotel."

"What's the club called?" she asked.

"Poppers."

"No kidding? My studio is a few blocks from there. It's in the Five Points neighborhood, and I've walked to Poppers before."

"Are there any hotels in the area?"

"Oh, plenty. And I know there are some Airbnb apartments and lofts in the area too. I've had family visit and that's where they stayed."

"Where do you live in town?"

"I live in my studio, actually. It's an old cabinet factory that I inherited from my grandfather who owned it in the 1940s. He shut the factory down in the 1960s and just used it for storage. My dad converted it into a workshop for him and his car buddies. Then, my dad passed away in 2007 and left it to my mom and me. Now the bottom floor is my studio, and I turned the second floor into a few apartments. I live in the biggest one, and a few artist friends live in two of the others. There's a painting studio in the corner and a pottery wheel and kiln in another. Then the forge and steelwork happens behind the warehouse."

"Holy shit, that sounds amazing!" said Jake. "Man, I'd love to own an old building like that."

"Yeah, you and every other asshole real estate developer in the state. Sorry, I didn't mean to call you an asshole."

Jake laughed and said, "No offense taken. I mean, it would be cool just to have an old building like that."

"I don't know how many of them have been trying to buy my building to either tear it down or tear everything out and convert it into small one-bedroom 'boho' apartments."

"Boho?"

"Bohemian. Five Points was hipster central a few years ago, and all those people want to do tiny living but still have running water. So they want tiny apartments. Fucking Millennials."

"Aren't we Millennials?" Jake said.

"Yes, and we're the *worst!*" Jackie said dramatically, flinging her arm to her forehead.

Jake smiled at that, his own eyes crinkling at the corners.

The flight attendant gave the flight safety instructions, and Jake and Jackie talked through the entire trip. He told her about life on the road as a standup comic, and she spoke of her life as a professional artist. A life that was partly possible because she owned her home and even got rent from her tenants. She didn't charge very much, she explained, because these were also artists, and housing could get expensive around Jacksonville.

Jake learned Jackie was a world-renowned artist, though, and her sculptures had been installed around the U.S., as well as Canada, Argentina, Luxembourg, and South Korea.

"Now I'm just looking for some ways to invest my money. I don't suppose standup comics know anything about wealth management, do they?"

"Actually, my old teammate, Alan Johansen, is a wealth advisor in Birmingham, Alabama. I can put you in touch with him. He's managing my portfolio and has gotten me into a couple of good real estate investments. Uhh, not tearing anything down. I own some student housing rentals in Minneapolis, and have partial ownership in a couple of car washes in Miami and a strip mall in Savannah."

"Savannah's only a couple hours from Jacksonville."

"Maybe I should go up there. I've never even seen the place."

The two talked about investments and some of the options Jake had seen over the last few years. The conversation turned to more personal subjects, and the two turned in their seats so they were facing each other, Jackie's hand resting on Jake's.

"So are you a member of the Mile High Club?" Jackie asked.

Jake blushed and stammered. "Uh, uh, uh, what?"

"Have you ever thought about, you know, screwing a total stranger in an airplane bathroom?"

"It's a little early in the book for that, don't you think?" said Jake.

"What?"

"What? I mean, I would love to, but we're going to land in fifteen minutes, and I'd like to think I'd take a little longer than that."

"Oh, jeez!" shrieked Jackie, laughing uproariously. "I didn't mean us! Oh my God, that's so embarrassing. I was just—I'm so bad at flirting and being sexy and I just said the first thing that came to mind! And I can't believe I said any of that."

Jake laughed with her and said, "Don't feel bad. I'll tell you a secret about myself. I'm bad at dirty talk unless I'm actually in the act at that moment. Like, right now, if we were trying to talk dirty to each other, I would stammer and get all embarrassed. But if I'm actually having sex, I can talk dirty like it was my job."

There was a chime overhead, interrupting the awkwardness that both of them were feeling. The flight attendant's voice came over the PA and said, "Ladies and gentlemen, the captain has turned on the seatbelt sign which means we will be landing in a few minutes. So if you could fasten your seat belts, please."

"If we could fasten our seat belts what?" said Jackie. "What will happen? That's an incomplete sentence, dammit!"

Jake laughed. "Marry me."

Jackie laughed with him. "It depends on your view of the Oxford comma."

"It's a must. Otherwise you get, 'We invited the strippers, JFK and Stalin,'" Jake said, quoting the old Internet meme on the subject.

Jackie squeezed his hand. "I've always wanted a June wedding. We'll keep it small, about thirty people total."

The two laughed and faced forward, but Jackie didn't release his hand, and Jake didn't pull away.

As the two were walking through the airport, hand in hand, Jackie said, "Well, this is where I leave you, Jake Nilsen. I have to go down and catch an Uber."

"Actually, I could drive you, if you'd like," Jake said. "I parked my truck here last week and I'm heading over to Poppers. Since you're close, I can give you a lift."

"I would love that. Thank you."

The two caught a shuttle to long-term parking, stowed their luggage in the back of the specially-locked truck bed, and Jake had Jackie punch her address into his GPS.

When they arrived at her building, Jake whistled admiringly. "Wow, she's a real beauty. I can see why you want to save her from the developers. And I love the sculpture out front. I'm guessing that's one of yours."

"Yes, it was the first metal sculpture I ever did, after doing concrete and limestone for several years."

"I can understand why your stuff is installed around the world."

"Aww, thank you. That's very kind."

"Say, I have to go check-in at Poppers and let them know I'm here and find a hotel, but I don't have a show until tomorrow. I've had a great time talking with you. Could I take you to dinner tonight?"

"Sure, that would be great. And I didn't want to offer earlier, because I didn't know you very well. But if you're interested, I actually have a very small apartment that's empty right now. You can stay there for the week. I'll loan you some sheets and a towel, and you can use that while you're here. No charge!"

"That would be great," said Jake, smiling a bright smile.

"Wonderful. Let me show you where to park then you can go up and I'll give you the key. You can check-in then come back and rest before we leave."

CHAPTER 4

"Hi, I'm looking for Cherie. Is she around?" Jake was in the bar area of Poppers Comedy Club. A few staff members were cleaning up and getting the place ready for tonight's open mic.

"She's in the back office," said one of the servers, pointing to a hallway with a sign that said "RESTROOMS" hanging over it.

"Is she in the men's or women's?" asked Jake.

"Let me guess, you're a comic," said the woman, rolling her eyes.

"Um, no," mumbled Jake. "I sell, uh, matchbooks." He hurried down the hall, spotting a third door that said, "Manager." He knocked and the door opened.

"Can I help you?" said the woman who answered the door. She was tall and blonde, a little heavyset, and wore tan pants and a women's polo shirt.

"Are you Cherie?" asked Jake.

"Guilty," said Cherie. "Are you Jake Nilsen?"

"No, Nil—er, wait, yes. Nilsen." *This is weird. Twice in one book? That* never *happens*, thought Jake.

"I was just looking at your headshot that your manager sent over. Plus he told me how to pronounce your name right."

"Ah."

"Cookie?" Cherie offered him one from a plate of chocolate chip cookies she'd been enjoying before he knocked.

"Ooh, don't mind if I do. I love chocolate chip. Thank you very much."

"You're welcome. I made 'em myself," said Cherie. They were excellent and Jake said as much.

"So, do you need a hotel tonight? I wasn't sure if you'd want a place. We've got an apartment, but it got annihilated a couple of weeks ago by Curtis Sanders and his girlfriend, Anna. Apparently, another friend of theirs, Debi, came to visit, and the three of them trashed the place with some marathon sex session. I got complaints from the neighbors and I'm having the place steam cleaned now. And redecorated."

"Shit, that's incredibl...y rude and terrible," said Jake, deciding not to admit to knowing Curtis. He and the other comic had a tradition of sharing their sex stories with each other in a competition. The loser had to buy the winner dinner, and Jake was worried this story would be a five-star meal winner. "Whoever this Curtis guy is, I hope he's ashamed of himself."

"Oh, come off it," laughed Cherie. "I know he's your friend. Sherie, the manager at Popcorn in Atlanta, is a friend of mine. She told me about the last time the two of you were in town. Alyssa says hi, by the way."[30]

Cherie winked, and Jake's face turned red as he smiled at the memory. Alyssa was the annoying-but-sexy server at Popcorn he had spent that weekend having athletic sex with.

"So what about that hotel, stud? We can set you up with a Best Western about twelve miles from here. It's cheap, but it's clean."

"No need," said Jake. "A friend has an apartment she's going to let me borrow while I'm here. She's just a couple blocks from here." Jake described the former warehouse and its proximity to the club.

"Oh, sure, I know that place," said Cherie. "There's a really cool sculpture out front."

"That's my friend's sculpture. I'll let her know you like it."

The two chatted a little longer before Jake excused himself to go back to Jackie's apartment to shower and get ready for dinner.

"Florida lobster tails for the lady, and for you, big guy?" said the server, looking at Jake expectantly, pen and pad at the ready. Jake and Jackie were at the Barnacled Hull, one of the local seafood restaurants near Jacksonville Beach. They were sitting in a booth near the open wall, looking out at the ocean and listening to the crashing of the waves.

"I'll have the mahi mahi with spicy rice," said Jake. "Thank you."

The server took their menus and left.

"Man, we don't have weather this nice in Mankato in November," Jake said, looking out at the ocean.

---

[30] See *Stand Up, Lie Down #5: Alyssa in Atlanta.*

"Is that where you were?" asked Jackie.

"My ten-year class reunion was this weekend and my parents talked me into going."

"No kidding? My 15-year reunion is coming up next year. I don't know if I'll go." she shrugged.

"Why not?" asked Jake.

"I didn't have a great high school experience. I was one of the arty kids. People either ignored me or hassled me. I just kept to myself or hung out with a few friends. What about you? I'll bet you were real popular in high school. That blonde hair and great body. Were you on the swim team?"

"Yes, I was on the swim team, but no, I wasn't that popular. I was also in the theatre, so neither clique fully included me. I was too actor-y for the swimmers and too athletic for the actors. I hung out with both groups, but I was the tagalong."

"And how was the reunion?"

"It was ... pretty great. I saw some old friends and got to spend some time with a few people I knew."

Jake could feel himself get a little melancholy, and he knew he would mope all night if he let the mood take hold. So he raised his beer in a toast, and Jackie raised her white wine.

"To art," he said. "May we always have beautiful things to look at."

"To comedy," said Jackie. "May we always have corny things to laugh at."

Jake snickered. "To comedy. But I was serious."

"Aww, thank you." Jackie blushed and looked out at the ocean. The evening wind blew in and blew her hair across her face. She combed it behind her head with her fingers. The two chatted for a few more minutes until their food arrived, and they dug in. They enjoyed the food for a while, and Jackie spoke up. "So what do you do when you're not doing comedy? Do you have a regular job?"

"No, I've just been living on the road for the last several months. I drive from venue to venue, do my shows, and then move on to the next one. This week, I flew home for the reunion, and I'm doing this show, then my tour is officially over. My agent thinks he can set me up with another seven or eight shows out west, but I'm still wondering if I want to go all the way out there or just stick with the eastern half of the U.S. for another year. Or maybe I'll stay somewhere for a month and relax."

"Lots of beautiful women out west," said Jackie.

"Lots of beautiful women right here," said Jake.

Jackie smiled and looked down at her plate. "So about the wedding," she said.

Jake turned pale. "Oh! Uhh, were you...?"

Jackie threw her head back and laughed. "Jesus, Jake, you look absolutely panicked! I was kidding, you dope."

"Ohh," Jake breathed a sigh of relief. "That was a good one."

"So when do you have to decide about the next leg of your tour?"

"I probably will take a month off and then go wherever he can get me booked."

"Where will you stay in the meantime?"

"Oh, I don't know. I might go down to Miami and visit the car washes, or head up to Savannah and finally see the strip mall. Or I may just fly home and hang out there."

"Eww, Mankato in December? I can't imagine being that cold for so long."

"It's not so bad. You get used to it."

"You're not cold now?" asked Jackie. She was wearing a light sweater and rubbed her arms to warm them up.

"No, are you kidding? This is beautiful. Are you cold?"

"It's getting a bit cool," she said. The temperature was seventy-two degrees, which Jake and all of Mankato, Minnesota, considered a warm spring day.

"Why don't you slide around here then. I'll keep you warm."

Jackie smiled and slid over to Jake, who put his arm around her. She leaned into him and breathed his scent in. It was a manly, musky scent, a combination of his body and his cologne.

"I feel safe with you," she said.

She took another deep breath of him and stroked his thigh with her fingertips. Jackie gasped as she saw the outline of Jake's eight-and-a-half-inch dick swell in his pants. Jake kissed the top of her head in response.

"Did... did... I do that?" she asked, looking up at him, a hint of nervous longing in her eyes.

Jake kissed her forehead. "I'm afraid you did."

She looked at it, and her hand moved toward it then jerked away as if it were a hot stove. "Can I touch it?"

"Yes. Please," Jake whispered hoarsely.

Jackie pinched it lightly between her thumb and forefinger and poked it to see how hard it was. It was like iron now, and Jackie knew how to work with iron. She squeezed it between her fingers and the heel of her hand, running it up and down the length of his shaft.

"I'd love to see this in person," she said.

"Check, please," he called to the server.

He dropped several twenties on the table, and the two left like the server was about to ask them to be on the cleanup committee.

CHAPTER 5

"You'll have to be gentle with me," Jackie said in Jake's ear as he kissed and licked her neck. She wrapped her legs around his waist, and he held her up in the large service elevator in her warehouse. "I don't know if I'll be able to get all of that inside me."

She had gotten a preview as Jake had driven them back from the restaurant. She pulled out his cock and had given him a slow handjob as they drove, stopping before he came, leaving his ballsack full of come.

"We'll take it as slow as you need," he said.

He cupped one of her breasts in his hand and held her up with his other. Her breasts were smaller but perky and firm, about the size of tennis balls. Each. They were each the size of a tennis ball. Not both of them together were the size of a single tennis ball. That would be weird. Plus, where would you even put the nipples?

Jesus, would you quit that? thought Jake. *I'm trying to concentrate here.*

Sorry, said the author. *I've been drinking.*

Jake had been sneaking tiny glances at Jackie's cleavage most of the night and had been hoping he could get a good look at her tits up close. He was about to get his chance.

Jackie handed Jake her key and said, "It's the door on the left."

Jake let them in and kicked the door shut behind him. He carried her to the couch and plopped onto it with her straddling his lap. Jackie lifted her skirt to her hips, and Jake helped her take off her t-shirt and bra. He kissed and licked her breasts, enjoying their size and shape, which, as described earlier, were like tennis balls. But they weren't yellow and fuzzy, just smooth and normal skin—

Seriously! Stop it! thought Jake.

Sorry, sorry. I'm good. Won't happen again.

He gently squeezed them, sucking one of her nipples into his mouth and pinching the other, making her moan. She ran her fingers through his hair and arched her back, urging him to suck and lick her harder. Jake pulled her back up and slowly lifted her skirt; she helped him, pulling it over her head. Then she unbuttoned his shirt and slid it over his head. He pulled her against his chest and wrapped his arms around her so he could feel her bare skin against his. She licked his ear and nuzzled his neck, giving small kisses and tiny sucks in the crook of his neck.

"I love the feeling of our skin together," he said. "You're so soft and silky and I love how you feel against me."

The two kissed and licked each other's neck, just enjoying the feeling of their skin against each other. Jake was able to reach his hands around to the opposite sides of her ribs, his left hand on her left ribs and right hand on her right ribs. He ran his fingers up and down her ribs, feeling each one like he was counting them as she drove her tongue hard against his neck.

"Oh, fuck, your tongue feels wonderful," he murmured.

He shifted his hands and kneaded her strong back muscles as she stayed mashed against him, grinding her cunt against his raging hard-on, still in his pants.

"I want to see it," she said. "Let me see your dick."

They stood up, Jake standing several inches taller than her. She undid his belt and opened his pants. Jake slid them down and kicked them off, and Jackie removed her lacy purple panties. She held Jake's cock like she was shaking hands with it and stroked it in an underhanded motion.

"This *is* a big one," she said. "I hope this will fit in my pussy."

"Do you want to suck it?" he rasped.

"I'm not very good at it," she said.

Jake sat back on the couch and pushed his hips forward. Jackie knelt in front of him and licked his head and shaft a few times before she put it in her mouth. She tried to take as much in as she could but could only manage a few inches before she had to stop.

"I'm sorry," she said. "I'm sorry, I wish I could suck more."

"Never apologize," said Jake. "I've got a beautiful woman putting my cock in her mouth. There's nothing I could ever complain about."

Jackie smiled and sucked him back in. She bobbed her head up and down, using her fist to jack him off as she sucked. Her hair fell and blocked Jake's view of the beautiful sight, so he pulled it gently back to reveal her green eyes gazing up at him as she worked his prick in and out of her mouth. He watched the suction she was putting on his dick, watched her cheeks hollow out with the pressure, and could feel his come rising. He was getting close to a release.

She would pause every so often, lick the sides of his shaft again for lubrication, then return to her sucking and pumping. Jake could feel the pressure build in his ball sack, and he squirmed in anticipation.

"I'm going to come in a minute, baby. Where do you want me to come?" he said, using the proper pronunciation of "come." He figured anyone who loved the Oxford comma would say it that way instead of "cum."

"Not yet," she said, removing his cockhead with a *pop*. "I want you to eat my pussy first."

Jake groaned in frustration. That was twice she had postponed his release. She sat down next to him on the couch and he took her place on the floor, nestled between her slender, powerful thighs. Jake pulled her hips toward him so they were on the edge of her couch. He kissed and licked his way up one thigh, sliding his tongue in the crevice where her leg and her pelvis met, and skipped over her wet cunt, licked the other crevice, then worked his way back down her other thigh.

"Oooooh, Jake. You missed my pussy. Please eat my pussy. Please," she moaned. Jackie squirmed as he further opened her thighs like he was opening a precious treasure, revealing her pink folds and swollen labia.

She rested her legs over his shoulders, her small feet resting on his V-shaped back. Jake licked the entire length of her wet cunt once, twice, three times, like he was eating an ice cream cone on a hot summer day. Jake lapped at her lips, pausing once in a while to suck her labia into his mouth. Jackie's juices flowed as he continued his tender ministrations to her wetness. Each stroke of his tongue slid over her hard clitoris, which he gently massaged with his thumb as he lapped at her lips.

"Ohhhhhh, Jake, lover, I'm going to come. You're making me come with your mouth. Ohh, you'd better stop, or I'll come in your mouth. No, Jake, ahhhhh! Jake, ahhhhhhhh! JAKE, STOP! I'M GOING TO COME IN YOUR MOUTH!"

Jake looked up and met her eyes but didn't stop licking. He smiled even as his tongue worked its magic, and he gripped her forearms with his strong hands.

"OHHH, GOD. YOU WANT THIS! YOU WANT ME TO COME IN YOUR MOUTH!" Jackie shrieked, writing in delicious agony as he continued sliding his tongue up her drenched pussy, flicking it over her hard pearl. "OH, FUCK, LOVER! I'M... OH GOD, GET READY... HERE I GO... IN YOUR MOUTH... I'M... OHHH! OHHH! AAAAAAAAA!!!!"

Jackie bucked and writhed as her first orgasm washed over her, and still Jake continued licking her, working her back up toward her second.

"OHH, Jake, I'm going to come again. Ohhhhh, what are you...? That's so good... What are you...? AAAAAAAAA!!!!" And she bucked her hips again, more violently than the first one, pulling him toward her with her feet, even as Jake held onto her arms. "I'M COMING AGAIN! I'M COMING—AAAAAA!!!"

"Oh, God!" she gasped, trying to catch her breath after the waves finally subsided. "No more. No more. I need. A break. Oh, fuck."

Jake sat back, grinning, his face shiny with her wetness. "You taste amazing," he said. "I loved licking up your juices as you came."

"I'm ready for you to come now, too, lover. Fuck my wet pussy."

Jake positioned himself so his eight-and-a-half-inch cock was at her entrance. He slid his cockhead up and down between her meaty labia, getting it wet with her fluids.

"Ohh, please, Jake. I can't take it. Please put it in me. Please shove that fat cock in me as far as it'll go."

"Do I get to come this time?" he said with a smile.

"Anything you want, lover. Please fuck me with that giant cock."

Jake slid his thickness into her a couple of inches which made her gasp: "HOOOOLY FUCK!" He slid nearly all the way back out and immediately pushed back in again, going in another inch.

"OH, GOD," she said. "Give me a minute. Just stay for a minute." Jake could feel Jackie's cunt muscles tense and relax, tense and relax, as she accommodated her lover's cock.

"Okay, do it again," she said with a nod. Jake pulled out to the same point and slowly pushed his way back into her pussy, watching her lips open to accommodate his veiny, hard rod. He made it nearly all the way in that time, so he waited again, flexing his cock and making it bounce.

"Ow, shit! What was that?" she said, laughing. "Did you bounce your dick in me?"

"Yep. Guy kegels." He bounced it again.

"Ohh, fuck. That feels weird. I love it."

Jake bounced it a couple more times then slid his cock out one more time. She could feel the emptiness where he had left her. Jake grabbed Jackie's hands and pushed one more time—"FFFFFUUUUCK!" she cried—this time driving himself into her so deeply, he was buried to the hilt in her hot cunt.

"Oh, God, you're in me. You're all the way in me," she babbled. "I feel so full. I've never had a cock this big in me. Oh, I love this cock. Fuck me, fuck me, lover. Fuck me with your big cock."

Jake was only too happy to oblige. Still gripping her hands, Jake slid out then drove himself forward, making her gasp again. He pulled out one more time and pushed in again. Out, in. Out, in.

"Ohh! Ohh! Ohh!," Jackie grunted with each thrust. "Ohh! Ohh! That's so fucking good."

Jackie's pussy grew to accept the fleshy invader and Jake was able to speed up his rhythm until he was pulling her toward him as he pushed himself into her, their bodies slapping with each powerful thrust.

"Ohh! Ohh! Ohh!" Jackie yipped. "I'M COMING AGAIN! OH, FUCK, JAKEY, I'M COMING ON YOUR BIG COCK! OHHHHHHHHHH!" Jackie thrashed and bucked as Jake grabbed her hips and continued driving himself into her eager cunt.

"I'm gonna come too, baby," he finally said. "I'm gonna come too! Where do you want my hot come."

"Come on me!" she said. "Pull out and come on me. I want to see it. You can come in me later, but now I want your hot come on my stomach."

Jake didn't need any more urging. He pulled out of her now-gaping pussy, grabbed his cock in his fist, and jacked off. He looked into Jackie's beautiful green eyes as she was breathing hard and stroking his forearms while he jerked himself to completion.

"This is for you, Jackie. I'm gonna come for you, Jackie. Oh, God, baby, take my come. UNGH! UNGH! UNGH! UNGH!"

The first thick shot of jizz shot out and left a rope several inches long, frosting Jackie's flat belly. "OH!" she gasped as she felt the hot juice hit her skin.

The second blast fired further and landed between her tits, leaving a trail longer than the first. "Oh, yessss!" hissed Jackie.

The third come rope landed almost as long as the second, on Jackie's breast and trailing down to her pubis. The fourth and fifth shots were just honored to be included, and they made a good showing, landing a few inches past Jackie's belly button.

Jackie quickly pivoted on the couch until her face was next to Jake's cock, and she sucked the remaining come out of the tip. Then she lay back as Jake sat back on his heels, both of them gasping for air.

"Oh, fuck, that's amazing," said Jake. "You look so fucking hot with my come on you."

"I feel dirty," she said. "Good dirty. This is what I wanted. I was actually fantasizing about it on the plane when we were talking. I just didn't dream it would actually happen."

"I'm certainly glad it did," said Jake, giving a little post-coital shudder. "I was thinking some of the same things."

"Oh yeah? You fantasized about coming on me?"

"On you. In you. In your mouth. Yes, I did."

"I want all of those, plus a few more variations," Jackie said, stroking Jake's arm. "In fact, if you can help me out in the shower, we can probably manage another of those."

Jake stood up and helped Jackie to her feet. She still had his come running down her torso. She scooped up some of his jizz on her finger and popped it into her mouth.

"Oh yeah, we can definitely manage those," she said, turning and walking toward her bathroom. "I know which one I want next."

"As you wish," said Jake.

"By the way," Jackie said as they stepped into the bathroom. "I don't have any plans for that apartment for a while. If you want a place to stay while you decide whether to go on your next tour, you're welcome to it."

"I may take you up on it," Jake said. He pushed the door closed behind him, leaving it open just a little bit.

Book Club Questions

1. Which of the cities that Jake visited would you most like to have sex in?

2. Which cities have you had sex in? Can you name them all without blushing and dissolving into nervous giggles?

3. Other than Jake, which of the characters was your favorite? And if Jake was not your favorite, why the hell not? He's a nice guy!

4. Does it seem plausible or implausible that Jake had sex with 15 women in eight cities? Does that bother you? Then why did you read all eight books?

5. Do your friends know that you read filthy smut books? Does your family?

6. Which of your friends would you secretly tell that you read filthy smut books? Why didn't you invite them to your book club? I mean, are you really even friends at this point if you can't invite your friends to read filthy smut books as a group?

7. Did you catch all the jokes? Which one was your favorite? Would you please tweet that to the author? She desperately needs validation.

8. How do these books compare to 50 Shades of Grey? Don't pretend you didn't read it. Why would you lie about that?

9. What are some scenarios that you would like to see Jake in? Tweet your best suggestions to the author. She's always looking for new ideas.

10. Would this all have been more believable if Jake had been a traveling encyclopedia salesman in the 1940s?

CHASTITY VELDT

Having years of humor writing and publishing under her belt, Chastity has turned to writing humorous erotica. Puns and fourth wall breaking are only some of the entertainment Chastity Veldt will bring her readers. With a passion for fun reads and awkward moments, her debut series "Stand Up, Lie Down" will delight erotica readers with a fresh new feeling.